T0365987

QUEENS & GODS:
DARK HORIZONS
BOOK I

MEAGAN FOLMAR

ARCHWAY
PUBLISHING

Archway Publishing books may be ordered through booksellers or by contacting:

Archway Publishing
1663 Liberty Drive
Bloomington, IN 47403
www.archwaypublishing.com
844-669-3957

ISBN: 978-1-6657-7027-9 (sc)
ISBN: 978-1-6657-7028-6 (e)

Library of Congress Control Number: 2024926329

Print information available on the last page.

Archway Publishing rev. date: 12/12/2024

PART ONE

Only the lake at the base of the gods' mountain could sparkle like other-worldly sapphires as it did that dazzling fall dusk. Only in this most sacred place where the immortals bestowed their tokens of favor or inflicted their great displeasure could there be such beauty and such torment. I knew better than anyone that great pain and I still suffered from it, long after the memory of my crime had faded into the ages.

My curse was that I could only watch, never interfere. It was a hard burden to bear on even the most beautiful of days, but it was nothing short of harrowing that evening. The gods may have known everything that transpired that day, but I alone knew the full consequences of their actions. What the costs would be and the sacrifices that would be demanded.

Everything would have turned out so differently if I had acted but the Fates were beyond my control. They spun the strands of destiny when the mood to be wicked struck them, weaving tighter and tighter before cutting the strings of life.

I only watched as the events unfolded that would doom so many in the years to come. I looked up at the gods' unblemished mountain that stretched high into the sky, much farther than any other mountain in Midrios with a grey mist that constantly shrouded its peak from mortal eyes. The lake shimmered brightly with power, and I watched Spyridon standing on the rich green grass next to the water. This holy leader had maintained his vigil for hours, only peering into the horizon as he waited for the right moment to act. The sun had been dragged by Anatole's golden chariot across the sky too slowly for his liking, but it now hung suspended right above the horizon, warning them not to proceed with its blood-red rays.

Spyridon suddenly turned to face his group of followers. Some of them wore white robes with golden chords to signify they were holy people on the path of enlightenment. Others wore the trademark red cloak and golden shields that marked them as Leondrian warriors. Two of the holy people held twin infant girls in their arms, cradling them while the Leondrians stood protectively beside them. From the fierce expressions in the Leondrians' eyes, they were ready to catch the girls if the two holy people carrying them dared to drop them or to spring into violence if an unwanted visitor showed up.

They had all committed treason by taking the late King's twin daughters without permission, but they had stolen them anyway with the full knowledge of what might happen to them all. Born three days ago, the twins only had their dead mother's love and their departed father's fracturing kingdom as their only significant inheritance. This was well-known by the present crowd, and they could not shake their apprehension. It was not their own deaths that scared them, but the fear of the future that made them willing to sacrifice their own souls.

I turned my attention back to Spyridon as he assessed the lake, but he clearly cared not for the desperation of his followers that clouded the air like thunder clouds in a troubled sky.

"It's time." Spyridon announced to the men and women's great relief.

For their plan to work, it must be timed perfectly and without interference. At the precise moment of dusk, between a day's death and a night's birth in the ashes. The moment that briefly acted as a gateway between worlds where mortals could try to meet with one of the gods at this sacred place.

The twin children were gently put onto wooden infant-size boats and Spyridon pushed them forward, towards the entrance of the god-made tunnel at the base of the mountain where the lake ended. The water, which had been the picture of still serenity a second before, suddenly spurred to life. Unnatural currents churned beneath the twins that made the entire lake devolve into chaos. Both tiny boats rose and fell precariously through the waves, a mere hair's breadth away from overturning and being lost forever.

But so long as one of the children was chosen as the next Queen of Leondria, no one would weep too much over the other girl's fate. Honor might demand retribution, but they justified their actions by telling themselves that such a death could only be the will of the gods.

The waves whirled and whirled until, as if signaled by some unseen hand, dampened into a single current that ushered both children into that tiny entrance that would lead them to a council before the gods. To a meeting that no other mortal was privy to attend. Spyridon watched the boats disappear with an intensity that rivaled the Leondrians' murderous expressions then his face smoothed over as if he had all the time in the world to wait. Even though he knew he was already being hunted for leading the others into committing this terrible crime. The girls' own mother scarcely had the time to look into her children's eyes and name them before her body succumbed to the toil of childbirth. Spyridon had then taken them when the rest of Leondria was too distracted to notice his treachery.

The moon crested the horizon and her full, pale face shone upon them all. The humans paid this no mind and waited for hours in silence while the gods within raged with fury. The mortals didn't dare to lie down to slumber or to take a single sip of the gods' water. They only watched the tiny entrance with the fervor that fanatics possessed. They knew what their purpose was so they could easily ignore the marrow-deep exhaustion and parched throats if it was for the greater good.

A watery grey slowly replaced the inky black night sky as dawn approached. Spyridon narrowed his eyes and kneeled, only a step away from the lake's edge. The others straightened and their anticipation rose as a white light pulsed from the tunnel. A few more moments passed before the two boats suddenly sailed back to the bank and into their eager arms. Only for Spyridon to find both twins alive and well with the mark of the Queen inked on both of their chests directly over their hearts.

2

"Are you ready?" Zosime asked.

Vasiliki glanced at her sister with a side-eye expression she had long ago mastered and asked, "Are you?"

"How can I not be?" Zosime teased in that characteristically light tone of hers, as if she didn't have a care in the world and winked. "We've spent our lives preparing for this."

This question was their inside joke since it had been drilled in their minds since childhood that the lethal soldiers of their city-state, Leondria—the protectors of their country, Midrios—must always be ready for anything.

"That's the question, isn't it." Vasiliki murmured soberly and knew the corners of her mouth had turned down.

The air around them practically hummed with anticipation from the few dozen other Trainees who had given everything for this long-awaited night. They had endured ten long years of Training, an arduous experience that had claimed the lives of many of their friends, to even get to this point. They had sacrificed their childhood for something that was considered even more precious than their lives: honor.

They were finally about to take the Trials, the final test of their Training. The details of which were a mystery because it was forbidden under penalty of death to divulge any details about it to anyone.

Vasiliki watched the others compulsively sharpen their spears or zealously patrol the camp's perimeter. As she observed them, she couldn't help but think of the lessons they had received that reiterated the importance of keeping their emotions under absolute control. But she thought that one only needed to pay close attention to their fidgeting hands and inability to keep still right now to know what exactly they were feeling that night. Or perhaps Vasiliki was being too critical since she had known each person here ever since they had all been thrown into the proverbial lion's den together years ago.

"Not much longer now," a familiar voice stated behind her.

Vasiliki and Zosime turned to find their closest friend standing a respectful distance behind them. Despite being twenty years old like all the other graduating Trainees here, Dryas overshadowed them all with his height and build. No one they knew, even the legendary Spears who oversaw their Training, could look him straight in the eye due to his physical stature. His hair was darker than a starless night sky and his ice-blue eyes flickered often with good humor.

"I think you're right," Vasiliki agreed as she peered into the tree line where the last rays of sunlight were now glittering, as if protesting the end of the day before night would fully take over.

Dryas was doing a much better job than the others at masking his nervousness but even he betrayed his emotions when the muscles in his crossed arms twitched with impatience.

"We'll get through this," Zosime said with a casual wave of her hand. "There's no need to worry."

Vasiliki had to glance up at her sister who stood a full head taller than most females. Zosime's skin was golden-brown, and her hair was the shade of mahogany which often curled in the sun. Vasiliki was also tan from spending so much time outside, but her complexion was a few shades lighter than her sister's with hair that better resembled the color of chestnut. They had similar bone structures, but their facial expressions could not be more different. Zosime laughed and teased whenever she could whereas Vasiliki's straight-lined mouth could only be tugged upwards when she was feeling good-tempered enough to humor Zosime's attempts to amuse her.

They may have been the daughters of the late King but there was no such thing as royalty in Leondria. While they hadn't received special treatment during Training, they had always stood out. They were meant to embody everything Leondrians valued most, and members of their family had to be ready to replace the previous monarch at a moment's notice. The situation with them, however, was radically different than with any of their

ancestors. Their father had died when they were infants and there had been
no one to replace him until they came of age.

"I'm not worried for myself." Dryas corrected mildly. "If I pass, I'll just
be another soldier. You two will be the ones ruling Leondria."

A cold sweat broke out on Vasiliki's neck, and she had to resist the urge
to scratch her chest tattoo of a triangle with a lion inside it, wondering yet
again why she bore the mark of the Queen when she wasn't even considered
a Leondrian yet.

Zosime reached out a moment later, squeezing Vasiliki's shoulder reassuringly. Vasiliki gave her an exasperated grimace and Zosime shrugged. It
was one of her common gestures, as if to suggest she couldn't help sensing
her emotions, but Zosime squeezed Vasiliki's arm reassuringly again anyway before letting go.

What made them truly unique wasn't the fact they were the late
King's orphaned children who were expected to rule Leondria after passing the Trials. It was their heritage, the superior strength that ran in
their veins as a result of being descendants of a goddess. While killing a
part-god was difficult, it wasn't impossible. Which is why their family's
numbers had slowly dwindled over the years until all that was left was
Zosime and Vasiliki.

"She's right," Dryas reassured her softly. "After all we've survived, what
is there left they can throw at us?"

That last line did make her feel a little better but did nothing to
dampen the dread in her chest. They had waited their entire lives for this
night but a part of her just wanted it over with already. But another part
of her never wanted tonight to end because then she wouldn't be weighed
down with the impending responsibility of being queen.

Perhaps that was why she felt nauseated instead of excited right now.
Vasiliki glanced at Zosime then took a deep breath. The last thing she
needed to do right now was to project her nervousness on her sister who possessed the rare and enviable Gift to sense other people's emotions. Zosime
was the one person she could never hide her true feelings from, and she
didn't want to do anything that could detract from her sister's focus. Losing
focus meant missing crucial details and that could impact Zosime's chances
of surviving the Trials.

"You have nothing to worry about." Zosime grinned and her tone was filled with such certainty that it could have been mistaken for a premoni-tion. "I'll always bet on you two."

Dryas turned his gaze to Zosime and returned her smile, his eyes spar-kling. They stared at each other for a few seconds before Zosime's smile faded and she quickly averted her gaze. Dryas dropped the smile as well, and his eyes went flat as he surveyed their surroundings.

Vasiliki returned her attention to the horizon, both to watch the last rays of light fade away and as an excuse to pretend she hadn't noticed the exchange. No one spoke for a few moments and Vasiliki couldn't stop her-self from calculating her own chances of survival.

If it wasn't for the superior strength running in her veins, Vasiliki doubted she would have made it this far, unlike her sister who naturally excelled at everything that Leondrians prized most. She inwardly rebuked herself for such defeatist ideas and reminded herself that she was a descen-dant of Lady Meraki, the Goddess of War. Becoming a Leondrian was Vasiliki's only legacy, but it was one she had to earn after a brutal decade of Training and proving herself one last time in the Trials. Only then would she earn the right to wear the red cloak or call herself a Leondrian.

Zosime lifted her head unexpectedly and announced, "They're coming."

Zosime snapped her head to the left and narrowed her eyes. Vasiliki followed Zosime's gaze and only had to wait a few moments before she saw what her sister had sensed. Then a tall, blonde figure emerged from the darkness and one of the most infamous Leondrians who ever lived stormed into camp with her hand resting on the sword strapped to her side.

"Make way!" Anastasia exclaimed in a tone that threatened swift pun-ishment to those who failed to obey.

The Trainees all parted from her path as she led another famous Leondrian to the center of camp. Everyone here knew how General Perleros had led them through the dark times that had almost destroyed them all. Vasiliki's eyes fell to the wild boar he carried in one arm then glanced at Dryas. She couldn't help but notice how his arms were crossed even more tightly against his chest and how a muscle in his jaw clenched. She quickly looked back at General Perleros when he and Anastasia finally stopped before the triangle-shaped pyre in the middle of camp.

"General!" everyone roared passionately, the sound dying off at a wave of his free hand.

Anastasia used the torch in her other hand to set the pyre ablaze. Flames quickly roared to life which cast a brilliant light upon Perleros's weathered face as he studied them. He towered over them from his sheer height alone which was exemplified by his muscular physique. His salt and pepper beard was meticulously cropped and no hair remained on the top of his head.

"You all know why you're here." he stated, his voice soft but rich with the quiet intensity of command that made him easily overheard. "Look to the east."

Everyone briefly turned their gaze in that direction as ordered before returning their full attention back to him.

"There lies the path to safety. *Anyone*—" he informed them, his penetrating gaze resting on Zosime and Vasiliki before looking at the others. "—may use it. This option will be revoked when the Trials begin. You'll return home as Leondrians, or you'll die."

He tossed the dead animal straight into the blazing inferno as if it weighed nothing and prayed, "We offer you this sacrifice, Lady Meraki. May you deem these Trainees worthy to die free."

Everyone made the sign of the gods—placing their left thumb, index, and middle fingers on their chests directly over their hearts, raising them to the center of their foreheads, down to a point on the right side of their chests, and back over their hearts in perfect triangles.

Perleros leveled his gaze on them all, the rise in the fire adding another layer of intensity to his face while serving as a stark reminder that wild boars weren't the only predators prowling in the night. He nodded to Anastasia, turned on his heel, and left without another word. Leondrians weren't known for their loquaciousness and Perleros was a Leondrian through and through. He didn't look back as he left, and Anastasia waited until he was out of sight before stalking to the opening of the eastern path.

"There is no room for weakness." she said tersely. "Make us stronger by leaving. We'll tell your families you perished in the Trials to save them dishonor."

No one dared to say anything to her, but she didn't seem to have been expecting a response. Zosime's eyes clung to Anastasia as she left without another word, leaving them all bewildered in her absence.

"Quitting is an option?" a fellow Trainee, Yiorgos, murmured in shock.

Zosime turned to him sharply and stressed, "No, it's not."

Yiorgos nodded quickly and they all turned their attention to the pyre. Their attention on the wild boar's carcass was only interrupted when Dryas suddenly approached the pyre and thrust a rat into the flames. He murmured a quick prayer to the Goddess of War before turning away. Everyone followed his lead by finding something to sacrifice to Lady Meraki before the fire from the pyre died out that night.

Nothing they found was as dramatic as effortlessly tossing a wild boar into the fire, but they offered up small rodents they found nearby with murmured prayers to Lady Meraki for a lion's heart, physical strength, and mental fortitude. Wine that the Spears had given them was passed around and everyone took a ceremonial drink to toast the gods.

"One more night. We've waited longer for less." Zosime remarked when she and Vasiliki found a moment alone.

"Then our lives begin," Vasiliki murmured incredulously. "Do you know what you'll do?"

Zosime shrugged, "Tomorrow is too far away to think about. Do you know what you'll do?"

Vasiliki had to work up the courage to quietly confess, "I have no idea and it scares me."

There. She said it.

Vasiliki didn't really expect a response. At least, she didn't expect anything besides a joke to relieve the tension or for Zosime to tell her not to worry about it.

To her surprise, Zosime merely whispered almost too quietly for her to hear, "Me too."

Tonight was their last night of adolescence. No matter how grueling the last ten years had been, Vasiliki suspected that the real work would begin tomorrow. Only the gods knew how terrified she was, not that they were listening much these days. So she confessed this fear out loud once, in her last night of adolescence, before becoming one of the Leondrian queens her people had waited twenty years for.

She just had to survive the night. Survive the Trials, which only happened to claim the lives of several Trainees every year without fail for thousands of years. But no matter what happened, at least she had Zosime by her side. Vasiliki's eyes grew heavy as the minutes ticked by and she watched the smoke from the dying pyre drift towards the never-ending sky as a light mist slowly drifted towards them. Her thoughts growing sluggish and dull, she closed her eyes and found herself drifting away.

Vasiliki opened her eyes and sat up, repressing the urge to groan in self-reproach for falling asleep. Stupid. She turned towards her sister only to find Zosime was gone from her habitual spot beside her. She frowned then slowly rose to her feet. Clutching the sword hilt strapped to her side and raising her shield arm, she discovered that the roaring bonfire was her only companion. Vasiliki grew uneasy as she looked around the empty camp, and she couldn't shake the thought that she was not welcome here. She drew her sword and advanced closer towards the tree line, her senses sharpening as her eyes scanned the surrounding area.

Was this the first test? She wondered. Where was everyone? Who had reignited the pyre?

A crackling of wood sent Vasiliki spinning around, shield and sword raised to combat any threat. Her eyes instantly focused on a dark figure that had been waiting on the other side of the bonfire. She kept her eyes on the dark figure and didn't move, readying herself for the being to charge when the figure suddenly dissolved. In the span of a heartbeat, the same figure reappeared right in front of her. Shocked and only having time to blink, the figure grabbed Vasiliki's arm before she could defend herself. Nothing but a full decade of Training in brutal conditions prevented her from screaming at the searing ice-cold touch.

The bonfire was instantly quelled, and a black mist materialized out of nowhere, surrounding them both like a cocoon. Vasiliki peered at the figure and realized that it was a woman clothed from head to toe in black rags. She couldn't make out any of the woman's features besides her all-black eyes that had no trace of color in them. She couldn't shake the feeling that some primal part of her subconsciousness recognized the woman, but she couldn't remember where, even as the pain from the touch mounted to agonizing proportions.

Having no idea where the words came from, Vasiliki's mouth moved without her meaning it to and she said, "About time. You kept me waiting long enough."

The woman cocked her head, the shadows and mist keeping most of her face a mystery. But Vasiliki could just glimpse the bottom portion of her face. She could now see how the woman's mouth had been literally sewn shut.

The words continued to tumble out of her mouth when she urged, "Help them. I know you're tired but don't forget where you come from. It's time to fight."

The woman jerked her arm away, as if the words had somehow burned her, and then an excruciating scream started ringing inside Vasiliki's head.

Vasiliki's eyes flew open, and her chest was heaving as her eyes darted all around her in search of the nearest threat. Vasiliki exhaled shakily when she noticed her sister sitting beside her. Camp was exactly the same as she remembered it before she fell asleep and she loosed a breath in relief that the nightmare was finally over.

Zosime, eyes wide and body shaking, stated, "You saw her."

"The woman in black?" Vasiliki whispered.

Zosime nodded and they glanced down at their left arms where a severe burn in the shape of a hand remained. They stared at each other in disbelief as the realization set in that they had shared the exact same dream with whatever dark figure that had marked them both. Zosime opened her mouth to say something when a resounding BOOM sent Vasiliki sprawling into the dirt.

3

Vasiliki gasped when she fell, her head snapping hard against the ground. The world was drowned out by a high-pitched ringing which wouldn't go away even when she tried clearing her ears. She slowly opened her eyes and raised her head, finding nothing but a swirl of colors that made her stomach twist up in knots. Her head started pounding and she focused on taking a breath to steady herself.

The ringing slowly started to fade, and Vasiliki could finally start making out other noises around her. She could have sworn she heard some deep sound ripple through the air that could almost have been mistaken for laughter.

She felt more than heard movement beside her and it took a moment for her to register that her sister was shouting.

Then her ears finally cleared, and she heard Zosime bellow, "MOVE!"

It was the kind of order given with such authority that no one could ignore it. Vasiliki found herself stirring in response and clumsily reached out to grab a spear. She gritted her teeth and heavily leaned on the spear to support herself as she heaved herself to her knees. Vasiliki blinked rapidly several times when she dragged herself to her feet, but the world wouldn't stop spinning. She spit the dirt out of her mouth and took another deep breath to steady herself. The dizziness still hadn't faded but she could finally at least make out shapes around her.

Vasiliki glanced around and saw something blue flickering in the middle of camp. She narrowed her eyes to focus on it and could now make out that it was the remnant of a great fire that had demolished their pyre into splinters.

Keeping her eyes narrowed while her eyes adjusted, she could now see that the others were reacting to Zosime's command. They sluggishly rose to their feet one by one while Vasiliki scanned the perimeter and frowned, wondering if everyone had fallen asleep.

They had. She seethed inwardly. How had this happened?

She gritted her teeth and focused on willing strength to her legs as she strode forward, her mind racing. No human had the capability to create an explosion like that. At this point, it was only instinct driven by a decade of Training that propelled her forward as she and the others formed a few lines facing the trees to the East with shields and spears held at the ready. Vasiliki's arms started trembling from the effort, which made no sense since the shield and spear had felt lighter than air before.

She didn't understand why falling from a nearby explosion was causing this strong of a reaction from her. Bile rose in her throat, and she was almost overwhelmed by its unpleasant taste. She swallowed it down with a grimace and found herself thinking about the ceremonial wine they had drunk before falling asleep. Wine that the Spears had so graciously given to them mere hours ago before strolling deep into the forest where she hadn't seen them since.

Vasiliki had allowed herself to drink an entire cup of it and she was now wondering if its sweet aroma now indicated something sinister. She struggled to recall what it tasted like which was difficult to do with her head swimming. She remembered that it had a richer taste than she was used to, but she was now debating if the sweetness was a natural part of the concoction or a poisonous addition.

If the wine had been truly drugged, that would explain all her symptoms and everyone falling asleep. Typical, Vasiliki thought, for the Spears to break the warriors down to their lowest point and then see how they perform on the most important test of their lives. She had just never heard of anyone poisoning wine, especially when it was used for a ceremonial toast to their patron goddess.

Vasiliki's eyes widened as the ground suddenly started shaking beneath them. She was almost swept off her feet when a disturbing ripple pulsated the air around them. Vasiliki had to focus to keep her balance as she squinted into the distance. But even with her excellent eyesight, she couldn't make out anything besides the trees in the darkness. She couldn't shake the thought that something unnatural was happening here, but she had no idea what it was or how to react.

Even after a decade of Training, she only had one question on her mind that sent a cold shiver down her spine: what was coming for them?

Vasiliki gripped her spear tighter, determined to maintain a steady grip despite her now-sweaty hands. Still, she saw nothing. She tore her gaze from the tree line just long enough to glance at her sister, who was also struggling to maintain her balance beside her. She frowned when she saw Zosime's eyes suddenly widen, and the ground unexpectedly stopped quaking in fury. Vasiliki readied herself to turn—to throw her spear—to do anything—when a terrifying voice she had never heard before suddenly spoke.

Have you come to play with me, little ones?

Vasiliki thought her heart might stop in her chest and she inhaled sharply as she slowly looked back to the tree line. She could have sworn that she had heard the voice in her mind—the words echoing inside her skull—but everyone was reacting as if they had heard it too.

That same strange voice rumbled with laughter and the sound was deeper than anything Vasiliki had ever heard escape from human lips. The voice possessed a certain bitterness that only one who had lived too long could have and carried such sinister finality that she knew promised death.

The blackness around them thickened and Vasiliki briefly glanced up to see that the moon and stars had winked out from the sky. She quickly returned her attention towards the tree line, as she sorted through her knowledge of various magical beasts. Not many magical creatures still openly roamed the lands the mortals had conquered, but those who still roamed Lady Meraki's Forest were nothing short of deadly.

You do not know who I am? It asked with amusement but with no trace of surprise. *Pity.*

The darkness slightly dissipated and Vasiliki swallowed as she looked up to see red eyes glaring down at them. The crimson eyes grew brighter as a scaly black head emerged from the top of the trees. The thing before them had slits for nostrils like a snake and its two glistening white fangs protruded from its oversized mouth like the last two stars in a fallen sky. The Creature flicked a forked tongue at them before widening its mouth, exhaling a steamy grey fog which drifted steadily towards them.

Vasiliki tensed as the fog crept closer and gasped when it made contact with her skin, the searing sensation so intense that she was convinced that her flesh was melting away from her bones. She glanced down to see what the process would look like out of morbid curiosity and was astonished to discover that the mist didn't leave any mark on her tanned skin. Only the burn from the woman in black and a few scars were visible on her arms.

She quickly glanced back up and she could now see the rest of the Creature's front profile as it took a step forward towards them. Vasiliki was fascinated to see that its snake-like head was followed by a long reptilian neck and tail with black scales that looked sharper than any blade's edge. These black scales merged into golden fur that reminded her of a lion's proud chest which matched its illustrious paws.

She wasn't prepared for the raging headache that followed when the Creature next spoke, and its voice reverberated in her mind like an accusation.

Have you seen the visions yet?

The fog now consumed her entire body, and Vasiliki's muscles locked up to the point that she couldn't move. She could barely even breathe with the fog clogging her nose and preventing air from entering her lungs. Despite how fiercely she tried commanding her limbs to move, they refused to obey, and she couldn't stop her eyes from watering.

The dizziness returned in full force, and she then wondered if her initial assessment had been wrong. It was still possible that the Spears had drugged them with the wine earlier, but it was also possible that this Creature had been slowly poisoning them for hours with this strange mist while they were sleeping. If that was the case, then it had deliberately lulled them to sleep but Vasiliki couldn't figure out why it bothered making a loud explosion that woke them up instead of massacring them when they were defenseless.

She could just barely make out the shock and horror on the faces of her fellow warriors through her peripheral vision and knew that this Creature was somehow talking to each of them individually. Calling it a beast would be an inept description with its intelligent eyes that seemed to be filled to the brim with ancient knowledge. Vasiliki glanced back up at the Creature and found it glaring at her personally. Its head slowly descended until its face came to almost face-level with her. It flicked its tongue again with disdain and its glare somehow deepened with even more loathing.

If it wasn't for the anger in its tone, the Creature's voice could have almost been mistaken as a whisper of warning when it stated: *Let's begin.*

She struggled in vain to move but her body still wouldn't obey her, so she had no way of defending herself when it blew a golden mist into her face. Vasiliki squeaked as the last of her air ran out and she felt something intangible inside of her be dragged to the surface.

She didn't know if it was her basic life force, her spirit, or her soul that had been drudged up but—whatever it was—felt like it was being ripped apart for inspection. What she did know was that her vision darkened and the last thing she saw before unconsciousness took over were those resentful red eyes, forever glaring at her in accusation.

CHAPTER

4

Vasiliki didn't know if she was dead or dreaming for the images she saw were clearer than any nightmare but too disjointed for her to be a departed soul looking down from the heavens. These images only flickered briefly before her eyes, scarcely stilling long enough for her to make out what they were before vanishing.

She saw a lion and an owl battling ferociously against each other. Each inflicted bloody injuries against the other but none could get the upper hand in their fight. Vasiliki saw the owl land a blow to the lion's heart and the lion retaliated with a swipe at the owl's head before the scene dissolved. Then there was a heartbeat of darkness before an entirely new image appeared.

She next saw brutal fighting on an unfamiliar, narrow mountain pass. Her horror rose when she noticed many fallen Leondrians, their bodies bloody and broken. She desperately tried to make out who they were—if they were anyone she knew—when her view was yanked farther back. The last thing she saw before this vision faded away was a man in a palace made of bones and, in front of him, were countless soldiers who clearly outnumbered the Leondrian forces.

This scene was quickly replaced by a Leondrian man stabbing a woman in the throat. A manic grin twisted her lips before the light left her eyes. The man's face was just out of view but there was something strangely familiar about him when he reached up to wipe the blood off his eyelids. Before he dropped his hands so she could make out who he was, this scene was replaced by a closeup of Zosime's battered face.

Her face was lined with exhaustion and blood, but her eyes flared with her characteristic wild spirit. She looked ready to fight the entire world, despite whatever injuries she had clearly sustained. Zosime's eyes suddenly widened in shock and pain and Vasiliki's view was widened just enough to see a hand wrapped around a dagger that was plunged directly into Zosime's heart. Vasiliki was able to see a scar of a falling star on the assailant's wrist right before Zosime's body sagged lifelessly.

Vasiliki gasped as this vision retreated and the world disintegrated around her. No, no, no. She almost cried out. Not Zosime.

Her heart was now beating wildly, and she couldn't ignore her rising panic. Was this some prophecy of warning? A gruesome type of humor to set her on edge with no ring of truth to it?

She wanted to reach out and claw the image back to determine once and for all what it meant or to learn how to prevent it altogether. Vasiliki's frustration rose as her efforts amounted to nothing. The image of the fallen Leondrians had concerned her but she didn't know if that was a view of the past or the future. The one with Zosime clearly took place in the future, assuming the vision was true.

Vasiliki echoed the words in her mind: assuming the vision was true. That was when she reminded herself that this was only a test. Zosime was fine.

At least, she would be as soon as Vasiliki could return her spirit to her body. There was no telling what that Creature was doing in the real world while her spirit was suspended in this strange state. It had asked her if she wanted to play which likely bought her some time but, just how much time they all had, she didn't know.

There was suddenly a flash of white light and Vasiliki found herself lying on the ground. Her eyes were burning from the lingering glare, and she had to blink several times before her vision started to recover. She frowned when her vision didn't adjust then she realized that it was the middle of the night here too.

She sat up and looked down at herself, immediately feeling the lack of weight from the missing shield, sword, and spear she had been carrying moments ago. An ache still pulsed in her head and an involuntary shiver ran down her spine, but she could at least see and think clearly again. Vasiliki then glanced around and noticed the fields of grape crops around her as she slowly rose to her feet. She clenched her fists, feeling exposed and vulnerable without having the shield strapped to her arm.

It weighed almost nothing to her, but she was so used to feeling the straps around her arm that fixed it in place. So used to having to be mindful of how she used that arm for everything to avoid denting what was considered a Leondrian's most important asset. A spear and sword were undoubtedly important, but the shield represented so much more as a tool for defense than a couple of weapons. Losing or otherwise damaging it had severe consequences, but Vasiliki again reminded herself that this was not the real world.

But she decided to treat this strange place like the real world because she had a hunch that any mortal injury here would be fatal to her physical body. So, she started patrolling the area, her eyes sweeping her surroundings the best she could with no moon or starlight to assist. She kept glancing around and turning in full circles as she walked, fully expecting an ambush as the hairs on the back of her neck rose. But despite time passing with no sign of anyone else being nearby, she couldn't shake her feeling of unease. She suddenly stopped in her tracks when she realized what was bothering her so much.

It was utterly silent here.

Vasiliki scraped her sandals against the ground, but she didn't hear any sound of dirt moving beneath them. She slowly reached out and plucked a grape and a few leaves, but again, it didn't make the faintest sound. She shook her head and tried clearing her ears, but it was as if all sound had been vacuumed away.

She also realized what else was bothering her. She was utterly alone. She and Zosime had practically never left each other's sides since their birth and, for the past ten years since Training began, it was forbidden to go anywhere alone. Full citizens were not compelled to travel everywhere in pairs, but it was a common practice because individuals did not exist in Leondria. People were either an extension of their family, a part of their unit, or the hands that worked together to serve Leondria. It had been ingrained in her mind since childhood that they were stronger together, not apart.

It was such an alien experience, especially coupled with the knowledge that she would have to pass and survive the Trials all by herself. She would have no backup. She would have to rely on her Training to survive because whatever came next could very well kill her, even if it was all happening inside her mind.

Vasiliki scanned her surroundings again and squinted when she spotted a small house in the distance. Walking as carefully as she could on the off chance that someone nearby could hear her movements, she slowly made her way over to it. A few minutes passed before she finally approached the house at an angle and circled it. She didn't find anything of note as she walked around it, seeing only a backdoor and more crops in the yard. When she finished circling the perimeter, she then very slowly approached the front door and gradually pushed it open just enough for her to be able to slip inside.

She still couldn't hear anything when she stepped inside the house and carefully shut the door behind her. She swept her gaze around the one-room house and saw a small bed in the farthest left corner, a crib in the center of the room, and a table with carvings on it pushed against the far-right wall. She took a few steps forward and glimpsed down into the crib where only ashes and remnants of a crumpled red ribbon rested inside.

Was something in here supposed to trigger some sort of reaction? She wondered in bewilderment to herself.

Vasiliki next approached the table and discovered a chisel beside six wooden carvings of all the gods and goddesses. She leaned in and inspected them, marveling at the artist's skill. She immediately recognized the carving of her patron goddess, Lady Meraki, and she picked up that carving first. She made the customary sign of the gods and studied the carving of her ancestor, the Goddess of War. She was the tallest of the three goddesses and was the only one adorned with full battle armor and a cape. She had a spear clenched in her left hand and a shield with a carving of a lion on it raised high in her right hand.

Just like the shields they carried in Leondria.

Vasiliki frowned when she noticed a chip in the breastplate and turned the carving a couple times over in her hand to see if there were any other defects. Her frowned deepened when she realized that the rest of the carving was flawless before she gently placed it back down and scrutinized the other carvings.

She next picked up the carving of Lady Apistia, the Goddess of Wisdom. She was the patron goddess of Apistia, the second-most powerful city-state in Midrios after Leondria. The carving depicted Lady Apistia wearing a flowing dress with her hair pinned up. One hand was outstretched towards

Vasiliki, palm-up, and there was a faint chip on the forehead. Vasiliki also inspected the rest of the carving and found her curiosity rising as she wondered why this was the only mistake in another otherwise flawless carving.

Vasiliki turned towards the carving of what could only be Lord Anakalypto—known to all as Lord Kal—the God of Wandering. He wore a plain robe that seemed to billow in an imaginary wind. Next to him was Lady Hermione, the Goddess of the Soil. Both of her arms were outstretched, as if to offer a hug, and her belly was round, as if well advanced in pregnancy. Next to her was Lord Adrian, the God of the Sea, holding a fisher's net. The last of the gods was Lord Demetrios, the God of the Sky, who was carved with his back hunched forward and head facing downwards while holding a ball in his hand, mimicking an act that could only be weaving starlight from a perished soul so they could glitter in the night sky.

The carvings evoked the mantra that had been fervently taught to all children in Leondria: serve the gods first. Self-sacrifice for the good of Leondria. Defend Midrios. Always love and protect your family. This was how one was taught to live their life in Leondria, but Vasiliki had always wondered what someone should do when these values inevitably conflicted with each other.

Vasiliki blinked when she noticed a seventh carving of a hand mirror by the edge of the table. Very little detail had gone into this one, unlike the carvings of the Six gods. Glass was a rare commodity and Vasiliki marveled why someone would bother chiseling such a thing.

The mirror. How quickly mortals forget.

Vasiliki flinched as that low, off-putting voice reverberated in her head. The depth of the voice and the way it echoed in her mind was like an earthquake that threatened to knock her off-balance and suck her into the ground where she would never see the light of day again. The blood drained from Vasiliki's face when red eyes suddenly materialized and glared at her from the wooden mirror.

How unearned your arrogance is.

Could this Creature actually read her mind, not just talk to her inside her head?

I can read everything going on in your little head. It answered her unspoken question. *Your deepest hopes and fears. A future queen? What a joke.*

Vasiliki dropped the mirror and flinched when the red eyes material-ized in the wall in front of her.

Midrios will burn after you take the throne.

Vasiliki shook her head vehemently and tried not to let the taunt sink in.

Are these not your fears? It taunted. *When your sister inherited the precious Gift to sense the emotions of others, and you did not? That you will never be good enough? That voice is right. You'll* never *be good enough. Even some of your superiors think it too.*

"I trust them," Vasiliki said as steadily as she could, trying to ignore how deeply the Creature's comments were cutting into her. "I will rule the best I can."

She didn't know it was able to laugh as mockingly as it did when it continued. *You don't even know of the secrets and betrayals.*

It was simply trying to get to her as part of the test, Vasiliki reasoned to herself. There were no secrets in Leondria, and her people were loyal.

The mocking tone in its voice quickly devolved into wrath when it demanded. *You doubt me when all else in this world will lie to you? When your people killed and drove away so many of the magical creatures that used to roam Midrios?*

The sheer anger in that last statement almost made Vasiliki's legs give out.

"I will rule Leondria and protect Midrios the best I can." she insisted with her best impression at bravado, but she knew the words stumbled clumsily out of her lips.

Oh?

"Help!" a woman's distorted voice cried out.

Vasiliki blinked at hearing something outside of her head for the first time in what felt like hours then moved without a second's thought. She turned, grabbing the chisel as she did, and darted to the door. Instinct drove her forward with the need to protect whoever it was that was in danger.

"Help me!" the woman cried out again then screamed.

Vasiliki yanked the door open to find a man's body face-down in the dirt. A young woman cowered several meters away, bloody arms raised to protect her face, as a taller figure bent over her with a dagger in hand. Vasiliki sprinted forward as the figure sliced the woman's face, using her natural speed and the element of surprise to knock the figure over before they could inflict any more damage. She pinned the attacker's arm to the ground, ready to twist the blade out of their grasp, before glancing up at their face.

She froze when she realized who she had pinned beneath her.

"Hello, sister." Zosime giggled with a wide, maniacal grin and a murderous glint in her eyes that were now mysteriously blazing crimson red instead of their typical red-brown-yellow hues.

Vasiliki's mouth dropped open and her mind went blank. Zosime took advantage of her astonishment by striking Vasiliki with her other hand and knocking her sideways before straddling her. Vasiliki grabbed Zosime's arms out of reflex as she brought the blade down towards Vasiliki's throat.

What are you willing to sacrifice for the sake of your sister? The Creature's voice purred in her mind.

The dagger dipped lower towards Vasiliki's throat, and she heard a child screaming.

You'd clearly sacrifice yourself. But what else? The Creature continued. *This woman? Her child? Your soldiers? Your queendom? How many will you allow to die for the sake of one person? Kill her and save them.*

Vasiliki grunted with effort, and it felt like her muscles were deteriorating as the voice continued berating her from the inside.

Between her and the rest of the world, will you let the world burn?

Zosime leaned in to apply more pressure, and Vasiliki bucked her hips in an attempt to throw her off.

You can't do what needs to be done? Then you will never be good enough or strong enough. Give in if you don't have what it takes.

Vasiliki ignored it and clenched her jaw. She didn't know what sort of apparition was trying to kill her right now, but it certainly wasn't her sister. She already hesitated once but she wasn't about to make that mistake again.

Liar.

She bucked again, finally managing to thrust the fake-Zosime off her. Vasiliki quickly dove to the ground to grab the chisel she had dropped during the struggle. She gasped when she felt herself get dragged back and glanced back to see the fake-Zosime's hand over her ankle. Vasiliki then shifted to her back and kicked her in the face. The fake-Zosime howled, releasing her grip on Vasiliki's ankle, and she scrambled for a few moments before her fingers wrapped around the hilt of the chisel. She then rolled away when the fake-Zosime leapt towards her and plunged it into her upper thigh.

The fake-Zosime screamed as she clutched her thigh, the wound only a couple inches below a major artery. Vasiliki panted as she took a few steps away from her and prayed that any wound here would not be inflicted on the real Zosime.

Vasiliki glanced down at her blood-stained hands and clenched them into fists to keep them from shaking. She knew the imposter wasn't her sister, but she couldn't shake the feeling that she had just betrayed Zosime. She refused to look it in the eye as the imposter clutched her leg in agony but didn't otherwise move.

A black cat suddenly materialized in front of her, and its red eyes stared at her with unwavering intensity as it peered into the depths of Vasiliki's soul.

I have seen your heart and mind, Vasiliki of Leondria. When the day comes that you must make this decision, you'll wish you had made a different choice.

She thought that was unlikely but said nothing. The black fur shivered with displeasure and, several heart beats later, the cat turned and walked towards the fields.

Follow me.

It was an unnecessary command, but she kept her mouth shut and followed anyway without comment. She paused for a moment as the cat took a path that led away from both women, deliberating if she should grab the chisel and dagger.

No, it must be a test.

To do anything but follow its commands would surely be deemed a failure, as she had learned countless times from the Spears. It deeply troubled her to leave behind two potentially life-saving resources, but she simply clenched her fists, tore her gaze away, and followed. The cat continued prowling forward, passing by rows and rows of grape crops before suddenly pivoting into a random aisle. She turned right after it only to have the ground beneath her vanish and her stomach rose into her throat as she fell into the unknown.

Vasiliki didn't know how long she was falling before hearing the ripples of waves beneath her, but she barely had time to register this fact or to make out anything in the darkness before she crashed through the sea's surface. She couldn't stop a bubble of screams from escaping her lips when extreme cold unexpectedly overwhelmed all her senses as she tumbled through the water. She sank lower and lower, trying not to retch when she accidentally swallowed salt water in the process.

It took all her self-control not to start coughing uncontrollably when her movements finally slowed. She was driven by the need to move and to get to the surface as quickly as possible where salvation awaited. She kicked with all her strength but accomplished little besides making her lungs and muscles burn from the exertion.

She tried to ignore the fact that she had no idea what she was doing and that her flailing only seemed to make her sink further down into the sea's icy depths. She fervently clawed at the water, trying to pull herself up to the surface but there was nothing to grab onto. It would have been so natural for her to climb a tree or to hike to the top of a mountain but the only real times she spent around water were during the periodic bathing times the Trainees had in a shallow pond.

Swimming lessons weren't exactly a priority for prospective soldiers who would do all their fighting on land. She was so tempted to scream again but she refrained when she realized how quickly her heart was beating in her chest and how badly her lungs were burning for life-saving air.

Continuing to claw at the water or trying to scream would only be a waste of air and energy that she couldn't afford to lose if she was going to survive. She didn't know if she had already been submerged for several minutes or not, but she instinctively knew that her time was running out.

Despite her body bellowing at her to continue fighting, Vasiliki made a conscious effort to stop moving. Her body raged at her supposed complicity, and she closed her eyes as years of Training began to prevail over her blind terror. If she continued panicking, there was no doubt in her mind that she would die. Succumbing to fear was a lesson the Spears had drilled into all the Trainees since day one. Panicking was the enemy and would kill her faster than a blade.

It wasn't quite possible to become calm, but she could at least regain her composure and reason her way out of this. She thought through her options but everything she could come up with wouldn't get her out of this predicament. There was no ground to run away on, no rope to climb up out of the water, no spear to thrust forward, and no air to scream for assistance.

She had flailed in the water in her clumsy attempt at swimming towards the surface, but that idea had failed miserably. She could try swimming some more but, even when she tried to pierce through the black water with her superior eyesight, all she could see in front of her was darkness. She had to bite her lips to keep from exhaling in frustration when she suddenly realized that she didn't even know which direction was up.

How could she possibly strategize a plan of attack if she didn't even know where the surface was?

The pounding in her head increased and she could feel her lungs tiring. She knew any regular mortal would have already passed out, but her heritage had blessed her with stronger lungs, so she knew she still had some time. An errant thought nagged in the back of her mind, and she tried to focus on it because it would only take another couple of minutes before she lost the battle for consciousness.

She knew that getting to the surface was the key, but she was confronted with the undeniable fact that she had no idea where the surface was. She remembered crashing into the water that had hit her harder than any fall on land and how she had tumbled many times under the waves before slowing. If she had been paying attention instead of being caught off guard, she would have been able to track how exactly she rolled then she would know which direction to go. She silently reprimanded herself for her stupidity, wondering what possible similarity there could be between drowning and fighting some evil phantom version of her sister.

She turned her head to look around again when she suddenly noted with surprise that it was also completely silent here. But this silence was different from the one she had experienced at the farmhouse. The silence there was unnatural and off-putting. Something hollow, something to fear without one of her essential five senses to alert her if someone was trying to ambush her from behind.

Between the pitch-black water and how weightless her body felt, the silence here was neither hollow nor eerie. It was peaceful.

Stay with me and keep me company. I'll take your fear and pain away. The sea seemed to sing in her ear, like a mother's comforting embrace. *Drift with me ... sink into my arms and look up at the stars every night.*

Oh, how she wanted to sink into a mother's arms and peer into the heavens to unlock its secrets. She could feel herself relaxing, a bubble of air escaping from her mouth as her lips parted in acceptance. This was not so bad, she thought to herself, and she wondered why she had been so afraid of this for so many years ever since she almost drowned as a child. She had felt a mother's arms around her then, but she knew that she had only imagined it when she had staggered away alone.

She found herself closing her eyes, ready to fade away into an endless slumber.

CHAPTER

5

As she waited to lose consciousness, Vasiliki envisioned a beautiful night sky with a bright moon and stars glittering like diamonds behind her eyelids. She mused to herself that perhaps the point of this exercise was recognizing when a task was impossible and accepting death as peacefully as possible.

I will protect you. The sea continued in its beautiful melodic voice. *Stay with me and study the skies.*

How beautiful, she thought, then her eyes suddenly burst open when the implications of that statement sank in.

Disappointment then rose bitterly in her chest as she yearned for a future she could never have. As much as she yearned for tranquility, she would never have it as a Leondrian. She knew without a shadow of a doubt that she would never be safe, never be at peace, and never be able to pursue her true interests. She would have to lead her people so that others can have what she herself could never attain.

No, this was nothing more than another illusion, Vasiliki realized, and she had to piece together what the first and second tasks had in common to survive this.

The silence itself couldn't be the only common link. But Vasiliki couldn't shake how entirely random the first task felt and how the "fight" had been nothing more than a façade. The real Zosime would have put up a much more valiant struggle and wouldn't have been taken down by a mere stab wound to the leg that wasn't even fatal.

The point of all this couldn't be about accepting the inevitable or out-witting something so much more powerful than her. Vasiliki mulled it over and realized that this all had to be about what choices she made. About how she reacted when confronting her darkest fears or put in impossible situations.

So the Creature had been telling the truth when it said it could read her mind and it probably knew perfectly well that she didn't know how to swim. She had regained her composure, if not entirely conquered her fear, so she there was some choice to be made here. She comforted herself with the logic that the Trials couldn't be unbeatable if scores of Leondrians before her had passed it already.

But what choice was there to be made here? Whether to drown or to drown?

She should continue trying to reach the surface where salvation awaited. But that wasn't the point, and it clearly wasn't working anyway. Staying still and waiting to die also wasn't an option so that left only one choice. She steeled herself to use whatever oxygen remained in her muscles to try to turn her body in a direction that she imagined was downwards. She would not wait for death to take her. She would do what was unnatural and charge towards it.

Vasiliki wouldn't have been able to say with any certainty whether she succeeded in flipping downwards or if she had only steered herself to the side before she tried pushing herself deeper into the sea's icy depths when something immediately caught her attention.

A giant yellow eye—larger even than the tallest trees she had ever seen—was staring directly at her. It wasn't just any shade of yellow either. They were the shade of molten gold that shimmered with destructive power, like lava bent on eradicating everything in its path. With the kind of intelligence that only came from seeing the rise and fall of civilizations throughout the ages.

Vasiliki's vision blurred and was even turning red at the edges, but the godly eye kept her undivided attention. She almost gasped when a sudden pressure enveloped her body, and she glanced down to find skin wrapped around her entire body. She hardly noticed the water moving around her and it felt like her lungs were close to bursting. Vasiliki squeezed her eyes shut as she focused on ignoring the pain.

She reflexably gasped when her face unexpectedly broke through the surface, and she swallowed as much air as she could. She would have begun shivering from the shock of frigid water coating her body in the cool air, but she only fixated on taking her next breath. Something she had taken for granted now seemed like the most precious resource in the world.

She grunted when something constricted against her body. The grunt turned into a gasp when the pressure from the hand wrapped around her body increased until she could barely breathe. She did her best to flail in an attempt to escape, but even her strength was no match against this figure that held her immobile.

She only dimly realized that she was being raised higher and higher in the sky until she was finally brought before the face of the giant who had saved her. She realized her mistake at once when she looked at the figure's face and knew that the blonde woman with golden eyes who had saved her was no ordinary giant.

It was the Goddess of Wisdom, Lady Apistia, who now held Vasiliki in her grasp.

"My Lady." Vasiliki breathed in awe, and she was forced to tear her gaze away from the goddess's eyes which were now radiating brighter than the sun.

Vasiliki never would have thought her first meeting with one of the missing gods would take place in some psychic vision when she was in desperate need of rescuing.

The thunder rumbling around her seemed to indicate the goddess's displeasure and the surge of lightning revealed some strange black sludge that was splattered across Lady Apistia's head.

Vasiliki swallowed and whispered, "Lady Apistia—"

Vasiliki was interrupted when a black crow landed on the goddess's arm right in front of her with the same red eyes the Creature had in its lion-serpent and cat forms.

It is not her. The Creature declared in her mind with enough venom to send a bright surge of pain in Vasiliki's head. *Even the gods do not dare to step into my domain, but I can show you the power they wield.*

Vasiliki could only manage a pained squeak as the hand increased its grip around her body and she heard multiple pops from bones that were threatening to break. She couldn't help but muse that it would be cruelly ironic if she had been saved from drowning only to have her bones crushed to dust and the splinters of whatever remained slip back into the sea's depths forever.

There truly was no prevailing in this task and Vasiliki would have sighed if she could. She did the only thing that she could do in that moment, and she lifted her chin at the crow, indicating that she didn't care what it did to her. This was no longer a matter of maintaining composure or keeping a cool head in an unwinnable situation. She didn't care if she ended up slain on a battlefield, drowned, or crushed. It didn't matter when or how she died because she would go out a Leondrian—with no fear in her heart.

Despite the pain, she did not allow herself to flinch when the Creature's voice flooded her mind with three words: *As you wish.*

Then the crow launched itself at her eyes.

Vasiliki hadn't realized she had raised her arms to protect her eyes until she knocked herself in the head with her shield. She toppled backwards and felt her back collide against the ground. She hastily glanced left and right, her chest heaving with adrenaline as she searched for the crow.

"Vasiliki!" a voice she would know anywhere cried out.

She had to blink a few times before she realized that she had collapsed right next to her sister. Zosime spared her a quick look with frenzied eyes and Vasiliki was relieved to see that it was her sister's regular eyes, not the insane red ones of the imposter from the first task. Vasiliki finally began to hope that she had escaped that mental prison and was back in the real world.

She glanced down at her body to appraise the damage and saw that she was soaking wet with brilliant black and purple bruises all over her body. Her shield was still strapped to her arm, but her spear was laying on the ground next to her. She looked around and saw that most of the Trainees were still standing in position, exactly as she had last seen them before she had been dragged into those psychic tests.

She clenched the dirt under her hands and inhaled sharply as the scents of Lady Meraki's Forest filled her nose. The sounds of the forest almost overwhelmed her after so much time spent in silence, but she cleared her ears the best she could to listen for any hostile movement. She warily grabbed her spear, waiting for the world to melt beneath her at any moment as she struggled to hoist herself to her feet.

Her drenched hair clung to her scalp and goosebumps lined every inch of skin from the lingering sea water rolling down her arms and legs. She forced herself to look up at the Creature who stood silently but almost seemed to be smirking at her with that serpent's mouth.

"You fall, you die." Zosime muttered and only then did Vasiliki notice three fallen bodies.

Faces she had seen every day were now face-deep in the dirt, lost forever from whatever challenge they had failed to overcome. The sky was still dark overhead, but it was now light enough for Vasiliki to make out the details of their bodies, so she wondered how long they had all been held captive in their own minds.

Vasiliki scrutinized the faces of all who remained standing. Only two remained in that strange sleep state with their eyelids fluttering rapidly from whatever torment they were experiencing.

She did flinch, along with almost everyone else, when they heard the Creature unexpectedly warn them. *Sacrifice demands one more life.*

Vasiliki looked at the last two Trainees in horror. The last two remaining were Yiorgos and Dryas. Yiorgos had been a steadfast presence in her life throughout Training, but Dryas was her closest friend. She knew it was wrong to hope for one to survive while the other perished, but she couldn't help but pray to all the gods to spare Dryas.

She inwardly raged in fury, certain that her prayers had yet again been ignored when Dryas rocked on his heels, as if the breath had been knocked out of his chest. His legs buckled and his knees collided against the ground with the kind of force Vasiliki knew only came from a corpse's dead weight. She almost cried out his name, but she heard his name escape from Zosime's devastated lips instead. Vasiliki couldn't tear her gaze away as his chest started falling towards the ground when he suddenly flashed out a hand to catch himself.

She almost missed it when Yiorgos collapsed next to Dryas and her heart leapt in hope when Dryas rose his head to stare at Zosime. She saw him gritting his teeth in effort as he rose to his feet and only then did she tear her gaze away to look at her sister again. It was only then that she noticed burns covering Zosime's entire body, including the one in the shape of a hand from the woman in black.

Vasiliki almost asked her what they should do next when Zosime looked away from her and leveled her gaze on the Creature.

Zosime broke the silence when she asked the Creature, "What shall we call you?"

Vasiliki had to suppress the sudden urge to tackle her sister into the ground so she would stop saying things that would get them killed. She braced herself the best she could while soaking wet, covered in nasty bruises, and—if she suspected correctly—poisoned by either the earlier mist or the wine. She almost dropped her spear when the Creature laughed, exhaling fire in its amusement.

Almost all of them flinched when its voice reverberated in their minds again. *It has been mortal ages since the last human dared to ask me that question.*

Vasiliki leaned forward, ignoring the burst of nausea and ready to spring if the Creature made a move towards Zosime. She didn't trust its temporary amusement and wanted to be able to act at a moment's notice.

Vasiliki could practically hear its laughter echoing inside her skull when it continued. *For your bravery, I will trade one answer for another and then your Trials will end.*

Vasiliki glanced at Zosime, but she was too staring intently into those disconcerting red eyes to notice Vasiliki looking at her.

Leave it to her sister to peer into the eyes of an immortal, god-like Creature and refuse to back down. Zosime inclined her head in assent to the Creature's challenge and Vasiliki shuddered as it sang, its deep voice reverberating in the air so intensely that Vasiliki's teeth clanged together. She felt liquid leak out of her eyes but knew the substance was too thick to be tears.

> *Who adorned the crown made of blood and bone?*
> *Wandered the world and cursed what was sown.*
> *Abandoned treasure first to ascend*
> *Last to slumber so as to defend.*
> *Decorated in black and burned to ash.*
> *Who am I?*

Vasiliki was speechless and her mind was a blank as she repeated the words in her mind.

"You place great value on your name." Zosime murmured, blood dripping from the corner of her eyes and rolling down her face.

There was no trace of amusement when it replied. *Names are powerful.*

Of course, it couldn't be something as simple as answering a straight-forward question. Vasiliki could reason her way to right answers with regular questions if she had time to think it over, but she was always terrible with riddles. What made matters worse was that this riddle was filled with even more contradictions than the ones she had heard before.

How does one curse things that were sewn? How does one that was abandoned ascend without assistance?

Not to mention, black apparel was taboo for those who died with honor. Funeral by fire was the only way to send one's soul up to the heavens and the bodies were always dressed in bright colors to celebrate their sacrifices to the gods. Only those whose spirits were not yet worthy to ascend to the heavens were decorated in black whenever possible and shamefully buried. The dead's only hope then was that their spirit would be reborn and find redemption in their next life.

Vasiliki knew they were in trouble when Zosime didn't answer right away but she stopped herself from flinching when the Creature asked a minute later. *What is your answer?*

Vasiliki knew that her sister was as stumped as she was when Zosime still didn't respond. Vasiliki went through various ideas in her head but none of them fit everything in the riddle and she ignored another burst of dizziness when the Creature exhaled fire again. *Anyone may answer if your future queens are unable to.*

Vasiliki thought through her options and wondered if it would be better just to admit they didn't know the answer or to just guess?

The Creature would simply resume the Trials if they admitted to not knowing the answer whereas it could all end now and she could prevent any further loss of life if they happened to guess correctly.

"L-Lord Anakalypto." Vasiliki called out.

The Creature flicked out a forked tongue in what Vasiliki could have sworn was contempt before it asked Zosime a single question. *Are you sure?*

"Yes." Zosime asserted without hesitation.

Vasiliki didn't know one word could hold so much power when it hissed at them both. *Liars.*

Vasiliki's legs almost buckled from the sheer rage of the following statements. *I already told you once the gods do not step into my domain. You should have listened.*

Without warning, the Creature struck. One of its giant paws swiped at the front line, its claws stretching out for the kill. Despite the speed and ferocity of the attack, this time they were ready for it. They all lifted their shields and held the line, but Vasiliki knew that playing defense was not going to help against such an adversary. They needed to take the offense if they wanted to triumph, and they needed to do it now.

The first line advanced, raising their spears as they did so, and formed a horseshoe around the Creature. They struck as the paw swiped again, thrusting their spears as deeply as they could.

Vasiliki marveled at how unaffected the Creature acted from the attack and wondered if its paws were really so thick that the spears couldn't penetrate it.

They aimed higher as the Creature stepped forward, but the spears bounced off the scaly skin. Red light glowed from its mouth as it breathed flame and they ducked behind their shields. The shields barely prevented streams of fire from swallowing them whole and did next to nothing to protect them from the heat of the blast itself.

Vasiliki felt the heat dim and she risked glancing up to find a blue light emanating from the Creature's mouth. The same color as the explosion from earlier.

"Move!" she shouted before ducking and rolling off to the side as the Creature launched four explosive infernos in quick succession.

The nausea and dizziness remained but Vasiliki could feel her thoughts clearing now that the lust of battle was rushing through her veins.

The fire and explosives were hard to fight against but could be avoided if they moved quick enough. Vasiliki narrowly dived out of the way of the last blast and prepared to sprint away from the next fire ball. But to her great surprise, the Creature didn't try to burn them to ashes again and only swiped another paw at them.

She frowned at this random change in tactics, confused that the Creature wasn't trying to set them on fire or exhale more of that paralyzing mist. It would make them disorganized, burn many, incapacitate some, and make them easier targets to kill. Vasiliki couldn't afford to spare more than a quick, sorrowful glance at a couple of her friends who had been too slow to dodge the fire. Whose bodies were already unrecognizable after being coated from the flames for too long.

She couldn't fathom why the Creature would suddenly try to clumsily swipe whoever remained standing with its furry paws. If it wasn't moving to eradicate them, she reasoned, then it must only be because it couldn't. Reason would then suggest that the Creature required some time to re-charge after too many blasts in a row. Not to mention that it was enormous which made it a slower target that they could exploit to their advantage.

She glanced at Zosime who was crouched several paces to her left, seeing a wild look in her sister's eyes. She knew then in that moment that her sister was about to do something crazy. Vasiliki opened her mouth to say something—anything—to stop her but Zosime dove into action before she could speak up.

Zosime darted forward while several people in the back line launched their spears directly into the Creature's chest. A few of the spears even stuck but the Creature remained standing, unfazed by the weapons sticking out of its chest. Zosime meanwhile leapt towards Dryas who was now kneeling with his shield held horizontally on top of his knee. She jumped onto the shield and Dryas launched her into the air.

She flew through the sky as the Creature swatted at several more spears that were thrown at its chest. Vasiliki knew she needed to keep moving and to attack but she only stood fast as she tracked Zosime's progress. The Creature could turn at any second and incinerate her, it could swipe her sister so hard that it would crack her skull open, it could—gods forbid—even swallow her whole.

Vasiliki could finally breathe again when Zosime landed high up on its chest, gripping the fur tightly as she used the lodged spears as footholds and the fur to pull herself upwards. The Creature reared its front legs, but Zosime held on tightly as she climbed slowly but steadily towards its neck. The Creature raised a paw but was unable to reach its neck to pry her off.

It shook wildly again, and Vasiliki could see from the ground how her sister's biceps strained from the effort of holding on. She didn't know what nightmares Zosime had to face earlier but she prayed to all the missing gods that she had the strength to maintain her grip.

The Creature's mouth widened, and Vasiliki hefted her spear when she saw a blue flash rising in its throat. She hurled the spear as hard as she could and could only hope that the poison in her veins and her sweaty hands wouldn't affect her aim. Her spear soared and she felt her heart stop when the Creature shifted at the last second. Instead of striking the Creature directly square in mouth to pierce its throat from the inside like she had planned, the spear hit its mouth off center. The Creature instead screeched and clamped down, shattering the spear into splinters instead of launching into another fire ball attack.

Vasiliki had bought her sister time, but Zosime had slipped from all the movement. Her eyes widened in horror as Zosime fell for a few seconds before she flung out a hand to grasp some fur. She miraculously regained her grip and Vasiliki watched her clamber quickly to the top of its neck. Zosime ducked her head as the Creature spurted vicious red flames down towards her. As soon as the flames died out, she grabbed one of its oversized fangs and swung, unsheathing her sword as she shot upwards, directly above the Creature's face. She gripped the sword with both hands and Vasiliki's heart quickened as she watched her sister fall towards the Creature's monstrous face. Its great jaws opened, and Vasiliki could see a flash of blue rise in its throat again.

Vasiliki knew she could do nothing but watch her sister be engulfed in flames before her very eyes. A great white ball of fire engulfed in blue flames spurted from the Creature's mouth and she had to look away from the blinding light. She knew it only needed seconds to kill Zosime once and for all then it could direct its full attention back on them. She forced her eyes open when a few seconds passed, and nothing happened. She had to blink before she finally trusted that her vision wasn't playing tricks on her.

Zosime was alive, standing on the Creature's face with her sword plunged directly in one of its eyes. Vasiliki felt another trickle of liquid leak out of her eyes when the Creature roared loud enough to make Lady Meraki's Forest shake to its core.

Vasiliki tensed as she prepared to run forward, unsure what she could do but knowing she had to do something to save her sister, when the Creature's legs suddenly buckled. She looked back up to see an airborne Zosime before losing sight of her when the Creature collapsed.

She was thrown off her feet when the ground quaked beneath them all from the sheer force of the Creature's body collapsing to the ground with a resounding THUD. She clambered to her feet as quickly as she could, her breaths coming in quick bursts.

Where was Zosime?

Vasiliki almost slipped from the uneven ground, but the Creature didn't move as she ran as quickly as she could towards it. She glanced around when she approached the body but didn't see her sister in the remains.

"Zosime!" Vasiliki shouted and she couldn't keep the desperation out of her voice.

She was greeted with silence, and she started running forward again when a voice stopped her.

"I'm fine." Zosime moaned as she popped up from a mountain of hair and jumped off its chest. "Its fur broke my fall."

Vasiliki heaved a breath of relief and chastised, "Give me a warning the next time you do something crazy."

"I was hardly going to give away my battle plan." Zosime countered lightly as she ripped the sword out of one of the Creature's unseeing eyes and sheathed it before jumping down.

Vasiliki glanced over at Dryas, who was also breathing easier now that Zosime was grounded.

"Later." Vasiliki told her sister with a meaningful look at the fallen warriors.

A heavy silence followed as they looked at their dead friends.

"Seven fallen." Dryas counted.

Vasiliki closed her eyes. Even one loss was one too many, but it could have been worse.

You still haven't figured it out yet?

A cold sweat broke out on her neck, and she slowly turned to find the Creature quivering with laughter on the ground. It was the most surreal sight of her life to watch it rise to its feet, its life miraculously restored. Vasiliki didn't have any more spears to launch against it and she frantically reached for her sword. Her heart beating in her throat, she didn't know how helpful a sword would be when the Creature's skin had already proven impervious to sharp objects and what should have been a mortal wound had already healed. But she knew that she had to try.

She had just unsheathed the sword when a voice akin to a venomous hiss flooded her mind. *Then you shall die ignorant.*

The Creature opened its mouth, and the last thing Vasiliki saw was a white fireball that engulfed her whole.

CHAPTER

6

Even Zosime's superior reflexes weren't fast enough to avoid the huge wall of blinding white fire that consumed her entire body. She screamed as her nerves burned away and her very soul was set aflame. Zosime knew she was dying but, when the pain kept rising without any signs of relief, she thought that this was her eternal punishment for failing the Trials.

There would be no honorable pyre to send her soul to the heavens for Lord Demetrios to weave starlight out of her soul. Nor would be a shameful burial where she at least had a shot at redemption in the next life. There was only never-ending pain for her failure and there was no doubt in her mind that she was dead.

She didn't know how much time had passed before the pain finally started to fade and the white flames vanished. Zosime raised a hand without realizing she did so then blinked when she saw that her skin was shimmering like one of the Six.

Zosime had to blink several times before her vision sharpened and she could survey her environment with clarity. She looked around in search of her sister and it was only when she saw that Vasiliki was unharmed that she could breathe easily. To her immense relief, everyone who had survived the final attack was still alive after being set aflame. Their emotions flowed through her body as if they were her own and she didn't sense any pain from them. Inheriting this sacred and rare Gift from her distant ancestor, Lady Meraki, could be quite useful at times, Zosime thought, since she could now focus her attention on the threat without worrying about anyone collapsing.

Zosime tensed as she took a few purposeful steps forward, gripping the hilt of her sword tightly, and turned in a full circle to take in every detail of her surroundings. The ground was so marred and cracked that it looked like an earthquake had wrecked the local area. This physical devastation was only enhanced by the trampled trees which were now lying in splintered branches on the ground. She quickly looked past the seven corpses, ignoring how several of her friends she had seen practically every day in Training were now dead, as she looked for any indication for where the Creature might have gone.

She couldn't afford to linger too long in her grief if it meant wasting a precious second that would endanger the rest of them. But it seemed like the Creature had vanished as mysteriously as it had appeared, and she didn't sense any other impending threats.

She closed her eyes and focused entirely on the Gift. It wasn't something she could control and certainly not something she could turn off and on at will. The Creature had been the only living being whose emotions she hadn't been able to sense. Zosime didn't know why that was the case, but the reasons didn't matter anyway. All that mattered was what that it had vanished and might still pose a threat to them.

She focused on the foreign emotions flowing in her heart but didn't sense any strange feeling that could be differentiated from the group of Trainees hovering behind her. She ignored their incredulity and grief the best she could in the hopes of getting any indication of where the Creature might be hiding. The Gift was hardly a honing beacon, but she thought she could get a rough estimate of where it might be since she could only sense emotions from those who were nearby.

She waited a beat. And another. Then another. Her optimism dimmed and, while she knew that she hadn't been able to sense its emotions earlier, a part of her hoped that she had just been too distracted to notice so she waited another moment just to be sure. She had been surprised twice tonight already and she didn't intend for that to happen again.

She slowly released her grip on the sword strapped to her side and turned back to the others when nothing happened. She blinked again as she fully took in their appearances. She had been ready to dismiss their initial glittering appearances as a remnant of the Creature's fire playing tricks on her vision, but everyone was still glowing brightly like they were one of the Six.

Zosime felt their awe then glanced down to discover that her own skin was radiating, exactly like theirs. She held up her arms to her face and turned them over, hesitating when she noticed that the burn she received from the woman in black had disappeared without a trace. Even old scars from Training were completely gone, her skin smooth and unmarked as if she had just been born. She felt rejuvenated, as if she had just received a full night's uninterrupted sleep and hadn't just spent the last few days stealing a few minutes to nap whenever she could.

She dropped her arms as the realization sunk in that the threat was gone and she could now experience this moment to the fullest. Her thoughts grew dull as this curious feeling of ecstasy filled her. Like an otherworldly energy had filled her up to make her feel powerful and the closest state to invincible that a mortal could obtain. Even the stars and moon had returned to celebrate their triumph, and the sky was brightening in preparation for the first rays of daybreak.

Zosime couldn't stop her eyes from glancing back at the seven bodies now that the danger had passed. She had waited her whole life for this night, but she hadn't expected her happiness at passing the Trials to be dampened by grief.

Zosime suddenly felt the hair on the back of her neck rise and heard bells ringing in her mind. She spun around, already unsheathing the sword at her side before anyone heard the rustling of leaves.

Except for the surprise attack by the Creature tonight, she could always sense when an adversary was about to strike. Except for the Creature, there was no being in this life she had met whose emotions she could not read. It had done things she had never thought possible, and even in this heightened state, she knew that the nightmares she had faced would haunt her. But she wouldn't think about the choices she had made that night. Not yet. Not at all if she could help it.

Zosime saw the others brace themselves for another attack when they heard a rustling of leaves and then Anastasia burst through the tree line, her armor covered in black blood. Zosime felt the others' confusion mirror her own as they wondered what Anastasia had battled while they had been held captive, but Anastasia's impassive face gave nothing away as she looked at them with a death-grip on her raised sword. She was close enough for Zosime to see something briefly flicker in her eyes and Zosime sensed something akin to both confusion and relief from her.

It took several seconds for Anastasia's shoulders to relax then a few more moments before she cautiously sheathed her blood-covered sword. She stalked forward and her eyes scanned all around them before her eyes fell to the fallen.

"Bury them." Anastasia ordered with no inflection.

Zosime blinked but didn't say anything.

Anastasia said flatly with a pointed look, "You know the law."

In other words, their spirits wouldn't rise to the sky and dance amongst the stars. They would receive neither recognition nor favor from mortals or gods. That was only reserved for Leondrians, particularly those who had fallen in combat or mothers who didn't survive childbirth. The seven fallen had been neither. They had been warriors, but they had not been worthy to earn the title of Leondrian so, under the law, they didn't deserve such honor.

Zosime turned and looked at the seven fallen. These were warriors she had lived with, ate with, and trained with for ten years. Zosime was no stranger to death—many did not survive the rigors of a decade of Training—but she could scarcely believe that she would never see her friends of many years ever again. Never talk to them again. Never feel their hopes and desires again. She had spent ten years with some of the best people she had ever met, and ten years hadn't been enough time with them.

Zosime said nothing as she knelt, placing her shield beside her, and began to dig as she did her best to harden her heart. Dryas didn't hesitate to join her and everyone else worked together to dig the seven graves of their fallen friends. She ignored the group's feelings of disbelief, sorrow, and marrow-deep pain. She could try to harden her heart as much as she wanted but she couldn't stop their sorrow from bleeding into her own chest.

Leondrians needed to rely on each other, so trust was a necessity and there was some room for vulnerability, but there was no tolerance for weakness.

Anastasia watched them while walking around what remained of camp. She maintained her stoicism, but her eyes were wary and Zosime could still sense her confusion. Anastasia unexpectedly turned and Zosime's cheeks reddened when their gazes met, and she quickly returned her attention to the task before her. She couldn't afford to let Anastasia catch her staring at her too often.

Zosime concentrated on digging and ignored how the dirt buried itself under her fingernails and how her hands were stained dark brown from repeatedly scooping out soil. She marked their progress by how deep each hole became and found herself slowing when the hole was finally big enough to fit a body. She and Dryas shared a knowing look then rose to their feet before slowly walking over to Yiorgos.

She felt Dryas's despondency, but she didn't know if he was aware that his life had only been spared at Yiorgos's expense. She would never breathe a word of it to him and she hoped that the Creature hadn't whispered it in his mind.

They handled Yiorgos's body as gently as they could, and she clenched her jaw when they had to scoop the dirt over him. They waited to cover his face last and then all trace of Yiorgos's body vanished from sight. Zosime looked up at the others who were finishing their graves. She moved to tuck a loose strand of hair behind her ear then frowned when she noticed that the dirt had suddenly disappeared from her hands, as if they hadn't just spent the last hour digging graves for their friends with their bare hands.

She chose to ignore it and instead dropped her hand against her side as she looked at the others. Vasiliki was the last to stand and Zosime almost missed the dirt vanishing from her sister's hands, as if her hands had been washed clean. No one made the sign of the gods or did anything at all except stand there in silence.

Zosime couldn't read whatever emotion Anastasia was feeling as she walked over to their group, but it reminded her of something akin to grim resignation.

When she stood directly in front of them, Anastasia leveled her gaze on the group and stated firmly, "As you know, it is forbidden to speak of the Trials. You will never talk about this to another living soul. You will *never* speak of the Creature to anyone, as decreed by the gods. If you do, the lives of the people you speak to about this will be forfeit. They will be buried with disgrace like your friends have just been, and you will be executed as a traitor."

She paused to let that sink in, glancing at Zosime and Vasiliki, and the message could not have been clearer: not even queens were above the laws of the gods.

Anastasia continued, "All that remains is to march back to Leondria before you earn the red cloak. You know what is expected of you when you put it on. Do not fail us."

The image of the imposing Anastasia was not something that anyone would likely forget. Zosime knew the image of Anastasia's blonde hair brilliantly shining from the first rays of dawn and her piercing blue-grey eyes staring fiercely at them all was something she could never forget. They all stared back at Anastasia and gave her nods of acknowledgment, but no one bothered to speak for they all knew the costs.

There had only been two instances in Leondria's history when someone had uttered a word about the Trials, and they had paid the ultimate price. It was one thing to be buried with shame and have a chance for redemption in the next life where it was possible to have one's soul ascend to the skies. It was another thing entirely to be executed as a traitor. To have been so disgraceful that one's soul was cut off from the gods forever without even getting a second chance of life where they would have a second chance to be accepted into Lord Demetrios's domain.

Zosime looked up at the same time that Anastasia turned to find the rest of the Spears returning to camp. Anastasia quickly approached them, and they murmured to each other in hushed voices for a couple minutes before they gave each other nods of finality. She could feel the rest of the Spears' eyes on the back of her neck as the group formed up in two lines.

Anastasia wasted no time with preambles when everyone was ready and merely ordered, "Move out."

Anastasia placed herself in front of the two lines the group made as they left camp. Zosime was still dazed by everything and only followed Anastasia's billowing red cloak as they walked away from the horrors they had seen and marched towards home. She was the beacon that Zosime would follow to the ends of the earth.

They wouldn't be walking such a distance, but the hours didn't quite slip away either. Zosime tried to lose herself into the movements of just putting one foot in front of the other as they forged ahead. She tried distracting herself with thinking *left, right, left, right* with each step she took to keep her mind busy every time the nightmares she had experienced that night flickered to the forefront of her mind. She snapped herself out of these memories whenever Anastasia's head would occasionally turn sharply to the left or right, as if she heard something they hadn't. Despite her alertness and

Zosime feeling resentment from many beings out of sight watching them, nothing ever emerged from the shadows to attack them on the trek back.

Lady Meraki's Forest was notorious for its dangerous beasts, so it was always dangerous to walk past the imposing marble archway that marked the entrance of the forest. Zosime allowed herself a lapse of discipline by glancing up at the archway as they passed it, marveling at everything the imposing and venerable structure that had stood the test of time represented.

It wasn't a long march from the marble archway to the gates that protected the Hearth like armor. Zosime still couldn't believe today had arrived as she passed the gates. She had dreamt about this moment so many times and the past ten years of hard work had all been so worth it to finally come back home with honor. The group's ethereal glow had dimmed with the rising sun but enough of it remained for their skin to still shine.

Zosime saw children gathering on the side of the streets who watched their approach with wide, admiring eyes. Her heart hammered with anticipation as they began the ascent of the final hill leading towards the beating Heart of Leondria. Zosime had to refrain from running the last leg of the march or to sigh in exasperation at their too-slow pace. If Anastasia hadn't been dictating their pace, she might have run anyway, no matter what the others thought.

They finally crested the hill, and the group came to a halt in a single horizontal line in front of General Perleros who had been waiting for them at the bottom step of the Heart. The Heart was the name for the granite building constructed in the form of a triangle with an open space in the middle of it where stones infused into the ground created the outline of a lion. This one-story building was the place where every Leondrian monarch lived, and the generals held their meetings.

Zosime glanced up to find that his face was impassive, as if they hadn't just faced the most important task of their lives and battled the god-like Creature. Anastasia didn't spare a glance back at them when she walked up to Perleros, made the sign of the gods, and stood beside him.

He paused as he took in Anastasia's appearance then softly addressed the group with a single order, "Kneel."

Zosime and the others immediately dropped to their knees. Perleros and Anastasia didn't hesitate to take the single step down to the ground and Zosime heard servants approaching. Perleros's assured footsteps echoed farther away and Zosime could only wait as he personally grabbed a red cloak from a servant, draped it on each Trainee in their group, and murmured something in their ears.

Only people who had passed the Trials could become Leondrians and be granted full citizenship as the most elite in Leondrian society. While Leondrians were at the top of their hierarchy, they also recognized they needed more than warriors to survive. Many throughout Midrios flocked to Leondria for its prestige or for protection but they served in important roles that they desperately needed to thrive while the Leondrians themselves focused on war.

Perleros spoke too softly for Zosime to make out what he said to each person but, based on how long she waited as he moved from warrior to warrior, she knew he was taking his time for these hushed conversations to have the most impact. Dryas didn't say much but Zosime could sense the rising tension between the two men at whatever Perleros had whispered in his ear. Vasiliki had remained quiet but serious, like always. Minutes passed before the golden sandals finally stopped directly in front of Zosime. Perleros crouched and Zosime raised her head enough to look him in the eye as he draped the red cloak over her shoulders.

He leaned in and whispered in her ear, "I saved you for last."

Zosime said simply, "They come first."

He nodded then declared, "We have forged you into a Leondrian. Now you must rule."

"I understand." Zosime breathed.

"Now the difficult part begins." he warned.

Zosime digested this and nodded, waiting for him to say something else. She could feel that something was bothering him, despite the cool exterior, but he said nothing further as he rose and centered himself in front of them.

Perleros announced, in that strange way his soft voice could carry for miles, "Rise, Leondrians."

The sun had risen to its highest peak in the sky when they stood for the first time as Leondrians, and the crowd erupted into cheers for the newest guardians of Midrios.

"May Mione officially begin!" he called out and the crowd's cheers grew even louder.

Their induction into the Leondrian ranks marked the beginning of Mione. Today was the beginning of a week-long festival celebrated throughout all of Midrios but was considered the holiest of holidays in Leondria. It was also the only holiday Leondrians celebrated at all, their only respite after a long year of never-ending work.

The festival was named after Lady Hermione who was revered as the ultimate harvester, provider, and mother. Leondrians, like any good Midrian, worshipped all the gods, but they were the most devoted to Lady Meraki. For the goddess who fell in love with a mortal and whose demigod child became the first King of Leondria.

Zosime didn't really know what her ancestors had looked like, but everyone knew that all of Lady Meraki's descendants possessed superior strength and shared one unique trait: her eyes. They were a godly combination of bright brown with shades of warm red and flecks of yellow that often gave people the illusion of burning bonfires. No one else in this world, save Lady Meraki, had such eyes.

It would be the first time she observed the holiday as an adult and the first time she truly celebrated it since Training began. She wasn't entirely sure what to do with herself and she found herself remembering how she used to celebrate Mione when she was a child. She had mainly run around and got into trouble which she wouldn't be able to do now. A Leondrian wouldn't be able to get away with the same things a child could.

She sensed Vasiliki's delight and disbelief but did not comment on it. She knew how much Vasiliki hated it when she sensed her mood which is why she tried her best to never let on the constant flow of emotions she felt from her sister, although her actions sometimes gave her away.

Perleros gestured for Anastasia to follow him and, after giving Zosime a scrutinizing look, walked up the steps into the Heart while the newest red cloaks dispersed in all directions to greet eager children and family members swarming the streets.

Something twisted in her gut, despite how common these kinds of glances were from him and some of the other adults. She could sense their grim apprehension, as if they were waiting for something ominous to happen, but she had no idea what that might be. It was as if they were waiting for her to do something terrible and those stares grew darker every time she did something they weren't expecting. What made matters worse was

that these stares were almost always reserved for her, and they only sometimes looked at Vasiliki like that. As if Vasiliki was the responsible one and
Zosime couldn't be trusted.

"What should we do now?" Vasiliki asked, shaking Zosime out of her
thoughts.

Zosime shrugged and gestured to the roaring crowd around them,
"Celebrate Mione."

"No, er, queenly duties?" Vasiliki clarified.

Zosime felt the routine jolt in her chest when she sensed the emotions
of someone approaching her from behind.

"You can't have queenly duties if you haven't even been coronated yet."
Dryas said lightly and she turned to face him.

Zosime could see Vasiliki thinking that point over before nodding.

With more confidence than she felt, Zosime declared, "They would get
us if they needed something. It's a tradition to celebrate."

It just wasn't a tradition for the daughters of the late King, the last descendants of Lady Meraki, and the only two people left in this world who
could claim the throne of Leondria to celebrate when there had been no
monarch to rule over their city-state for the past two decades.

Zosime knew better than to ask Dryas whether he would prefer to
spend the holiday with his father instead of with them. Not with the wariness and resentment that always pulsed deeply within him anytime he was
around Perleros. His mother had died long ago, like theirs, and his younger
sister was still a Trainee so she was not allowed to celebrate with them.

The three of them had almost always made up their own unit who
would face anything together. Zosime could feel many of her fellow
Trainees—now Leondrians—experiencing elation for being reunited with
family members they hadn't seen since they were ten years old. She could
also sense parents, aunts, uncles, and siblings craning their necks in search
of their children who now laid buried in Lady Meraki's Forest.

"Let's go," Zosime suggested so she wouldn't have to feel their despair
when they realized that one of their family members wouldn't be coming
home.

Vasiliki didn't need to be told twice since she naturally avoided large
groups and Dryas was content to do whatever they wanted. They ducked
away from the crowd and walked right out the gates. Zosime didn't intend

to wander far and found the perfect spot to rest on a nearby hill. She turned to face the two of them then smirked before allowing herself to fall backwards onto the grass. She closed her eyes and just lay there, enjoying the sun's rays caressing her face. She heard them sit down next to her and she felt their contentedness. Times like these were when the Gift felt like a blessing instead of a constant burden.

To her chagrin, it wasn't long before she sensed someone approach. She kept her eyes closed but she could clearly sense Balthasar's delight as he walked up to them. The pride he felt for his brother radiated like the sun and Zosime didn't bother to suppress her smile. He didn't offer any word of congratulations, nor did they expect him to. This may be a week of great happiness and celebration, but one should not be congratulated for merely fulfilling their duty.

"Dryas," Balthasar greeted, and she opened her eyes to see him grinning at them. "Welcome to the ranks, brother."

Dryas rose to his feet and embraced his brother and Balthasar warmly pat him on the back a few times. Zosime and Vasiliki also stood, and Balthasar respectfully inclined his head at the two of them.

"Stop being a loner and let's go celebrate." he teased Dryas.

Dryas hesitated as she glanced at her, and she sensed his concern about returning to the Hearth too soon. For someone who didn't possess the Gift, he often surprised her with his knack of knowing exactly what someone was feeling in any given moment. That or something in Zosime's face had given away her fear of running into one of the families earlier and he had noticed it. She gave him a nod to show that she was ready to return and the four of them headed back to the gates.

Zosime couldn't ignore her dread as they strolled back and she worried that not enough time had passed for the grieving families to return home. But to her immense relief, she didn't sense any sorrow when they walked past the gates again. Those who had lost Trainees in the Trials had likely gone home to grieve quietly, she thought.

She could now see the stares from her fellow Leondrians that followed her and Vasiliki everywhere they went. The air was heavy with expectation since the two of them were finally eligible to take their places as Queens of Leondria.

Yet, every single one of their ancestors who had ruled before them had ruled alone. There had never been two queens at the same time, and Zosime didn't know of any kings or queens who began their reign the day they donned their red cloaks for the first time. Despite the stares, Zosime felt a sense of rightness at being able to walk within the Hearth again.

Leondria encompassed a decent portion of land which included farms, Lady Meraki's Forest, and the Training Center. As Trainees, they had been limited to the Training Center which was located outside the gates so she had only been able to stare longingly at the Hearth from the distance for the past ten years.

She had waited so many years to return to where she had grown up and what she considered to be the spirit of Leondria. Very little had changed since she had lived here as a child, to her great relief.

Zosime never wanted to leave again.

As they walked, she could sense how the brothers' estrangement from not seeing each other for years was already starting to melt away. Balthasar nonchalantly led them through the crowd until they were standing by the Heart. Zosime overheard some whispers from the crowd that the annual Council meeting was about to begin as they made their way to the front. She spotted Anastasia and Perleros standing off to the right before the crowd became completely silent and the Council emerged from the Tower.

They moved in absolute silence, their sandals not making a sound against the ground as they walked towards the front of the crowd. Leondrians parted as the seven Council members walked in a single line towards the Heart and then turned to face everyone in the city. They wore all-red robes that covered every inch of their bodies and white fabric covered their faces underneath the red hoods. Any trace of individuality was gone, and not even Zosime could differentiate one from the other.

Only the mightiest of warriors could move without making a sound or see perfectly with something impairing their vision. Only the greatest of Leondrians could become a member of the Council. Those whose selfless-ness, greatness in battle, and absolute devotion to duty qualified them for this life-long position but at great cost. All those on the Council forfeited their names and were simply referred to as the Honored Nameless Ones.

They were essential for Leondria's government, which was composed of a single monarch who was a descendant of Lady Meraki and the seven mem-bers of the Council. These two branches of the government kept balance by providing a single ruler for everyone to unite behind while preventing any reckless monarch from leading them to catastrophe. This balance was achieved by requiring the monarch to receive the Council's approval for certain actions, such as declaring war or making official alliances.

"The first day of Mione has begun." the Council intoned together, and everyone made the sign of the gods. "Long may we serve Lady Meraki."

"Long may we serve Lady Meraki!" bellowed every Leondrian.

When the roar died down, the Council declared at the same time, "There is only one item on our agenda today."

Zosime sensed everyone's anticipation grow and the Council said, "Zosime, daughter of King Atreos, and Vasiliki, daughter of King Atreos, stand before us."

Zosime and Vasiliki broke away from the crowd and walked forward until they stood directly in front of the Council. Even from this close distance, Zosime couldn't pierce the white cloth to see the Council members' faces.

"Kneel." they ordered.

Zosime and Vasiliki fell to their knees, holding their left fists over their hearts and waited. Seconds passed in silence before the Council finally declared, "Rise, Queen Zosime of Leondria. Rise Queen Vasiliki of Leondria. Long may they serve."

Zosime felt Perleros's surprise and a strange sort of gratification from the Council, but she ignored these competing emotions as she rose to her feet and turned to face the crowd. Every Leondrian, besides the Council, was still kneeling with their left fists placed over their hearts.

A beat passed before the crowd suddenly roared, *"Long may they serve!"*

CHAPTER

7

Zosime thought for sure that the Gift would become numb after the bombardment of emotions she felt during Mione. There wasn't a single person who didn't feel something and didn't feel it profoundly. She mainly sensed the same three emotions from everyone she passed: Joy. Relief. Anticipation.

Despite the strangeness of having two people rule for the first time in their history, Zosime could tell that her people were comforted by her joint coronation with Vasiliki. That this event signified to them that times were finally returning to normal.

Zosime wasn't sure what "normal" was since she had been part of the generation that never had a Leondrian monarch in charge and had never met Lady Meraki. She could feel how badly the older generations yearned for it though and Zosime intended to do her best to provide it for them. Not that she cared much for tradition for tradition's sake, but she did care about serving her people.

The autumn sun was glowing like amber in the late afternoon on that first day of Mione and Zosime's head turned when she caught movement in her peripheral vision. She turned just in time to see Balthasar nudging Dryas before tilting his head toward one of the market stalls they were passing by. Dryas followed his gaze then his eyes lit up in delight.

"Go on." Balthasar laughed but Dryas hesitated when he glanced back at Zosime who hadn't immediately moved forward.

"Let's get some! I'm absolutely starving." Zosime said with a little too much conviction to be taken at face value and Dryas raised a disbelieving eyebrow at her.

"Excellent." Balthasar laughed and nudged him again.

Zosime smirked and asked Vasiliki, "How about you?"

"Er—sure." Vasiliki agreed and Zosime playfully pushed her forward. It wasn't hard enough to be a shove, but she did apply enough pressure to drive Vasiliki a couple steps forward.

"Do you like lamb?" Balthasar asked when Vasiliki recovered her footing just in time to avoid hitting the man in front of them in line.

"It's perfectly fine." Vasiliki answered politely, if not a little insincerely. Balthasar raised a skeptical eyebrow and Zosime blinked from how similarly he reminded her of Dryas with the gesture. Vasiliki cleared her throat and said a little more convincingly, "No, really."

"It's okay—" Dryas began, as if it meant nothing to him, but Zosime sensed his disappointment.

"It's your favorite." Vasiliki shook her head adamantly and continued a little forcefully. "And I'm hungry."

Zosime sensed her sister's discomfort from being in the spotlight and decided to change the subject.

"Does Daphne intend to compete in any of the contests tomorrow?" Zosime asked as they moved up a place in line when the Leondrian in front received their meal.

Zosime hadn't known Balthasar well since he had graduated from a different Training class but, in the process of catching up today, she had learned that he had married a couple years ago.

Balthasar hesitated before replying, "No, she isn't."

"Why not?" Zosime asked, intrigued when she sensed that he was holding something back.

Dryas frowned then his eyes widened in realization moments before Balthasar said quietly, "She is with child."

"Congratulations!" Dryas praised and Balthasar looked around to ensure no one had overheard them.

"She was feeling too nauseated to leave the house today, but she'll probably join us tonight." he explained in an undertone. "But we're not sharing the news with everyone just yet."

"Praise the gods!" Zosime said enthusiastically but only loud enough to be just above a whisper. "Lady Meraki and Lady Hermione have blessed you both. How far along—"

They were interrupted when the next person in line was served, and it was then their turn to order. She was surprised when she felt Vasiliki's bitterness until she remembered her sister's resentment toward their extended family. The last of their mortal family might have all passed away decades ago, but they did still have six immortal relatives they had never met.

Zosime was resolved to do her best as a queen, but she couldn't do anything about making Lady Meraki return. No one had seen Lady Meraki, or any of the other gods, for twenty years which was unheard of. Nor had they been given any explanation for why the gods suddenly disappeared after millennia of walking among the mortals. Zosime had heard whispers when she was a child that Lady Hermione and Lord Kal would still visit random mortals, but only rarely and only while in disguise.

"Queen Zosime." The vendor grunted as he handed her a plate with piping-hot lamb.

She gave him a respectful nod as she took it from him, and he nodded back before he started preparing the next plate.

Leondrians were never charged for such amenities since there was an understanding that non-Leondrians like this vendor would provide them with food in exchange for guaranteed protection against harm. Leondrians may be the sworn defenders of Midrios, but they couldn't prevent all forms of violence from erupting throughout the entire country. So those who feared being the victims of some rogue killer wouldn't have to worry about such things by living so close to the renowned warriors.

While the Leondrians never had to physically exchange anything for these services, she knew that the non-Leondrians residing in her borders often bartered with each other for supplies. Their services were highly valued but, while they may live in Leondria's borders, they were under no circumstances to be considered Leondrians. They did not go through Training, did not survive the Trials, and did not earn the honor of wearing the red cloak.

"Queen Vasiliki." The vendor grunted as he handed her sister the plate and the group headed to a nearby table.

Zosime was relieved to feel her sister's bitterness fade as they ate, even if it was only because she was now distracted by her distaste towards the lamb. Zosime personally thought it was excellently cooked, but she knew her sister preferred other food.

From her seat, she saw that the streets were practically deserted. Today might have been the beginning of their beloved festival but the first day of Mione was focused on families reuniting and spending time together before the bonfires that night. The real fun, Zosime thought, would begin tomorrow.

She enjoyed herself as they slowly ate and chatted, but she couldn't shake the emotions she was sensing from Dryas and Balthasar. While they had been more than gracious by sharing their time with them on this family day, she could tell they had sorely missed each other. She could tell how deeply the brothers yearned to catch up alone and she gave Vasiliki a meaningful look when they were too engrossed in an inside joke with each other to notice the exchange.

Vasiliki took the hint and gave her a small nod.

"Would you mind if we met back up with you in a couple hours?" Vasiliki asked tentatively.

"Are you sure?" Dryas asked and Zosime felt a twinge of regret from him, as if he thought that he had been ignoring them in favor of his brother. "We'd be more than happy to explore or do whatever it is that you want to do."

"We explored plenty today. I just want to see our old rooms." Zosime said smoothly to show that he hadn't been neglecting them.

"Assuming we're allowed in." Vasiliki added.

Zosime raised her eyebrows and replied in a tone that was too grave to be taken seriously, "We'd best find out then."

Zosime sensed Balthasar's amused skepticism and his gratefulness to have some time alone with Dryas.

"Whatever makes you most comfortable." Balthasar smiled and Zosime sensed his sincerity when he continued. "Will you join us tonight at the bonfires?"

"Can do." Zosime smiled back politely.

She nudged Vasiliki's arm, and they walked slowly back to the Heart where they had just been proclaimed as queens.

Zosime had sensed how others felt awed reverence towards the Heart, but it was simply home to her. She and Vasiliki had grown up there until they were taken away to Training when they were ten years old. She had spent so many nights of the last decade dreaming about this place and her heart quickened with longing expectation as they approached it.

They walked up the three steps to the main landing where the entrance was always guarded by two Leondrian guards who inspected visitors before permitting them to enter. But certain people, like the queens or generals, weren't ever stopped since they had previous authorization to enter. The two guards weren't supposed to react unless stopping people for authorization, but they unexpectedly inclined their heads towards them as they passed.

Zosime and Vasiliki inclined their heads back and the guards then made a remarkable impression of resembling marble when they stiffened and returned their gazes forward. Zosime understood that they couldn't be seen as relaxing on duty, and she appreciated that they took a moment to greet them. Mione may have been the only holiday that Leondrians recognized but there were always guards posted at the gates and at the Heart. She sensed their longing to be home, but they must have drawn the short straw to be on duty today.

She then approached the dark brown, wooden doors which had indentations on it in the shapes of lions and triangles. Zosime pushed the door open and was briefly overcome by a flash of déjà vu as they walked inside.

She felt like she was ten years old again and could have sworn that she was reliving a memory of the two of them running down the halls. Well, of Zosime running down the halls in the hopes that her sister would chase her, but Vasiliki only ever followed her at a brisk walk. That had always been the case with the two of them growing up, with Zosime jumping forward and Vasiliki hanging back.

Zosime glanced around and was relieved to discover that her home was just as she remembered it. As a representative of Leondria's beating heart, it wasn't designed to be some meaningless spectacle. It was functional and durable, which was clear from the hard stone that lined the walls and floor. There were sparse hallways with various rooms lining the corridors, each one serving a specific purpose. There was the Generals' meeting room, rooms for special visitors, rooms for the monarch, rooms for the monarch's children, a special room dedicated to commemorating their family history, a dining room, a kitchen, and a weaponry room.

Instead of exploring these rooms, they headed directly for their bedrooms. For security reasons, their chambers weren't right next to each other, so Zosime gave Vasiliki a brief parting nod before walking further down the hallway.

Zosime took a very quick breath when she stopped in front of her old room. She only hesitated briefly before opening the door and stepping inside. She made sure to keep the door open so the torches from the hallway would bring some light into the otherwise pitch-black room. Glass was a rare commodity, so the architects hadn't bothered making windows when they built it.

She glanced around the room and blinked when she noticed that it was spotless. Some servants must have come in to clean recently because there wasn't a speck of dust to be seen after ten years of vacancy and the freshly washed sheets on the bed were tightly tucked in.

Zosime kneeled before the large chest that sat by the foot of the bed. She popped it open and found clean crimson tunics, red cloaks, white sleeping robes, torches for the room, polishing materials, and some other supplies. She closed it and stood, taking in the rest of the room. There was a chair pushed off to a corner, a sconce to hang up a torch, and a weapons rack, but her chambers were otherwise empty since anything else would be a useless frivolity.

She didn't move for a while as she was overcome by a rush of memories from her childhood. But there were no tutors or guards following her every move now. Nor were there any Spears to dictate every minute of her day as they did during Training. She was suddenly struck by the realization that she could do anything she wanted right now.

She still had to live up to the responsibilities of being a Leondrian and to be a good queen for her people but that would be no trouble. She only had one dream in her life and that was to wear the red cloak. Now that she finally had it, she didn't know what that meant for the future. But tomorrow was too far away to think about so she wouldn't waste a thought on it until she had to.

She couldn't quite shake the smile tugging at the corners of her mouth when she padded down the hall to check on Vasiliki sometime later. Vasiliki hadn't bothered to shut the door so Zosime leaned against the doorframe and looked at her sister who was clearly lost in thought in the middle of the room. Vasiliki's eyes cleared when Zosime cleared her throat but neither said anything at first.

Zosime could feel her twin's detachment and she raised her eyebrows at her in wonder. She felt that typical flicker of resentment whenever Vasiliki realized that she was reading her emotions, but Vasiliki just never understood that the Gift wasn't something she could just turn on and off at will. It was something ingrained within her, and she could force herself to stop sensing other people's emotions like she could command her heart to stop beating.

Vasiliki didn't comment on this and merely said a little too flatly for Zosime's liking, "It's strange being back, isn't it."

Zosime resisted the urge to react. She didn't understand how Vasiliki was feeling so disengaged on the most important day of their lives. As if donning the cloak had been some burden for her to endure instead of cherishing.

Except for the Leondrians' strict adherence to follow tradition to the letter, Zosime loved everything about being a Leondrian. She loved sleeping out in the elements, doing physical challenges, being the toughest warriors in the land, and always pushing themselves to be better protectors for Midrios.

But her sister always had her head stuck in the clouds instead of seeing what was right in front of her. Deciding against pushing the subject which would only start an argument, Zosime instead jerked her head towards the hall a couple times and suggested, "Don't want to miss the party, do we?"

"No." Vasiliki replied quietly but it was clear that her heart wasn't in it.

"I think we've killed enough time here." Zosime joked as she walked away from the doorframe and ignored her rising irritation towards her sister's attitude.

Vasiliki didn't respond and silently followed her down the halls. When they walked onto the landing, Zosime paused. From this point at the top of a hill, she had a perfect view of the Hearth. She could even see Leondrian territory stretching out beyond the horizon where the Training Center and the farms were.

It was so beautiful, and she was forcefully struck by how grateful she was to be back home.

Zosime tore her gaze away from the distance and surveyed her people as she stepped down the three steps to rejoin them on the ground. Now that twilight was upon them, people were now starting to crowd the streets again. She felt their excitement and there was a noticeable difference in their usually reserved demeanor. They were lighter, freer, and there were more smiles than Zosime was used to seeing.

This was a time when they could all let their guards down and revel in much needed leisure time. People could partake in more wine than they otherwise would and relax but, even during this time of great celebration, under no circumstances should a Leondrian be caught lapsing in their discipline.

Zosime led Vasiliki towards the housing division of the Hearth. But instead of turning left where the rows of houses were, Zosime took a right where several tables surrounded small, triangle-shaped pyres. She was in the middle of looking for a free table when she caught movement in her peripheral. She turned towards the movement and found Balthasar waving for the two of them to join him.

She made a beeline towards him, ensuring to keep a healthy distance from the burning pyres where people were giving portions of their food in sacrifice to Lady Meraki, and saw Dryas and Daphne sitting on either side of him. She felt Dryas's spark of happiness and Daphne's curiosity when the two of them approached.

"My queens, this is Daphne, my wife." Balthasar introduced while Zosime sat down across from Dryas.

Daphne made the sign of the gods and said, "It is an honor to meet you, my queens."

"The honor is mine." Zosime replied and returned the gesture.

She knew next to nothing about her, only some tidbits she had heard earlier in the day from Balthasar. Such as Daphne and Balthasar marrying soon after they passed the Trials together. It had been clear based on how he talked about her that he had the highest respect for his wife. Seeing the two of them together, Zosime could now feel how deep that love connection was, as if their very hearts were intertwined.

Daphne had the characteristic muscled physique, tanned skin, and dark brown eyes of Leondrians. But where most Leondrians were defined by their hard facial contours and stern expressions, Daphne's face was soft. It wasn't the kind of softness that Zosime equated to weakness, but there was something about her features that reminded Zosime of the first green spurts of a budding tree that had just sprouted from the ground. There was something soothing about her, despite the sharp perceptiveness gleaming in those brown eyes.

"I'm glad you're feeling better." Vasiliki said politely.

Daphne smiled good-naturedly and waved a hand, "Morning sickness doesn't agree with me."

Daphne laughed when Balthasar quickly glanced at her and admonished lightly, "You already told them, my love."

His lips twisted up in amusement and he sheepishly conceded, "I suppose I did."

She must have been in the early stages of her pregnancy since Daphne still wore the red Leondrian uniform instead of the white pregnancy robes that women wore from their second trimester until their child was weened. Unless, of course, such women became pregnant again right afterwards and started the cycle all over again. Many women took that honorable path until they went through menopause while other females preferred to return to the ranks as soon as they finished breastfeeding. But it was understood that everyone, pregnant or otherwise, always had the golden shield of Leondria strapped to their arm.

Daphne suddenly craned her neck then chuckled, "You came on a good night."

Zosime followed her gaze where a slightly older Leondrian was finishing up his meal a few tables away from them. She felt herself drawn in by the others' anticipation but didn't know why they were feeling so excited.

Zosime turned back to Daphne and asked, "Why's that?"

"Flavian is quite the storyteller." Daphne smiled knowingly but somehow not with smug superiority.

"He's the best!" Balthasar exclaimed and continued quietly so only their small group could hear. "When the Spears weren't watching, he would tell us the best stories during Training."

"Does he tell stories every night?" Vasiliki asked.

"Not always." Balthasar answered with a shrug. "Just frequently."

"How do you know when he'll tell a story then?" Vasiliki asked Daphne uncertainly.

Daphne glanced back at Flavian and gestured, "Look at his eyes."

Zosime looked at him and she felt more than saw his eagerness as he glanced around the tables multiple times. Flavian swallowed another bite of his roasted lamb then walked over to the nearest shared bonfires.

"May we live to die free, Lady Meraki." he prayed before tossing the most succulent part of the meal into the fire.

He moved to return to his table when Balthasar cried out, "A story!"

Flavian's gaze snapped over to Balthasar then protested with feigned modesty, "I couldn't."

Zosime could sense Flavian's delight and how much he looked forward to nights like these, which was also evident in the crooked smile that now lined his face.

Many around them joined in the request for him to tell a story. Flavian pretended to buckle under the audience's expectations when he held up his hands in mock defeat and agreed, "Alright, alright."

He walked over to stand in front of the fire and Zosime noticed Leondrians from other pyres walk over to be in easy earshot.

Flavian clapped his hands together in delight and asked, "Are there any requests?"

"Tell us one about King Alexandros!" a few demanded. "Tell us about Leondria's founding."

Flavian mulled these suggestions over then shook his head, "I think one about Lady Hermione would be the most appropriate for tonight."

No one argued with that, so he composed his thoughts for a few moments then launched into the history of how Lady Hermione brought the cycles of days and nights through her children. Zosime hadn't doubted Balthasar, but she blinked in surprise at just how good Flavian was at public speaking.

It was true that Leondrians shouldn't seek attention, but he was such a captivating storyteller that this flaw was easily forgiven. Zosime became utterly absorbed and just fell into the story, almost as if she was living it herself, and just listened in contentment while the bonfires burned late into the night.

—

Zosime awoke to a pounding knock on her door, and she bolted up in bed. Nausea coiled in her stomach, and her head was slightly spinning. By the gods, she thought, maybe that last cup of wine had been a mistake.

"Zosime!" Vasiliki called out.

Zosime staggered when she stood and glanced at her chamber pot, relieved she hadn't thrown up and let the servants know she had over-indulged the night before. She stumbled in the general direction of the door then opened it, blinking from the torchlight in the hallway.

Vasiliki took in her appearance for a moment then stated, "They're about to start."

Zosime inwardly cursed, thinking that the lack of light in the room must have thrown off her inner clock, but she only gave Vasiliki a terse nod. She realized that was a mistake when a spike of pain laced the inside of her skull, and she felt Vasiliki's eyes on her when she quickly grabbed her sword and shield. She sensed some concern and a little bit of judgment, but Vasiliki gracefully didn't say anything as they hurried down the hall. Zosime hastily strapped on the sword and shield before they ran into anyone else, and they soon stood outside where the rising sun now crested the horizon.

Today would be the beginning of the contests. The real fun. For the rest of the week, there would be sprint relays, timed treks up the closest mountain range on the other side of Leondria and Lady Meraki's Forest, push up contests, and many other tournaments to prove everyone's strength.

Vendors lined the streets with water pouches, wine, and food which Zosime gleefully accepted. She furiously gulped down some water and bread as she and Vasiliki followed the crowd outside the gates then resisted the urge to sigh in relief as her headache started dissipating.

"There you are!" Dryas called out and Zosime followed the sound of his voice until she found him and Balthasar in the middle of the crowd.

"I've waited a long time for this, brother." Balthasar clapped Dryas on the back.

"He has." Daphne teased lightly. "But I don't know why."

Balthasar couldn't stop himself from laughing when he said, "My wife seems to doubt my skills."

"Not at all." Daphne rested a hand on her stomach. "But you won't win with the queens competing."

Balthasar kissed her on the cheek and rested a hand on her lower back as they walked forward.

"I'll get top three." Balthasar winked.

"Now that, I am confident of." Daphne agreed with a loving smile.

"Let's go." Zosime encouraged to Vasiliki when she sensed her hesitation. "Tree throwing will be so much fun."

"You should do it." Vasiliki said. "I'll be happy watching you."

Zosime stared at her but didn't respond. She was only willing to push Vasiliki so far out of her comfort zone and it was too exhausting to do even that some days.

Daphne turned back, clearly overhearing the conversation, and pursed her lips. She hesitated for a moment then urged respectfully, "You should join in, my queen."

"I'm fine." Vasiliki disagreed awkwardly. "I'd rather watch."

Daphne's pained expression didn't go away, and she said gently, "Your people need to see you in action."

Zosime sensed Vasiliki's ripples of uneasiness but also a resigned sense of duty from the sincerity emanating from Daphne's words.

Zosime could tell that Balthasar agreed with Daphne, but he only shrugged and turned to Dryas, "Come, brother. Let's see just how badly I crush you."

Dryas was clearly reluctant to leave Vasiliki when she was uncomfortable, but he followed Balthasar when Vasiliki gave him a nod to show that it was okay for him to leave.

"Don't be fooled." Daphne sighed when the brothers were out of earshot. "They would agree with me, but you're basically a sister to them, Vasiliki."

Vasiliki looked down then finally said, "Adelphie's only has a year left in Training."

"That's a long time away from people you love." Daphne said kindly. "And ruling involves stepping into the spotlight."

Zosime could feel how keenly the brothers missed their sister, even if it was a subject they didn't mention out loud. The only time family members were allowed to see Trainees were during funerals of close relatives because permitting them any more breaks from Training would weaken them.

Vasiliki looked away when Daphne suggested, "Think about it."

Daphne walked towards the brothers and Zosime sighed, "She's right, Vasiliki."

Zosime didn't look back to see if Vasiliki followed her when she rejoined the trio and cracked her neck as she waited. Zosime knew her sister. Even as a child, Vasiliki avoided large crowds, but Zosime hoped that she would come out of her shell soon. Not that it was shyness holding her sister back, but it felt almost like some compulsive need to analyze every little thing before acting.

Zosime's veins crackled with life as the crowd cheered and shouted playful jeers at the competitors, and she thought that she could live off this energy forever.

"Better be warming up, brother." Balthasar warned.

"Don't need to if you're my competition." Dryas rolled his eyes with a playful smirk.

Everyone roared when Perleros gave a nod, signifying the beginning of the event. Without further ado, the people ahead of them started throwing their trees and Zosime was impressed by how well everyone did. They had arrived later than the others so the three of them would be competing last, but they passed the time with lighthearted heckles.

"Is that the best you can do?" Balthasar teased Flavian after he threw his tree.

Flavian wiped the sweat off his brow and gestured to him, "Like you could do better, Sergeant."

"Oh, we'll see." Balthasar replied good-naturedly then, after bumping elbows with Dryas, he warned, "Better not throw out your back, little brother."

Dryas only scoffed before bending down to pick up his tree and lifting it up over his head. He took a single step forward then threw it as far as it could across the clearing. Balthasar squinted as they watched it land farther than all the other trees that had been thrown so far.

"Gods' blood." Flavian swore under his breath. "There goes top three."

"Watch and learn." Balthasar winked as the crowd roared then he bent down to pick up his own tree.

He paused for a moment before throwing it and they watched it land several feet farther than Dryas's. Dryas may have been the taller and stockier of the two brothers, but Balthasar was deceptively muscular for his lean frame.

All eyes now turned to Zosime, and she could feel the anticipation rise in her chest. Without further ado, she picked up the tree, smoothly lifted it above her head, then launched it across the field. The tree easily soared past everyone else's and crashed against the ground, several of the branches splintering beyond recognition on impact.

She turned to look at her sister who had been hovering behind her and she felt her resolve harden before Vasiliki stepped forward to claim the tree next to Zosime. The crowd quieted and watched her intently as Vasiliki picked up the tree, her gaze focusing into the distance. Zosime could see that Vasiliki wasn't struggling with the weight but that she merely wanted to take her time with the task, like with everything she did. Vasiliki took a breath before cocking her arm back and launching the tree into the air. It soared like a bird born into flight then smashed right next to Zosime's half-crushed tree.

They had tied.

The crowd went wild in their excitement before finally quieting when Zosime heard someone walk up to the final tree. Her heart leapt when Anastasia approached the tree next to them. Anastasia didn't seem to be looking at anything in particular when she effortlessly lifted the tree into her arms. Anastasia narrowed her eyes at the distance in a moment of concentration then catapulted the tree across the field without breaking a sweat. It soared in the air and landed hard against the ground—noticeably further than everyone else's but significantly behind the sisters' trees.

The crowd roared again, and Balthasar smirked at Daphne, "Third place."

"I never doubted you." Daphne laughed then kissed Balthasar.

The tree throwing may have been the first official contest of the day, but Zosime lost count how many times she passed by groups of Leondrians engaging in unofficial physical contests. One had to watch their step as Leondrians spontaneously engaged in pushups, sit ups, and planks throughout the Hearth.

"Is that the best you can do?" was one of the regular taunts she would hear.

"Just getting warmed up." would be a common response, despite the obvious sweat dripping down their faces.

Dryas and Balthasar weren't immune to this energy and Zosime saw Daphne shaking her head in amusement as the brothers would push each other to their limits.

Zosime sensed Vasiliki slowly relaxing as the festivities continued. Zosime was immensely enjoying herself, appreciating what a nice change it was to be herself. It could be such a struggle sometimes to maintain the expression of grave soberness that the rest of the year demanded of her. Not that she didn't take her duty seriously, but it was difficult to repress making jokes or smiling anytime she wanted.

This had by far been the best week of her life. It may have taken a couple days for Zosime to adjust to sleeping indoors, but when she did, she was always the first one to wake and be ready for the day. She relished finally feeling as one with her people, seeing old friends again, and feeling nothing but joy from everyone around her.

Well, from almost everyone around her.

Zosime couldn't shake the feelings of uneasiness from Perleros and Anastasia, nor could she escape the grief of certain people who had lost a Trainee in the Trials. She understood why they felt anguish for obvious reasons, but she couldn't figure out why Perleros and Anastasia were still feeling disturbed. She had a hunch it had something to do with the Trials and the black blood that had stained Anastasia's armor. But they hadn't told her anything about it and she didn't know why it was bothering them when everyone knew that dangerous beasts roamed Lady Meraki's Forest.

She kept waiting for Perleros or Anastasia to come tell them what to do next, but they never did. She couldn't shake the feeling that she was being watched but they never approached her. Zosime wasn't ready for the week to end but time seemed to slip through her fingers like water until it was all gone.

The final day of Mione came much faster than she wanted, and everyone's mood was already dampening in preparation for another hard year. She noticed Dryas and Balthasar glancing at her and Vasiliki more frequently on the final morning of the festival as the sun steadily climbed up the sky until noon approached.

"My queens." a familiar voice said from behind her.

Zosime's heart skipped a beat, and she turned to find Anastasia making the sign of the gods. Zosime quickly recovered herself and returned the gesture. The two of them could almost be mistaken for sisters with their same height and willowy build, if it wasn't for Anastasia's blue-grey eyes that very clearly indicated she wasn't a descendant of Lady Meraki. Neither did her blonde hair match Zosime or Vasiliki's brunette locks.

"It's time." Anastasia stated.

Zosime and Vasiliki gave the brothers and Daphne a parting look as Anastasia led the two of them away.

"Time to announce the new year, my queens, then to attend a meeting with the generals." she informed as she led them back to the Heart. "Do you know the words?"

Zosime and Vasiliki glanced at each other and shook their heads. Anastasia quickly muttered the instructions then waited with the others as Zosime walked up the three steps of the Heart to address their people. Zosime looked out at the large crowd that had assembled before them, and they stared at her expectantly.

When Vasiliki didn't speak up, Zosime cleared her throat and announced, "Mione has now ended. Fighting for the new year now begins."

She paused and looked at Vasiliki who finished, "May each day be devoted to Lady Meraki and to serving Leondria. Long may we serve."

The crowd echoed the words: long may we serve. The sisters glanced at each other uncertainly before making the sign of the gods. Zosime glanced over at Anastasia who gave the wooden doors behind her a meaningful look, so Zosime turned on her heel and entered the Heart.

She and Vasiliki barely made it a few steps inside when Perleros emerged from the shadows. The older man gave them the sign of the gods and greeted, "Time for a meeting, my queens."

They followed him down the hall and into a spacious room designated for the generals' meetings. Leondrians moved fast but Zosime was surprised by how quickly they had assembled, considering the pronouncement had occurred only a couple minutes ago. The chattering ceased and all the generals made the sign of the gods when Zosime and Vasiliki walked in behind Perleros.

Zosime could feel their expectations and uncertainty. Not uncertainty in themselves but in their untested queens. Zosime and Vasiliki had never seen battle or led Leondrians before. Age was not a huge factor when assessing one's leadership skills, considering the relatively high likelihood of Leondrians dying young. But the fact remained that the queens were the youngest in the room with no experience and Zosime could sense that did mean something to them.

Leondria hadn't gone on any campaigns since the death of King Atreo twenty years ago. As a result, Leondrians who may have otherwise died in battle were able to age and many now possessed streaks of silver in their hair or beards. There was no need for introductions here since everyone in Leondria knew who the queens were, and Trainees were consistently drilled on who was in their chain of command.

"It's an honor to serve you as we did your father." General Penelope announced, an old woman whose hair was now dominated by grey hairs instead of brunette ones. She looked like her best years were behind her and Zosime sensed a tiredness in her, as if her energy had long ago dissipated.

Zosime glanced at Perleros when she felt a sudden wave of sorrow and shame from him, but his face remained as impassive as stone. His eyes flickered to hers and, when they made eye contact, she felt him tighten the reigns on his emotions until she only felt focus from him.

"It's time to create the objectives for the year." Perleros stated.

The generals were now actively staring at the two of them, but they were greeted with silence. They had spent their lives waiting for orders and obeying commands, but it now seemed like they wanted them to just start issuing commands.

"May we proceed, my queens?" Perleros hinted.

She could sense Vasiliki's discomfort as keenly as her own and Zosime found herself nodding to Perleros's question.

Zosime turned towards the doorway when she heard footsteps and saw Anastasia enter the room. Zosime didn't comment but couldn't help but wonder why she was there. She was a Spear, one of the elites who had been hand-picked to instruct Trainees and lead them to the Trials. She should have returned to her post in the Training Center, not be listening in on a meeting with the queens and her generals. But no one else objected when Anastasia walked to a corner and silently watched them, so Zosime returned her attention to the generals and ignored her rapidly beating heart.

"The farms reported having enough crops to support Leondria through the year." General Thea, another woman with wrinkles around her eyes but who looked young enough to still be in her prime, said matter of factly. "But they harvested less than anticipated and we should consider rationing."

Zosime frowned then said slowly, "Okay."

"How much did they harvest?" Perleros asked.

"About three quarters their typical amount." General Thea answered promptly.

"We can do quarter rations and reserve however much we can spare for the winter, if the queens authorize it." Perleros suggested with a significant look at her.

"Authorized." Zosime replied with more bravado than she felt in that moment and sensed a flicker of approval from a couple people in the room.

She knew she had a long way to go to earn their trust but, based on that reaction, she knew it was decisive authority and confidence they valued.

"It will be done." General Thea said coolly, as if such a feat was trivial.

Zosime's eyes snapped to General Oscar when he stepped forward to address them. He still looked to be close to Perleros's age but, based on the fewer grey hairs and wrinkles on his face, was the younger of the two.

His emotions felt sharper than the others, as if he was more on edge than they were. His brown eyes glimmered when he said, "It is an honor to serve you both like we did your father, my queens. Your arrival marks a return to our roots, and we should discuss the matter of finally resuming expeditions—"

"Such discussions are premature before the queens even tour the rest of their city-state." Perleros interrupted brusquely and, to Zosime's surprise, with severe dislike rising in his chest.

She felt General Oscar's simmering contempt towards him, but he only nodded in reluctant acquiescence to his superior officer.

"We'll coordinate separate tours for each queen." Perleros added and everyone nodded in agreement. "When would you like to see your lands, my queens?"

"The sooner the better." Zosime responded eagerly.

The room grew silent and Perleros looked expectantly at the queens who glanced uncertainly at each other.

"No further matters, my queens." he said then, after a beat, ordered to the other generals, "Dismissed."

They made the sign of the gods and gave the queens parting glances, leaving only Zosime, Vasiliki, Perleros, and Anastasia in the room.

Perleros stared at the queens for a long time before he finally advised, "Always watch and listen."

"Yes, General." Zosime said.

"Yes, General." Vasiliki repeated quietly.

He then gestured towards Anastasia while looking at Zosime and said, "Anastasia is now a member of your personal guard. If you approve."

Zosime's heart quickened even more but she still managed to agree, "Yes, General."

Anyone else standing next to Perleros may have been overshadowed by the mammoth-sized man but Anastasia's impenetrable expression and deadly grace created the illusion that she stood just as tall as him.

"You graduated Training." Anastasia said after a moment of silence. "Don't wait for Perleros to speak for you. You're the voice for your people now. Use it."

Zosime wasn't the type to have trouble making decisions but acting on instinct in the heat of the moment was one thing. Learning to give orders to the very same people who had regimented her entire life before this was something else.

She just had to learn to speak up because her people were counting on her now, and she wouldn't be able to live with herself if she let them down.

Mione may have just ended, but Zosime already knew that it was going to be a long year.

CHAPTER

8

Zosime was used to having all her time organized for her, but she had no idea where all her time went after Mione. It turned out that a lot went into ruling Leondria that she hadn't anticipated. Training plans required her authorization, vendors in the market needed to have their passes to serve food renewed, she had to attend every meeting with the generals where they wanted her orders for everything, and she was called to resolve even minor disputes.

She was also expected to lead Leondrians through physical exercises with Vasiliki every morning. But that was one duty she didn't mind at all. In fact, she was grateful for this release of energy since she didn't have free time to work out throughout the day anymore. But once these daily two-hour morning exercises were over, the rest of her day was occupied with other tasks. She was so busy that she hadn't even seen Vasiliki much for the past few weeks outside of meetings and the nightly bonfires.

There had also been deliberately separated due to security concerns. Zosime and Vasiliki were the only two people left of Lady Meraki's mortal line so many of the generals had agreed with General Oscar's suggestion in their second meeting for the queens to spend time apart. Zosime knew that they weren't particularly concerned about anything terrible happening to their queens in the Hearth, but she could sense their never-ending worry for their safety.

Zosime couldn't honestly say that she felt prepared for her new role, and while she charged ahead confidently, she couldn't shake the feeling of being lost. She wasn't used to spending so much time away from her sister and, as a result, she felt as if a part of her was missing. There had only been a few times when they had been separated in their lives, but this felt different from those prior experiences. Longer and as if it would never end. It also complicated day-to-day matters as well. Such as certain disputes being decided by one sister without the other knowing until later.

Except for Anastasia following her like a shadow everywhere, Zosime stood alone for the second time in her life. Those winter camping trips to the mountains where the Spears would periodically check on her to see if she had frozen to death didn't count in her mind. The first time she had ever really stood alone, she thought, was during the Trials.

Not that Zosime often thought about the Trials. In fact, she tried her best to suppress those memories as much as possible even if they almost always caught up with her in her nightmares. She had made choices there, even if they were only in her mind, and she now had to live with the knowledge of what she was capable of.

Zosime clenched her fists. She didn't want to think about that. Didn't want to think about how real the blood on her hands had felt and how she would have sworn before all the gods that what she had experienced had felt so real that she sometimes confused what happened in the Trials for reality.

"My queen." Anastasia said, snapping Zosime back to the present.

Zosime had been receiving an earful from two farmers who had been getting into a heated argument. One of the first farmer's goats had apparently snuck out of a pen and trespassed on the second farmer's land, eating some bad grapes before ramming down the front door of his house. According to second farmer, the goat had thrown up all over the floor and "destroyed a priceless table" before keeling over dead while the first farmer furiously asserted that the "priceless table" was in fact "a battered stump not fit for a donkey to eat at." Both wanted reparations for property damage, and both wanted Zosime to make the other pay all the costs.

"Yes, Anastasia?" she asked, grateful for the interruption since it was becoming difficult to keep a straight face.

"Are you all set for the generals' meeting?" Anastasia asked, her face the perfect emblem of seriousness. "We're running late."

Zosime turned back to the farmers and inclined her head towards them, "Come to the Heart immediately after morning exercises tomorrow and we'll resolve the issue then."

The farmers reluctantly agreed and immediately proceeded to insult each other as Zosime walked away. The last thing she heard before getting out of earshot was that he "should be grateful since the goat's droppings were much-needed decorations that brightened the room for the jackass living there."

She bit her lip so no one could hear her laugh as she and Anastasia walked back to the Heart and found everyone waiting for her when they strolled into the meeting room.

"The goats are wreaking havoc again, generals." Zosime said by way of explanation with the faintest trace of a smile.

Vasiliki shook her head, and Zosime sensed her amused exasperation.

"Report." Zosime commanded the room when no one else found this statement as comical as she did.

"We have finished gathering food from the farms and they are now stored here for the winter." General Thea responded.

Zosime found herself growing concerned, remembering a comment from the first meeting about rationing. She hadn't known it was a big enough problem to warrant this much relief radiating in the room and made a mental note to keep an eye on the situation in the spring. Since the problem was now resolved for the next few months, she would focus her attention on pressing issues in the meantime.

"The Spears have delivered a favorable report on the next graduating class of Trainees." General Oscar said. "They only predict a few casualties in the upcoming winter."

Zosime nodded, thinking of her own experiences living off the mountain range. Trainees had to camp there for the winters to prove their mettle and demonstrate their survivor skills. Many died from exposure and dehydration, but older Trainees learned how to sustain themselves on those desolate mountain ranges.

"Do we know why we have been yielding less crops in recent years?" Vasiliki asked with a frown and Zosime blinked, thinking they had moved on from that subject.

"We receive what the farmers give us and there is nothing to suggest they are hiding food from us." General Thea said.

Zosime could tell this was really bothering Vasiliki, but her sister kept her tone calm when she urged, "We should ask them if they have any theories."

"It will be done, my queen." Perleros said patiently then continued. "We have also finalized preparations for the Queen's tour."

Zosime almost fidgeted with excitement at the thought. As much as she loved the Hearth and made the most of her time in the Training Center, her heart had always yearned to see the rest of her lands and meet more of her people.

Zosime opened her mouth when Perleros unexpectedly stated, "The preparations are all ready for you to begin your tour in the morning, Queen Vasiliki."

Zosime snapped her mouth shut and caught Perleros assessing her reaction.

"Shouldn't Queen Zosime be joining us on the tour?" Vasiliki asked and Zosime felt Vasiliki's concern at the idea of Zosime being left out.

Affection rose in her chest at her sister's thoughtfulness, and they waited as the generals looked at each other, hesitant to answer right away.

"It would be too much of a security risk, Queen Vasiliki." Perleros answered, softly but with a tone that left no room for argument. "We have you listed to tour Leondria first then Queen Zosime will receive her own private tour a couple weeks after you, my queen."

"Your safety is our primary concern," General Penelope added. "Especially until either or both of you marry and bear children."

Zosime felt a pin drop and she didn't need to look at her sister to know that Vasiliki was blushing.

Zosime was also for a loss for words and only stuttered, "Well—that is—er—"

She had never been more thankful to anyone else before in her life when Perleros interjected smoothly, "That is a separate issue for a different time, General Penelope. Our queens need to complete their tours then we can start discussing potential matches."

The old woman nodded in acceptance and Zosime almost collapsed in sheer relief.

Perleros redirected his attention to Vasiliki and asked, "My queen?"

Vasiliki cleared her throat awkwardly and said honestly, "I would be honored to attend the tour, General Perleros."

Zosime knew Vasiliki didn't want to go anywhere near as much as she did, but she held her tongue. She begrudgingly told herself that Vasiliki also wanted to tour Leondria and that she would just have to wait her turn. As much as the waiting made her heart quicken in jealousy and her toes curl in impatience.

"If there's nothing else—" Zosime hinted, and the generals shook their heads. "Dismissed."

The only way she could have left the room faster would have been to run out and she exhaled in relief when she was out of sight. She was not ready for any discussion about matrimony or children and found herself cringing in revulsion at the thought.

"What are you thinking about?" Vasiliki asked and Zosime spun around.

Zosime sighed and rubbed her forehead, "Needed to get out of there."

"We have some time before dinner." Vasiliki suggested. "Let's wait in my room."

Zosime wholeheartedly agreed with that idea and could feel her sister's nerves as they walked over to her room and closed the door for privacy. Vasiliki lit a torch before sitting on the side of the bed and Zosime collapsed into the chair in the corner of the room.

"That was something." Zosime finally declared.

"Yes." Vasiliki replied, scratching her head. "It was."

They sat in silence for a moment before Vasiliki lifted her head and inquired, "Goats?"

Zosime couldn't stop herself from smiling and proceeded to tell Vasiliki the whole story.

"So it went *baaah baaah* then projectile vomited all over the floor." Zosime laughed. "And now they want me to determine who owes the other what tomorrow."

Vasiliki closed her eyes, and Zosime saw the corners of her mouth lift slightly before she said, "I'll just have to wait to hear how it all gets resolved when I get back."

Jealousy twisted in Zosime's gut, and she stated a little more coldly than she intended, "Right."

Vasiliki frowned and opened her eyes, "Are you alright?"

Zosime didn't feel like talking about it, so she hastily replied, "I was just thinking about our friends. We don't really see them anymore and I don't know how they're doing."

Vasiliki's face grew grave in contemplation, and she stated, "I've been wondering the same thing. We ascended so quickly I wonder how much it's held us back."

Zosime sensed her sister's inner turmoil and almost frowned. It was hard to understand her when she got like this.

Zosime asked her with as little irritation as she could manage, "Why do you think that?"

"Everyone else in charge has had experience with leading. Commanding." Vasiliki shrugged then continued. "All our friends are now at the bottom of the Leondrian hierarchy, learning what to do one step at a time but we skipped all those steps. Now we stand at the top with no idea of what their life is like now."

"Not no idea. We went through Training and the Trials, just like everyone else." Zosime corrected.

"You know what I mean." Vasiliki muttered.

"I don't." Zosime disagreed and she felt a flicker of irritation from her sister.

"It really doesn't bother you?" Vasiliki asked incredulously.

Zosime frowned in genuine confusion, "What should bother me?"

Vasiliki shook her head in disbelief but said nothing.

"Adapting to change is a part of life, Vasiliki. It's who we are as Leondrians. Duty calls and we answer. We may not have the same experience as the others, but we'll learn by doing." Zosime said, not understanding why this was frustrating her sister so much.

Zosime felt a flicker of resentment from Vasiliki and Zosime leaned forward, continuing in a reassuring tone while suppressing the jealousy stirring in her chest, "There is nothing to be worried about tomorrow."

Vasiliki's face flattened and her hands tightened in her lap, "I'm fine, Zosime."

"You'll get to spend an entire week outside in the sunshine and receiving a full tour of Leondria." Zosime forced some optimism in her tone. "You can tell me all about the tour when you get back."

They were suddenly interrupted by a rapping at the door and Vasiliki rose to her feet to answer it.

Anastasia made the sign of the gods when Vasiliki opened the door and greeted, "My queen."

Vasiliki pulled the door further open, and Anastasia scanned the room where she noticed Zosime for the first time.

"My queens." she corrected herself then readdressed Vasiliki, "We leave at sunrise for the tour, my queen. You will be accompanied by three Leondrians for your personal guard."

Vasiliki outwardly took this in stride, but Zosime could keenly feel the uncertainty bubbling under the surface.

"Wouldn't you remain with Zosime as her personal guard?" Vasiliki asked a moment later.

"Ordinarily, yes." Anastasia agreed. "But General Perleros made an exception this time, unless Queen Zosime objects."

Zosime felt another stab of jealousy but only said, "If General Perleros thinks the extra protection is necessary, then not at all."

"He'll be taking over as your personal guard for the week we'll be gone." Anastasia added. "He just wants to take extra precautions, considering."

It was unusual since personal guards always remained nearby their charges, but Zosime could adapt, especially for such a short stint. He probably would have never suggested it if it was a farther journey or required extensive time away from her.

Anastasia must have picked up on some of these feelings because she inquired, "Is there anything you require of me, my queen?"

Vasiliki looked down and only said, "No."

Anastasia briefly pursed her lips and advised, "Follow our lead but we will obey your commands."

Anastasia glanced at Zosime who reflexively stiffened and nodded respectfully before walking away.

"Try to enjoy yourself, Vasiliki." Zosime suggested. "Let's go eat."

Vasiliki responded by snuffing out the torch before following her out.

—

Dinner couldn't have ended fast enough for Zosime, and Vasiliki was even more pensive than usual. To not elicit any unnecessary questions from the others, Zosime quietly patted Vasiliki on the shoulder before leaving the table and heading to her bedroom.

She didn't even bother lighting the torch in her chamber, simply taking off the shield and sword and hanging them up in darkness. And without delay, she fell into bed. She closed her eyes, hoping to fall sleep early, but knowing it would likely be another unrestful night. Whenever she did start drifting into unconsciousness, she could hear echoes of the Creature's voice reverberating in her mind and her eyes kept flying open throughout the night as a result. At least she was being disturbed by her own dreams instead of waking up in confusion whenever she slept nearby others, whose emotions bled into her unconscious mind.

Zosime finally sighed and sat up after waking for the fifth time and cracked her neck as she rose to her feet. It was pointless to expect to go back to sleep at this point so she shuffled over to her shield and picked it up. She rifled through her trunk for cleaning supplies and dutifully went to work polishing her shield.

She scrubbed for as long as she could until she guessed that enough time had passed for people to start getting up for the day. She then put away the polish and strapped the shield securely to her arm before walking out of her room.

Even though it was still dark outside, Anastasia was already waiting at the bottom of the steps, and she made the sign of the gods when she saw Zosime. They didn't speak and Zosime returned her attention to the horizon. Dawn would not arrive for another couple of hours, and she was suddenly starkly reminded of the history story that Flavian told on the first night of Mione.

The world had been a dark place many years ago, both literally and figuratively. The sun used to roam close and far away without rhyme or reason and many beasts had tormented the land before the Leondrians drove them away into Lady Meraki's Forest and other Midrian islands. The sun didn't begin its routine journey from one side of the horizon to the other until Lady Hermione's and Lord Adrian's first child, Anatole, was born.

He had been a child of light who couldn't bear the darkness, so his parents built him a special chariot for his birthday for him to saddle up the sun to bring light as he pleased. What began as a personal obsession to drive the chariot across the sky each day became a duty to bring light to mortals and immortals alike.

It wasn't until his sister, Selena—another being of light—was born that he was finally willing to put down the reigns and permit the night to come. But at least the world wasn't enveloped in total darkness again because his sister now rose in the sky with the moon and their pale light radiated alongside the stars.

Zosime always identified more with Anatole than with Selena. Zosime didn't fear the night, but she always preferred the daytime. She didn't want to hide herself under the cover of darkness. She wanted everything to be out in the open and for her to be able to stand boldly as herself in the bright light of day.

But the shadows still clung to the deepest parts of her heart, and one supposedly couldn't appreciate the light without experiencing the dark.

She didn't have to wait long before Vasiliki joined her on the landing and stood next to her. Zosime sensed her anticipation, tinged with never-ending uncertainty. They only had to wait a few minutes in silence before Jedrick, Vasiliki's personal guard, walked towards them with a few horses in tow. Jedrick was several years older than them and bowed his head in respect as he handed one of the reigns to Vasiliki.

Jedrick didn't often speak as he efficiently executed tasks like everyone else who worked full time around the Heart. He had been nothing but respectful towards them yet sometimes the emotions she sensed from him made her think he viewed her as someone who still needed to grow up. The same way Anastasia seemed to look at her at times, which bothered her more than she ever wanted to admit.

Zosime was reminded of this feeling when Anastasia said to her, "General Perleros will still be here for anything you need, my queen. We will be back in a week."

"Gods be with you." Zosime said, trying not to trip over the words.

She sensed something flicker in Anastasia's chest that Zosime couldn't identify but Anastasia only made the sign of the gods.

"It's time, my queen." Anastasia announced to Vasiliki who then led her horse around.

Zosime couldn't help but admire how majestic the animals were. They had been used for campaigns years ago to help carry supplies, but it was rare for Leondrians to actually ride them, because it would be undignified to rely on another being's strength as a mode for transportation. But at some point in their history, horses had become a symbol of the Leondrian monarch. So, while it would be a sign of weakness to ride horses everywhere, it had become an acceptable method of travel for kings and queens. Perhaps the sight of them on horseback reminded people they were part-goddess or perhaps it made for a better story at the campfires. Zosime didn't know but didn't spend too much time dwelling on the matter.

She had never gone horseback riding until Jedrick began giving her lessons a few weeks ago to prepare her for the tour. She hadn't known what to expect and was surprised to discover that horses felt emotions remarkably similar to humans.

"Careful now, my queen." Jedrick had cautioned the first time he had brought a horse over to her outside the gates a few weeks ago. "Always approach them from the front and always with a calm state of mind, else your bad temper becomes theirs."

Zosime had been extremely skeptical of this remark since she was used to feeling the emotions of living beings, like goats. They held nasty tempers of their own without influence from anyone and she thought he had been exaggerating until she felt a spark of curiosity from the horse.

"What's your name?" she had then asked the animal respectfully.

The horse had lifted its head and sniffed deeply in Zosime's direction before Jedrick answered, "Eleftheria."

Zosime had laughed in approval and Eleftheria had retorted with an indignant neigh. Zosime had then quickly smothered the laughter to not offend her and felt Eleftheria's impatience when she mounted her at Jedrick's instruction. Zosime had felt how eagerly Eleftheria wanted to run so, ignoring Jedrick's advice to take it slow, Zosime pushed her knees against her sides to show she could gallop as fast as she wanted.

She hadn't expected the ride to be exhilarating or to feel as one with Eleftheria's wild spirit as she galloped as hard as she could until Jedrick managed to pull up beside her and grab the reigns. She felt Anastasia's and Vasiliki's disapproval when they caught up to them on horseback several seconds later but neither she nor Eleftheria cared what they thought in that moment.

Chasing the wind had tasted like freedom and there was nothing else in the world quite like that feeling.

Vasiliki did nothing of the sort now as she mounted her horse calmly with the others. Perleros stood closely beside Zosime, and he exchanged a quick look with Anastasia as Vasiliki cautiously nudged her horse forward.

Zosime reminded herself again that Vasiliki would only be gone a week, and her turn would come soon after as she watched the group trot into the distance.

Zosime dropped the smile when her sister was out of sight and realized it was almost time to lead her people through the daily morning workout. She could think of no better time to release this pent-up energy than after watching Anastasia and Vasiliki ride off together to see the rest of her lands without her.

CHAPTER

9

Perleros had many years ago grown accustomed to functioning on only a few hours of rest a night. Few Leondrians could boast about consistently receiving an uninterrupted night's sleep but not many could rival Perleros's ungodly schedule. He couldn't even remember the last time he slept through an entire night. Perhaps at some point before Training, when he was a small child?

Who could remember such a trivial thing at his age.

While never-ending work had just been a natural part of his life for the past twenty years, he couldn't help but notice the toll his tedious schedule was inflicting on him. He knew the lack of rest was catching up to him and he was now feeling the full brunt of old injuries, especially the ones he received from the fight with Typhon a few years ago.

He would never forget that fight for as long as he lived or the terror that had shaken him to his bones. He still remembered the stench of burning flesh and seeing old friends of his burn alive in a matter of seconds until he could no longer recognize their blackened corpses. Wearing the red cloak meant being part of a community, having an unbreakable bond of brother and sisterhood. But even he couldn't distinguish his fallen friends from one other after Typhon had finished with them.

It was a memory he often thought of but who could forget such a thing? It had been the second time in Perleros's life that he had been certain that he was about to die. He hadn't feared dying itself but what had sent shivers of alarm down his spine was the thought of failing his people. He had let Leondria down twenty years ago when he failed to save his dearest friend, King Atreo. Those consequences still haunted them to this day, but at least they had dodged catastrophe when a war with the gods had been averted at the last possible second.

Perleros slowed then came to a stop at the main foray in the Heart. Despite standing on solid stone, he could almost feel the ground rumbling beneath him as he recalled the scene. He was standing as close to King Atreo then as he was from the front door now when he saw his friend die. He remembered freezing in horror and then having no idea what to do next when his entire world tilted sideways in the span of a second. Perleros didn't think of himself as an arrogant man, but he had never before been so humbled than when he saw first-hand the palpable rage of two wrathful goddesses on the precipice of battle.

He had replayed the scene in his mind over and over again, but he couldn't stop himself from mulling over everything he could have done differently to save his friend. His King. But he always started inwardly cursing himself for how slow and naïve he had been. If that wasn't bad enough, he had to relive his failure every time he saw his friend's twin daughters who were now utterly unprepared to rule. Vasiliki was too cautious and hesitant with everything whereas Zosime often rushed into situations without thinking.

They were still young and had time to mature but Perleros knew how quickly life could change at a moment's notice. He couldn't help but wonder what the next catastrophe would be and how long they had until it came. One thing he had learned countless times during his four-decade tenure in this life was that he could always count on another disaster happening.

"Resting, Perleros?" Oscar jeered and Perleros suppressed a sigh.

Perleros thought it better to get this interaction over with and turned calmly to face the man who had made it his life's mission to torment Perleros for his failures. Oscar waited a moment before stepping away from the dark shadows clinging to one of the hallway's corners where the torchlight didn't reach. Oscar's brown eyes glared up at him in accusation and his mouth twisted in strong dislike. It wasn't the scowl by the average sized man that made Perleros wary. He had too much on his plate to worry about such trifling matters like whether his subordinates liked him.

They had never been on friendly terms as young men, but Oscar had never forgiven him for Atreo's death, not that Perleros could blame him. No, it wasn't Oscar's dislike that kept him awake some nights. It was Oscar's vision that worried him. The hunger that glittered in Oscar's eyes when he talked about the future and his evident eagerness the few times he talked about the possibility of renewing campaigns.

At least Oscar was loyal enough to limit how much he showed his hostility to Perleros to times when no one else was around. Like now. He had always been careful not to overstep the mark too much in public, but Perleros often worried what he would do if he got the queens on his side and slowly turned Leondria's less virtuous side to something much darker. Leondria wasn't meant to be some great empire where the other city-states were subservient to them, nor was it meant to be run by those who thirsted for more power. Leondria was a protector, not a blood-thirsty conqueror.

"General Oscar." Perleros said with a military crispness that would make the bitter fall wind outside envious.

He always did his best to maintain his cool demeanor, but he also didn't possess infinite patience. Perleros only wanted to go home and lie down for a few minutes, both to alleviate the radiating sharp pain in his neck and to acquire some much needed rest.

"How's the neck?" Oscar asked but Perleros knew the man well enough to know he was mocking him instead of asking out of kindness. It also didn't help that Oscar's mouth was now curved up slightly in self-satisfaction.

"There is no burden the gods can give me that I can't handle." Perleros replied.

"Is that right?" Oscar tilted his head with a predatory gleam flashing on his face. "Is that what the people think?"

Perleros did have to admit to himself that Leondria was going through a period of great change and that its reputation had taken a great hit. There was a significant decrease in the amount of people who had sought their protection in the last few years and Perleros didn't fail to see the connection between these dwindling numbers and the battle against Typhon they had very nearly lost. The people's confidence in their ability to protect them, he knew, had been badly shaken and that certain parts of Midrios were still re-building.

He couldn't help but remember Zosime begging him to let her go and fight beside them before he and a group of Leondrians left to face the god-like monster. Her reaction hadn't come as a surprise to him, but he had been astonished by Vasiliki's reaction. Vasiliki typically kept her head down and followed orders to the letter but even she had implored him—almost to the point of insubordination—to leave the Training Center to go with them. Perleros had done his best to lead, follow Lady Meraki's commands, and abide by Leondria's traditions but he had considered taking them with him for a few moments.

He hadn't wanted to strip any Leondrian of their right to protect their people, but they weren't Leondrians yet. They were stronger than any living mortal breathing which could make all the difference between them surviving or being slaughtered. Despite doing his best to hold Leondria together without everything collapsing around him, he thought about bending the rules just this once.

What had clinched his decision to order them to stay behind was his promise to their mother weeks before her delivery. How she had begged him to look after her husband and unborn children if she didn't survive the birth, and he would never forget the desperation in her eyes when she had dug her long fingernails into his shoulders. They may only be a few years away from adulthood, he had thought, but Perleros couldn't ignore how young the two teenagers had looked.

He had left soon after on the journey north and, even now, he could still smell the fire and the blood from the fight. He remembered being surprised by the sheer power and force behind Typhon's blow when he had struck Perleros. He had dimly felt himself soaring through the air then being overwhelmed by a blinding pain when his neck slammed against fallen debris. He had known that he needed to get back up to fight but his legs wouldn't obey his commands, and his chest wouldn't move when he tried to breathe.

He had continued to struggle against his disobedient body but nothing he did would make his legs move. He had demanded his limbs to get up again and again. He knew he had to will himself to stand and fight until all the life was choked out of his body and his flesh melted away from the fires Typhon hurled at anything that moved.

But his body had only ignored him. He had at first believed that his inability to move was from the shock of the impact but then the unsettling thought that his injury was much worse than he initially realized crossed his mind.

He had then looked up when he caught a flicker of movement in his peripheral and ignored any thought of self-pity when he saw Anastasia. He had blinked in surprise, thinking she had perished when she had been flung into what remained of a smoldering building seconds before he had crashed against the rock. In that moment, she bore an uncanny resemblance to a wrathful Lady Meraki when Anastasia emerged from the fire with blazing blue eyes and soot covering her blonde hair.

Respect and sorrow had risen in his chest, and he hadn't been sure which one he felt more in that moment. He hadn't known her or her parents that well, but he felt so much pride for the young woman as she limped towards Typhon. The ungodly monster had cackled when he saw that she was the last one standing, and she responded by straightening her limp into a determined walk. Blood had coated her arms and legs, but she clenched her spear with a strength that surprised Perleros.

The monster and girl had merely stared at each other for a few moments before she screamed then unleashed an attack on the monster like a one-woman hurricane. He had blinked several times in an unsuccessful attempt to clear his vision, but he hadn't been able to stop the blackness from creeping in the corner of his eyes. He had kept waiting—hoping—for Lady Meraki to appear and destroy Typhon. However, even after all but one Leondrian had been slaughtered or too injured to move, his goddess never showed.

Perleros hadn't been able to stop himself from wondering if they were being punished again for King Atreo's death.

His thoughts had turned to his children when the darkness started descending in full force. They would be orphaned now, and he would have failed them again with his untimely death, as he did before when he couldn't save their mother from succumbing to a sickness he couldn't cure. Balthasar had been old enough to understand everything and Adelphie had been too young to really remember her mother, but he could always see the look of accusation in Dryas's eyes every time they saw each other.

His sight was all but gone when Anastasia had knelt beside him after dealing the finishing blow to Typhon that Perleros hadn't been able to see. He had been certain that he was moments away from death but the only thing he could think about was that Anastasia had saved them. Because of her, his children and everyone else in Midrios would live to see another day.

He had lost consciousness at some point, and he hadn't initially believed that he had survived when he woke up some time later. It had been nothing short of miraculous. It was supposed to be the greatest honor for a Leondrian to die in battle, which he didn't disagree with, but he couldn't help but think that dying in battle after living a long life would be preferable to the young departing this mortal plane too soon.

He must have overestimated the extent of his injuries when he hit his neck because he had been able to walk and breathe again soon after waking up. He had thanked the gods for Anastasia's victory over the monster and thanked them again for giving him the foresight to bring her with them at the last minute. From what little he had seen before passing out, she would be an invaluable asset. She was a Leondrian's Leondrian and he had promoted her immediately upon their return home.

He had then taken her under his wing and later assigned her as a Spear in the queens' final year in Training. To her credit, she never let the attention she received from her fellow warriors go to her head despite the infamous status she now held. She simply continued to quietly serve and protect without fuss or demand for recognition.

He knew she would be a great mentor who could keep his friend's daughters safe.

"No answer, Perleros?" Oscar jeered. "Do you really believe that's what the people think?"

Perleros grunted, not feeling any desire today to spar with Oscar, but Oscar was clearly in the mood to provoke him.

Unsatisfied with his response, Oscar stalked up to him and demanded, "Are they showing any *signs*?"

Perleros's eyes flashed but merely said through gritted teeth, "No."

Perleros hated to raise his voice or otherwise lose any sort of control. Having to shout showed an incapacity to lead and he fervently believed that a quiet command was all one needed to be effective.

"No signs of the queens going mad?" Oscar pushed and Perleros leveled his full gaze on Oscar. "No loss of control or red eyes?"

"No." Perleros repeated even more firmly.

Oscar opened his mouth and Perleros took a step forward, ordering with soft intensity, "Enough, Oscar. If the queens start showing signs of madness, I will keep the generals informed."

Oscar's jaw clenched and he warned, "We will *all* be watching. We don't need them turning out like their father."

Oscar begrudgingly inclined his head since Perleros did outrank him then stalked away. Oscar pushed the boundaries when they were alone, but so long as he didn't cross them when they were in public, Perleros could tolerate his bouts of anger. He could permit the glares, the resentment, and the animosity because he couldn't disagree with him. Perleros had never forgiven himself either for what happened to their king, and he was now responsible for his children. He couldn't allow himself to fail his friend again by failing his daughters.

He had come perilously close to failing them when they had just been born and he couldn't afford to let that happen again.

While it had been years since Perleros had lost his wife, all he wanted in times like these was to hold her in his arms and forget about the world. But he knew he didn't have the luxury of comfort anymore, so he simply walked towards the exit.

He had problems to deal with and daylight was burning.

CHAPTER

Vasiliki's heart was pounding in her chest, even long after they had left the gates. This was completely new territory for her. Literally. Throughout her life, she had only been inside the Hearth, the lake by the Hearth, Lady Meraki's Forest, the nearby mountain range, and the Training Center. She knew these areas were only a fraction of Leondria and that fraction made up only a sliver of her country, Midrios.

She was keenly aware of how much she had been barred from visiting and she was still stunned by the idea that she was now allowed to see it all. She did her best to keep her face outwardly impassive, but her curiosity was running rampantly. She had always wondered what the rest of the world looked like, especially what lied beyond it. What lied past the souls glittering in the night sky, beyond Lord Demetrios's domain in the sky, beyond this realm that even the gods had never been to. She had always wanted to uncover the secrets of the universe, but duty commanded her to keep her sandals planted on the ground and her eyes straight forward on her people.

She was doing her best in her new role, but she knew that everyone could see that she was struggling. Stepping from the role of Trainee who obeyed orders to queen who was now suddenly expected to command seasoned generals wasn't something that came naturally to her. She just wasn't comfortable with the demands of making decisions in the heat of the moment without time to think over the consequences. This skill to confidently give orders came so naturally to Zosime that Vasiliki couldn't help but be awed by her at times.

She could never be like that.

Not when Zosime was always the first one to speak up and Vasiliki found her mind constantly wandering. She wondered what people would think of this unique time in Leondrian history.

What would define her reign, besides being the first Leondrian co-ruler with Zosime?

It was a question that had plagued her for weeks, and she still didn't know the answer. She doubted future generations would remember her name, not that it mattered. She didn't want notoriety or fame. All she wanted as queen was to keep her people safe but, beyond that, she just didn't know.

She shifted herself on top of her horse, still finding the movements a little jarring. Anastasia rode beside her, and her shoulders were more tense than Vasiliki was used to seeing. She also noticed how Anastasia was constantly surveilling their surroundings. It was clear that, despite whatever was bothering her, Anastasia was still soaking in the sights and Vasiliki couldn't blame her.

Her lands were gorgeous with its marvelous mountains, the rich green grass and trees, the peaks and valleys of its rolling hills, and the majestic blue sky. Everything about it was beautiful, even if Lady Meraki's Forest watched them ominously from the distance. Vasiliki suppressed a shiver and turned her gaze away from that darkly alluring place. She had heard stories of parents taking their ill children to the edge of the forest in the hopes of finding a cure, but she had never understood why before.

But now she did.

She could remember the heat of the white flames engulfing her entire body and feeling like her soul had been set aflame. She didn't hear herself screaming but she knew that she must have been, from the shock alone if not from the pain.

Then the flames had dissipated, and she had opened her eyes. She had been greeted with darkness then bright bursts of light, and she could scarcely believe that she had been accepted into Lord Demetrios's domain. She had not been able to ignore a nagging thought in the back of her mind that she would fail the Trials and be unworthy to ascend to the heavens. Then she had blinked a few times to clear her vision and discovered that they were all glowing. As if their inner-most essence was shining for the whole world to see which didn't fade for a full day.

The migraine that had laced the inside of her skull, the exhaustion, the cold, and every other source of pain she had been experiencing moments before had vanished. Every scar she had acquired from Training had also been wiped away and she felt like she had just been reborn.

She knew now why those parents did what they did. Knew their desperate hope that the Creature would heal their children of their maladies, so they had a chance of one day becoming Leondrians. The overwhelming majority of such children were not granted such mercy, and their tiny graves were never visited. Becoming the strongest mortal protectors of Midrios required sacrifice and there was no tolerance for weakness, even from children.

Vasiliki also noticed how Anastasia's hands would tense over her reigns every time she glanced at Lady Meraki's Forest. Vasiliki shared her sentiment, not harboring any friendly feelings from her single experience there. What did surprise her was how much Anastasia's attitude towards the place had changed since she hadn't seemed that fazed when she had led them in the forest before her Trials.

Perhaps it had something to do with the blood she noticed on Anastasia's armor when Vasiliki had awoken from the fire. That strange, black blood. She had figured that Anastasia had run into one of the many hostile magical beasts that roamed Lady Meraki's Forest, but she hadn't expected to see the concern in Anastasia's eyes when she had burst through the trees to check on them. As if she was ready to fight death itself to protect them.

Vasiliki hadn't asked her about it since she wasn't sure if that was too close to the forbidden subject of discussing the Trials. She did remember Anastasia and Perleros walking away immediately after their cloaking ceremony and not seeing either of them for a while. They had resurfaced for the official events, including the arm-wrestling contest where every Leondrian stood in line for a chance to arm wrestle their monarch. It was a tradition almost as old as Leondria itself since everyone had apparently wanted to test Alexandros's, the first half-god's, strength. It then became one of the most popular events of Mione, and monarchs were even spontaneously challenged to arm-wrestle throughout the year for fun.

There had been confusion on whether Vasiliki or Zosime would be the one to arm wrestle everyone then Zosime had sauntered to the table and raised an eyebrow in challenge at the large crowd. That had been enough for a long line of people to form to face Zosime while Vasiliki had melted into the crowd. Everyone, without fail, lost to Zosime. Dryas, Balthasar, Anastasia, Perleros, Oscar, Thea, everyone.

There had been some encouraging hollers when Balthasar and Anastasia faced Zosime, but Zosime still won those matches easily. Vasiliki tried not to attract attention, but she had been nudged forward after everyone else had gone and then the crowd wanted to see if Zosime would prevail over her sister.

Vasiliki hadn't said anything when she had sat down before her sister. Zosime had smirked and wiggled her fingers at her while Vasiliki deliberately rested her elbow on the table before clasping hands with her. She had dreaded the outcome, even with the tie of the tree throwing contest earlier. They hadn't usually gone head-to-head and not all part-gods were created equally, so she wasn't sure how her strength would compare to her sister's.

After all, Zosime had been the one to be blessed with the Gift and Zosime was the one who possessed this strange power of premonition to warn her whenever an attack was about to occur. She was the one with all the confidence and the one who looked and acted the part of queen so much better than she did. Zosime was the natural warrior, a better Leondrian. She didn't overthink everything like Vasiliki did or find her mind wandering in directions that it shouldn't. She didn't feel the need to ask questions, to discard the mantle of queen, or take off the red cloak to study the universe.

"Are you ready, sister?" Zosime had asked with a smile.

Vasiliki had only looked into Zosime's eyes—an identical copy to her own—and inclined her head to show that she was ready. She had resisted the urge to rub the mark on her chest and tried to suppress a rising feeling of resentment. If the generals had waited to ask her when she was old enough, she would have deferred the position to her sister then she would have gladly pledged her allegiance to her.

The queen was supposed to be the living embodiment of everything Leondria stood for, but Vasiliki always fell short. Why was she also marked by Lady Meraki as an infant for the position of queen when she clearly didn't measure up?

She had felt her sister begin to apply pressure against her hand and her hand had moved a couple inches before Vasiliki responded with pressure of her own and returned their hands to the middle. She felt Zosime increase the pressure more and more and Vasiliki responded in kind. She had heard people placing bets on who would win but neither of them gained traction over the other.

Sweat had started to drip down both their foreheads as they both applied their full force against the other but neither one could force the other one's hand to move an inch. At some point, they had just called a stalemate, and Vasiliki had calmly withdrawn her hand.

Vasiliki was shaken from her thoughts when Anastasia unexpectedly said, "It can take years to become truly comfortable with wearing the cloak."

Jedrick turned his head towards Anastasia but didn't comment. There was no warmth in her voice, no softness of any kind. It wasn't the voice of one trying to be kind, nor was it the voice of one trying to comfort someone younger and much more inexperienced. It was simply matter of fact.

"It can take years to learn how to lead." she continued in the same tone. "One usually learns from watching others and slowly rising up the ranks."

"Yes." Jedrick agreed when Vasiliki didn't immediately respond. "Those without that luxury can always turn to people they trust to ask questions."

"Which they can do anytime." Anastasia offered.

"I see." Vasiliki replied.

It was surreal to receive this permission to ask questions when that part of herself had always been chastised growing up. She had never been able to suppress it, so she had learned to keep these questions to herself.

Anastasia started to slow her horse as they approached the first farm and Vasiliki followed suit. The family who lived there quickly left their house and eagerly waited for their arrival. Vasiliki's horse resisted slowing down but she was finally able to bring her to a full stop then dismounted.

"My queen." the farmers greeted with awe and made the sign of the gods.

Farmers may not be Leondrians, but they held great deference for their customs and courtesies. None who resided in Leondria were disrespectful to them, but Vasiliki could tell which service providers were only interested in protection and which ones wanted their descendants to become Leondrians by how much effort they put into learning their traditions.

"The honor is mine—" Vasiliki raised her brows in question.

"Andres." he replied eagerly and added hastily. "My queen!"

"The honor is mine, Andres." Vasiliki said and had a hunch that Andres fell into the latter camp.

More people emerged from the field and they all quickly jogged forward for their chance to meet her. They were all tanned from the sun, like her, and she could see the effect that years of hard labor had on their bodies.

"Please, my queen, come inside." Andres invited and they handed the reigns of their horses to a few people who must have been his children. Vasiliki and her guards followed him across the grass and through the threshold of his home. "Would you like to have some wine? Grapes? Cheese? Anything I can serve is yours."

Vasiliki gestured to her guards—Anastasia, Jedrick, and Orrin—and stated, "I would be honored after *they* eat."

"Of course!" he cried as they sat down at the dinner table then started pushing food and drink on them.

Vasiliki merely gave her guards a look before they could protest and silently refused to touch her food. The gods had long ago decreed that it was a grave insult to insult a host's hospitality, but she wouldn't allow herself to partake until her guards had eaten something first. A host always ate last out of respect for their guests, but Vasiliki thought it improper to even look at her food before they had taken a few bites of their meal since she was their queen.

Vasiliki finally allowed herself to pop a grape into her mouth once she saw the others had made a dent in their meals. She relished the burst of sweetness in her mouth, savoring the taste of her favorite fruit.

Vasiliki realized that she should probably strike up a conversation with her host, but she didn't know what to say. She took a few sips of wine as her mind raced and found herself grateful that Leondrians weren't expected to be make small talk. Still, she knew that she needed to do something.

Out of ideas and desperate to make a good impression, Vasiliki said to Andres, "Tell me about your family."

Andres's eyes sparkled and he didn't need any more permission to launch into his family's entire backstory. He gestured to each family member and rattled off names, beginning with his wife beside him, their seven children, his mother, his brother, and his brother's children. Then, when Vasiliki thought he was about to finish, Andres started telling them so many anecdotes about each family member that Vasiliki marveled how he was able to talk so much without stopping to breathe.

"Our family has lived in Leondria since my grandmother emigrated here. Only three more generations before our family is eligible to go to Training. Each child grows stronger than the one before!" Andres finally paused when his brother cleared his throat and sharply elbowed him in the side.

Non-Leondrian families were required to live in their borders for at least seven generations before they could ask for their child to be admitted into Training. If that child was one of the few who were permitted to enter Training and if they later passed the Trials, they would become the first one in their family to wear a red cloak and every successive generation would then be required to live and die as Leondrians.

Or be hunted down for the ultimate act of dishonor and betrayal, but it rarely ever came to that. Vasiliki could only remember one time in recent memory where two Leondrians deserted but they had only done so since their child had been born deformed and wouldn't have survived in their society.

"I hope to see it." Vasiliki said diplomatically and the brother released a quiet breath of relief.

Vasiliki had long been eager to leave but didn't want to be rude, so she took her chance to give Anastasia a meaningful glance. Thankfully, she got the hint.

"We will need to move on to stay on schedule, my queen." Anastasia announced quickly and the family's faces dropped in disappointment.

Vasiliki rose from the table and gave Andres a small smile, "May the gods bless and reward you for your hospitality. I hope for the opportunity to break bread at your table again."

"The honor is ours, my queen." he said breathlessly.

Vasiliki was deliberate in her movements as she left, making sure not to move too quickly or slowly to offend. She and her three guards mounted their horses, and she inclined her head again at them again but didn't look back as they trotted away. She couldn't ignore the uncomfortable fullness in her stomach with the horse's jostling and looked at Orrin who was biting his lip. She raised an eyebrow at him, and he quickly turned his head away.

"Less open ended questions next time." she said to herself aloud. "Noted."

She had meant it as a serious critique—to show the others she had learned from a mistake—but it caused a much different reaction than she expected. Orrin started losing his composure, his shoulders shaking with suppressed laughter and Jedrick started rubbing his mouth to cover his grin.

Even Anastasia's lips rose in amusement as she agreed, "Yes, my queen. The good news is we only have a few more places to visit today before we stop for the night."

That was a relief to Vasiliki who wasn't sure how much more chatter she could tolerate. While Anastasia was true to her word, Vasiliki was still bombarded by more people than she expected in the next three farmhouses they visited. The hosts pushed as much wine and cheese on her as they could, but none were as overwhelming as Andres was. She had learned to pace herself so she wouldn't insult her hosts by turning down food while also keeping herself from vomiting.

She had tried to be careful with her wine intake, but the world was spinning by the end of the day. She was grateful when they finally stopped for the night and had to make a conscious effort not to stumble or slur her words.

She watched the sunset after they finished setting up camp and how the golden rays of light streaked across the sky in a last act of rebellion before the night descended upon them. She found herself wondering if Anatole still dreaded the last leg of his journey right before stepping off the chariot to allow the moon and stars to emerge every night. Or perhaps he loved his sister too much to mind.

She sympathized with his fear of the dark, but the night had so many mysteries to be unraveled and so many questions to be answered. There were countless discoveries waiting for them beyond their world and the souls in the night sky shone more brilliantly than the brightest rays of dawn. She could only imagine what life would be like if she could wake up every day at dusk to study the stars.

She chastised herself for that errant thought and forced herself to re-count the events of the day so she could focus on her duty, not her innermost desires. She had heard her people rejoice so many times which was strange to her since she went from being a minor with no responsibilities to a ruler of thousands only a month ago.

It had been even odder to see so many tight-knit families living and working together under the same roof. To see parents playing with their children with an endless depth of parental concern shining on their faces.

They had physical bonds that held them together by breaking bread together every day. Vasiliki was accustomed to the intangible bonds, the ones that were forged from spilt blood and sacrifice. The ones that couldn't be easily defined or explained.

Watching these parents had made Vasiliki feel empty, which was a feeling she hadn't felt since the first day of Mione. Her parents died when she was born so she never knew that loving parental caress she had seen so many times that day. She looked up at the sky as the night descended, a part of her hoping that she would find her parents' souls dancing among the other stars, but she didn't know if they cared enough to watch how their daughters were doing.

Her thoughts took a dark turn as she thought about her extended immortal family, who had never once bothered to show up in her life. She didn't know why the gods had disappeared, but she hoped to one day find out the answer to that mystery. Her mind revolved with so many other questions she had, and she glanced at Anastasia who was sharpening her sword on the other side of the small bonfire they had built.

"How may I serve, my queen?" Anastasia asked, lifting her gaze from her sword.

Vasiliki drew in a breath and asked, "Am I—allowed to visit the Training Center?" That was something she had been curious about—but who was she kidding—that wasn't what she really wanted to know. She continued before Anastasia could respond, "Are there limits to where I can go and what I can do?"

Even Jedrick and Orrin looked up at that question and they all waited for Anastasia's response.

Anastasia looked at her for a moment then answered, "There are three things you must always do: protect your people, obey the Council's final decisions, and serve the gods. We aren't going past the Leondrian borders for this mission but those are the only three things you are limited in doing. Everything else you are—allowed—to do but great queens listen to their advisors."

Vasiliki blinked when Anastasia added, "Visiting the Training Center occasionally is good, but coddling isn't. The Spears know what they're doing."

Vasiliki nodded and Anastasia returned to sharpening her sword.

Sometime after they returned from this trip, Vasiliki would pay the Trainees a visit. She knew that many wouldn't survive Training, but she wanted all her people to have the opportunity to meet their queen and know who they would be fighting beside in the future.

Vasiliki found herself enjoying this quiet time by the fire with the night sky glittering above them as Anastasia, Orrin, and Jedrick wordlessly sharpened their weapons. She was used to hearing raucous laughter by the bonfires back home with thousands of Leondrians gathered at one time to share stories.

She enjoyed this even more, hoping to one day earn their respect and share in that silent, inviolable bond that clearly bound the three of them together. But perhaps that was impossible with her position and Vasiliki would just have to learn to live with that.

She didn't know at what point she had drifted off into unconsciousness, but she was shaken awake for her turn on night shift before she even realized that she had fallen asleep. She clambered to her feet to join Orrin on watch for the last two hours of the night. They said very little to each other, but he gave her a small smile at one point that seemed to border on approval.

It seemed as if no time at all had passed before the rest of their party awoke and were ready to begin the second day of the tour. Vasiliki was more careful with her food and drink intake this time, but it was more or less the same as the day before. So much thankfulness and awe of having a ruler back in charge.

Vasiliki had heard more than once that day that having a monarch back after twenty years meant that the bad times were now over. The country-wide terror of Typhon's return was still fresh in their minds, so everyone naturally knew Anastasia's name. Anytime Typhon's name was invoked, Anastasia's name was mentioned in tandem. The hero renowned across the lands from saving them all from disaster.

Vasiliki couldn't help but notice how Anastasia never volunteered her name unless explicitly asked and wondered if she also struggled being in the spotlight.

Anastasia received the second-most attention and signs of respect after Vasiliki with countless grateful comments along the lines of "You saved us all."

Vasiliki remembered those dark times well. She had implored Zosime not to disobey Perleros's order to stay at the Training Center after they had pleaded with him to let them go with him. She harbored her own objections to his order but conceded that he knew more than her. So she obeyed and it took all her powers of persuasion to convince Zosime not to defy his order. What finally made Zosime listen was that, if the group who left to fight Typhon failed to kill him, then the two of them would be the last lines of defense for Leondria.

Now it seemed that the dark times were over, so long as the grain shortage didn't worsen and the rumors that the laws of hospitality were holding less sway in recent years weren't true. Vasiliki saw nothing of the sort from her own people, even if there were fewer farms the farther they moved away from the Hearth.

It was on the third day of their tour that Vasiliki found herself standing at the edge of Leondria's furthest eastern border, looking up at the tallest mountain range in Midrios. Vasiliki was well-acquainted with the mountain range by the Hearth where she had to survive many winters without provisions. But this mountain range, the one that separated Leondria from Apistia, stood so high that its peak was shrouded by clouds in the sky.

She wasn't sure why it felt so otherworldly to her. Perhaps it was because the gods lived at the top of this mountain and her skin broke out into goosebumps at the thought. Was her family standing directly above her right now, watching her stand at their front door?

Did they know she was waiting for them?

She glanced around hopefully but only saw her guards. Even though she knew better, she nudged her horse to the side and kept an eye out as she led her horse across the base of the mountain.

After a few minutes, Orrin suggested respectfully, "Perhaps it's time to turn back, my queen?"

Vasiliki paused before responding, "Not yet."

There was a guarded look in Anastasia's eyes, but she only followed closely behind Vasiliki next to Jedrick.

Vasiliki slowed when she approached a large lake and felt a flash of déjà vu. She blinked several times, trying to understand why this place suddenly felt so familiar and why she felt a spark of long-buried terror, as if she was moments away from drowning even though her feet were firmly planted on land.

Still, she waited, but she couldn't explain why. She finally shook her head and turned away from the lake.

"Let's go." she muttered, and she urged her horse to trot faster.

She should have known better, she thought resentfully to herself. Her parents died when she was born, her extended family disappeared, and Zosime was always leaving her behind by being so much better than her at everything. She shouldn't have expected for the gods to suddenly show up, as if Lady Meraki would suddenly run down the mountain side and welcome her with open arms.

Vasiliki shook her head again and thought that the sooner they left this place, the better.

Anastasia called out, "My queen!"

Vasiliki glanced back in surprise and saw Anastasia straightening in her saddle. The others were now on full alert as they scanned their surroundings for a threat. They may still be in Leondrian territory, but this part of her city-state was mainly deserted and significantly closer to other territories in Midrios.

Anastasia's hand rested on her sword strapped to her side as her eyes narrowed and she brought her horse in front of Vasiliki's in a way that would shield her from an attack.

Vasiliki could then make out some sort of shape in the distance that was slowly prowling towards them. Anastasia's grip on her sword tightened and she leaned forward, as if to spring into action when she suddenly frowned as the shape drew closer.

"Is that a cat?" Jedrick's brows drew together, shifting his horse to stand more in front of Vasiliki's as well.

Vasiliki frowned at the large grey cat in their path which made the hairs on the back of her neck stand up. She felt—a shock of recognition?—and Vasiliki found herself drifting forward as her ears started buzzing. She wasn't sure when she stopped her horse again or when she dismounted, but she soon found herself staring into the cat's inhumanly gray eyes beneath her with the cat staring intensely back at her. Her body slackened in surprise as she stood there, enthralled by the feline's gaze.

She was too mesmerized to move when the cat shivered and began to grow taller and taller. The cat's expansion was grotesque, something inhuman, but Vasiliki's eyes didn't waver from its gaze that looked like wandering thunder clouds. Its eyes flashed and the cat didn't stop growing until it was at eye-level with her. And yet, Vasiliki didn't move or blink, as she felt another flash of déjà vu. As if the cat was someone she knew but she couldn't quite remember where from.

Flickers of images and sensations soared through her mind. Isolation. Wandering. Discovery. It suddenly hit her where she knew him from, granted she had never actually met him before.

"Lord Kal." Vasiliki breathed and the cat shuddered.

Her uncle in his animal form.

Vasiliki felt the enchantment break when Anastasia abruptly grabbed Vasiliki and shoved her behind her with more force than she was expecting. Anastasia glared at Lord Kal, and he stared mournfully back at Anastasia. He tore his gaze away from the angry woman and glanced at Vasiliki again before turning and prowling away, vanishing from sight.

Vasiliki suppressed whatever emotion was surging within her and ignored the fact that another family member had abandoned her yet again. Without a single word spoken or a single explanation for the past.

Orrin was uncharacteristically struggling for words, and he hesitated for a long moment before asking, "Was that—"

"Lord Kal," Anastasia said with a clenched jaw. "Let's go."

Vasiliki almost gaped. Anastasia had just met one of the Six and yet her fists were still clenched, and her tone had been hard, not awed like the others. Which didn't make any sense.

Unless Anastasia had met Lord Kal before, and it had clearly not gone well.

CHAPTER

II

"Sing my name, my muse. Once you sing my
name, summon your powers, my muse.
Once you summon your powers, speak my future, my muse.
Sing and speak all so I may know my fortune.
My beautiful maidens—speakers of prophecies
and truth—weavers of divine Fate.
Slip into your power! Spin the wheel!
Summon your prophet powers and tell us what
we want to know most dearly!"

On and on the curious or the condemned would cry out for answers of their future: does she love him back? Would their crops survive? Would they acquire riches and fame? Could they win the gods' favor? Would the gods ever come back?

Those last two questions had been asked countless times in the years following their disappearance and were only occasionally inquired into now. Very few questioned the gods' power but almost all now doubted that they would ever return. A new generation had been born and raised without the gods' presence, and it was clear they lacked the faith and servitude of their ancestors.

Many had flocked here over the years but never for the purpose that it was built. *To serve the gods.*

Spyridon was just a man who had dedicated his life to their service. Unlike most, he had never forsaken his faith and remained devoted to the gods. There had once been a time when he had whispered to the gods, and they answered him, but that had been when he was a much younger man.

He still murmured to them but only the wind ever replied now, singing just loud enough for him to hear. Every time it did, Spyridon's eyes would roll to the back of his head as an image appeared in his mind. Lord Kal had blessed him long ago for his dedicated service and Spyridon had acquired a shadow of his prophetic powers as a result.

Spyridon heard the man at the temple's entrance finish his plea for the muses to tell him his future but ignored the subsequent cackling and prayers. He thought that the mortals should all know better by now than to ask them for anything and felt no sympathy for the taunts the man who invoked their call was now receiving. These muses weren't mortal women or goddesses, but some form of higher being who somehow inspired fervor from foolish mortals who usually called them the Weavers or the Fates.

Like the gods, they had the ability to change their physical appearances at will, but he had only seen them take on the forms of beautiful young maidens or withered crones.

"Please, weavers." the male voice continued.

Spyridon was already tuning out the man's begging, having heard so many selfish requests over the years that he only half-listened to them now.

Spyridon never knew why the three weavers joined him after he had built the temple twenty years ago. He did know that the weavers loved to plague the mortals who dared to ask about their future. Sometimes, they would even seek out mortals in dreams whose fates they had long ago woven into their wheels. At least until their instrument of weaving life and death had been broken by a vengeful goddess years ago.

"What do I need to do to ensure my family's prosperity?" the man beseeched.

The three weavers replied by cackling maliciously then chanting, "Should we cut the string of life?"

Spyridon stepped around the grey limestone column, seeing the weavers dancing around a middle aged man in their maiden forms.

The women's white dresses stood out like a beacon piercing through a heavy mist against the temple's grey walls and Spyridon's ashen-colored robes. Their clothes hugged their slender womanly bodies in ways that he knew inspired others to write the most beautiful music or take the foolhardiest actions. Spyridon wasn't impressed and he couldn't fathom why artists flocked to them for inspiration. Physical beauty was meaningless because what truly mattered was how deeply one devoted themselves to the gods.

"He was right." the man finally said bitterly when it was clear that he could no longer stand the weavers' strange chant and dance. "I asked the wrong questions."

The wind immediately rose around Spyridon which sent his eyes rolling to the back of his head. An image of a different man tanned from years spent toiling under the sun, working for his family, and serving the gods with all his heart sprung behind his eyelids. This man's head was bent in servitude and his brown eyes were trained on the task in front of him. Spyridon couldn't shake the inexplicable feeling that he was a true believer with an important purpose.

Then the wind whispered in his ears: *send him to Leondria.*

Spyridon opened his eyes when the wind died down and he blinked, taking a moment to ensure his footing was stable before walking towards the man still being ridiculed by the weavers.

"Who so advised you?" Spyridon demanded.

The man who dared to ask for prophecies looked up at Spyridon and his eyes widened, his mouth flailing in discomfort as the weavers continued their eerie giggles. Spyridon had long ago grown accustomed to their presence and was only interested in getting an answer from the man.

"The gods demand you to answer." Spyridon ordered with a raised chin when the man didn't immediately respond.

The man hesitated then, after a fearful glance at the weavers, reluctantly whispered, "Angelos."

"Send him to me." Spyridon commanded.

The man flinched, slowly backing away from the chanting weavers then turned to flee down the steps Spyridon had carved into the mountain years ago.

"We will know if you don't." Spyridon warned dangerously which made the man pause.

"Shall we cut the string if he doesn't?" the weavers shouted gleefully, and the man started sprinting down the mountain.

Spyridon turned on his sandals and walked to the other side of the temple, passing by marble sculptures of the Six and one of an abandoned male with no face. He pushed open the single pair of silver glass doors that separated the inside of the temple from the balcony facing the gods' mountain pass.

He had chosen this place well, he thought to himself.

It was high up enough in the mountains that the mist shrouded the temple from scrutiny from people on the ground while not being so low as to obstruct his view of the gods' mountain. If he was extremely lucky during one of the seven times a day he walked onto the balcony to pray, he would even catch glimpses of the gods' golden palace.

He dutifully prayed to the gods then thought about the wind's most recent command to send this man named Angelos to Leondria. He remembered the last interaction he had with the Leondrian Perleros and how the gods had spared him from the general's wrath twenty years ago. Spyridon had known that taking the King's daughters meant there was a strong possibility of being executed as a traitor by the Leondrians if they found him, but he had received a command from the wind to take the children to the gods' mountain so he had obeyed it.

While he had been spared a brutal death and a traitor's execution, the others who followed him had not been so fortunate. But their sacrifices had not been in vain since the girls had both been marked and the gods' will had been done. Spyridon admired the Leondrians' immeasurable devotion to Lady Meraki but thought that their single-minded allegiance to only one of the gods at the expense of all the others was egregious. In this temple, all the gods were served equally.

He paid little attention to the time but knew he wouldn't have to wait too long for the man named Angelos to arrive. Only a handful of days passed until he heard the weavers taunting someone new and he knew that the time had come. He left the balcony and walked to the front of the temple where he immediately recognized Angelos from the vision that the wind had sent him.

"Cut the string! Cut the string!" the weavers laughed, and to Spyridon's surprise, Angelos didn't flinch at their threat.

Everyone knew that a weaver cutting a string meant imminent death, but Angelos only stared at them warily instead of reacting desperately like most did.

Angelos looked at Spyridon as he approached and asked, "How may I serve the gods?"

The weavers paused in temporary bewilderment and quieted as they scrutinized Angelos with newfound curiosity.

"Are you familiar with the fate of Lucas?" Spyridon asked as he turned away, waving an expectant hand for Angelos to follow him.

"I am." Angelos said as they walked down the hall.

"Do you know it well?" Spyridon stressed as they approached the glass doors.

"I am an Apistian." Angelos replied as if the answer was obvious, and Spyridon nodded before pushing the doors open.

Thunder roared and lightning crackled violently as a storm brewed around them out of nowhere, but Spyridon paid it no mind when he stepped outside onto the balcony. He knelt at the outdoor altar that was directly facing the gods' palace, barely feeling his knees hit the hard floor or his soaked robes clinging to his skin. He knew his white hairs were now plastered to his balding head but at least his routine fasting kept his thin frame from putting too much pressure on his old bones in this kneeling position.

Spyridon bowed his head and closed his eyes as he moved his lips in prayer. As he did, the wind lifted even more, and the storm's thundering grew so loud that he was sure that everyone in Midrios could hear the tempest raging around him. He opened his eyes just in time to see bright green flames roar to life on the altar of their own accord.

He rose to his feet and watched the flames grow higher and higher, impervious to the pouring rain. They had now grown so high that all in Midrios could see them if they only knew where to look. Spyridon peered into the godly fire for a moment longer before slowly turning towards Angelos who had been silently watching him by the doors the whole time.

"The gods demand your service." Spyridon demanded and his eyes flickered to the sculpture of the abandoned man for a few seconds before he returned his gaze to Angelos. *"Go to Leondria. Death for Midrios is coming."*

PART
TWO ⊕

CHAPTER

12

Alastair walked down the bustling Apistian streets and watched people of all sizes, races, and creeds pass by him. His steps were measured, like always. No minute detail was beneath his appraising gaze and no idea was too small for him to turn over in his mind. One could not glance at Alastair without finding a teasing smirk, a look of superiority, and wheels constantly spinning behind his calculating, turquoise-blue eyes. He was taller than average, and the shade of his skin fell somewhere between the color of copper and ebony.

He had been raised in Apistia—named after its founder, the Goddess of Wisdom—but he did not love his city-state because he was born here. He strove for its glory because of all the qualities that already made it unique. People throughout Midrios, and even some other countries, came here. It was a haven for the inventors, the scholars, and the geniuses.

There had once been a time when they had lived without walls and all had been welcomed here, but that changed a long time ago.

Thousands lived within Apistia's borders and it was common to see crowds lining the streets or gathering around new unveilings of art. There were many engravings of owls, sculptures of Lady Apistia, and buildings that did their best to touch the sky.

They strove for ingenuity and had invented democracy, the amphitheater, and the university in the process. They were a city-state of firsts, even if that barbarous Leondria did technically predate Apistia. Except for that minor detail, it was clear to all with a functioning brain that Apistia was the superior city-state in every way.

He continued analyzing the crowd's movements as he strolled down the familiar streets. It was always wise to observe one's surroundings and prudent for an elected representative to understand their constituents. To keep a finger on the pulse of the issues that would inevitably arise on the Senate floor.

His adversaries wouldn't be complacent so neither would he. Especially not after everything he had seen done to his family and the fools who didn't plan ahead.

He stopped by a large group that had assembled around a boy not much older than ten flawlessly playing the Fate of Lucas, the notoriously difficult trademark song of Apistia. Alastair was impressed by how quickly the boy's small hands flew across the violin's strings, especially when he noticed burns lacing his fingers and the inside of his palms.

Lady Apistia wrote the Fate of Lucas and, while emotions were unbecoming since such things distracted the mind, even the most cold-hearted Apistian would find themselves deeply moved every time they heard the song properly played. All musicians here inevitably tried to play the Fate of Lucas, but few could pull off its technical difficulty. Only the truly best could move an entire audience to tears and it was one of those rare circumstances where such emotional displays would not be held against them.

The boy plucked the last string in the song and Alastair turned away as the crowd clapped fervently with a few tears in their eyes. He didn't make any further stops and soon found himself approaching the Senate building. While every structure in Apistia was impressive, Alastair thought the Senate building was one of the most magnificent pieces of architecture ever constructed. There were meticulous engravings of owls up and down the six tall, white marble columns where sculptures of the gods stood at the top of each of them. These sculptures were capped by a triangle-shaped roof which gave the impression that the gods were holding up the building and looking over them.

A sculpture of Lady Apistia stood at the bottom of the seven flights of stairs, and it was uncanny how the white marble mimicked a wet dress flowing in a gust of wind. Lady Apistia's hair was characteristically pinned up and one hand was outstretched with the palm facing the sky. The eyes in the sculpture were blank, as was customary, since even the greatest of artists wouldn't dare to try to capture a human, let alone a goddess's soul.

Alastair thought it would be a striking work of art if it was a sculpture of a mortal woman, but it failed to do Lady Apistia justice.

Without the irises, the sculpture simply failed to capture the sheer power and intelligence that he remembered radiating from those golden eyes. Eyes that promised imminent salvation or absolute destruction. The artist captured the goddess's typical stony expression but some of the nuances were lost. Like how her face would sometimes flicker with impatience when someone was acting foolish or how her lips would momentarily tug upwards with amusement when she had sprung some intellectual trap that someone had fallen for.

Everyone who walked past her sculpture up to her Senate would then know that wisdom seekers would be welcomed while warning away those who might have been foolish enough to waste their time.

Alastair took his time walking up the seven flights of stairs but still passed some others who struggled with the climb. He nodded at two Senators—Ermis and Iason—he saw talking by the entrance. They quickly ducked their heads, going back to whispering to each other, and Alastair smirked. He could recognize the signs of a last-minute deal when he saw it, but he would exploit that to his advantage later. He would take his time and watch how this meeting played out before making his move.

He walked up to the two glass doors which were stained with various shades of blue and gold, signifying the skill of the much sought after glassmaker. Even the most irresponsible Apistian usually took great care in opening these priceless doors but there had been a few prior incidents where the doors needed a touch-up or had to be replaced altogether from age. It was no matter, however. They had the resources and expertise to remake the unique door again.

Alastair carefully pushed open the doors and stepped inside. The foyer was full of people but was no more crowded than usual. There was still plenty of space to freely move about as he strolled towards the Senate chamber. Under each blue and white stained glass window, there were carvings of famous Senators, of the most erudite Apistians in their history, and of Lady Apistia with Jason.

Some of the passersby would stop to admire the art but most exploited their opportunity to accost a Senator before their weekly meeting. Alastair's sharp eyes never failed to notice when a bag of silver passed hands or when an attractive son or daughter happened to accompany one of their parents to "just talk" with their representative. Those were the sloppy ones though.

He did find himself greatly amused when he saw a stranger speaking fervently to someone he knew well.

"Senator, the time to act is now." the man urged.

Alastair had heard that line before many times. Everyone wanted immediate solutions to their problems even if most of their issues didn't warrant immediate action. Alastair had to suppress a laugh that this man had chosen to corner Senator Sophie of all people. The wily, cunning woman didn't retain her seat in the Senate for over two decades by not playing the long game and outsmarting everyone in her path. Of all his political adversaries, she was by far his favorite since she always put up a good fight which entertained him in some of the most tedious meetings.

Few knew how to play the game of politics and they were both masters at it.

He continued walking by them, close enough to overhear their conversation while on his way through the second pair of blue and gold glass doors to enter the Senate floor. He quickly lost interest in the man's assertions that the Senate needed to work together for Apistia's welfare when Sophie's eyes flashed to his. Amusement and contempt flashed across her face and Alastair raised a teasing eyebrow at her.

Alastair had just walked past them when he overheard the plea, "—Apistia needs to work together with Leondria."

Alastair stopped dead, uncharacteristically stunned. Now *that* caught his attention.

He had never heard of anyone ever suggesting for Apistians to work with those blood-thirsty murderers. They may have been historically instrumental in prevailing over attacks on their country but what they had once stood for and what they had become were two very different things.

Alastair felt more than saw the man's gaze focus on his back and Alastair remembered that he needed to move forward. He forced his legs into action, recovering himself as he entered the Senate chambers. Three-fourths of the room had seats exclusively reserved for the Senators with benches in the last quarter of the room open for any Apistian citizen to silently watch the proceedings.

He walked down several rows of steps until he found an open seat in the Senator section. He crossed his arms over his light blue chiton as the other senators began entering the room while they attempted to give off the impression of unaffected dignity.

A Senate session was supposed to start at noon when the sun was at its highest point in the sky, but some senators would try to make a power move by arriving right after a meeting was supposed to begin. It had become a relatively recent trend since no one had dared to waste Lady Apistia's time by showing up late back when she did attend Senate meetings.

She had been a force to reckon with and no one wanted to provoke the quick-witted goddess. It had been amazing to see her in action when he had watched the Senate meetings in the back of the room as a child.

That had been a long time ago though and Alastair was now a grown man who no longer had to be silent at these meetings. He thought showing up late was a senseless tactic and he preferred to arrive early for these meetings for three reasons:

1. He could observe everyone which gave him an opportunity to read the others and acquire an advantage over them.
2. The Navy had long ago ingrained in him the importance of punctuality, so he had too much respect for time as a military man.
3. Those who arrived late always missed something. It could be a senator's stance on an issue, what problem they were dealing with that day, or how to read the shifting loyalties in the room.

He wasn't surprised when he saw movement in the corner of his eye and a pale woman in her mid-thirties wearing dark blue peplos sat down next to him. Tossing her silver-laced brown hair behind her shoulder and her brown eyes glittering in anticipation, she shifted ever so slightly towards him. He had known that foolishly stopping dead in the corridor earlier would put a new target on his back but a part of him was curious to see how she would proceed with the assault.

"Sophie." he greeted, his tone jovial but dripping with sarcasm.

"Alastair." she replied with equal lightness and pretended to take a moment to look around the room. "Perfect time for a session."

"I couldn't agree more." he said.

"Really?" she asked with feigned surprise and raised her eyebrows mockingly. "I was concerned the cold weather was getting the best of you. I could have sworn that you looked disconcerted moments ago."

Ah, calling him emotional. He knew she could do better than that.

"I was merely stunned to have been on the receiving end of your *lovely* gaze." he retorted lightly.

She exhaled in amusement. They both knew her days of beauty were behind her and that it was her mind, not her looks, that most often intimidated people.

She replied, "I am sure the constituents who elected you would be pleased to know their senator is so rational and cool headed."

Ah, now a mockery of how well he lived by their Lady's values and a nod to his age because he must be naïve and idealistic since he was a decade younger than her.

Her eyes slid towards him, and he could see her savoring each word as she went for the kill, "Especially after hearing about the Leondrians."

He only put a hand over his heart and stated, "I am touched by your concern, Sophie. I wouldn't have expected such an emotional display from you."

Despite all his unpleasant memories of the Leondrians, he wouldn't be easily baited or provoked. He couldn't be in this line of work.

"How often the young and inexperienced mistake strategy for concern." she chided. "But it is wise of you to let go of your grudge against the Leondrians. They only murdered your father, after all."

There it was. The proverbial knife he had been expecting. Her contempt for his father still hadn't ceased despite his death twenty years ago and whose ire she had long ago redirected from his deceased father towards him. Though he knew she had more respect for his political skills than his father, who allowed his idealism to cloud his better judgment.

"If you had been paying attention, you would know it was foolishness that killed my father." Alastair corrected evenly. "You would know since you were there. Unless that lesson was too subtle for you to discern, Sophie."

He winked at her as he saw controlled rage flare behind her eyes for the first time that day.

"I'll let you ruminate on that." he whispered as there was a loud banging of a gavel to quiet the Senate chamber. "Do let me know if you learn something worth sharing."

The senators all rose and made the sign of the gods while chanting, "By Lady Apistia's grace, may our meetings be blessed with wisdom and knowledge."

They all sat down. Alastair saw the rage in Sophie's eyes rapidly melt into cool disdain and he knew that her mind was plotting the next three moves against him.

The session began and Alastair noticed many bewildered looks thrown his way since his and Sophie's rivalry was well-known. He listened to everything that was said, but his mind wasn't entirely in the meeting since he was preoccupied with other thoughts.

There was a time when all he did was fantasize about getting revenge against his adversaries. Against the Leondrians who murdered his father which caused his family's imminent downfall. Against Sophie and the others who used this to their advantage to spearhead a campaign against them and drove them to poverty.

He thought about what he would do if he ever ran into the Leondrians again. He had scraped for every piece of news about Leondria in the subsequent years, even long after he had joined the Navy. Much of what he had heard was only general news of little interest until Typhon's unexpected rise a few years ago.

Many in Apistia had chosen to flee into the open sea in a fierce storm rather than face his fires. Alastair hadn't been surprised by the high casualty count but what he had found odd that, except for Typhon's rampage, this city-state of would-be conquerors had firmly stayed inside their borders the past couple decades. Perhaps Lady Apistia had struck such fear into their hearts that they had been cowed into submission, but Alastair suspected there was more to the story than that.

"Are there any other issues a senator would like to bring up today to add to the next meeting's agenda?" the moderator asked.

Sophie rose gracefully beside him, her voice booming in the chambers, "There is an issue I would like to raise for the Senate's consideration."

Alastair snapped his full attention towards her, expecting something insidious but not knowing exactly what. His mind raced with possibilities as he watched her eyes sweep the room she now completely commanded. Only he was close enough to catch her lips slightly curl up in anticipation before her expression rippled into complete neutrality.

"Apistia has stood the test of time. We are second to none in terms of technology, medicine, using democracy as a model of government, and acquiring knowledge. Many flock here for honorable reasons but there are some who have set their eye on us—not to educate themselves—but to take by force that which they cannot build then destroy that which they cannot understand." she declared, and Alastair noted how the room hung on to her every word. "Leondria now has two queens ruling those *renowned warriors*. We remember all too well what happened to us the last time Leondria had a monarch in charge. We are too shrewd to ignore evidence or to wait for the Leondrians to make another move against us."

She let her words hang heavy in the air, drudging up fear and uncomfortable memories.

"While we have built walls and we have established a Navy, we do not have an army." Sophie pointed out and her voice grew grave. "Only the mountains to the west shield us from the Leondrians but they could always cut through or around them to approach our walls, like before. Lady Apistia protected us once before from them, but we must be wise enough to defend ourselves, especially considering the gods' withdrawal from mortal affairs these past twenty years."

The anticipation in the room grew and Alastair noted more than one senator who had leaned forward in their seats towards Sophie.

"We do not know what these new queens' intentions are, but it is likely they have the same or most of the same advisors as their father. They are young. Inexperienced." Sophie's eyes flashed eagerly with opportunity. "Malleable. Easy to observe to deduce any sinister plans and easy to mold to best serve *our* interests. There is one tenet that anyone who has studied Lady Apistia and our history knows keenly well that I would ask this Senate to contemplate before I present my motion for consideration. One can better anticipate the changes in the wind when one steps outdoors and watch the movement of the leaves. This wise Senate should consider sending a message to these queens to form an—alliance—with Leondria. To keep our eyes close for any movement of the leaves so we can best strategize how to change the course of the wind."

There was a stunned silence as her words sank in, but Alastair knew Sophie better than to believe she was doing this for altruistic reasons. He may not have heard the beginning or end of the conversation that stranger had with Sophie outside the Senate chamber, but Alastair also knew better than to believe that Sophie would be persuaded to do anything like this based on one conversation with a stranger minutes before a Senate session.

"Before the rest of the assembly takes a vote, I would like for one Senator to make his vote known as he is the one who stands to gain or lose the most from it." Sophie continued, gesturing to Alastair.

The whole room was now staring at him, and he knew that she had trapped him. He could vote in favor of her proposal by standing or vote against it by remaining in his seat. If he stood, it would be construed as an emotional response because he would then be seeking an opportunity for revenge. If he remained sitting, it would be construed as an emotional response because he would then be running away from his father's killers. He almost smirked at her and couldn't help but appreciate the strategy.

"How do you vote?" she finally asked. "Senator Alastair, son of Aetos."

Alastair reminded himself that politics was all just a game of moves and countermoves. He had a lot to lose with either option he took but he could also turn this to an opportunity to exploit to his advantage. Alastair then stood which caused an immediate buzzing in the chambers. The others didn't wait for the moderator or for Sophie to ask for everyone else to vote as Senators in the room started standing to show their support. It wasn't long before a quarter of them were now standing in favor of the proposal. A third. Almost half.

"The vote has passed and will be added to the next meeting's agenda." Sophie announced when a slim majority of the Senate finally stood in support of the proposal. "This session shall now be adjourned."

Technically, only the moderator was allowed to end any Senate meeting, but Alastair smirked at her audacity. Sophie gave him a man-eating grin before descending a few steps to talk to some of the others. He could have joined her but anything he said now would be questioned for bias so he would bide his time to play this just right. He turned towards the entrance as the crowd started filing out and kept his face blank when he saw that the man who had cornered Sophie earlier was sitting in the back.

Watching him.

"Follow me." Alastair said when he reached the top of the steps and the man obeyed without hesitation.

Alastair kept his pace measured as they walked outside the building and started down the long flight of stairs.

"What is your name?" he inquired with a side glance at the stranger.

"Angelos." the man replied. "I come with urgent news."

So he had gathered, Alastair thought wryly to himself.

"The gods have sent a message." Angelos continued almost frantically and grabbed Alastair's arm.

Alastair stopped, raising an eyebrow at where Angelos rested his hand. He wasn't concerned, knowing he could handle himself if Angelos started an altercation, but not liking the familiarity of the gesture either.

"You must work together with Leondria." Angelos urged, and Alastair's gaze wandered to the distance, towards the westward mountains where he knew Leondria waited.

"Do you see it?" Angelos demanded. "Do you still see the smoke from here?"

Even though the unnatural green fire in the westward mountains had extinguished days ago, there was still white smoke drifting across the sky. Anyone who had not seen the mysterious flames during the storm might have mistaken this smoke as the remains of an ordinary fire, but Alastair knew better.

Everyone knew that there was a temple for the gods there that belonged to the holy man, Spyridon. Alastair did not know him well, despite his name being whispered from time to time, but didn't need to meet the man to know that he was a zealot.

"Spyridon saw you in a vision." Angelos whispered.

The white smoke lingering by the holy man's temple was the one thing that gave Angelos's claim that the gods had sent him any sort of credibility, but the assertion was still very thin at best.

"Don't you see that you are instrumental for what comes next?" Angelos pushed and Alastair raised a skeptical eyebrow.

"Did you hear the words from Lady Apistia yourself?" Alastair asked but already suspected the answer.

Angelos briefly hesitated then answered, "No, but we know that Spyridon serves only the gods."

"No mortal is above self-interest." Alastair pointed out coolly.

"How is serving the gods not also serving our people?" Angelos demanded. "You saw for yourself what happened in the meeting."

"Senator Sophie has her reasons for doing the things she does." Alastair corrected.

"You serve the gods." Angelos insisted, not addressing Alastair's last remark. "Go to Leondria and broker an alliance. Events are already in motion."

Alastair rested a hand over his heart and protested, "I serve myself. Ask anyone inside."

"Don't worry." Angelos squeezed his arm and glanced at some senators who gave them curious looks when they passed. "I understand how you must handle the Senate."

"No Apistian would make that journey for a first audience with the queens. At least, not without proof that you were sent by the gods." Alastair said skeptically.

Angelos returned his gaze to the mountains and the smoke, his expression distant, before asserting, "I'll handle the queens. You just do your part."

Alastair scrutinized Angelos as the strange man hurried down the rest of the steps. He had waited twenty years for Lady Apistia to return but he would not get his hopes up without hard evidence illustrating that she was coming back. Regardless of whether Angelos was telling the truth about this supposed message from the gods, Alastair had a sneaking suspicion that things were about to get interesting.

CHAPTER

13

Anastasia kept her eyes on the fire while listening for any threat. Not that she was expecting any attack with a crowd of Leondrians surrounding the bonfires with their shields strapped to their sides. But she was Queen Zosime's personal guard, so she always had to be ready.

Gods knew there was so much they didn't know, and someone would use that to their advantage to strike against them, if they were given the opportunity.

Anastasia watched the two queens and couldn't help but notice the tension quietly ripple between them that only seemed to slowly grow with each passing day. She thought that part of the problem was the clash of their different personalities and not figuring out how to smoothly make decisions together. Anastasia would wait a little while longer to see if this was something that would resolve on its own or if she would need to intervene. The queens learning to overcome their differences on their own would better enable them to solve problems in the future than if Anastasia prematurely intervened.

It hadn't reached a point of becoming a full-fledged problem yet. If she saw anything that suggested otherwise, then she would step in. Doing anything to hold their hands before that moment would be coddling and any waiting afterwards would be detrimental so she would wait a little longer before deciding whether she needed to step in.

This tension between the two only seemed to worsen since their return from the tour, which was also around the same time that Anastasia had noticed the new looks Vasiliki started shooting in her direction. The occasional puzzled, inquiring glance after they had run into Lord Kal on the way back from the eastward mountains.

Anastasia couldn't stop her fists from momentarily clenching when she thought about him showing up unexpectedly in that strange feline form. He knew what he did to her, and she would never forgive him for it.

"Anastasia!" Flavian suddenly exclaimed and she looked up, already half-expecting what he was about to say.

He gestured for her to stand and encouraged, "Tell us the story of your triumph over Typhon!"

Anastasia shook her head, and her heart became heavy with dread as Flavian pleaded, "C'mon, ma'am, it's a favorite!"

Anastasia usually enjoyed listening to the nightly stories by the bonfires, but the re-telling of her triumph over Typhon was something she would rather forget. She had only faced him once, but she had lived the experience over and over again from the hundreds of times the story had been told and the thousands of times she had re-played it in her mind.

"You may tell it if you wish." Anastasia finally said quietly, and Flavian's eyes sparkled.

She needed to do something with her hands, and she focused on detaching herself from the situation. She understood that many who had not seen battle wanted to bask in glory, but she could never say out loud that the fight with Typhon had been one of the worst days of her life. Anastasia's gaze fell, and she couldn't stop herself from remembering the blood that had coated her arms.

Couldn't help but remember how her muscles felt like they were being shredded from the inside-out. She could practically hear Typhon's cruel laughs and her eyes flashed to a piece of wood on a nearby bonfire that had crackled unexpectedly. She knew many feared the Creature as something malevolent, but it was simply misunderstood.

Typhon was the true monster.

The sight of Typhon physically ripping apart some of the best people she had ever met and hearing their screams of agony was something she would never forget. Nor would she forget the days leading up to the fight with him.

She remembered so clearly, even now, how the changes in the wind had deeply disturbed her for the weeks leading up to the confrontation. She hadn't known why it had bothered her so much but her worry that something was wrong had only been reinforced when she heard from one of the Spears that Zosime had been on edge for the past month. Not sleeping and continually warning them that their doom was upon them. The Spear had shaken off the warning, believing she was cracking under the pressure of Training, but Anastasia hadn't been so sure.

She had remembered seeing the girl in passing a few times in Training and had seen her total commitment to becoming a Leondrian. Anastasia had doubted she would suddenly start succumbing to the rigors of Training out of the blue and knew that demi-gods often possessed godly powers they didn't always understand.

But no one could ignore the trembling in the ground around them a short time later and when people from the north had started fleeing in droves to Leondria for protection.

Anastasia had been amazed that the Council waited so long to approve a team of Leondrians to go face the monster. They all knew the odds were worse than grim and, despite the age and battle experience differences between her and the rest of the group, Anastasia had quickly befriended the seasoned warriors.

Gallows bonding, she supposed. Her strength had set her apart from the other Trainees growing up and she had done her best to assimilate as mama had warned her to do with her dying breath. She could also remember the Creature's voice reverberating in her mind during her Trials when it warned: *don't let them see you for what you are.*

The younger people here just didn't understand what it was like to be responsible for the fate of millions and to be a hairbreadth away from failure.

She looked up and blinked when she caught Perleros staring at her. There was no sympathy in his eyes but there was grim understanding there. He and Oscar were the only other Leondrian survivors of Typhon's wrath, and she was sure he also felt pain every time the subject was brought up. Because it wasn't a story or an engaging history lesson for them. They had lived it and, while they had ultimately prevailed, seeing such terrible things had broken some part of them that could never be made whole again.

Anastasia wearily watched Flavian rise to his feet and face his eager audience with a grin. People started making calling out to "Start from the fight!" "Start from the mountain shaking!" "Start from the warriors marching off to the fight!"

Flavian shook his head at the shouted suggestions and clapped his hands together, "Any good story starts at the beginning."

The others quieted down eagerly even though, Anastasia thought bitterly, they had heard this story so many times before they had to have it memorized by now.

"Before Lady Hermione's children were born, the world used to be a very dark place. This is before her son, Anatole, received the golden chariot to drive the sun across our horizons and long before her daughter, Selena, ascended to the night sky to bring us cycles of sun and moonlight to the world." Flavian began and spread his arms with a dramatic flair. "Many people were little better than beasts and magical creatures roamed the land with impunity. People were cut down left and right and no one blinked an eye. But of all the powerful magical creatures that roamed these lands, one figure was unlike all the rest. Only one struck universal fear and almost brought about our downfall."

Anastasia closed her eyes for a moment then begrudgingly opened them when Flavian continued, "No one really knew how or exactly when Typhon was born but all we can say for certain is that he came to life on one of the islands surrounding Midrios. There have been many beasts that have stood on two legs or even spoken our language like a human being, but none were like Typhon. The monster that stood on two legs and swung two arms like a mortal but had a hundred lizard heads that spewed something even worse than fire."

"Lava!" a little girl's voice cried out and Anastasia heard a young woman who must have been her mother shushing the child.

"It was lava." Flavian acknowledged, unfazed. "Some say he was born inside a volcano when the lava inside was sitting dormant for too long. Some say he was born from the ashes of a volcanic eruption and rose as something even worse. No one from that island lived to tell the tale and no one dares to step foot there. What we do know is that he was born with an unquenchable thirst for destruction and found himself unsatisfied after killing everyone on that small piece of land and razing it to the ground."

Anastasia braced herself but couldn't stop the flash of fire from skirting across her vision.

His voice deepened as he said, "He looked to the horizon and made the world around him shake and the wind itself tremble as he swam in the seas.

The water obeyed his commands and swirled into the greatest typhoon ever seen that followed him into the mainland where he even drove back Lady Apistia when he struck her city-state. He killed everything that crossed his path in a fierce storm of water, wind, and lava. Sometime during his trail of destruction, he found a monstrous woman with a poisoned soul and their union resulted in many monstrous creations that still roam Lady Meraki's Forest to this day. The gods soon realized that there was no stopping Typhon, and he would destroy all of Midrios, so they came together and fought in a ferocious battle, ultimately shackling him, and forcing him into a deep slumber deep beneath a mountain where he remained for thousands of years."

"But he awakened!" that same little girl's voice cried out and the same woman dragged her away from the group, murmuring stern words to her as she did.

No one said anything to stop her, knowing that the girl would need to be taught discipline, even if it meant missing the rest of the story.

"But he awakened and broke free from his shackles a few years back." Flavian proceeded without skipping a beat. "His full strength had not yet returned but the strength he did have was more than enough to decimate and terrorize the people of Midrios. Those who were fast enough to escape Typhon's wrath fled to Leondria for sanctuary, but many were cut down long before they arrived here. The people begged the gods to intervene again, but they never came. They have still never been seen since their disappearance twenty years ago, with one exception."

Flavian's eyes slanted towards Anastasia and Vasiliki. The news of them seeing Lord Kal during their tour had spread like wildfire but Anastasia only replied with a stony expression.

He got the hint and moved on, "One could see the thunder and lightning raging above the gods' mountain which made many wonder if they would finally emerge, but they ultimately had faith in our strength as Leondrians to battle the threat this time."

At that point, Anastasia stopped listening and she couldn't stop herself from reliving the experience all over again.

She had felt the shift in the wind a few years ago but had known it was no typical change of the seasons. It hadn't been the regular cool breeze of fall but something ominous that had kept her from enjoying the impending

Mione festivities. Typhon had broken free right before Mione and started to inflict the full extent of his wrath in the middle of the festival. And yet, the Council had refused to authorize them to wage war until after the holiday ended. Anastasia's skin had been crawling by this point to act, but she knew her opinion wouldn't mean anything to anyone as someone who had only worn the red cloak for a year.

She had recognized that she didn't have the battle experience of the seasoned warriors who had been chosen to go on the expedition. But she had known that she was strong and that she could make a difference. She had known it in her bones, but she also realized that she would have to convince the one in charge to permit her to come or she would be ordered to stay behind.

General Perleros had announced the day before the group of Leondrians going north and that he would be leading them personally in the fight against Typhon. She had known that she would have to appeal to him directly at the right time when he wouldn't have the chance to change his mind so she had waited until the morning of their departure to corner him when he would be at his most vulnerable. She had managed to intercept him as he was walking down the three steps of the Heart to march towards the troops who were waiting for him by the gates.

"General." she had greeted solemnly, and he had only looked at her impassively.

As if he was seeing everything and nothing at all. As if everything in this life was both precious and meaningless to him. As if he had already embraced his own death and his children's likely doom.

She had seen the realization dawn in his eyes and said curtly before she could open her mouth, "I've already taken all the volunteers that can be spared."

There was reluctance and regret in his eyes. Anastasia had heard that the two future queens had also begged him to come, and she knew he would be wary of more requests to volunteer from other Leondrians.

There was no point in arguing with him since that would only hurt her cause. Leondrians took orders. They didn't argue with their superiors, especially a new Leondrian to the highest ranking one. There was no point asserting that her safety was immaterial because that was their way of life. It was their duty to put their lives on the line for the greater good.

"You can help fortify our defenses." he had suggested as understanding flickered in his eyes.

"I am a Leondrian." she had said more to herself than to him. She didn't see the point of being born stronger than most if she couldn't use that strength to protect the place that she held most dear in her heart. She had recovered herself and felt steel rise within her as she insisted, "I won't hold you back."

That was the true issue, whether she could hold her own and not compromise the others' effectiveness to work together in battle.

He had studied her for a long moment then, when she saw the briefest flash of grief in his eyes as he looked at her, she knew then that he would approve her last-minute request.

"We leave now." he had finally said and looked at her as if she was already dead and gone.

She had only tightened her grip on her spear and asserted, "I'm ready, General."

She had followed him down to the gates where so many Leondrians stood ready to go in two files by the gates. She had noticed a lot of people frown at her in surprise when she melted into the back of the first line before Perleros gave them the order to move out.

They had begun marching immediately and Anastasia didn't once look back at the Hearth. She hadn't needed the painful reminder that this was probably the last time she would see her home and she wouldn't give anyone a reason to doubt her resolve.

She had soon felt someone watching her and she quickly glanced to her left to see who it was. They were walking next to the Training Center and all the Trainees had formed a line, making the sign of the gods as they passed. It had taken Anastasia a moment to discover that it was Zosime's red-brown-yellow eyes that were staring at her in a mix of surprise, horror, and respect.

Anastasia had then returned her attention to the Leondrian marching in front of her and ignored the girl's gawking. She had just focused on walking, knowing they had multiple days of hard marching north to reach Typhon, even if they took little time to rest. He had broken free on the eastern side of the mountain but had inexplicably turned west to wreak havoc and destruction instead of turning his eye back on Apistia to settle old scores.

Time was of the essence, so they had marched quickly as the sun journeyed across the sky. The sun's movements had seemed slower than usual, as if Anatole was dragging it across the sky as slowly as possible to squeeze every drop of light for the Leondrians as possible. She didn't know why the gods had slipped behind the curtain of mist at the top of their beloved mountain, or why they refused to in their darkest hour, but she could see that at least some of them weren't oblivious to the mortals' affairs.

Anastasia hadn't felt fatigue when they finally stopped late in the evening on that first night. While the others immediately began cooking the supplies they had carefully packed, she had slipped away from camp and gone hunting. She wouldn't take up their limited resources since she was a last-minute addition, and it hadn't taken long to find imprints on the ground. She had carefully followed the tracks for about an hour until she found the lynx that they belonged to. It had initially ignored her, but when she pulled out her sword and began approaching it, it had charged towards her.

It had been a quick fight and the animal had fallen on top of her after she drove her sword into its belly. It had mewled in pain for a moment before going still and she barely noticed the extra weight when she carried it back to camp. She had said nothing to the others as she skinned the animal and placed the strips of muscle onto the fire she had just built. As she waited for the meat to slowly turn brown, she had cut deep into the animal's chest and ripped out its heart.

She had then tossed the heart into the fire and prayed, "I offer you this sacrifice, Lady Meraki. May we continue fighting another day and die free."

She had watched the fire consume her sacrifice and looked up when she noticed several people staring at her.

"I haven't seen that look from the younger generation before." one of them had said. She had vaguely recognized the seasoned warrior who had more grey hairs on his head than brown, but it took a second for her to remember his name.

"We always devote a sacrifice to our Lady at every meal, Captain Tobias." Anastasia had replied quietly.

"Yes." Tobias had agreed. "But the younger ones do it as a matter of ritual because of what they're taught. They don't say it with the intensity you just did."

Anastasia had merely declared, "I live to serve."

Tobias had tilted his head, but he and the others said nothing as they quickly ate then went to bed. They would only have a few more hours to rest before resuming their march and no one wanted to waste this precious time with small talk when they could be sleeping. Anastasia had forced her eyes to close, but it felt like no time at all had passed before they were awakened and ordered to get moving.

She had heard the cracking of joints as the older Leondrians stood up and Captain Tobias had joked, "Typhon has nothing on age."

Leondrians had a good tolerance for humor, and it was encouraged for esprit de corps so long as it didn't impact their readiness. The group began to feel lighter the closer they got to Palapao, and Anastasia didn't notice the passing time until they were one more night away from their absolution. They would either succeed and the children could grow up to take their place one day or they would fail, and all would be lost. There would be no middle ground and it reduced the pressure on them now that the waiting was almost over.

The whole group had been thrumming with anticipation by the time they stopped for the final night. They knew they likely only had hours left in this mortal form, and despite a life of discipline, the notion was liberating. Their main concern had been at the prospect of being stuck in a spiritual plane between this world and the next if there were no survivors to give them a warrior pyre or even a shameful burial. But the group had focused on other thoughts, like the sunset being the most beautiful thing they had ever seen.

Everything had become magnificent since they knew it was likely the last time that they would do the very things that made them human. A normal battle was one thing—a likely slaughter against a larger-than-life beast with destructive powers that rivaled the gods—was something else entirely.

The others had opened up more than she had ever seen before when they stopped for the last time. A final rest—a last refuge—to regain their strength before confronting Typhon the next morning. Anastasia had noticed more than one blister-ridden foot when sandals were removed and stiffness in their movements from the days of hard marching, but no one complained. To her great surprise and delight, the older Leondrians had invited her to join them by the fire that final night as they shared stories.

For the first and only time, she had felt fully included and was reveling every second of their limited time together. Very few had been able to sleep that night so they distracted themselves with laughter, which had slowly subsided as the dawn approached.

Some anticipation had remained when they formed up one last time and strode the final distance to Palapao, but it had been mainly replaced by the grimness that they had been fighting back for days. Anastasia had felt her uneasiness return with full force as the morning light quickly darkened with storm clouds and the wind had become so violent that the trees themselves shook.

They had smelled the smoke before they saw the devastation of what remained of the once proud Palapao. Bodies had littered the ground, and it had seemed to Anastasia that the entire country was burning. And yet, despite the freshly burning fires and the vicious wind, Typhon was nowhere in sight. This had set Anastasia further on edge as they carefully stepped over bodies and debris of fallen buildings to look for him, but she couldn't shake the feeling that he was close.

"Did we scare him off already?" Tobias had wondered aloud.

"Stay alert, Captain!" Perleros had chastised.

Anastasia had then felt a flash of heat soar by her cheek, and Tobias was suddenly engulfed in white and red flames. He had let out a screech of agony, but he collapsed before Anastasia could rush to his side and she knew that he was dead when he his screams of anguish silenced several seconds later.

She had slowly turned, and her eyes widened when she saw Typhon in all his wicked glory. He had stood taller than life with four humanoid arms and two humanoid legs with too many lizard heads for her to count. Two of these arms were fully extended for all to see the scaly dark red wings attached to it and a long, thick tail that ended in spikes. There were only lizard heads where a face should have been, and all of their eyes were staring directly at them.

As if he had found his new source of prey for his malicious amusement and couldn't have been more delighted. In that moment, she had suddenly recalled how intimidating the Creature had initially been to her during the Trials, but she knew beyond a shadow of a doubt now what true evil was.

Typhon hadn't been discarded based on his appearance then used for self-gain without a care in the world on how he felt about it.

She could feel the basic malevolence of his soul from the sour taste of the wind, and she knew there would be no rest for anyone until he was slain.

"Form up!" Perleros had ordered which snapped her out of her daze.

They immediately formed a few lines and raised their spears, but Typhon only cackled from a hundred different mouths then spit lava at them. She had to take a step back as the Leondrians in front of her were hit. For a second, she thought that the armor had shielded them but then she inhaled the stench of burning human flesh and watched their bronze skin melt away right in front of her.

The winds had strengthened as well, sending many Leondrians flying into trees and rocks, breaking bones like these renowned warriors were nothing more than rag dolls. Anastasia had seen Oscar get tossed somewhere but lost track of him as she launched her spear towards the monster. It had soared through the air and somehow impaled one of the many lizard heads. The other heads had screeched then, before she could react, she found herself airborne for several seconds before crashing into a nearby burning building.

She had been dazed when she finally lifted her head to see the fire creeping towards her. Blood had already started pouring down her arms and one of her legs was sprained, if not broken. She had let out a gurgled scream when she tried standing and had a sneaking suspicion that one of her hips had been dislocated. She had started coughing from the smoke and knew that she had to move right away, or it would all be over.

She had gritted her teeth and managed to stand, dragging a useless leg behind her as she forced her way back outside. She hadn't been able to stop the coughing fit but could finally start breathing better when she was back outside. She had quickly appraised her surroundings and realized that she now stood alone. There were corpses everywhere and Perleros looked seconds away from death himself.

Only a handful of minutes had passed since they arrived and yet everyone else was already dead or too injured to move. She hadn't been able to stop tears of rage from falling down her cheeks when she saw Typhon scoop up a few of the charred Leondrian bodies and swallow them whole.

She had tightened her grip on her spear and glared at the monstrous beast. She would rather be cast out, die in the belly of the beast, or burn alive before permitting him to destroy everything she had worked so hard to build. So she had started dragging herself towards him and, as the pain started to fade, her gait became determined as she walked over to the now-laughing Typhon who had finally seen her.

The Creature's warning from her Trials had then sprung to the forefront of her thoughts: *don't let them see you for what you are.*

There weren't any witnesses left, she had reasoned to herself, so she could permit instinct to take over. The thought had made her chuckle for a moment and then she screamed in righteous indignation as she ran towards him.

She would rather die than fail.

She would rather wander the spiritual plane for a thousand years than give Typhon free reign to destroy Leondria.

She would rather risk ex—

"Mighty Anastasia then slayed the beast." Flavian said, swiping his arm in the air so dramatically that it shook Anastasia out of her nightmare.

The fire in front of her crackled and she almost flinched. She reminded herself that she had survived, and she took a few measured breaths to calm herself down. She couldn't unravel right now in front of everyone, she inwardly reprimanded to herself.

She hadn't sought glory in slaying Typhon, but it had made her a legend when the survivors of Palapao emerged from their hiding places once they realized he was dead. It made her as much of an individual as Leondrians could be without notoriety, considering the circumstances behind the story. She hadn't abandoned her place in the line to try to kill the monster on her own. She hadn't left on a vigilante mission to seek out the monster for her own glory. She had only done what needed to be done but she had accomplished it in such a way that set her apart from all the others.

"May Lady Meraki continue to bless us with strength." Flavian prayed, a typical ending to a battle story, then cheered, *"May we fight to die free!"*

Everyone roared with him, and Anastasia repeated the words quietly. No matter what she had seen, done, or been through, she would always believe in those words. She would always fight for her right to die free.

So many things had pulled her in so many directions in her life, but she would continue to serve until her dying breath.

She caught Vasiliki giving her that now-familiar appraising look, as if

Anastasia was a mystery she wanted to unravel. Anastasia just had to pray that the queens wouldn't delve into what should remain in the past.

Vasiliki and Zosime murmured to each other, and Anastasia followed when they rose to their feet. Anastasia and Jedrick silently escorted them to their rooms and then wordlessly walked back to the housing section. They gave each other a nod as he strolled towards his house where his wife and young children were waiting while she made her way to hers. A single Leondrian like her would ordinarily be required to live in the barracks but they had made an exception for her.

She glanced up at the moon when she opened her door, feeling another shift in the wind that eerily reminded her of the calamity that was brought to their doorstep three years ago. She couldn't put her finger on why a sense of uneasiness rose in her chest, but she couldn't get rid of that nagging feeling that something was wrong.

Perhaps it had something to do with the strange creatures that had surprised her while the queens were taking their Trials. Not the typical run-of-the-mill malevolent beasts she had been expecting but something else entirely that she couldn't explain, even months after the queens' Trials. She only knew that something with black blood had knocked her off her feet and required a surprising amount of her strength to kill.

What she had immediately feared was that there were more of those things that were after a much more valuable prize: the future Queens of Leondria. While Anastasia had made sure not to stray too far from the Trainees with the other Spears also patrolling nearby, she had immediately began sprinting as fast as she could to check on the Trainees. She wouldn't interfere with the Trials themselves, but she wouldn't let monsters kill them while their minds were held hostage.

She couldn't help but think that it was a shadow of what was yet to come. Everyone knew it was forbidden to discuss the Creature or the Trials themselves, so she had been very careful in describing what she saw to Perleros upon their return to the Hearth.

He hadn't known what to make of it either.

All she knew was that this was a time of changes and, if misfortune was on the rise, a time of reckoning. This thought troubled her throughout the night, and while the next morning came too soon for her to get any rest, Anastasia strapped on her shield like every other day and pinned the red cloak to her shoulders. Every Leondrian who had experienced the toll of real battle and studied their city-state's history knew the heavy cost of wearing the red cloak and she felt it now.

She walked out of her house and started making her way towards the Heart when someone called out her name.

"Anastasia!" Flavian shouted and she turned to face him, frowning as he jogged towards her. "You should come to the gates."

"Were you on guard duty?" she asked, and her eyes narrowed when he nodded in confirmation. "And you left your post, Sergeant?"

"No one else is up yet and my partner still has him under watch—" he started explaining then urged. "I think you need to see this for yourself, ma'am."

He may have been one of the generals' nephews who bended the occasional rule but he had never done anything like this before so she decided to hear him out. She gave him a nod and followed him to the gates where she saw a Leondrian guard's eyes trained on someone Anastasia had never seen before.

Anastasia stopped in front of the stranger and narrowed her eyes, "Identify yourself."

"My name is Angelos." the man said with an inclined head.

"State your purpose." she ordered as she took in his disheveled appearance. "What is your business here?"

"I have an urgent message for the Queens of Leondria." Angelos declared breathlessly and Anastasia blinked in surprise. "War is coming."

CHAPTER

14

Zosime's eyes flew open and her began chest began heaving as she tried to escape from the powerful red eyes that had haunted her dreams yet again. She could feel the dark circles under her eyes but that was nothing new since Zosime was used to not sleeping through the night. Her heartbeat slowed and she sighed before pinching the bridge of her nose. She exhaled and turned over, closing her eyes again in the hopes of getting another couple hours of sleep.

Nightmares or not.

Several minutes passed in vain before she sat up in irritation. She rubbed her temples where a headache was starting to emerge and resigned herself to the fact that she wasn't going to get any more rest that night. Her chambers were too dark to discern what the exact time was, but she had developed an inner clock after growing accustomed to the darkness of her old room again after years of sleeping outside.

Her inner clock was telling her that morning was still hours away.

It was in these moments when sleep was an elusive mistress and she had to wait such a long time for the day to come that she felt the most restless. It was too early to lead the daily morning exercises, go to an advisor meeting, approve a permit, resolve a conflict, listen to stories around the bonfires, or talk with Vasiliki.

"It's okay." she whispered to herself.

But she couldn't ignore how she was staring at the blank wall in an empty room with nothing to distract her. She couldn't stop the Creature's words from the Trials from echoing in her mind... *Mere words? Do you really think that will be enough?*

Zosime's fists clenched.

Do you place so little value on loyalty? Are you so easily provoked into violence?

She suddenly swung her legs off the bed then sighed in resignation. She would never forget that night for as long as she lived. She distinctly remembered how her eyes had fluttered shut when she and Vasiliki were waiting for the Trials to begin and opening them sometime later to find everyone in camp gone.

What had sent her hand flying to her sword's hilt after discovering the empty camp was when she sensed a stranger's presence. Her inner alarm bells hadn't started ringing to warn her of an impending attack, but she hadn't been able to shake the feeling that someone was watching her. Her eyes had scanned her surroundings but even her superior eyesight hadn't been enough to pierce the darkness to find whatever was waiting for her.

She had waited with bated breath for several moments then frowned when no attack came. If the person had wanted to attack her, they would have done it by now. They had the tactical advantage, knowing exactly where she was when she didn't know who or where they were. But still, nothing happened. Zosime had the distinct impression that the figure was hiding from her, instead of trying to ambush her.

"Come out." she had called to whoever lurked in the trees, not interested in a long stalemate.

She had been greeted with silence, but she noticed that a strange mist now hugged the ground by her feet, almost as if it was in awe of her. She would have been more concerned in other circumstances, but her warning bells still hadn't started ringing, and she hadn't sensed any ill-will from the stranger. Or any particular emotion at all—which was odd—so she had focused all her attention on the Gift until she could finally identify an emotion from them.

It had been the whiff of terror she had sensed that compelled her to sheath her sword and lower her shield before repeating reassuringly, "Come out. I mean you no harm, friend."

Terror and heartbreak had seemed to rise from the person and Zosime had said softly, "You need not fear me. Come out."

A few moments had passed where nothing happened and Zosime thought that the figure wouldn't emerge after all.

Then a woman had suddenly materialized in front of her and Zosime's eyes had widened, her arms automatically starting to raise to defend herself when she forced herself to stop. The woman had been a tantalizing figure, clad all in black with a hood draped low over her face. The darkness and mist had seemed to envelop the woman in a way that Zosime couldn't explain. The woman's hands had been corpse-white, and she had a strange style of sword strapped to her side, but the woman made no move to attack her.

Zosime had blinked as her heart skipped a beat and she felt a flash of déjà vu. She hadn't been able to stop herself from asking, "Do I know you?"

It had been a strange question to ask because surely no one could ever forget the sight of such a figure. But Zosime had been certain that she knew this woman from somewhere. Zosime had taken a few steps closer to the woman who had stiffened but hadn't otherwise reacted.

Zosime hadn't known if it was madness that drove her forward, but she couldn't stop her hands from slowly reaching out and pulling back the hood. Her eyes had widened when the hood fell back, and she almost gasped in horror. The woman's black eyes were the only source of color in a face that was whiter than death and her mouth had been literally sewn shut.

"Who did this to you?" she had whispered, horrified.

The woman had only looked down then moved her head slowly from side to side. Zosime had opened her mouth then gasped as her eyes rolled back without her meaning to and some strange force started making her mouth move against her will.

"About time. You kept me waiting long enough." Zosime had found herself saying.

The world had darkened and Zosime didn't know how long her spirit had been separated from her body before she found herself coming back to herself. She had struggled to wrestle control of her body when more words kept pouring out of her mouth, unbidden, "Help them. I know you're tired but don't forget where you come from. Time to fight."

She had felt searing pain—the likes of which she had never felt before—then had sat up in the real world, shaken to her bones. It had only been when she had looked into her sister's eyes that she knew she had escaped that strange dream. But then she had seen the twin handprint on Vasiliki's arm and knew that the experience had been more than a mere dream.

Was it a prophecy? Zosime wondered. A warning?

She didn't know and there had been no sign of the woman in black in the months since. Nightmares hadn't bothered her before the Trials and now she couldn't stop having them or keep herself from dwelling on them.

The frustration rose in Zosime's chest, and she began pacing around her room.

It was too early for her to walk into the city since queens weren't supposed to go anywhere without at least one guard by their side, but she desperately needed to do something to pass the time. She immediately stopped her pacing and picked up her shield from the weapons rack, polishing it with vigor.

She really wanted to talk to her sister about the woman in black, but it was forbidden to discuss the Trials and now she didn't know what to think about it. She could practically hear Vasiliki mulling in her mind that it could have been part of the Creature's mind games and her reasoning for why it shouldn't be taken as anything more than a test.

But Zosime didn't think so.

She couldn't explain why but the Creature eerily reminded her of the woman in black and, while the Gift didn't seem to function around either of them, she had felt some sort of connection between the two. She didn't know how or why but she fervently believed that the two events were unrelated to each other.

But she couldn't talk to Vasiliki about it since it did happen during the Trials and she hadn't seen her sister much lately anyway, even after Vasiliki's return from her tour weeks ago. Zosime had initially been grateful to have her sister back, but the resentment came rushing back when Vasiliki told them about meeting Lord Kal.

People called Zosime's ability to sense other people's emotions a gift, but it was Vasiliki who was truly blessed. Vasiliki didn't have her every move watched, Vasiliki wasn't forced to wait to see their lands, and now one of the Six had decided to visit her after a twenty year hiatus.

Zosime worshipped the gods just like any good Midrian and she had wondered a few times if they would ever come back. But she had too much on her plate to really concern herself on why they left, and she had stopped anticipating their return a long time ago. She didn't resent their disappearance like Vasiliki did and it puzzled Zosime why her sister would care so much when she had never met them before.

At least, not until now. The report had shocked Zosime, not to mention everyone else. Vasiliki had just ridden out to the gods' mountain and one of the Six had shown up.

The news had spread like wildfire throughout the Hearth and, Zosime suspected, to the rest of Leondria. Zosime had tried dragging out more details from Vasiliki in private, but she didn't have anything more to tell. Vasiliki did share that Anastasia was apparently furious with Lord Kal, but she suspected that Vasiliki had only been projecting her own feelings based on the turmoil she sensed from her.

Vasiliki was too concerned about the family they shared blood with instead of the family they had spilt blood with over the years.

She suddenly realized that she had been vigorously scrubbing the same spot on her shield for the last several minutes and that no further polishing could make it sparkle any brighter.

Zosime sighed.

She knew she wasn't supposed to go anywhere by herself, but she just couldn't take waiting in this room anymore. Firmly making up her mind to get out of here, she quickly strapped the shield to her arm and strode out of the room. She kept her footsteps as silent as possible as she crept down the hallway. It wasn't uncommon to find the occasional servant or high-ranking Leondrian walking around inside the Heart, but she had long ago found another way to sneak out. She didn't know who created the secret exit in the building, but she had used it to her full advantage ever since she had discovered it as a child.

Zosime could remember this one time when she was four or five when a simple game of hide and seek with Vasiliki had turned into a manhunt. Vasiliki had methodically, if not predictably, searched every room but Zosime had snuck out and waited for half an hour before returning to her room. She had then done her best impression of bewildered innocence when she was finally discovered, pretending to have been there the whole time.

She wasn't a child anymore who was trying to win some game. She just needed fresh air to calm the storm in her mind.

Successfully evading the servants, Zosime snuck into her family's history room. Most of the rooms here were only designed to be large enough to be functional but this one was spacious. There were precious family heirlooms, gifts, and artwork, the few that could be allowed for Leondrians without appearing materialistic.

She didn't stop to look at anything in particular as she darted straight for the large rug pinned to the back wall. The rug depicted Lady Meraki standing with her mortal husband, Alexandros, holding their infant son, also named Alexandros, on top of the tallest hill where this building was now erected.

Zosime didn't waste any time looking at it and focused on pressing the weak spot in the wall behind the rug and climbed in. Clearly someone else in her family long ago also needed to get fresh air alone and she gratefully walked down the narrow steps inside the walls before pushing a weak spot in the wall that led outside. She slipped out of the narrow gap and carefully pushed the wall back in place until there was no trace of an opening. Unless one knew where to look.

Zosime then inhaled deeply, reveling the wind on her skin.

She just needed a little time to unshackle her burdened soul from that stifling room then she would return and start her day like the good, disciplined queen she was supposed to be.

It was exhilarating to walk around alone for the first time in years and her heart lifted. She hadn't snuck out of that hole since she was a child, and it was exhilarating to not have a guard tailing every step she took. She could hear Vasiliki's chiding voice in her head about breaking rules, but it would be a brief and desperately needed excursion then she would go straight back without causing any trouble. She shoved down the rising annoyance at the thought of her sister's judgment and did her best to hug the side of buildings to stay out of sight, even though not many people were up.

She walked around for some time until her thoughts finally settled. She didn't know how long she wandered but knew it must have been for a while when she noted the lightening sky. It was still a little early, but she would need to double back soon to return to her chambers without being discovered.

She hadn't realized she had strolled by Anastasia's house until she heard her voice and her heart immediately quickened at the sound. Zosime frowned at what she heard but didn't say anything when she saw Flavian and Anastasia stalk towards the gates surrounding the Hearth.

She sensed Flavian's urgency and knew something very important was about to happen, so she followed them. It was a short walk from Anastasia's house to the front gates and Zosime studied the strange man who waited there as she slowly approached. The stranger looked like he had spent many days out in the elements, but she sensed that his conviction was inexhaustible. She heard Anastasia's demand for identification and then felt his bombardment of emotions. Desperation. Sincerity. Devotion. Fear—not for himself, perhaps—but fear *for* something she couldn't make out.

"I have an urgent message for the Queens of Leondria." the man declared breathlessly. "War is coming."

Zosime froze for a second then took a few steps forward to ask, "Where?"

Anastasia reached for her sword and whirled faster than Zosime could track before she stopped, eyes widening when she recognized Zosime.

"My queen." the three Leondrians said, making the sign of the gods.

"War is coming to Midrios, Queen Zosime." Angelos whispered breathlessly. "Death is coming for us all unless you do something about it."

"You make no demands of our queen." Anastasia threatened quietly as she angled her body between Zosime and the man. "Where is your proof of who you are or your claim?"

"Did you see the fire?" he rasped and Zosime could tell by the sound that he had not drank any water recently. "By the gods' mountain pass? The storm?"

Anastasia's jaw clenched and Zosime vividly recalled that storm from weeks ago. She had seen the abnormal green fire that defied the great storm but hadn't known what it meant.

Anastasia echoed her thoughts when she pointed out, "That was weeks ago."

"It takes time for a mortal with no warrior training to approach the Apistian Senate then make the trek to Leondria." Angelos stated then looked behind Zosime. "Where is Queen Vasiliki?"

Anastasia's frown deepened and she said, "We will verify your story, assuming it's true at all, before we allow you to speak to our queens."

"There is no time to waste!" he admonished and Zosime sensed his rising urgency.

"Anastasia." Zosime said.

"My queen?" Anastasia asked without tearing her gaze away from him.

"We can hear what he has to say." Zosime suggested.

Anastasia's eyes flickered to the other Leondrians then back to Zosime before answering with a slight emphasis in her tone, "We can verify his identity and claim first, my queen."

Zosime couldn't think properly around her. Her heart was beating fast in her chest, but she kept her eyes trained on Angelos. His emotions were sincere, and her alarm system wasn't ringing to warn her of some sort of trap. While she respected Anastasia and desperately wanted her to think well of her, Zosime couldn't shake this feeling that Angelos meant them no harm.

"Bring him into the Heart and call the advisors." Zosime decided, not daring to look at Anastasia as she started to turn away.

"A moment, my queen." Anastasia's voice rang out.

Zosime paused and turned back in surprise. Anastasia had never contradicted her in front of others before.

Anastasia trained her eyes on Angelos, giving him a piercing glare that threatened the worst of deaths if he tried anything. She started patting him down, searching for weapons then stepped back unsatisfied when she didn't find anything.

"You walked here from Apistia with not even a dagger to protect yourself or to scavenge for food?" she asked incredulously.

"The gods watched over me." he replied humbly with a bowed head.

"An Apistian who walked across the mountains instead of taking a boat?" Anastasia asked suspiciously.

The man hesitated for a moment then simply repeated, "The gods watched over me."

Anastasia's face darkened further but she didn't say anything else on the matter. She positioned herself in between Zosime and Angelos then ordered the guards to remain at their posts but to send word if there were any further developments.

Zosime slowed her pace for the clearly exhausted man, so it took several minutes before they reached the Heart where she noticed Vasiliki and Oscar whispering to each other with grave faces. What made Zosime frown was how the two of them quickly backed away from each other and the feeling of secrecy emanating from them.

"Who's this?" Vasiliki asked, moving to step forward when Oscar repositioned himself to stand between her and Angelos.

Before anyone could speak, Zosime replied smoothly, "This is my guest."

Oscar pursed his lips and Zosime felt his flash of anger. If he had been able to say or do anything before Zosime did, she may not have been able to claim guest right. Now Angelos was under her protection, and she could listen to his story without interference since any breach of host etiquette would be an offense against the gods themselves. In the old days, the gods would punish offenders personally and there had been some instances where a breach of such etiquette had been enough provocation to instigate a war.

Oscar shot Anastasia a look and she said, "This is Angelos, son of—"

Anastasia glanced at the man who answered, "Angelos, son of Hector."

Anastasia continued, "Angelos, son of Hector, approached our gates and was stopped by the guards. He comes bearing a message for the queens and I searched him."

Zosime felt Oscar's indignation grow when Anastasia added, "That is all I know, General."

Zosime caught the brief look Oscar and Vasiliki shared before Oscar whispered angrily to Anastasia, "We'll talk later."

"You've had a long journey." Zosime said to Angelos, gesturing towards the entrance. "We have food and water for you."

She could sense how desperately he wanted to share more of his news but couldn't refuse a direct invocation of hospitality.

"Welcome, guest." Vasiliki said with more politeness than conviction as they walked inside.

"The honor is all mine." Angelos said.

Anastasia hovered close by, her eyes watchful, while Oscar stalked several paces away to whisper with Perleros who had been waiting inside. Zosime caught Perleros's gaze as the four of them entered the breakfast room. Anastasia stood silently in the corner while Vasiliki, Zosime, and Angelos sat down at the table. Servants flittered in soon after, hastily placing food and drink at the table and bowing hastily before exiting the room.

Angelos only stared at his food and Zosime gestured for Angelos to start eating after several moments passed. Based on his thin frame, he must not have had many consistent meals lately.

Vasiliki broke the silence and asked, "Where do you call home, friend?"

"Apistia, Queen Vasiliki." Angelos answered and slowly bit into some bread.

Zosime could sense her sister's spark of interest towards that city-state on the other side of the gods' mountain then felt this curiosity shift to suspicion.

The corners of Vasiliki's mouth turned down for a moment and she asked, "Our heritage is evident with the eyes, I know. But how do you know our names, friend?"

Zosime heard footsteps and turned to see Perleros standing at the doorway, clearly now caught up on the situation.

"Your names are no secret, Queen Vasiliki. Everyone in Midrios has eagerly waited for your ascension for twenty years." Angelos replied.

"I did not make my meaning clear." Vasiliki clarified as she stared at him, questions clearly spinning behind her eyes. "I mean we did not introduce ourselves individually. Are our faces so well known?"

"Ah." Angelos said, comprehension dawning on his face, then explained. "Spyridon described you both to me before he sent me to serve the gods."

Zosime felt recognition from Perleros when the name Spyridon was uttered which quickly shifted to deep-seated rage. She looked at Vasiliki who looked and felt as bewildered as she did.

"We do not know your master, Angelos." Zosime said.

Angelos frowned then looked at Perleros whose face was even more grim than usual. Irritation and distrust rose in his chest when he looked at the highest ranked general in Leondria.

"He knows." Angelos declared, his tone not quite disrespectful but clearly not neutral either.

Zosime looked at Perleros who reluctantly affirmed, "I do."

The air hung heavy around them following Perleros's uncharacteristic show of anger. Vasiliki awkwardly bit into some cheese while Angelos sat stiffly in his chair with Perleros hovering close by. Anastasia remained a silent observer.

Zosime leaned forward and poured wine into a goblet. All eyes in the room tracked her movements as she pushed the drink towards Angelos and asserted, "You need this more than we do."

The breakfast did not resume its initial familiarity even if both sides lived up to the customary demands of hospitality. Angelos ate and drank slowly, as if knowing the interrogation that was forthcoming and wanting to enjoy this moment for as long as possible.

There was a faraway look in his eyes when he finally finished his last sip of wine and said, "I am honored to have broken bread at your table, but I understand you and your advisors might have some more questions for me."

"We do." Zosime said and stood.

He slowly rose in turn and announced heavily, "I am ready."

Zosime frowned, sensing strange detachment from him but said nothing as they walked into the receiving room down the hall where the rest of the generals were waiting for them.

"What is this message for us, Angelos, son of Hector?" Perleros asked, not spitting out the words like someone else might have but with enough hardness to illustrate his slipping control over his anger.

The faraway look in Angelos's eyes didn't fade but his voice was strong and clear when he answered, "War is coming."

"Apistia is declaring war?" Thea demanded, aghast.

"No." Angelos said after some murmuring from the other generals.

"What is this tiding of war then?" Oscar grilled. "If Apistia does not intend to strike us?"

"It was not Apistia who attacked Leondria." Angelos said darkly then declared. "I warn you of a country far to the east who has emerged once again with designs to conquer the world."

Once again? No person in their right mind would dare try to attack Leondria once, let alone twice. Zosime felt Perleros's anger and remorsefulness, so she knew that whatever Angelos meant by what he said must have contained some shred of truth.

What important subjects for a general to hide from his queen. This threat to the east and whatever this business with Spyridon was about.

"Afshin has arisen—" Angelos continued.

"Afshin is dead." Perleros cut him off and Angelos blinked.

"Yes, but his son, second of his name, has grown in the past two decades with dreams of besting Leondria and with a greater taste of bloodshed." Angelos elaborated.

"How could you possibly know this with such certainty?" Oscar demanded. "Unless *you* have divided loyalties."

"I have wandered near and far from our home." Zosime caught

Anastasia stiffening as Angelos continued. "I have climbed mountain passages and sailed the seas and have seen and heard and lost it all too many times to count. But I have always returned to my beloved homeland, and I have *always* served the gods."

Angelos said this last part with such conviction it almost made Zosime start.

"So I can say this with complete certainty in front of the generals and queens of Leondria, lest the gods strike me down where I stand: Afshin, second of his name, is amassing the largest army anyone has ever seen." Angelos concluded and the generals looked at each other.

Nothing like this had been mentioned in any advisor meeting before and the generals' hostility melting into mere skepticism was what most troubled Zosime. She glanced at Perleros who did not outwardly react, but she could sense his suspicion and animosity towards the man.

"Have you brought any sort of proof to support your claims?" Thea asked and Zosime tore her gaze away from Perleros.

"No." Angelos admitted. "But my story rings true and there are many cries from the lands to the east that can be heard from across the Karkaros mountains. One need not have omniscient eyes to see the devastation Afshin has wrought across the lands beyond the mountains. Apistia is also aware of the threat, and they are taking steps to act."

Oscar scoffed, "One need only see by sending Leondrian troops beyond Midrios's mountain guardians? Yet not a single friend has joined you."

"He holds those lands tight in his grip while conquering more countries as he moves west towards us. With how quickly he is moving despite the many miles that separate you, he will reach us in the next few years." Angelos announced. "With Midrios divided, he will overwhelm us with ease unless you act now."

Zosime didn't know what to make of his assertions, but she could sense the depth of his sincerity. She saw him look at all of them in turn before he lowered his eyes in grim acceptance.

"I come here with no friends and nothing to offer to show my honorable intentions." Angelos noted then shook his head with a light laugh. "It could be a falsity, or I could have my own selfish motives. But every word I speak is true and *now* is the time to act. To unite Midrios from civil war and stand together against this great threat."

The room was silent, but Zosime didn't think one needed to have the Gift to tell that Angelos was fighting a losing battle. She was struck by his conviction but also wasn't wholly persuaded by his explanation. She held no love for Apistia, but no hatred for it either like some in Leondria. It was founded by her aunt, after all. She did, however, think that they tried too hard to show off, based on the few rumors she had heard about them.

It was hard to take people like that seriously, especially when they only sent one messenger who disliked Leondria's highest general and without any proof of imminent war. If it wasn't for the sincerity emanating from the middle aged man, she would have dismissed him outright. And based on his frustrated disappointment, he was aware of this.

"We can offer you comfortable lodgings." Zosime offered. "To recover from your long journey."

"We need to act now." Angelos reiterated.

"Do you have anyone you can call to testify to your veracity or evidence you can retrieve to support your claims?" Vasiliki inquired.

"I have talked to the Senate." Angelos replied. "They discuss whether to ally with Leondria."

Oscar's eyes gleamed when he said, "So that is a no to Queen Vasiliki's question. If you had support from your Senate, you wouldn't have come alone."

"The Senate takes her time." Angelos retorted. "But Afshin does not. Spyridon has seen it in a vision."

This was a little far-fetched for Zosime and, evidently, was too much for some of the generals.

"The same one who took our queens from the cradle and fled across the country for an experiment?" Thea asked, not a little acidly. "This is the man you would have us believe?"

Angelos looked all around the room then looked down, as if to prepare himself for something dreadful. He murmured more to himself than to anyone else in particular, "He was right. There is only one way to convince you."

Perleros took a step forward right before a knife flashed into Angelos's hand, and he murmured, "For the gods."

Zosime didn't see Anastasia's hand before she was shoved with such force that she fell halfway across the room. Zosime's eyes widened as her mind processed what just happened while Anastasia unsheathed her sword. Meanwhile, Perleros launched forward towards Angelos, but before Perleros could reach him, Angelos plunged the dagger into his own heart. He let out a cry of pain and collapsed as blood began spurting from his chest.

Perleros held Angelos's arms down, but the man offered him no resistance as he struggled to move his chest up and down to breathe.

"Madness! Lies!" Oscar seethed.

Angelos only shook his head a couple times, as if to contradict Oscar where he lacked the strength to speak before his chest fell one last time and the light left his eyes. Perleros warily put two fingers against Angelos's neck and waited. When nothing happened, Perleros warily stood and turned to check on his queens. Zosime blinked and climbed to her feet, unsure what to say now. According to the stunned look on Vasiliki's face and the shock emanating from her, she knew her sister was just as lost as she was.

The silence was broken when Oscar turned to Anastasia and exploded, "How could you not find the dagger?"

Anastasia shook her head in incredulity then sheathed her sword, turning to appraise Zosime. She felt exposed as Anastasia's eyes roamed across her body before finally nodding, as if to reassure herself that Zosime was unhurt. Anastasia's eyes then fell to Angelos's body.

"Lazy inspection, Anastasia!" Oscar reprimanded when Anastasia didn't respond.

"She checked, General Oscar." Zosime informed him.

"Not well enough, my queen." he disagreed.

Anastasia lifted her gaze and returned Oscar's glare coolly, "There was no dagger."

"Our queens could have been killed!" Oscar roared in indignation. "Take responsibility for your carelessness!"

Zosime felt a twinge of—anger?—from Anastasia but she maintained her coolness as she repeated calmly but firmly, "There was no dagger."

Oscar opened his mouth, but Perleros interjected, "Enough. Recover yourself, Oscar."

Oscar flushed but snapped his mouth shut, having displayed too much emotion than what was acceptable. Zosime looked at the corpse and couldn't shake the feeling that Angelos did not mean them any harm. At no point had she sensed maliciousness towards them.

"Apistia sent him." Thea said. "We need to act before they strike."

"It was Spyridon who sent him, not Apistia." Perleros corrected and the generals' eyes widened. "It sounded like they're as wary of us as we are of them."

Vasiliki finally asked quietly, "Who is Spyridon?"

"Someone dangerous." Perleros said. "Who stole you as infants and almost killed you both. He serves only himself."

Zosime looked at Perleros, sensing he wasn't telling them the full story and said, "Afshin."

An uncomfortable silence descended as Oscar's eyes drilled into Perleros's.

"Afshin, first of his name, died twenty years ago." Perleros finally answered. "On the battlefield against your father, King Atreo. Your father fell soon after."

Zosime nodded for him to continue and then caught Oscar giving Perleros a slanted look with an expression that she couldn't decipher. The rage that was emanating from him towards Perleros was palpable, something deeper than mere resentment.

She returned her attention to Perleros who finished, "He had a dream of conquering us and brought over an army to make us submit. We did not."

"But he evidently had a son with grander dreams." Oscar scoffed.

"Intel isn't our strong suit." Thea pointed out then added. "And we have rarely left Leondria's borders in the past couple decades."

"We can start acquiring intel now." Vasiliki suggested to Zosime's surprise. "See if his story holds truth."

Thea inclined her head in agreement and Penelope slowly nodded.

"We'll assemble a small group and head northeast. See what we can find out." Perleros said.

This was a suggestion the others concurred with and then their eyes rested on Angelos, the dagger still protruding from his chest and his blood pooling around his body on the floor.

Perleros turned to Anastasia and ordered, "Bury him. Then report to me to explain how this happened."

Angelos would receive no honor here for his cowardly act. They would not waste the wood on someone who committed suicide so there would be no pyre to send his soul to the heavens.

In that moment, Zosime couldn't shake one of the Creature's accusations during the Trials and it echoed in her mind like a never-ending bell: *do you place so little value on loyalty?*

Zosime watched Anastasia pick up Angelos's body, sling it over her shoulder, and walk out of the room, purposefully avoiding her gaze. Loyalty meant everything to her.

15

Dryas opened his eyes and blinked as he adjusted from the sensibleness of dreams to the absurdities of the waking world. He sat up on his cot and rubbed his eyes for a few moments before standing and getting dressed. The room was bustling as the others got up to prepare for the day. Every day started the same: morning workouts, bathing, and then training exercises, unless he was on guard duty at the gates.

Some parts of life hadn't changed since Training, but it almost felt like stepping into a new world. There were still high expectations of him, and the days were still vigorous, but his day to day was much less regimented than before.

He possessed more freedoms than he did when he was a minor.

There were still more restrictions than if he were married or promoted to a higher rank. But so long as he showed up when and where he was supposed to be and did his duty, he was more or less left alone. He was an adult now and was expected to act like it.

There were strict curfews for new Leondrians, so they hadn't been allowed to stay out after dark to join the older Leondrians at the bonfires. The only time he was allowed out of the barracks after dark was when it was his turn to be on guard duty at the gates.

He understood and didn't complain. Privileges were earned and he was fine being patient until the rest of the restrictions were gradually lifted. He only wished that he could see Zosime and Vasiliki again, but he understood their positions kept them apart. Even if he could, he would make no demands of them. They were too important for him to monopolize their time.

But he couldn't ignore how much he missed his two dearest friends. He had one older brother and one younger sister but, due to the gaps in their ages, he had spent little time with either of his siblings until recently. He had worshipped the ground Balthasar walked on when he was a child but rarely saw him in their adolescent years since they were in different Training classes. Adelphie was still nine years old in his mind, even though she was a teenager who was now a year away from taking the Trials. They rarely saw each other but—when he was very, very lucky—he had been able to hear her sweet melodic voice singing at night.

He and Balthasar were now making up for lost time and were waiting to do the same with Adelphie. He would have visited her in Training if it wasn't absolutely prohibited. So he had no choice but to wait until when— no, *if*, he reminded himself—she survived the Trials.

There were no guarantees in this life after all.

He learned that all too well when his mother died. Then again throughout Training and another time during the Trials when the weak didn't survive. It was a cruel world that demanded sacrifices, so loyalty meant everything to him.

He had been getting along well with the other Leondrians, but he couldn't help but notice that he hadn't been able to talk to Zosime and Vasiliki since the last day of Mione months ago. He saw them in the mornings from afar but never had the opportunity to interact with them like he used to.

He understood their new positions took up a great deal of their time, but he hoped they wouldn't think of him in the years to come as just an old childhood friend. But he would continue to serve, and he would be ready should they ever need him.

Dryas grabbed a clean red cloak from the trunk at the foot of his cot and pinned it to his shoulders. He strapped on his shield and made his way to the door, passing by rows of impeccably made beds on his way out of the barracks. Quick to rise, quick to get ready, quick to pack up, and quick to leave. That was the Leondrian way.

He and a few dozen other Leondrians lived in one of several barracks located by the gates. They jogged out the door and gathered up outside where it was still dark out. The Leondrian officer in charge of their barracks stalked to stand in front of them where he bellowed for them to form two lines and then to be ready to "run until your feet are raw and bloody" which received a chorus of laughs.

A run, Dryas thought. Perfect.

Winter now fully held them in its chilly embrace, frost lacing the grass and light snow sprinkling the ground. Dryas found the coolness invigorating without too much of a drop in temperature to be miserable. Not that winters often got too bad in Midrios. There were the rare years where there had been major snowstorms, but it rarely ever came to that. Perhaps it had something to do with Midrios being surrounded by water on three sides with hundreds of islands off its coast that the sea prevented extreme cold from becoming an issue.

Dryas only allowed himself a small smile as they all began to run. His blood started warming from the exercise when they left the Hearth behind, and they chased the receding moon. His longer legs could be a disadvantage in long runs, but he loved this feeling of outpacing the wind anyway.

He lost himself in it for a while before feeling a prickle on the back of his neck and turned his head to discover a fellow Leondrian named Elena watching him.

She raised an eyebrow at him in challenge with the corner of her mouth tilted up just enough for him to notice that she was smiling at him. She was a year older than him, and was someone he had talked to in passing once or twice.

They both returned their attention forward before someone noticed and Dryas focused his attention solely on the run again. It was so invigorating, and he found himself disappointed when they turned back towards the gates since he knew the run would be ending soon. He could do this all day and this twelve mile run was ending sooner than he wanted it to.

He could see Zosime ahead of them all, blazing even brighter than Anatole dragging the sun in his golden chariot. Her red-brown-yellow eyes were shining in one of those rare unguarded moments when she glanced back to check that she wasn't running too fast for the rest of them. He knew he should value discipline above all else as a Leondrian, but he looked forward to those times when she showed her wild spirit that no one had been able to tame more than anything else.

Seeing those moments of untamed passion meant more to him than anything else in this world. He could see that fire now as she ran but could tell that she was also restraining herself to not leave them all behind. He caught the sun's first rays glittering on the horizon as they crested one of the many hills in Leondria and they slowed themselves to a walk as they crossed the gates back to the Hearth.

He dragged his eyes away when she took off back to her home at the top of the tallest hill in the Hearth with Anastasia while he and the others began heading back to the barracks. His eyebrows rose when he unexpectedly caught Vasiliki's gaze as they started to turn.

She gave him a small, sad smile and his heart lurched. He knew she was aware of his feelings towards her sister and suspected she supported a match between them. But he would never push Zosime, and he knew she had her reasons for not returning his longing gazes.

And he loved her too much to push it. Valued her friendship too much to jeopardize it. It was much better to treasure the friendship he still had instead of losing it altogether. There was something unreadable in Vasiliki's eyes but the closest word that came to his mind to capture her expression was *soon*.

They would see him soon. Knowing Vasiliki, she was feeling guilty for not seeing him much lately, but he gave her a nod showing he understood.

She reluctantly turned away with Jedrick and Dryas walked back to the barracks with the others to clean up before his guard shift. He went through the motions of bathing in the communal pond behind the barracks since they hadn't earned the right to use the bathing houses yet and changed into fresh clothes. He soon found himself leaving the barracks to head to guard duty when he found one of his favorite people waiting for him.

"Morning, little brother." Balthasar greeted warmly. "Figured I'd walk you to the gates."

Dryas grinned in turn, and he asked, "How's Daphne?"

"Tired." Balthasar mused as they started walking. "But she's a warrior. She's mainly happy to not be sick every morning anymore."

Balthasar had told him all about the early stages of the pregnancy during Mione with a certain joy and nervousness that only a first-time parent had. He had heard about his brother getting married a couple years back through the grapevine, but he had been ecstatic to see his brother so happy when they were finally reunited. He was also proud to call Daphne his sister by law and seeing how well she fit into the family in his daily visits to their home.

"Enjoy the run?" Balthasar asked.

"Better than you did." Dryas teased, knowing how much his brother hated running.

"I'm faster than you." Balthasar nudged him and chuckled.

"In your dreams." Dryas rolled his eyes and gave him a sly grin. "Old man."

"Look here," Balthasar laughed. "You little—"

"Balthasar!" Andreas, an older Leondrian assigned to guard the Heart, called out.

They turned to face him and one look at Andreas's face told them that this was not going to be a social visit.

"Duty calls, brother." Balthasar sighed and clapped him on the shoulder. "Come over for lunch after your shift."

Dryas nodded and Balthasar hurried away. He could see Balthasar good-naturedly catching up with the other Leondrian as they headed in the opposite direction. Dryas suspected there must have been some special orders for his brother, but he didn't say anything as he walked the rest of the way to the gates.

Everyone had heard about the strange Apistian who had just walked up to their gates to talk to their queens a few days ago. Many had seen the body Anastasia carried over her shoulder afterwards and the corpse's blood dripping down her back and legs. Servants had moved quickly to clean up the trail of blood Anastasia left as she purposefully stalked outside the gates. No one knew where exactly she buried him, but she had returned a couple hours later with her skin covered in dirt and blood with such a grave expression on her face that no one dared to approach her.

Whispers had begun circulating around the Hearth in the aftermath of the incident but, even stranger than some suicidal Apistian killing himself in front of the queens, was how Vasiliki and Anastasia had met Lord Kal. Rumors of whether the gods would finally be returning and even quieter murmurs discussing the prospect of war had spread like wildfire.

Dryas wasn't privy to the meeting of the generals and queens, but it was obvious to everyone by how they acted that they were appointing a group to gather intelligence. To determine if this country far to the east and Apistia legitimately posed a threat to Leondria.

Dryas nodded to Flavian, and they made the sign of the gods to each other. Even chatty, story-telling Flavian had been reserved lately as all the Leondrians wondered what their future would hold. Dryas kept quiet and stayed vigilant at his post, keeping his eyes trained forward to survey everything in view and doing his best to ignore his intuition that he was about to say goodbye to his brother again.

16

Balthasar had a sneaking suspicion on the reasons behind his summons when he and Andreas strode away from Dryas. He had quickly engaged Andreas in conversation, but the exchange rapidly dwindled into silence when they walked up the three steps of the Heart. He could hear their steps echoing down the halls after they entered the building, and he gave Andreas a serious nod when they stopped just shy of one the meeting rooms. The older man then patted him on the shoulder a couple of times before walking away.

Balthasar didn't see the point of delaying the inevitable, so he went ahead and entered the room. He found Perleros, Zosime, and Vasiliki waiting for him inside. But there was no room for familiarity here because it wasn't his father and his brother's friends that stood before him now. It was his commanding general and his queens.

Balthasar made the sign of the gods and recited the customary address, "How may I serve, my queens?"

Queen Zosime took one look at him then said, "You've heard the rumors, Balthasar."

Balthasar nodded. Everyone had heard the rumors from the past few days.

There was only expectation in Perleros's eyes when he addressed Balthasar, "You've been assigned to a small group of Leondrians for a mission to go east. Your objective is to gather intelligence for any credible threat about Afshin the Second."

"Yes, sir." Balthasar responded.

Vasiliki warned him with a sympathetic look in her eyes, "I can't promise you'll make it back for the birth of your child. Can you live with that?"

Balthasar saw Zosime blink in surprise whereas Perleros's face only remained outwardly impassive.

"I won't fail you." he promised quietly then quickly added. "My queens."

Zosime nodded then declared, "We leave tomorrow."

Vasiliki's eyes widened and Perleros's head snapped towards Zosime.

Vasiliki cleared her throat and clarified with a slight emphasis in her tone, "Don't you mean *they* leave tomorrow?"

"No, *we're* leaving." Zosime straightened and mirrored Vasiliki's tone. "They and *I*."

"My queen." Perleros said and Balthasar noticed how tense his father's shoulders were. "This group will be entering foreign territory with unparalleled dangers."

"A ruler stands by her people." Zosime raised her chin, eyes flashing at the fatherly tone. "Why should they take risks for me if I won't do the same?"

Balthasar knew his father well enough to be certain that he wasn't going to visibly lose his temper, but he also knew that his patience was wearing thin. He saw a vein stand out in Perleros's neck, and he worried that the stress would aggravate the old injury that Typhon had inflicted. Balthasar's back twinged at the memory, and he shifted on his feet. He didn't know Zosime very well, but he thought fondly of her, almost like a second sister, and it was moments like these that he understood why his brother was so smitten with her.

Granted, an untamable spirit wasn't always a suitable quality in a queen. But there had also been strange signs in the last few years so having someone unwilling to bow her head might be someone Leondria needed now.

His father looked unwilling to argue, even if it was just in front of Balthasar.

"Go, son." he ordered, and Balthasar remained silent as he made the sign of the gods again and then turned on his heel.

He had never left Leondria before, let alone Midrios, and he had no idea what to expect beyond those far-away Karkaros mountains. He didn't even know what to expect beyond Leondria. He knew that he should anticipate danger, certainly, but he didn't know what specifically to prepare for.

He walked outside into the blinding sunlight and carefully made his way down the winding streets. He knew better than to talk to Dryas while he was on duty, which was one of the fastest ways to receive a beating and the reprimand of a lifetime for distracting the guards. Even if he was tempted to receive such a punishment, Balthasar had noticed Dryas's suspicious face when he was called away earlier and figured this would be a better conversation to have in private.

He turned into the housing section of the Hearth where many homes were lined up perfectly side by side. There were rows after rows of one-story houses built specifically for married couples and their inevitable children. The houses themselves were designed in the shape of triangles with three wooden steps leading to a wooden door, a smaller and cheaper version of the Heart that would allow for expansion. He strolled down seven rows then turned, passing six houses before walking straight up to his home.

"My love." Daphne greeted him with a wide smile as he walked inside.

Her belly had a noticeable bump now and she all but glowed. She had her red cloak on over a white robe which was the customary uniform for pregnant Leondrians after their first trimester.

"My love." he kissed her then held her against his chest.

If the gods struck him down at that very moment, he would have died a happy man. He could have spent every moment of his life in her arms and not want for anything. But he knew that he couldn't, and he thought sadly of the child whose birth he would likely miss.

He didn't know if she intuitively sensed a shift in his mood or if there was something in his posture that gave him away, but she suddenly looked up at him and whispered, "What is it?"

He begrudgingly took a step back so he could look her in the eyes while still holding on to her hands then told her the news.

Balthasar waited but Daphne didn't say anything. She was looking down, not meeting his eyes, but her grip was iron tight, as if she alone could stop him from leaving. She finally closed her eyes and exhaled, nodding in grim acceptance.

"Duty calls." was all she said.

Balthasar squeezed her hands and kissed them both before letting go. He strolled over to his trunk at the foot of their bed and slowly leaned over to open it. His back cramped in response, and he grabbed a new crimson tunic. He slowly straightened then proceeded to take off the shield, red cloak, and red tunic that he had been wearing. He carefully set down the shield then cast the sweat-drenched clothes onto the bed. Grabbing a clean red tunic, he was about to put it on when he felt a soft touch on his lower back.

He paused then promised, "I'll be more careful this time." When he saw her wince, he reassured her, "It wasn't your fault. You didn't do it on purpose."

She quickly turned away, removing her hand from the spot on his lower back where he knew a scar rested.

He frowned for a moment then carefully put on the clean shirt and re-fastened his cloak. He sat down on the bed, deciding to spend the time waiting for Dryas by polishing his shield and some other weapons. He would have loved nothing more than to lie down, but he knew such an act would only make Daphne feel worse. Instead of resting his back which had started flaring up during the earlier run, he put away the dirty clothes into the sack for laundry and went straight to polishing.

"I'll grab lunch from the market." Daphne suddenly announced sometime later and hastily left the house with a hand resting on her stomach.

He sighed and let his hands fall. She had never forgiven herself for the unfortunate incident a few years back that had prevented him from going off with the few dozen Leondrians assigned to fight Typhon. She had to know he never resented her for the terrible accident.

Maybe she didn't, he thought to himself as he recalled the incident. He had told her not to blame herself right after getting hurt, but he hadn't said anything recently.

He sighed then permitted himself to lie down for a few minutes, exhaling in relief when the pain subsided a little.

These recurring flare ups were irritating to deal with, but back pain was nowhere near as agonizing as being burnt alive or being torn to shreds so he didn't complain. Only three had come back from the fight alive, after all, so he knew that he likely would have suffered such a fate if he had gone with them. He only wished he could have helped them and fulfilled his duty.

But he had lived because of some freak accident that happened a couple days before the group left. And he had to carry that burden with him every day.

At least Perleros had survived, and he was grateful for Anastasia every day for saving his father's life. She had been a more or less constant presence in his life since they started Training at the same time, but he didn't know that much about her. Balthasar tried to get along with everybody, but the other Trainees had kept their distance when she seemed to naturally excel at every rigorous Training exercise while they struggled. She had then grown sterner in her interactions after her mother died, and grown even more reserved after the Trials.

Grief and Training affected them all differently, he thought to himself. His father had been the first in his family to be accepted into Training as the seventh generation descendant of immigrants and had projected the importance of strengthening the family legacy onto Balthasar throughout his childhood.

Balthasar had once cared about nothing else, but that obsession had fallen away years ago. He would fulfill his duty, but he didn't care about rising as high as he could through the ranks anymore.

He has happy with his wife, his brother, and his impending child's birth. That was all he needed.

Balthasar then heard the doorknob turning and quickly sat up as Daphne walked back inside with food in her arms. He hurriedly moved to her side to help and noted how she seemed to have recovered her composure as they put the food down.

Balthasar assessed the table and raised an eyebrow at her, "Dryas's favorite?"

She gave him a small smile and admitted, "I thought he should be in the best mood possible before you told him."

He agreed with her, suspecting that Dryas wouldn't take the news well and would immediately blame Perleros. His little brother was astute so it wouldn't take long for Dryas to see their father's hand in Balthasar being assigned on a dangerous expedition for Leondria's welfare. Which would likely expedite his promotion from a sergeant to the officer ranks.

He started making some preparations as they waited, and he and Daphne shared a look when there was a knock at the door half an hour later. She gave him a small smile as he moved over to the door and opened it where he found his brother waiting.

Dryas stood a full head taller than him which was disrespectful for a younger brother to be, but Balthasar warmly ushered him inside. It was unnerving at times how similarly Dryas looked like their father. They both stood taller than most men with broad physiques and ice-blue eyes that seemed to peer into a person's soul. Balthasar guessed that, after a couple more years of filling out, the only two things that would distinguish his brother from his father would be some grey hairs and wrinkles.

Balthasar favored his mother and didn't inherit many physical characteristics from his father. Where Perleros had light blue eyes, Balthasar's were dark like a running river. Where Perleros seemed to dwarf most people with his height, Balthasar only stood a little taller than average. Where Perleros's broad physique resembled an unmovable boulder, Balthasar was lean like a willow. Balthasar knew he shared the same coloring as his father, as well as some freckles and the same hard jaw, but that was about it.

Balthasar gestured for Dryas to sit, and he saw his brother's eyes widen in delight at the piping hot lamb meat ready to eat. He and Daphne shared a smile at his expression and the three of them sat down together. Balthasar gave him a wink and Dryas smiled boyishly as he served himself.

It was good to see that smile, he thought to himself.

Joy wasn't something they had experienced much in their family since their mother died. Balthasar was mainly relieved that his mother was no longer suffering, even if he wished she was here to see his own child come into the world. He knew, however, that Dryas had directed his grief towards their father. Had blamed him for not being able to move the heavens and earth for a cure.

How young he was, Balthasar thought, to think that his father was more than the mortal man he was.

Balthasar took his first bite of the lamb and closed his eyes for a moment to savor the taste. He knew it would likely be months before he had another meal like this, and he wanted to enjoy every moment of it. A delicious meal with his beautiful wife and little brother. He used his free hand to squeeze Daphne's leg then took another savory bite of the lamb.

Dryas's eyes began to narrow when Balthasar finally swallowed.

Balthasar flashed him a grin and asked, "How was guard duty?"

Dryas slowly put down what remained of his lamb's leg and his eyes narrowed further. His gaze then fell on the weapons that were arranged on their bed in meticulous order, shining and recently sharpened, and his mouth tightened.

"You're leaving." he said more than asked.

Balthasar and Daphne shared a quick look and Balthasar confirmed, "Yes."

He could see the wheels spinning in his brother's eyes then the shift to accusation as he made multiple connections.

Balthasar sighed, "Don't blame father."

"Why not?" Dryas shrugged and his shoulders stiffened. "The family's legacy means more to him than the *actual* family."

He wanted to reiterate that such an assertion wasn't true, but he also needed Dryas to understand how the world worked.

Balthasar stared at his brother and asked him softly, "What would you know about legacy or family when you've only worn the cloak for a few months?"

Dryas's jaw clenched but he didn't break off the stare while Daphne rested a hand on Balthasar's arm.

"Cut him some slack, Dryas." Daphne recommended. "Perspectives change as you get older."

Dryas shook his head and glanced down at the lamb for a moment before ultimately pushing the plate away.

Balthasar opened his mouth to encourage Dryas to finish his lunch when Dryas changed the subject, "Do you know how long you'll be gone?"

Balthasar shrugged and estimated, "Months? Maybe a year?"

The brothers stared at each other, each passing moment growing more strained between them, when there was a sudden knock at the door. Balthasar shifted in his seat to stand when Daphne firmly pushed his shoulders down.

Her patience had evidently run out because she gestured to both of them and commanded, "Talk. Now."

She rose from the table and started walking over to the door. A part of him wanted to laugh but an even bigger part of him wanted to sigh in exasperation. He knew he wasn't going to change his brother's mind, but he wanted him to know that he meant well.

"Dryas—" he began to say when the door opened.

"My queen!" Daphne exclaimed in surprise and Balthasar blinked. "Please, come in."

Balthasar caught the look of anticipation on Dryas's face as they both stood.

"I'm honored to be welcomed into your home, Daphne." a female voice responded.

Dryas's face quickly dropped, and seeing Balthasar looking at him, quickly hid his disappointment. Daphne opened the door wider and gestured for their queen to walk in.

"I didn't mean to interrupt." Vasiliki declared after glancing at the leftover food on the table.

"Not at all." Balthasar said, making the sign of the gods.

"I won't impose much longer." Vasiliki said. "I know you're preparing."

"You're welcome anytime, my queen." Balthasar insisted and he couldn't help but notice the way her shoulders were slightly slumped. As if the weight of all her responsibilities were pressing so hard against her that she couldn't stand perfectly straight.

"I'm giving you your farewell gift now." Vasiliki announced and Balthasar's eyebrows rose in astonishment. Before he could insist that a gift was not necessary, Vasiliki continued. "I bear a message from your sister."

"Y-you saw Adelphie?" Dryas stammered.

"I can't often bear messages to you for obvious reasons." Vasiliki gave them a pointed look.

He knew she couldn't afford the appearance of favoritism and he gave her a nod in understanding.

"But, just this once," Vasiliki hesitated. "I asked her if there was a message that she wanted me to pass along to her brothers."

"What did she say?" Dryas asked eagerly and Balthasar flashed him a warning look.

Dryas had to understand that Vasiliki wasn't his good friend anymore. She was his queen and had to be treated as such.

Vasiliki answered in a regal tone that he hadn't expected from her, "She says that every time you look up at the night sky, she will be singing for your safe return, and she prays for you both every day."

Balthasar finally allowed himself to smile and his throat grew tight, marveling on how she had maintained her sweetness after all these years of Training.

She was so young when Balthasar last saw her, but he remembered so clearly how she would sing those high, melodious notes to the sky almost every night. Much to their father's chagrin and their mother's delight.

It was faint but, for the first time, Balthasar saw a queen where his brother's best friend had stood moments ago. Vasiliki had a long way to go, he thought. She needed to stand taller and learn to give commands assertively without a second thought, but he could see a shadow of the ruler she could become. If she found the inner strength and confidence she desperately needed.

There was an awkward silence where he could tell that she wasn't sure what to do next. He thought about inviting her to stay for lunch, but he then worried about blurring important boundaries that Dryas needed to respect. If his little brother only saw Vasiliki as his queen, having her over for lunch would be innocent. But he didn't and he needed Dryas to understand how things operated as an adult.

Vasiliki ultimately cleared her throat and then inclined her head at them.

"Rest well." she advised Balthasar and trailed off before stating. "I will speak to my sister about—I'll speak to her."

She hesitated as she looked at Dryas, the desire between talking to her friend and maintaining her composure as queen clearly warring with each other.

"I'll see you tomorrow." she finally said to him, sadness edging her voice.

She nodded at Daphne who opened the door for her, and Vasiliki's red cloak billowed in the winter wind as she left. Dryas frowned as Daphne walked back over to them and sat down again.

"What did she mean?" Dryas asked.

"Come, finish your lamb." Balthasar suggested as he sat back down next to his wife.

"What happened with Zosime?" Dryas pushed, concern rising in his eyes.

"She told me she was coming with us." Balthasar answered reluctantly. "Father and Queen Vasiliki are trying to talk her out of it."

"I see." Dryas muttered and Daphne reached across the table to squeeze his hand.

Dryas didn't react to the gesture and Daphne withdrew her hand.

From what he had seen, Balthasar highly doubted Queen Vasiliki would be able to change Queen Zosime's mind even if it would be best for everyone if she didn't go. Her presence would cause complications and, even with her superior strength, would likely put the group in more danger. He was prepared to protect and serve his queen, but he would spend the rest of today treasuring this precious time with his family.

While he didn't particularly care about the family legacy, he was a Leondrian first. What he cared about was doing what was right, fulfilling his duty, and protecting his family, whether it was those he was related to by blood or those he shared an unbreakable connection with. So if that also meant making his father happy and receiving a promotion to the officer corps after a long mission away from home, then so be it.

But today he was going to do what made him happy and enjoy this time with his beloved wife and brother. Tomorrow, he would say goodbye, do his duty, and take one step closer to the bright future his father envisioned for him.

17

Balthasar had scarcely closed the door behind him when Perleros turned to Zosime and declared, "My queen. It is vital that you stay in Leondria."

Zosime sensed his worry but didn't care for the condescension in his tone. She knew he was concerned for her well-being, but she was his queen who was responsible for the fate of thousands, and she knew what her people needed.

"It's vital I go." she disagreed. "For Leondria's future."

"The group is qualified, my queen." Perleros stressed. "They can determine if the threat is credible. You're needed here."

"I can keep them safe." Zosime rebutted.

"*You* need to be safe, my queen." Perleros retorted. "A queen is not expendable."

Zosime raised her chin and demanded, "Why should they take risks for me if I won't do the same? Leondrians may live a life of danger but none of them are expendable."

She sensed Perleros's exasperated frustration and physical pain. There was a part of her that thought it was strange that she could argue with him now, considering how it would have been taboo to disagree with a superior only months ago.

"No Leondrian is expendable." Perleros agreed quietly. "But you can't be replaced, and your people need you here to rule."

Zosime gestured to Vasiliki and pointed out, "Vasiliki will still be here to look after things. I'm not leaving Leondria without a ruler!"

She saw Perleros's hands twitch in his lap then still. She sensed Vasiliki's distress devolve into anger, but Zosime was too preoccupied with Perleros to pay it much mind.

"You should not risk your life over a mad man's tale." he said. "He was unstable."

"Better to risk my life verifying if Leondria is in danger than the whole country being ambushed." Zosime vehemently disagreed. "Everything will be taken care of here."

Vasiliki stood up, shaking her head before declaring, "I'll return."

Zosime blinked in surprise and watched her sister leave the room. She knew that Jedrick would follow Vasiliki to wherever she was going, but she hadn't anticipated her abrupt departure.

Perleros watched Vasiliki leave before returning his attention to Zosime. She could see and sense yet again that all-too familiar feeling of concern and suspicion radiating from him. Pushing down her resentment, she only stared back at him and dared him to challenge her. She had made this decision, and in the sights of all the gods, she was following through with it.

Zosime grew impatient waiting for him to see her point of view then waved her hand to show that the matter was closed, "This is a command, *General.*"

Perleros remained silent for several seconds before finally replying coolly, "Yes, my queen."

She bit her cheek when that feeling of worry from him didn't fade but refrained from asking him about it. Refrained from asking him why he always looked at her like she was moments away from ruining everything.

He suddenly stood and declared, "I must inform the other generals, my queen."

He made the sign of the gods and left. Zosime glanced around the room, feeling its emptiness as she waited for her sister. When half an hour had passed and Vasiliki hadn't returned, Zosime started to wonder where she had gone. After an hour, she started growing concerned and she was ready to go looking for her when Vasiliki stepped back into the room.

Vasiliki looked at Zosime then asked with crossed arms, "You're still planning on going?"

"Yes." Zosime confirmed and she felt the fury soar in Vasiliki's chest.

"Best prepare then." Vasiliki advised coldly then turned to leave.

"Wait." Zosime called out and Vasiliki paused.

"We'll be fine." Vasiliki murmured to Jedrick, who waiting just outside the room, and slowly turned towards her when there were no other ears around.

"Why the anger, sister?" Zosime asked, puzzled.

"*Why,* Zosime?" Vasiliki erupted, throwing her hands in the air. "*You* ask me why?"

Zosime blinked and crossed her own arms defensively, "I don't understand."

Vasiliki's fists clenched and she seethed, "Why do you do these things?"

A muscle twitched in Zosime's jaw. Even Vasiliki thought that she was being impulsive. Her own sister didn't understand how badly she needed to go. It wasn't from some childish thirst of adventure or an excuse to act irresponsibly but to ensure that they didn't get blindsided again.

Zosime remembered how closely Typhon came to destroying them all. Now she had the power to do something to protect Leondria, instead of waiting helplessly on the sidelines. She wouldn't allow harm to come to her people out of some willfulness not to recognize a major threat just over the horizons.

If she couldn't do her part to keep her people safe, then she didn't see the point of being called queen. Vasiliki might have been the cautious one, but Zosime had to be sure war was the only path forward before condemning so many of her people to death. Her warning bells hadn't started ringing yet which had never failed to warn her of a threat before, with one exception.

She had thought her heart might stop altogether with how violently her warning bells were ringing inside her head for a full month before Typhon broke free from his chains beneath the mountains. Perhaps it was too early for the internal alarm system to go off now or perhaps it had started glitching since she wasn't warned when the Creature ambushed them.

She had to be sure before acting this time.

She wouldn't be able to stand that feeling akin to madness if she had to again wait several weeks with no one believing her warning that a great danger was coming for them. She couldn't go through that again.

"Do you not remember Typhon?" Zosime asked. "Do you not remember our entire childhood?"

"Of course, I do!" Vasiliki retorted. "But they're our advisors. They have more experience than we do and have our best interests at heart."

"They have their heads buried in the sand." Zosime snorted. "Such a focus on tradition that they don't think outside the box or move in a different direction when the times demand it!"

"So you know better than General Perleros?" Vasiliki scoffed. "You didn't stop to think how it would impact Balthasar, who General Perleros had designated as the mission leader."

"We're Leondrians, Vasiliki." Zosime was dumbfounded that she had to explain this to her. "Sacrifice comes with duty."

Vasiliki added in a dangerous tone, "You didn't think how it would impact me."

Zosime frowned in confusion, "You won't be in danger. You'll be fine here."

Vasiliki shook her head and muttered, "You're missing the point. Again."

Zosime opened her mouth and Vasiliki held up a hand, "If you don't get it by now, you won't. Just get ready and I'll see you off tomorrow unless you come to your senses."

Vasiliki didn't look at her when she stalked out of the room.

Zosime may have had the power to sense emotions, but she had never possessed the ability to read minds. This distinction had never been clearer to her than in this moment when two people she thought the world of were angry with her for doing what was right.

She only looked out the open door, not knowing what she had done wrong and hurt that she was left utterly alone by the two people who she thought would understand.

———

Zosime strapped the shield to her arm and looked around her bedroom for what was likely the last time for a long time. Her bag was packed, her weapons were sharpened, and she was now ready to embark on the mission. It had felt like she had just returned home from Training and now she was leaving again.

She allowed herself a little while longer to savor this moment before letting go. She blew out the candle and pushed her door open, not looking back as she strolled away. She walked out of the building and stopped on the main landing.

The group hadn't wanted to draw attention to themselves, so they had decided to leave in the middle of the night when everyone would still be sleeping. Zosime slowly walked up and down the landing, occasionally looking out at her slumbering city-state, as she waited for the others to arrive. She only had to wait for a few minutes until she saw Balthasar, Daphne, Dryas, and Perleros making their way towards the Heart.

Zosime was fully aware of the strained relationship between Dryas and his father, and it was strange to see the two of them walk close by each other when they had spent most of their lives estranged. Based on their positioning, they had made sure to stand on either side of Balthasar instead of walking side by side as they approached her.

"My queen." Perleros greeted respectfully but there was no warmth in his tone.

"General." she replied in the same tone.

"My queen." Dryas greeted blithely.

Zosime smiled back, "Dryas."

Perleros flashed his son a disapproving look and the warmth fled from Dryas's face. He shifted further away from his father, and they now stood coldly in different directions. She wanted to diffuse the tension, and almost opened her mouth to say something when she heard footsteps behind her.

She turned to find Vasiliki waiting a few feet away from her, standing stiffly and avoiding her gaze. They hadn't spoken since their argument yesterday so there was an awkward silence before Zosime finally said, "Hold it together while I'm gone."

Vasiliki nodded seriously but did not offer any words of comfort. Prayers were not welcome here. They had a mission to do and only the Fates knew if their life strings would soon be cut so any prayer that could draw their attention or be meaningless anyway weren't wanted.

Zosime could sense Vasiliki's distress over her safety, even if neither of them had forgiven the other.

"Are you ready?" Zosime asked in a colder tone than she intended, still angry at her sister's insults yesterday but not wanting it to wholly define their departure.

She sensed a great sadness well up inside her sister's chest, but Vasiliki didn't say anything. When she didn't respond after several seconds, Zosime turned away and discovered that the rest of the group had arrived. Anastasia stood alone off to the side while Flavian, Alec, and Nicholas were saying their farewells to their families.

Balthasar embraced Daphne, bending slightly so their foreheads touched. The husband and wife each rested a hand over her rising stomach, and they gave each other bittersweet smiles. When he found the strength to leave, Balthasar stepped away from Daphne then turned to his brother. He hugged Dryas for a while and Zosime sensed their reluctance to part from each other. They finally let go and Balthasar gave his father a respectful nod before joining the rest of the group off to the side.

Zosime couldn't stand the sorrow rising in Dryas's chest or the mournful look in his eyes as he stared at his brother. Not able to tolerate it any longer, Zosime stalked up to him.

Dryas's eyes widened when Zosime pushed his shoulder and demanded, "What are you doing?"

She sensed surprise from everyone and a ripple of concern from Perleros.

"Z—my queen?" Dryas asked, confused.

Zosime couldn't keep up the façade and her stern face morphed into a grin when she asked, "You coming?"

She wouldn't be the one to separate the brothers and she would be more comfortable having her closest friend accompanying her anyway.

She sensed the group's displeasure, but the decision had been made and she gestured for Dryas to follow. Something akin to disapproval flickered in Anastasia's chest but she said nothing. Zosime shook her head at their reactions but didn't comment because it was time to go. The others would see that he wasn't like all the other newbies, and she knew that Dryas would prove his worth to them.

She knew it in her bones.

She marched forward, leading the group out of the gates and the guards let them pass without a word. She maintained the brisk pace for a while as she led them through the darkness, her mind churning too much to pay much mind to how much time was passing until Anastasia crept up from behind her.

"My queen." Anastasia said and Zosime snapped out of her memories, noticing the rising sun for the first time.

Zosime glanced at her and, after sensing her continual displeasure, stated, "It's too late to send Dryas back now. He's coming with us."

Anastasia's blue-grey eyes peered into her own and she replied, "I know, my queen. We obey your commands."

Zosime blinked, now wondering what she was wanting to talk about.

"Your eyesight and strength are superior to us regular mortals." Anastasia explained tactfully and tilted her head to the group behind them. "Could you slow down for the others?"

Zosime looked behind her to find her cohort struggling to keep up and inwardly cursed, immediately slowing down. In her haste to leave, she had forgotten about adjusting her pace to compensate for the others.

"Of course." Zosime said, reddening slightly. A few moments passed in silence before she asked. "You don't approve of him coming, do you?"

"No." Anastasia answered honestly. "Unless he can pull his own weight and think on his feet quickly."

"I know he will." Zosime said fervently.

"It is not me he has to prove himself to, my queen." Anastasia corrected. "The others are the ones who must accept him."

They cut off their conversation as the group ran to close the distance between them. They had ruled out taking horses, ultimately deciding that it would bring too much attention to them and would require too much care on a mission to foreign territory. A part of Zosime was disappointed they didn't because there was nothing quite like the experience of galloping across the land while tasting freedom in the wind.

"We should proceed through the farmlands, my queen." Balthasar said when they finally caught up and caught Zosime glancing over at Lady Meraki's Forest.

Zosime looked back at him and declared, "That way is just asking for trouble."

Anastasia nodded in agreement but didn't say anything else to her after that and the group didn't start any conversations as they continued their march. They walked for several hours like this, and the sun had reached its midpoint in the sky when Zosime sensed gnawing hunger from the group. She could ignore her appetite for hours but, after waiting and waiting for them to speak up, she finally stopped.

Spinning around to face the surprised group, she asked, "Is anyone hungry?"

"I'm fine, my queen." Balthasar answered and Dryas followed his brother's lead by shaking his head.

"All good, my queen." Flavian lied.

The others quietly agreed and Zosime raised an eyebrow at them. She tapped a finger over her heart a few times and said good-naturedly, "There's no point lying to me. I have the Gift, remember?"

They cleared their throats, embarrassed, but still none admitted they were hungry. Zosime had a hunch that no one wanted to be the first one to admit weakness.

An amused Anastasia gave them an out, "The queen is wondering if anyone would have any objections if we ate lunch now?"

"Oh, not at all." Flavian responded immediately, now that his honor was no longer at stake.

"I wouldn't dare." Balthasar smiled.

"I could eat a horse." Alec chimed in while Nicholas shook his head at him.

"We'll just need to pass this farm then we can build a fire to hunt—" Anastasia said quickly when she was interrupted by a delighted outcry.

"My queen! Anastasia!" a male voice hollered from a nearby field.

Zosime noticed Anastasia take a deep breath and she asked, "Do you know him?"

"We met on Queen Vasiliki's tour." Anastasia answered and paused in search for the right words. "He's … chatty."

"I see." Zosime said, somehow refraining from smiling.

She could only imagine Vasiliki's and Anastasia's faces when they realized they were the guests of an extrovert. Her heart fell for a moment when she remembered their frigid parting, but she shook it off when she saw the man burst from the fields.

"What's his name?" Zosime whispered as the man hurried over to them.

"Andres." Anastasia murmured back.

Zosime had remembered trotting by this farm when she had been taken on her personal tour but now she knew why Anastasia had then hurried the horses until they were a couple miles away.

"How do you do?" Andres cried out ecstatically, clumsily making the sign of the gods when he approached them.

"Quite well, Andres." Zosime replied and he beamed when she said his name. Remembering Anastasia's desire to circumvent this farm, she continued. "We were just passing through—"

"Nonsense!" Andres disagreed. "My queen, you deserve the best, not some drivel you'll spend hours hunting. Please, come in." he gestured towards his house. "We aren't done with chores yet, but we will have some snacks for lunch. It is supper you will truly enjoy."

"Truly—" Zosime began, surprised by his energy and vigor. "We have a long journey ahead and could not impose until supper—"

Andres either wasn't getting the hint or wasn't taking no for an answer because he waved a hand and insisted, "Impose a full day and night, my queen! Come inside and rest, guests."

Gods blast it, he had invoked hospitality. She traded a look with Anastasia behind his back and the group reluctantly followed him inside.

"I must offer my sincere apologies, Anastasia." Andres cleared his throat. "I had no idea who you were the last time you were here."

"No offense was given." Anastasia said.

"I should have recognized you last time, but my excitement overtook me." he continued and waved for them to sit at the table. "We've never had the queen visit before! But you're one of the best heroes Midrios has ever seen. My gods, your slaying of Typhon is still told almost every night here! You don't know how much I've wanted to apologize since I've found out it was you who visited—"

A woman walked in through the back door and paused, stunned by the unexpected guests.

"Andres?" she called out, but it was hardly louder than a squeak.

"Excuse me." Andres murmured and hurried over to her, whispering fervently into her ear.

Her inquisitive expression morphed into recognition when her eyes rested on Anastasia's face. She whispered something quickly back and Zosime sensed her embarrassment. Based on the interaction and what she felt from both of them, the woman must have been his wife.

Zosime overheard him telling her, "They have a long journey ahead, Iris. It's our duty to provide what relief we can."

She bit her lip and, conscious of her guests, gave them a polite smile before quickly going back outside. Andres turned back to his guests and Zosime decided to cut in before he asked Anastasia for a retelling of her battle with Typhon. Seeing him open his mouth, Zosime asked, "How is your family?"

"Has the babe been born yet?" Anastasia added smoothly.

"Last week!" he crowed. "She's a strong, healthy girl!"

Eyes sparkling with pride, he began telling them all about his oldest daughter's pregnancy. None of this seemed to surprise Anastasia so Zosime began to wonder if he had a habit of repeating himself.

He continued, "—It was her first pregnancy and she handled it so well. She has her mother's eyes—"

Zosime sensed the other people in her group's polite attention but the only one who was interested in the constant babble was Balthasar.

"How was the birth?" Balthasar asked when Andres did stop for breath.

Andres asked shrewdly, "Having your first?"

Balthasar nodded and Andres beamed. He opened his mouth to answer when Iris returned with a few young children, bearing plates of fruit and cheese. Zosime inclined her head in appreciation when the food was placed on the table and waited for them to sit down.

"Pardon us, my queen." Iris said. "We weren't anticipating your arrival, and we already ate."

Zosime doubted this was true based on the rumble of hunger she sensed from her and the children but didn't think it would be appropriate to pull the same move on them as she did on her Leondrians earlier.

"No worries at all." Zosime smiled, hoping to put her at ease.

Perhaps she was just uncomfortable breaking bread at the same table as her queen. Zosime did feel some anxiety from her and didn't want to make her feel worse, especially in her own home.

"Please, eat." Andres insisted and Zosime picked up a slice of cheese.

"Anyway—" he turned back to Balthasar after he bit into an apple. "To answer your question—"

Zosime didn't find any fault with Anastasia's observation that Andres was chatty, but he did seem to mean well. He was definitely eager, and she sensed his devotion to them as representatives of Leondria. He kept talking throughout the meal, but Zosime could sense there was something he desperately wanted to talk about.

"Is it true—" he swallowed when he finally exhausted himself with the subject of his children and Zosime sensed him build up the courage to finally ask. "That you met Lord Kal?"

There was a very long pause before Anastasia replied darkly, "Yes."

Blinking rapidly, he asked, "With your own eyes? One of the gods after twenty years?"

"Andres!" Iris snapped, horrified, and Andres shifted in his seat to look at her standing by the door. Recovering herself slightly, she asked in a more dignified tone, "Can you help me with the last of the chores? We only have so much time before it gets dark."

"Of course." he replied and turned back to Zosime. "Please forgive me, my queen. Help yourself to anything you want."

Zosime couldn't stop herself from staring at Anastasia when she sensed her anger.

"Sounds like they'll be a while." Balthasar commented dryly when Andres joined his wife outside, scratching his head and glancing at Zosime.

"We're probably obliged to stay here until tomorrow morning." Anastasia said heavily in an undertone, the rage dissipating in her chest. "He'll insist on giving us lodging after supper."

"We should discuss our route then." Zosime said and Anastasia and Balthasar exchanged a look. Zosime frowned and asked Anastasia, "You have a map, right?"

Anastasia nodded and pulled out a rolled-up scroll she had tucked away in her breast plate. She put it on the table and put a couple cups on the corners of it to keep it lying flat. Zosime studied it, seeing the outline of Midrios's mainland with certain symbols on it to signify mountains and city-states.

"We're here." Anastasia pointed to a spot above a small triangle to illustrate where the Hearth was located. She then traced a line up to a set of ridges that Zosime took to symbolize the mountain chain separating Leondria and Apistia. Anastasia then traced her finger to the right where the ridges ended until landing on the northeast Karkaros mountains that separated Midrios from other countries. "We'll be taking this path out of Midrios."

Zosime shook her head and pointed out, "I understand the need of our current route to avoid Lady Meraki's Forest but to go up and around the mountains will add a lot more time." She then traced a line straight across the first set of mountain ridges and stopped at the coastline before going up the Karkaros mountains, "We could go straight across then up."

"Or—" Zosime returned her finger to the coast then dragged it across the blue dye signifying the ocean. "Take a boat, bypassing Karkaros altogether."

Anastasia and Balthasar shared another quick look then Balthasar said hastily, "None of us sail, my queen."

"A fisherman or sailor would." Zosime declared. "We can trade a ride for protection."

"If they accepted such a trade." Balthasar pointed out. "This path would take us through Apistia, and we don't want to draw attention from less than friendly city-states."

Zosime knew little about Apistia, besides whispers she heard now and then. They were weaklings who relied on intellect and trickery. They preferred to spend their days drinking and lazily lying around the coast. They had corrupt people in positions of power who only cared about receiving favors and money without any sense of loyalty. According to the whispers, at least.

"I can take care of any threat." Zosime reassured him.

Dryas cleared his throat and Zosime glanced up, seeing Andres holding a pitcher. Anastasia snaked out a hand and retrieved the map, smoothly tucking it back into her breast plate. Zosime thought this was unnecessary since she didn't sense anything malicious from him, but she didn't comment on it either.

Instead, she flashed Andres her most charming smile and asked, despite thinking there was nothing else he could possibly add to the subject, "Do you have time to tell us more about your granddaughter?"

He beamed, pouring them more wine and said, "I can do better than that, my queen. I can fetch her so you can see her for yourself."

He set down the pitcher and strolled back outside.

Anastasia took this chance to lean in and murmur to Zosime, "Our mission is to gather intelligence, my queen. There are traders in Palapao who could have information and we wouldn't need to worry about treachery like we would in Apistia."

Zosime hesitated.

"Sometimes the path forward is slow, but it is the only proper way to achieve the objective." Balthasar whispered and Zosime's frown deepened.

To her great surprise, Dryas remarked, "You wanted to be sure, right?"

She glanced at him and reluctantly nodded, ignoring the flicker of surprise she felt from Alec and Nicholas at Dryas's question. She hadn't expected her friend to say anything after being quiet the whole morning, knowing he was feeling self-consciousness for being a last-minute addition to the group and wanting to prove his worth to the others.

"You can't be sure if you rush." Dryas added softly, and after Balthasar glanced at him reprovingly, he added. "My queen."

"Okay." she finally agreed and, while still thinking that the expedient route would be the better choice, decided to trust their judgment. "We'll go the long way."

18

Vasiliki was not the type to stoop to anger, let alone hold a grudge, but the passing days were not enough time to abate the rage that had settled in her chest. She occasionally felt resentment, yes. Nor could she deny feeling abandoned when she had suddenly been forced into ruling Leondria all by herself. While she was used to this latter feeling, she was quite unused to that raging hot creature that stirred in her chest whenever she thought about Zosime these days.

She always put Zosime first, but Vasiliki couldn't ignore the signs anymore that her sister was only preoccupied with her own impulses. When Zosime decided to do something, she did it without any regard for the consequences. Time and again, she put Vasiliki in some untenable position without sparing a second to think about how her actions affected her. Then there was the time when Zosime was so clearly upset that Vasiliki had been chosen to tour their lands first, even though she only had to wait a few weeks for her turn. For the first time, Vasiliki was put first—noticed first—and her sister couldn't even be happy for her.

Vasiliki just couldn't take it anymore.

Especially when Zosime had so casually tried assuring Perleros that everything would be taken care of back home while she was gone. Because Vasiliki would be here, doing the sensible thing as always. She had been trying her best to speak more in meetings lately, but she so relied on Zosime to lead them. Zosime was bright and magnetic like Anatole and Vasiliki feared that, with her sister gone, the respect for her authority would crumble. Then all would see that she couldn't handle the responsibility.

Why, why, why did Zosime have to leave?

She supposed that Zosime couldn't help herself. But there had been no justification for what she did right before she left. What in the name of all the gods had she been thinking bringing Dryas along on that dangerous mission at the last possible minute? Vasiliki didn't need the Gift to know what everyone was feeling in that moment. She could read it plainly enough on all their faces.

Vasiliki had nothing but confidence in Dryas's abilities and she only wanted the best for him. She had missed her friend more than she could ever admit out loud, given her new position. It had been so hard at times not to talk to him when she saw him in the distance every morning and she had planned on arranging a visit with him soon when Zosime had haphazardly taken him with her.

Despite the confidence she had in him, she couldn't ignore the fact that Dryas didn't have the experience for such a delicate mission and Zosime was placing him in unnecessary danger.

She didn't know if she would be able to forgive her sister if she got their friend killed.

Vasiliki's heart started beating fast at the thought of Zosime's recklessness and faster still from the responsibility she had thrust upon her. For years, it had been the three of them and now she stood alone. Vasiliki now unwillingly carried the burden of ruling over thousands when she had struggled every day with being queen.

She knew that she had relied on Zosime these past few months, but she was realizing just how much she needed her.

She had to fight against that voice in her head during every meeting now that yearned to cry out that she needed time to think. Needed time to breathe before making a decision. But there was never enough time, and her voice would fail her whenever she needed it most.

Like when Angelos had told them about the threat from the east or when he plunged the dagger into his own heart. His claim of war may or may not have been the words of a madman, but Vasiliki couldn't shake the thought that they held the rings of a fatal prophecy. With all her skills and abilities, it seemed that the gods had smiled down on Zosime, but Vasiliki feared that Zosime's luck would soon run out. She was at least comforted by the knowledge that Anastasia was there to protect Zosime, despite whatever mysterious past she had with Lord Kal.

Vasiliki hadn't forgiven her sister's thoughtlessness, but if she let her good thinking prevail over her anger, she was forced to admit that her sister had good intentions. For the most part. Vasiliki's thoughts took a dark turn when she recalled General Oscar's warning when he had approached her that fateful morning when Angelos had changed everything.

She had woken up early and quickly gotten ready for the daily morning workout. Vasiliki was never late, but she had been surprised when she had walked onto the Heart's landing and didn't find Zosime already waiting for her there. She knew her sister didn't sleep well most nights and had waited for a little while before she had heard General Oscar call out her name. She had turned towards him and inclined her head when he approached her.

"Did you sleep well, my queen?" he had asked while making the sign of the gods.

"Yes, General." she had replied, surprised both by the fact that he had approached her and by the question itself. "You?"

"As well as could be expected." he had said evasively which had made Vasiliki frown.

"Is something troubling you?" she had asked, concerned.

General Oscar had hesitated, opening his mouth for a moment before shutting it and looking away. "Forgive me. I shouldn't have approached." he had shaken his head and continued unconvincingly. "It is nothing, my queen."

"All my generals should approach if there is an issue to solve." Vasiliki had said gently.

"I don't know if you can, my queen." he had replied.

"What is it?" Vasiliki had asked. "If it's within my power to fix, tell me."

"Even if it might hurt you, my queen?" he had countered with a sad smile, and Vasiliki's eyebrows rose.

"If I'm doing something wrong," she had said quietly, her heart hardening as she thought about how much she was failing in her duty. "It's best I know."

"No, my queen." he had reassured her quickly.

"What is it then?" she had asked, both confused and curious on where he was going with this conversation.

She didn't know what he could ask that would hurt her if it wasn't a reprimand of her performance. He had again hesitated, and Vasiliki had followed him when he walked several paces over to the side of the landing that was far enough away to be out of the guards' earshot.

"If I may ask—" he had trailed off for a moment then inquired. "How is Queen Zosime doing?"

"Great." Vasiliki had responded automatically but couldn't keep the surprise out of her voice.

She hadn't been able to help herself from marveling at the question. Zosime had adjusted to the mantle of queen so much faster than Vasiliki, who was still trying desperately to catch up.

"I've been very impressed with how you've handled the transition, my queen." General Oscar had praised, and Vasiliki had felt a rush of shock. "You've kept such a steady hold of yourself. The others have noticed, too."

General Oscar had then waited a moment and Vasiliki was given the impression that he wanted her to say something. While she had been flattered by the unexpected compliment, she was more interested in what he had to say about her sister.

After a moment, she had asked, "Are you concerned about Queen Zosime?"

"I am, my queen." he had said. He had then cleared his throat then proceeded delicately, "If I may speak freely?"

"Granted." she had allowed.

"You know her best, my queen." he had remarked then continued. "Has she been adjusting well? We are aware that you two didn't have the traditional experience before your coronation so we just need to know if we need to provide her with more guidance."

"She's been fine." Vasiliki had reiterated.

"No—impulsive decisions?" he had pressed. "Nothing that might concern you?"

Vasiliki wanted to deny the questions outright but found herself hesitating.

Taking a step forward, he had declared, "We only wish to serve, my queen."

Vasiliki had opened her mouth to respond when Zosime had then sauntered up to them with Anastasia and Angelos in tow.

"Think about it." he had whispered before they quickly stepped away from each other.

And she had. She had given the matter a lot of thought and she couldn't truthfully deny Oscar's claim of impulsiveness. Not with her sister giving Angelos guest right before the advisors could vet him, despite the security concerns. Not with her insistence on going with the group the day before they left to potentially very dangerous lands. Not with her inviting Dryas to go with them moments before they left.

Vasiliki couldn't ignore her sister's actions anymore, but it was out of her hands now. She could now only wait for Zosime to stroll back through the gates with the same self-assured smirk and raised teasing eyebrows. She could only wait for her sister to come back with news on whether the threat was real. Or wait for the group to come back with her lifeless body because her recklessness had finally cost Zosime her life.

So Vasiliki would have to wait all winter, as she had spent her whole life waiting for people that had walked out of her life without ever coming back.

Her life was a vigil that never ended, yet she must forever remain at her post for the sake of her people. She did her duty without complaint but how her heart yearned to spend her time studying the stars instead of being dragged into the spotlight day after day.

She couldn't ignore the nagging thought that she wasn't good enough for the job. That she wasn't the person the Leondrians needed to lead them. But she was all they had for the foreseeable future, thanks to Zosime.

Every day she awoke in the dark, led the daily morning exercises, and met with her advisors. She had asked for word on her sister, and she was greeted with the same answer: *no update, my queen.*

She did do her best to make time to visit the Trainees now and then, although she made a point not to single out Adelphie again. She was resolved to not abuse her position by showing favoritism. However, she didn't see any issues with visiting Daphne now and then, under the pretense that Daphne didn't have her husband there to support her through the rest of her pregnancy. She was bearing his absence well enough even if Vasiliki could see the subtle cracks in her facade that showed how hard she was taking her husband's prolonged absence.

She was the closest thing Vasiliki had to a friend right now. Not that she would ever be permitted to say such a thing out loud either. Daphne was one of her subjects, not someone for Vasiliki to bother on personal visits even if Daphne never seemed to mind. It had been a much-needed refuge from the world, and she was always grateful whenever Daphne, in her white pregnancy robes and red cloak, let her inside her home.

Like today.

They hadn't talked about anything specific and there had been a few long stretches of silence when all they did was drink water or polish their shields.

Vasiliki could feel her spare time growing short, but she couldn't help but ask, "Is there anything else you need assistance with, Daphne?"

Despite Daphne's protests, Vasiliki would offer every time she visited and would do the occasional chore to Daphne's amused exasperation. Jedrick would usually stand in a corner of the room, keeping quiet without looking at anything. The only times he moved from the corner were when he wordlessly assisted Vasiliki in one of these chores.

Daphne waved a hand with a smile then rested it on her now swollen stomach, "Between you and my parents, I am well off, my queen."

Daphne's eyes clouded over and Vasiliki could tell she was lost in memories of her beloved Balthasar. Vasiliki quickly glanced at Jedrick who also looked alarmed that Daphne might be moments away from tears.

"How is—" Vasiliki fumbled for a topic for a moment then asked wildly. "The pregnancy?"

Daphne sniffled then took a deep breath to compose herself. Daphne cleared her throat and continued, "It's—I don't even know how to describe it. The greatest honor."

Pregnancy had always seemed strange to Vasiliki but that was a common theme she had heard. That it was one of the greatest of honors.

"Have—" Daphne hesitated.

Vasiliki straightened, both grateful that Daphne was regaining control of herself and wondering what she had to say. Vasiliki gave her a small smile and gestured for her to continue.

"Has anyone broached the subject of your marriage?" Daphne asked slowly.

"Yes." Vasiliki answered after a pause. "Briefly."

"Have there been any arrangements yet?" Daphne questioned.

Vasiliki resisted the urge to fiddle with her hands and answered as calmly as she could, "No."

She was not ready for this conversation. She knew that there were many people younger than herself who were already parents. She also knew that many Leondrians married very soon after donning their red cloaks for the first time. Duty would soon command her to do the same—marry and have children to further Lady Meraki's line—but her heart pounded at the thought. She was already drowning now and the thought of something that frightening was just too much for her right now.

It would also be different if there was someone who interested her. It amazed her every time she saw two Leondrians share that bond that went deeper than the one all Leondrians had, the look in their eyes when two lovers glanced at each other. But the idea of crossing into that great unknown without a shield to protect her or a great love to give her to courage to take the leap on top of her responsibilities just made her heart pound harder in her chest.

Vasiliki must have been broadcasting her thoughts on her face because Daphne smiled in understanding and reassured her, "You have some time. Marriage should be about devotion."

Vasiliki shifted in her chair uncomfortably and agreed, "Yes, love."

Daphne shook her head and laughed softly as if love was a concept Vasiliki was too young or too orphaned to understand, "No. Not love."

"Isn't it love that changes the world?" Vasiliki asked bitterly, feeling her shortcomings in that moment now more than ever. "That's strong enough to move mountains and which binds us together?"

Daphne's mouth dropped open for a moment in surprise at Vasiliki's sharp tone. Even Jedrick looked over and Vasiliki shut her mouth before she said another foolish thing.

Daphne appraised her for a moment then said without a trace of humor, "Love *alone* isn't enough."

Daphne's eyes grew distant, and she suddenly sighed, "If love alone was enough, the world would be a simpler and better place. But it isn't. You need to be devoted to each other. Willing to sacrifice, even dishonor yourself, for the other person. To pay attention to what they need and be devoted to your marriage for the rest of your life. Even with the best matches, it's no easy thing."

"Dishonor yourself?" Vasiliki echoed, confused.

Daphne blinked and Vasiliki had the impression that she hadn't meant to say that part.

"I only meant—" Daphne said quickly, and she lost her train of thought for a moment before finishing. "You'd be willing to do anything for them, even sacrifice your own soul."

Vasiliki blinked, not knowing what to make of that and Daphne quickly glanced down at the table.

"I see." Vasiliki said quietly.

Daphne looked up and smiled, "The gods have blessed me with a great love. They will surely bless you as well."

Vasiliki highly doubted it. She didn't form those attachments like others did. Could never be truly open to have that kind of relationship with whoever she did marry since she had to hold so much of herself back every day to be the Leondrian her people needed her to be. But she inclined her head in appreciation of the sentiment.

"I have to go." Vasiliki said reluctantly, knowing she had squeezed every ounce of her free time that she could spare.

"You honor me with your visits." Daphne said.

"You honor *me*." Vasiliki corrected and rose to her feet, Jedrick following her every step once they had left the house.

Vasiliki may not have ever been in love before or know much about the subject in general, but she was well acquainted with sacrifice. Her people needed her, and she would do her best by them, even if she yearned for a future that she could never have. Studying the skies and unlocking the secrets of the universe would have to wait. Indefinitely.

Vasiliki resisted the urge to sigh but kept her head as high as she could as she walked back to the heart for her next task of the day.

There was just never enough time.

CHAPTER

19

Zosime knew that patience was not her strong suit, but she felt perfectly within her rights to believe that Andres's weakness was not appreciating other people's time. Her feet were itching to hit the road again, but Anastasia had correctly predicted that Andres had insisted on them staying for dinner then spending the night.

He had invoked hospitality and now Zosime's hands were tied. A direct refusal of hospitality was a grave insult so guests usually only needed to give their hosts strong hints about their lack of time and that would be that. Zosime did as such, remarking how much she appreciated his home and his food but that they possibly couldn't infringe on them any longer, but it was of no use.

So their group awkwardly took up space in his house, and all the while, Zosime sensed concern from Andres's family. She could also feel their reverence towards her but their distress and irritation towards Andres didn't fade either.

What she found odd was that she sensed his family's hunger when Zosime went outside to assist with the chores with the farm animals. But they always insisted that they were fine, even when Zosime caught them feeding the baby with goat milk.

"Did you hear that?" Anastasia suddenly asked after Zosime lifted the final bale of hay into one of the pens.

Zosime frowned, "I didn't hear anything."

"I thought I heard something—" Anastasia looked towards the fields. "Some animal."

Zosime blinked and looked around, "I don't see anything."

"Permission to survey the perimeter to be sure, my queen?" Anastasia asked with a pointed look. "I wouldn't want some predator sneaking around our host's lands."

"Yes. I'll join you." Zosime agreed, getting the feeling that Anastasia was giving her a hint, and waved a hand to the others. "Nothing will get past the two of us, carry on."

They walked deep into the fields in silence before Zosime finally built up the courage to ask, "Did I insult them?"

Anastasia raised an eyebrow at her and pointed out, "Wouldn't you be able to sense that, my queen?"

"I sensed their distress." Zosime responded, surprised that Anastasia didn't give her a straight answer. "The Gift doesn't always give me the full picture. Just certain emotions they're feeling at the given moment."

Zosime sensed Anastasia's interest and dreaded being asked questions about it. Everyone had been fascinated with this ability growing up and she could never adequately capture how the Gift worked. Others woefully misunderstood her best attempts at describing it and only thought of it as an honor. Being a Leondrian was an honor. Being their queen was the true gift. Not sensing everyone's emotions all the time, which often bled into her dreams and kept her from fully resting.

"It's because they don't have enough food for us." Anastasia explained. "So they have to fast to not mistreat their guests."

Zosime stopped dead in her tracks which made Anastasia still.

Dumbfounded, Zosime said, "I thought they were skipping lunch for chores or saving their big meal for dinner."

Anastasia shook her head, "There's not enough food going around these days. Do you remember the early reports from your first couple meetings with the generals?"

Zosime thought about it for a moment and finally answered, "There's been less output the last few years, right?"

"Yes, my queen." Anastasia answered promptly.

Zosime bit her lip as she felt a flash of anger. She had tried politely leaving and not burdening Andres, but he had insisted they stay and now she was taking food out of her peoples' mouths.

"I thought we had enough food stores to last through winter." Zosime finally said.

"A lot of it goes to the Hearth for storage." Anastasia clarified. "To go to the Leondrians, the Council, and the servants to keep everything up and running. Or, if they get attacked or experience hard weather, we have provisions we can give back to them as insurance. It wouldn't be an issue most years, but our presence is dwindling their supplies."

"Yet we can't go back to the Hearth to replenish their food." Zosime shook her head and sighed. "And we'd have to repeat the process every time someone invokes hospitality."

"It would be a grave insult of their honor, my queen." Anastasia agreed then a sly smile rose on her lips. "But if we killed a predator stalking their lands, it wouldn't be unexpected to bring it back to present to our host."

Zosime's heart lifted, and she grinned, "It would be positively rude of us not to."

Anastasia's blue-grey eyes sparkled in response and Zosime's mouth almost dropped open in astonishment. Anastasia's expressions were always guarded, and she never sensed any sort of joy from her, so to see her eyes glowing like that was almost like watching her jump ecstatically up down.

Anastasia began walking again and Zosime glanced at her before asking, "You didn't hear anything, did you?"

Then Zosime heard something rustling nearby and immediately placed her hand on her sword. Anastasia shook her head and cautiously approached the source of the sound, slowly withdrawing her dagger from her side then leaping gracefully into the tall grass. Zosime charged forward a few steps when she heard the animal scream in pain then stopped when Anastasia stood again.

"Would you like to see the terrible beast, my queen?" Anastasia asked after yanking the dagger out of a furry throat.

Zosime did so, glancing down at the body for several long seconds before staring at Anastasia in disbelief.

—

The two of them quickly caught the others' attention when they strolled back towards the house with the dead animal slung around Anastasia's shoulder.

"My queen!" Andres breathed after taking in the blood and exclaimed. "You didn't need to hunt. We have enough to provide for you!"

"This terrible predator was threatening your lands." Zosime disagreed.

Andres frowned and repeated slowly, as if not believing his ears, "Terrible predator?"

"Yes. It was trespassing, eating your grass which would starve your livestock." Zosime insisted seriously.

"A goat?" Andres asked, clearly confused.

"Terrible beast." Anastasia said with a grave expression that made it look like she had just slayed a powerful monster.

"Absolutely." Zosime continued in the same tone. "We wanted to repay your hospitality by presenting you with this gift."

Andres looked like he was at a loss for words for several seconds before he finally grinned.

"The mighty Anastasia strikes again." Andres chuckled and Zosime sensed an unexpected flash of darkness from her. "We can have extra for supper then."

Anastasia followed him wordlessly as he walked towards the back of the house. Zosime caught Dryas looking at her with amusement and he raised a skeptical eyebrow at her.

Zosime shrugged and said derisively, "Goats."

They had to wait a little while for dinner, but she was pleased that the whole family joined them to eat this time. Andres continued telling them stories throughout the meal and stayed up late to ensure they were entertained. Zosime sensed his wife's exasperation and worry but she was ultimately able to persuade him that their guests needed rest.

Andres had been adamant about the Leondrians taking their beds, despite Zosime's polite protests. So she reluctantly agreed to take his bed and stared up at the ceiling for a while before drifting to sleep. She woke up the next morning surprised that she slept decently with only the occasional slip of worry from the family bleeding into her dreams.

Iris must have given Andres a stern talking to because he was noticeably subdued when they sat down for breakfast. Zosime had gone over how to approach him about their need to resume their mission without being obligated to stay here any longer past the morning. But he beat her to the punch when he had his children bring in a sack of food for them to take with them when they finished eating breakfast.

"For your journey." Andres said worriedly.

"May the gods bless and reward you for your hospitality. I hope for the opportunity to break bread at your table again." Zosime recited.

"The honor is mine, my queen." Andres said and they rose from the table.

Zosime inclined her head to each member of his family while Balthasar took the sack from the children. She really didn't want to take it when they could fend for themselves out on the road, but honor kept her lips sealed.

The family gathered to watch them leave and Zosime found her burden so much heavier than the day before. She sensed the group's wariness as well and they marched in silence, not commenting when other farmers emerged from their homes to wave as they passed them by. If it wasn't for the sack slung over Balthasar's shoulder, Zosime was sure that some of them would have offered them food and hospitality. But they only waved and some cheered as they walked further down the farmlands.

The food stack sustained them throughout the day, and they only stopped when it was time to set up camp for the night. Nicholas quickly prepared himself for bed, insisting that "his ears had taken enough of a beating already." Even Flavian was too tired to tell a story that night, so they quickly ate and went to sleep with a couple guards taking shifts to patrol during the night.

Several days passed in this manner since farmers would routinely approach them to offer them food or to talk with Zosime. She could feel their progress slow and again yearned for the horses which had kept away those not on the list to visit during her tour of Leondria. It wasn't that she didn't want to see or hear from her people, but her impatience was growing. She needed to gather intelligence to categorically support or deny Angelos's claim of war and now her people were preventing her from doing her job. She would gladly hear their burdens after her return and meeting with her advisors, but she could think of no polite way to tell them to wait.

The group did start relaxing as the days passed and Flavian soon returned to giving nightly stories around the campfire, entertaining the group's requests for certain history retellings. She didn't sense any more outright hostility towards Dryas, but she could still tell that the others hadn't accepted him either. What had most surprised her was Balthasar's severe disapproval, but he seemed to be taking the opportunity to instruct his little brother whenever he could.

She often saw the two of them whispering during the daily walks or by the nightly fires while the others kept their distance from the last minute addition to the group. When he wasn't giving Dryas advice, Balthasar would spend time with the others, and she sensed how well-respected he was. She initially found it astounding that he hadn't already been promoted to a higher enlisted rank or accepted into the officer corps. But then she remembered that, with them staying in their borders the last couple decades, that there hadn't been many vacancies in the higher ranks that they otherwise would have had if they had been going on expeditions with inevitable casualties.

She understood then why Perleros had been so insistent on Balthasar going with them as the mission leader—until Zosime decided to join them—and why Penelope pushed for Flavian to be in the designated group. Succeeding on such an important mission would be enough for the other leaders to accept such a big promotion that would have caused friction without a prior opening to fill.

Zosime preoccupied herself with her mission as they slowly crept towards Leondria's territorial boundaries and didn't concern herself too much with the group's current dynamics. She knew the early discord was already waning, even if there was still some unfriendliness in the older Leondrians' interactions with her dearest friend.

They were close, she thought restlessly, as they steadily approached the gods' mountain.

They were so close to leaving home and being one step closer to accomplishing their objective. As much as her impatience was getting the better of her, her heart still became heavy from the idea of leaving her beloved Leondria.

Dusk had arrived when they finally stood before the holy mountains and Zosime found herself staring up at it in awe, for the second time.

"My queen." Balthasar said and Zosime turned to look at him.

"Should we camp here for the night?" he hinted, and she sensed the group's growing agitation at the prospect of leaving Leondria for the first time.

"There's still enough daylight to continue for a couple hours." Anastasia disagreed and Zosime thought she sensed weariness from her.

It could be so hard to read her at times, this woman of unyielding resolve and cold iron. It was also difficult to think straight around this legend who exemplified their values so well.

"The lake is just up ahead, ma'am." Balthasar pointed out politely, giving Anastasia a scrutinizing look. "Enough water for us to drink and store."

Anastasia's face only grew graver, and she shook her head, "I wouldn't drink it."

Zosime frowned at that comment, and she could tell that Balthasar was also struggling to understand this strange warning.

"We can boil it, ma'am." he suggested respectfully. "To cleanse it of anything that would make us ill."

"It's the gods' water, sergeant." Anastasia explained. "No fire in the world is powerful enough to purify it."

"Yes, ma'am." he said and Zosime sensed how his trust in Anastasia overcame any confusion he had in her cryptic warning.

Zosime caught Anastasia glancing at the mountain and her jaw clenched.

"There will be travelers foolish enough to drink it. We should continue a couple more hours then rest, my queen." Anastasia suggested.

"We'll be stopping here for the night." Zosime decided. "But there will be no drinking from the lake."

"Yes, my queen." everyone acknowledged.

"Flavian, Dryas, go hunting. Alec, Nicholas, establish a perimeter." Zosime ordered.

Zosime often paired up Flavian and Dryas since he had taken Dryas's last-minute presence the best out of everyone and the two of them nodded before setting off together.

"They need to eat." Zosime explained to Anastasia when everyone else had set out to work. "And I doubt any sick traveler who drinks from the lake could overpower us."

"Yes, my queen." Anastasia responded quietly but there was still a weariness to her that Zosime couldn't explain.

Balthasar quickly dug a hole to set up a small pyre so the winter winds wouldn't extinguish the flame. Alec and Nicholas gathered rocks and sticks, busying themselves for the night as they waited for Dryas and Flavian to return. The two weren't gone longer than an hour or two before they returned with a dead lynx.

Flavian smirked and asked the group, "Who's ready for dinner?"

The rest of the night was uneventful as they ate and went to bed soon afterwards. Zosime and Anastasia had first watch, and she found herself growing concerned when Anastasia never lost that feeling of wariness. When her shift ended a couple hours later, Zosime had then woken up Alec and slept fitfully for the rest of the night.

When she awoke with dawn's morning rays caressing her face, she had the distinct impression that Anastasia hadn't slept at all. Zosime sat up to discover that Anastasia was still patrolling the perimeter instead of Nicholas who was supposed to be on the last night shift. She didn't say anything to her though as the group consumed the rest of the lynx for breakfast and covered up the hole where they had made the fire.

"Let's go." Zosime said when they had finished packing up and continued their trek north.

She hesitated for just a moment when they left the gods' mountain behind which marked the end of Leondrian territory. For everyone except Anastasia, they had left home behind for the first time in their lives. The sun steadily rose but the chilly wind didn't abate at all as they walked for hours in the fresh snow.

While it was a mild winter day, Zosime hadn't really expected to run into anyone so she was surprised when she saw a man with a young boy pulling a cart towards them in the early afternoon. The father and son quickly stopped in their tracks when they saw them, and their eyes instantly widened.

While she had been surprised to see anyone out in this part of the country, what most astonished her was the spike of fear she felt from them both. She noticed the man's muscles tighten and how fiercely he trembled as she felt cold ice settle in his chest that had nothing to do with the weather. Concerned, Zosime hurried forward and approached him.

"Tell me the problem, friend." Zosime said and, in a flash, Anastasia was standing beside her.

His brown eyes widened further, and his mouth opened and closed multiple times before he whispered, "Take what you want. We won't fight."

Zosime's brow furrowed, and she glanced behind him for any evidence of pursuers before asking, "Did someone chase you? Harass you?"

"Take what you want." he repeated in terror, and the child scurried behind his father's leg.

"I don't want anything from you." Zosime said, aghast, and sensed the man's exhaustion underneath his panic. "Where are you headed? I can carry your cart for a while."

She knew they needed to continue north for their mission but her concern for this clearly terrified man overcame this thought.

The man started shaking and he begged, "I have done nothing to provoke your anger, queen. I'm just a trader who got lost in the snow. I didn't mean to tread too close to your lands. Please, spare my son."

Zosime couldn't understand why he was so afraid when they were here to protect him. She watched him in shock and had no idea what to say when he murmured the word *please* over and over again.

Balthasar stepped up to stand beside her and whispered, "He wishes to be left alone, my queen."

Zosime desperately wanted to help him, but she didn't know how. She would ordinarily have insisted on providing her assistance but, since this man was not one of her subjects, she couldn't give him commands. Clenching her jaw and looking in the other direction, she stepped out of his path, and he then dragged the cart as quickly as he could away from them.

"We'll be approaching Palapao soon, my queen." Balthasar informed her after the father and son were no longer in sight. "We might find answers there."

Zosime didn't comment on his attempt to make her feel better and said with some forced degree of optimism, "Next time."

She couldn't shake the encounter from her mind for the rest of the day as they walked north. She didn't speak at all except to order the group to stop for the night and to set up camp. She sensed Dryas's eyes on her, but he didn't say anything to her as Balthasar started preparing their meal.

She couldn't get over the fact that the man had been afraid of her. Leondrians protected people. It was their mission to defend Midrios and to serve the gods. The whole encounter just didn't make any sense to her. She replayed this scene in her mind as she leaned against a log, barely listening to the others chatting as she stared into the fire.

She didn't know at what point she closed her eyes or when the comfortable blanket of sleep descended, but it did not remain in place for nearly as long as she hoped. Instead, this comfortable blanket was unexpectedly ripped away from her and was replaced with the feeling that something was horribly wrong. Alarm bells started screaming in her mind, but her body did not jerk awake as it always did before.

Fear settled in her chest when her eyes disobeyed her command to open, the feeling only worsening when she heard strange sounds in the darkness. A whirling, a snapping, and the sound of wood breaking.

That's when she heard vicious laughter from multiple people and an old female voice croaking in malicious delight, *"Have you come to play with us?"*

PART
THREE

CHAPTER

I never held any love for winter, despite my talents for it. I never cared for its cold cruelty that sent many to their early graves. Never wanted to see this magnificent country withering under its chilly touch or watch the land retreat into itself for months at a time. What I most yearned for each year was what came after the last trace of snow melted away. There was nothing in this life as sweet as Midrios in the spring or seeing your beloved holding a rose to her lips after confessing her love to you.

How I longed to see my lady of spring with her chocolate eyes and cherry-red smile that was so beautiful that even the greatest of roses would blush in her presence from the shadows. But she was long gone and there was nothing that could bring her back to me.

I may have seen the world's imperfections long ago, but I never sought out the darkness. It just came to me when I least expected it and it has since shackled me, body and soul. Grief and well-meaning misjudgments weren't accounted for in my sentencing. The gods could be cruel like that. But at least I now understand the cycle of life much better than when I still walked among the mortals countless years ago.

I see the patterns that others miss and how each decision ripples into the future. I know why the lion and the owl have been at odds with each other, long before war was laid upon Midrios's doorstep. I know why the gods have retreated from the mortal realm and what their final act will be before withdrawing once again. But that will be revealed to the mortals in time, no matter how desperate they are for their help.

I watched Zosime and her group leave the Hearth to embark on their journey to gather intelligence. A part of me wanted to weep and beg them not to go but perhaps I had been so afflicted by my sentence at this point that most of me was indifferent. If it wasn't for the fact that my favorite to watch was a member of this group, the one who would suffer so much before shedding their physical form once and for all.

I could see how each of them struggled with their internal battles and how they were compelled to halt in accordance with the law of hospitality. They may have felt annoyed by the delay but what was heart-wrenching was what happened after they left their host's halls.

They didn't see how a neighbor walked to Andres's house to ask about missing livestock and how he gleefully told her about Queen Zosime's visit. They didn't see how excited he was to spill over every detail of their visit. What great guests they were and how concerned he was about them taking the long way out of the country. He wanted her to know what a thoughtful subject he was, providing his queen with extra food to sustain her group as they went up and around the mountains before going to Karkaros. And how he prayed every night for their safety and for his family's health through the rest of winter.

The group didn't see how this report would spread like wildfire by farmers and traveling traders. How it was heard by unfriendly ears throughout the country.

The Fates may not have the same power they once held with their malfunctioning wheel that once weaved destinies for gods and mortals alike, but they still had cards they played behind the scenes.

And I could do nothing but watch and pray for a better future that I knew will never come.

CHAPTER

21

Alastair knew things were about to get interesting as he waited in the Senate chamber for the meeting to begin. After weeks of intense infighting, the Senate was now ready vote on Sophie's proposal. Alastair really enjoyed a good debate and seeing the game being played out, but he really had to resist the urge to tap his foot at times at how slowly the Senate was moving on this important issue. He knew better than to expect the Senate to move quickly when it came to their domestic security, but he reminded himself to not let his impatience overcome his better judgment. He had a reputation to uphold, after all.

Strong reputations carried power and that meant everything in this dog-eat-dog world.

The delays had afforded him time to gather intelligence and he was now convinced the evidence pointed to one probable conclusion: that Angelos was right. He couldn't help but frequently think about the roaring fire that rose unnaturally high in the sky at that cracked holy man's temple next to the gods' mountain during that fierce storm a while back.

As he had waited for the Senate to finish debating every possible point about proposing an alliance with Leondria, Alastair had been covertly speaking with his connected friends and traders from the east who had heard hordes of whispers about Afshin's threat that corroborated Angelos's claim. They had also informed him that not much was known about Angelos's past but that he was currently an Apistian fisherman and family man with no ties to Leondria or Spyridon that they were aware of.

But with all the information he had collected, there had been no update on Angelos himself. Alastair knew he had left for Leondria, but no one he had talked to had seen him since. Not even his worried wife who had taken over the business in her husband's long absence.

"I don't know where he is Senator." she had told him, and he had noted the dark circles of strain and exhaustion under her eyes. This worry had quickly turned into anger when she muttered a moment later, "His imbecile friend never should have gone to that temple then begged Angelos to go see that fanatic."

Nothing in her tone or demeanor had suggested to Alastair that she was lying which had been an interesting development to him.

"He sounded like an honorable man and a better friend." he had said sympathetically.

"Please find him, Senator!" she had begged him frantically before resting her hands over her eyes when they heard a baby start to wail from inside her house.

"All will be well." he had said kindly, recognizing the signs of a person close to losing their composure, and reassured her. "We will look for him."

Tears had welled up in her eyes and she gave him a small, grateful smile before going inside to take care of the child.

He didn't bother telling her that, if her husband had gone to Leondria, then he was likely long dead by now. Unfortunately, the Leondrians had cracked down on their security the past couple decades so Apistia didn't have good spy contacts who could pass back information to confirm whether Angelos had arrived. It was possible Angelos was delayed in his journey, but Alastair found himself more convinced with the passing days that the queens had inherited their father's bloodthirstiness by killing the Apistian messenger.

It wouldn't be the first time.

He kept this knowledge to himself as the other politicians argued whether to extend an alliance with Leondria. Alastair could tell that Sophie was talking to other Senators to erode his influence based on their superior smirks and the occasional off-handed remark about emotional biases. As a result, Alastair had to be even more meticulous than usual so he wouldn't lose any more influence from her interference. He had seen first-hand what happened to his own father when he had lost the support of the Senate and Alastair wouldn't make the same mistakes.

Prokopios had really asked him a few weeks back after Alastair had invited him over to his house for dinner, "You really trust Leondrians?"

Alastair had remembered snorting, "You can't trust Leondrians. What you can count on is them having a disciplined army which just so happens is a very useful tool when facing an adversary in war. You've heard the same rumors I have and who is coming for us."

"They'll be just as likely to put a knife in my back than in the enemy's." Prokopios had grumbled. "Afshin could be reasoned with. The Leondrians have repeatedly demonstrated that they cannot."

"You're volunteering to go on the front lines?" Alastair had gasped then exclaimed. "How patriotic of you, good sir!"

Alastair hadn't been able to stop himself from hurling the jab at the old, overweight senator who had outlived his usefulness to Apistia a long time ago.

Prokopios's face had reddened at the insult, and he had insisted, "They'll burn our fair Apistia to the ground and enslave us."

"Perhaps," Alastair had allowed before continuing. "*After* the battle, once they have fulfilled their self-interest in not being enslaved themselves by Afshin, who has demonstrated that he will gladly offer us the opportunity to submit to slavery before bringing his troops in to kill us before we finally agree to surrender our liberty. One would hope an erudite Senator like yourself would be able to pick the correct time to outwit a bunch of Leondrian grunts and two inexperienced queens without compromising Apistia's chance of success in war."

That last statement had made the other Senator's face purple in rage before Alastair handed him a cup of wine and state with a superior smile, "Senator Prokopios, they run around outside and throw sticks at each other every day while we spend all our time honing our mental sharpness and improving our Navy. What chance could they have of outmaneuvering us?"

Alastair preferred verbal sparring with smart senators to escape boredom, but he also found talking with the witless ones like Prokopios delightful. Such people didn't require any degree of intellectual effort, but they did provide unmatched entertainment, especially when he saw a spark in their eyes when they thought they had caught up to him. It was amazing how much they enjoyed being mocked before Alastair helped them to understand the bigger picture then they did exactly what he wanted them to do.

Alastair almost laughed in his seat in the Senate chambers as he recalled that conversation, still impressed by the foolishness of that question. One didn't need absolute trust with temporary allies when facing a common enemy. The only Leondrian he could absolutely trust was a dead one, but he was confident that they would look out for their own self-interests. He didn't know anything about the two new Leondrian queens or how far their bloodthirstiness went but he could reasonably assume they valued survival.

No, he could never trust Leondrians, but their army would be essential if Midrios was invaded again.

He also couldn't pass up the opportunity to meet these queens in person, assuming they did agree to ally with Apistia. He was forced to admit to himself that children were not automatically guilty for the sins of their parents, but if these queens had turned out like their father, then Alastair would bide his time until it was the right moment to strike.

For his family. For himself.

Alastair didn't make the rookie mistake of looking around the Senate chambers to watch it fill up when he knew so many would be watching him. It was one thing to survey his surroundings on a normal day, but it was quite another to look desperate on a vote he was accused of being emotional about. So he emulated his best expression of boredom and only glanced at the others through his peripheral vision.

This was one vote that no Senator dared to arrive late for. Alastair suspected that if anyone other than Sophie had proposed this alliance then it would have been rejected out of hand. He knew everyone had an opinion on the matter and predicted that it would be a close vote, one way or the other. Many Senators had slowly come around to the idea of extending an alliance with Leondria, but many hadn't. Which was disappointing but hardly surprising.

The room was buzzing with hostile disagreements until Sophie entered the room a few minutes later and glided down the rows of steps like she didn't have a care in the world. Everyone was silent as they watched her take center stage, spread her arms wide, and greet, "My fellow Senators."

Alastair could see everyone lean forward in their seats with rapt attention, but he made sure to only cock his head just enough to show polite interest.

Sophie clasped her hands together and continued, "I made a proposal before this esteemed assembly and—as you all well know from our procedures—reserve the right for final comments to persuade you to vote in favor of it." she paused for a long moment before declaring. "But we have already long pondered its ramifications from every angle."

Sophie appraised the crowd who was practically on the edge of their seats by this point with calculating eyes and stated, "You have heard them all before and have had time to think the matter over. I will not insult your intelligence or waste our precious time by reiterating every point in favor of the proposal."

Alastair raised an eyebrow at that, and he heard a few bewildered murmurs. It was so common for Senators to belabor the merits of their case that their speeches were expected to last for at least two hours. Some were so desperate or loved hearing the sound of their own voices so much that they droned on for a full day and voting had to be postponed to the next meeting. Sophie was never desperate, always embodying the perfect picture of cool serenity, but she knew how to use tactics to her advantage.

After allowing the crowd to absorb this shocking development, Sophie remarked, "I will close by clarifying one thing I have heard questioned during deliberations. This is not a proposal of appeasement made from fear. Such unworthy emotions would, of course, be beneath this logical body. This proposal is in fact one that espouses the values that we and our patron goddess live by every day: logic and wisdom. Vote in accordance with what Lady Apistia created when she established the best city-state in Midrios. Vote *wisely*. Vote in favor of the proposal."

She bowed her head and Alastair was now surrounded by stunned faces from both the senators around him and a sliver of the public who was watching silently in the back. That must have been the shortest speech in the Senate's history and now there was no time for stalling or to overthink which way to vote. While she had advocated for detached, logical thinking, he could see how carefully she had picked her words to evoke the deepest sense of loyalty and patriotism from the senators. He knew now based on their expressions that many would now vote out of emotion instead of detachment.

Very well done, he thought.

"All in favor?" she asked.

Alastair gracefully rose to his feet and saw that some rose quickly while others hesitated before clambering to their feet. More and more Senators stood until a quarter of the assembly was standing. Half. Alastair craned his neck until he could see Prokopios on the other side of the room. Their eyes met and Alastair raised his chin slightly and knew his eyes were flashing in warning. Prokopios bowed his head for a moment and Alastair fought to keep his fingers from clenching before Prokopios slowly rose to his feet.

Dozens of senators then sprung from their seats after seeing the old senator stand and now two-thirds of the Senate was standing in favor of the proposal.

It was good to see that Prokopios remembered owing Alastair a debt. He had certainly waited long enough to collect on it. He would have preferred to wait a while longer but perhaps Prokopios deliberately didn't vote earlier to redeem that favor now. Cunning, even if Alastair had gotten him out of a tight spot years ago from his own foolishness. Right when he began to think that Prokopios might have scraped together some intelligence since the last time they spoke, he noticed the older man quickly glancing over at Sophie. She didn't react, even if her eyes darted ever so slightly back at him before he quickly turned his head away from her.

Ah, Prokopios was not so astute after all, Alastair thought to himself. Sophie must have known Prokopios owed Alastair a favor and hatched a plan to force Alastair to call in that favor now instead of later on when he might need it more.

Sophie spread her arms and proclaimed, "The proposal has been adopted. It is now passed and binding. We should send a messenger in the spring to Leondria to see if they acquiesce to our *alliance*."

Sophie smirked at the word alliance and there were chuckles around the room. Leondrians were known for their strength, not intelligence. They should be easy enough to manipulate. If the Apistians played the game just right, they could even dismantle the Leondrians altogether. Especially without them being able to hide behind Lady Meraki for protection anymore and having inexperienced queens at the helm.

But Midrios's survival came first, and Alastair was willing to work with his enemies for as long as necessary to protect Apistia before satisfying his own personal desires. His city-state and country were counting on him, and he would act as his oath of office demanded of him.

Then he would indulge, drinking from the well of revenge like the sweetest of wines.

"The next necessary step is to decide on a messenger." Sophie announced. "Someone with the erudite prowess to survive an odyssey to and from Leondria."

The room grew silent, knowing the true question was who would be daring enough to embark on a dangerous journey from Apistia to Leondria where they might kill yet again.

Alastair smirked as he thought of ideas.

CHAPTER

22

Zosime was getting tired of walking. Not tired in the physical sense, of course. She could walk for hours without discomfort, but she was growing restless that they had done nothing else for days. It wouldn't be so monotonous if they were running. She would be content if she could feel the pounding of her golden sandals against the ground, her heart galloping in exhilaration, and the wind teasing her hair. But the others wouldn't be able to keep up with her so she resigned herself to walking.

At least Flavian was a great source of entertainment every night when he would retell their history so vividly that it felt like she was living it herself. She did have to pull him aside a few nights ago to tell him not to relate the story of Anastasia and Typhon again during their mission when she had felt Anastasia's reaction. She had felt his immense surprise about her making such an order, but he hadn't repeated the story since.

Zosime felt—pain? No, resentment? Was it anger?—from Anastasia anytime it was told. She couldn't ban it back home with thousands of Leondrians around, but she could forbid its telling in their small group to spare her feelings on this mission.

She really wanted to know why Anastasia felt so negatively about something that had brought her so much honor. But she learned long ago that people resented it when she revealed that she knew what emotions they were experiencing at any given moment, so she decided not to say anything on the matter unless Anastasia brought up the subject first. The gods knew there were things that Zosime didn't want to talk about.

Have you come to play with us?

She didn't know how long ago she heard that strange voice, but it still disturbed her. The mere thought of it now sent shivers down her spine and made her eyes dart in every direction to survey her surroundings.

"Are you alright, my queen?" Anastasia asked.

Zosime turned towards her and found her frowning in concern. She swallowed then replied, "I'm perfectly fine."

Anastasia suddenly reached out and rested a hand on her arm, which stopped her mid-step. Stunned, she didn't say anything when Anastasia took a few steps closer to her. Leaning forward to whisper in her ear, which sent another round of shivers down her spine, Anastasia murmured, "Do you want to play a game with me?"

Zosime froze and Anastasia pressed her lips against her ear before straightening to look at her eye-to-eye.

"I said—" Anastasia laughed playfully like a light rain in May. Her golden locks and blue-grey eyes that had been radiating brighter than Anatole in his golden chariot died away and the color in her cheeks faded to a pale white. Her eyes widened in time with her lips to form the most haunting expression of sorrow that Zosime had ever seen.

Anastasia's mouth opened but a very different voice came out, starting off low before veering into a high giggle, almost like an old woman stuck in a half-memory of being a young girl, "Have you come to plaaaaaaaaaay with us?"

Fear instinctively coiled in Zosime's stomach which was quickly replaced with rage when she demanded, "What did you do to her?"

The world flickered inexplicably around her and Zosime fought to regain control of herself. For a fleeting moment, terror reared its ugly head and she suddenly wondered if she was still in the Trials. If she was still being tested to see if she was worthy to become a Leondrian and if the last handful of months had just been a strange continuation of those mind games. If she closed and opened her eyes right now, would she find herself in Lady Meraki's Forest with the Creature's red eyes flashing above her?

Anastasia's mouth opened and a cackle escaped from her lips. Dryas, Balthasar, Flavian, Alec, and Nicholas—who had been standing off to the side watching the exchange silently—formed a ring around them and began chortling in glee. Zosime suddenly remembered what had happened next in the Trials: asking the Creature its name, the fight, the flames, and the march back home.

None of that could have been imagined, Zosime thought resolutely to herself. She knew in her bones that she had truly awoken after living two of her worst nightmares and that the Creature had released her from its terrifying embrace. As real as this nightmare felt, she knew that it could only be taking place in her own head and that something else must now be holding her prisoner.

"Leave my dominion." she demanded with her chin raised in defiance. "My mind is my own."

Anastasia turned to Balthasar and chirped, "She figured it out, sister."

"We can still play!" he laughed and danced lithely, as if he was a young girl who could balance herself on top of beams of light.

Zosime cocked her fist back and summoned all her strength to punch this imposter pretending to be Anastasia. Her arm soared towards the amused face when her fist connected with air where the phantom-Anastasia had stood a moment ago.

She blinked and whirled to find that everyone was gone. The ground then began to rumble and she lost her footing. Bracing herself for the impact, she flung out a hand to slow down her fall right before she landed hard against the ground. The wind was knocked out of her for a moment then she looked up to find herself in an unfamiliar temple of white and grey where three crones were dancing around her in a triangle.

She felt her knees give out and she struggled to stand only to realize that her arms and legs were bound by brown ropes while the three strange women continued to dance. She glanced down at herself to discover that the rope wrapped around her was made of human hair. But unlike any other rope, no matter how hard she tried, Zosime couldn't break its hold on her.

A sudden feeling of helplessness soared in her chest as her efforts to escape continued to fail. There had only been one other instance where she hadn't been able to break free from some strange mental prison, but Zosime had at least been standing beside her fellow Trainees then. Here, she was lying in the prone position, utterly bewildered, alone, and unprepared for what was coming next.

She looked back up when she heard a strange whirling sound followed by what sounded like something getting cut.

Snip! Snip! Snip!

"Who is the harbinger of death for us all?" the youngest of the three crones sang.

"Who knows? Who knows?" the other two laughed. "We do!"

"Who is Zosime of Leondria?" the youngest cried out while approaching her.

To Zosime's horror, she could do nothing to stop this youngest crone from pushing her head down and ripping out a piece of hair.

"No one! No one! Just another string to be strung!" the other two laughed again.

"Queens and gods are not above the fate of our wheel." the youngest belted out while raising the hair she had just ripped out from Zosime's head up in the air for her sisters to admire.

Zosime's eyes watered in pain for a moment before she frantically looked around the room and discovered a strange instrument that stood behind the youngest crone. It was a conglomerate of many silver circles inside a major sphere that wasn't spinning properly and was so large that it almost touched the ceiling. All the circles had strands of hair linked around them and some of them intertwined with hairs in other circles. The back side of the entire sphere was a wall of hair, all woven together in individual braids of varying shades and textures like a loom. Many of the smaller wheels were smashed or dangling loosely, and it looked like the entire contraption was one breadth of wind away from falling over into pieces.

"Who dies? Who dies? the other two sang to each other. "All but one."

One by one, all three crones turned their heads towards her and their eyes burrowed into Zosime's very soul. Silver shears suddenly flashed into the youngest crone's hand before she demanded, "Who do we hold responsible for our broken wheel?"

The other two continued glaring at her when they chanted, "Zosime! Zosime! Zoooosime!"

Warning bells went off in her mind and she heard a loud *SNIP* before her eyes flew open. Zosime blinked rapidly as her eyes adjusted and she frantically looked around her while clenching the sword's hilt, ready to withdraw it at a moment's notice.

Zosime jerked her head to her right when she heard Anastasia ask, "Are you alright, my queen?"

Zosime blinked several times again, tensing as she waited for her to approach. She wondered if she would have to relive this nightmare over and over again and if she would soon find herself tied back up. She waited for several seconds with wide eyes for something to happen—for that beautiful face to distort and cackle maliciously—but nothing did. She then realized that they were all still sitting around the fire waiting for dinner to be ready, not the middle of the day like in the nightmare.

"My queen?" Anastasia asked again, this time with more concern. Her blue-grey eyes then widened and she stood, turning in a full circle as she studied their surroundings. "Do you sense an attack?"

The others then stood and rested their hands on their swords as looked around in search of any threat.

This was real, Zosime told herself. It had to be. She wiped away a little drool from her mouth, realizing that she must have dozed off while the others were talking.

"Vivid dream." Zosime finally said and cleared her throat. "I don't sense anything."

This seemed to placate everyone but Anastasia and Dryas, who both reluctantly sat back down but didn't press the issue. Balthasar went back to tending to the roasted rabbits cooking over the fire, Flavian stared longingly at the food, Alec began sharpening his sword, and Nicholas stretched his legs by the fire while fiddling with his knife.

"Chow's ready!" Balthasar announced a few minutes later.

After receiving their portions, everyone grabbed a large piece of cooked rabbit and hung it over the fire.

"We offer this sacrifice to Lady Meraki. May we live to die free." they all murmured reverently before dropping the juiciest portion into the flames.

They all then hovered close to the fire for warmth to counteract the winter breeze that stubbornly clung to the air around them.

"Tell us a story, Flavian." Balthasar suggested after taking a few bites of his rabbit.

Flavian grinned as he devoured his food and held up a hand in jest, "Hold onto your shield, Balthasar. When I finish eating."

"Losing your touch, Flavian?" Alec raised an eyebrow and Flavian narrowed his eyes at him.

"I guess Flavian is getting too old." Nicholas sighed. "Or too boring."

Balthasar lowered his face to hide his smirk while Flavian straightened in indignation. He then resembled a starving man that hadn't eaten in days when he swallowed the rest of his meal whole, despite the steam emanating from the meat and stood up.

Folding his arms, he demanded a little hoarsely, "Would we prefer a tragedy or a comedy tonight?"

The wizened voices still fresh in Zosime's ears, she ordered, "Not a tragedy."

"How about an adventure story?" Balthasar suggested nonchalantly despite the surprise she sensed from him by her command.

Nicholas grinned and asked mildly, "Aren't we already on one?"

"Bored already, Nicholas?" Flavian retorted.

"How about a retelling of the First Passage?" Dryas offered, his eyes still not leaving Zosime's since she had first woken up, and Nicholas shrugged indifferently.

"It's a good story when told right, assuming Flavian hasn't lost his touch." Alec joked.

Zosime hadn't heard that one in a while and it could be just what she needed to distract her from the nightmare clinging to her thoughts. She gave her nod of approval which prompted a spike of excitement from Flavian who took a moment to compose his thoughts before beginning, "Our first king of Leondria—King Alexandros—had three sons: Theofylaktos, Chrysanthos, and Agapitos. All three were young when their mother was killed and were all deeply affected by her death. King Alexandros became king and established Leondria but, as he grew older, he saw that he and his sons aged the same way as normal humans, even if they possessed god-like strength. His mind often turned to the question of succession. To continue what he had built in honor of his wife and to ensure the continuation of their line. He didn't want a weak system based on the eldest child automatically being chosen without proving themselves, especially if there was a child born afterwards that would be stronger and better suited for the position.

One of his sons fully believed in what his father was building but had no interest in ruling so he served by joining the Council. Another son would have taken over to make his father proud but lacked the temperament for the position. The third son had all the right qualities but didn't want to lead. King Alexandros knew his time in the mortal world was ending, which he kept secret from his goddess mother and his sons until his deathbed.

He had made it compulsory for all his sons to become Leondrians, but he would not force the mantle of kingship on them for then all under their protection would suffer. He had avoided the title when he was younger, and tragedy still followed. One who is forced to become king when they have no desire to rule is no king and he knew better than to force his sons into it, for then all his sacrifices would have been for nothing. Someone could only rule once they had embraced their duty. So he called this son before everyone and, not knowing of his father's plan, knelt before his king in front of his fellow Leondrians, the Council, and Lady Meraki."

Zosime couldn't help but notice how the fire crackled with that last statement.

"'My son!' King Alexandros had called out loud enough for all to hear. 'Your strength and loyalty are unparalleled, but your mind has wandered from your strong heart. You have been too distracted to reach your full potential to fulfill your duties as a Leondrian.' His son had gone still, expecting a formal reprimand before all or a proclamation that he would be named as his successor, despite his wishes to the contrary.

'Turn in your red cloak.' the king had then ordered, and the entire crowd froze in shock, including his two brothers. Numbed and confused, this son slowly rose and, with shaking hands, removed the red cloak from his shoulders and offered it to his father. 'You are stripped of your cloak and your title as Leondrian. You will leave Leondrian lands, and you will embark on a Passage until you bring back something of value to Leondria. Return before you do so, and your life will be forfeit.'"

Flavian's hands gestured around them, letting the silence add to the suspense before continuing, "The crowd was still stunned silent and they could scarcely believe their ears when King Alexandros proclaimed, 'One of your peers will offer you a gift to take with you on your journey.'

At first no one moved and then one brave Leondrian stepped forward and untied the ribbon holding her hair in place. Scarcely breathing, he held still as she tied the white ribbon around his wrist and pressed a kiss to the palm of his hand. She melted back into the crowd and King Alexandros boomed to the crowd again, 'Now he will receive the blessing of a goddess.'

All stared at Lady Meraki—radiating brighter than sunlight—who stepped forward to appraise her grandson. 'You are lost but you will find your way, my grandchild.' Her eyes glowed as she pressed her thumb against his forehead, and he seized for a moment as some intangible gift flowed from the goddess into the mortal. 'I bless you.' the goddess announced, and the crowd released its breath when Lady Meraki stepped away. The king took a moment to make the sign of the gods to her before returning his full attention to his son and declaring, 'I gift you your shield to remember Leondria's strength. You will now walk out the gates and not come back until you return with these gifts and a proper offering for Leondria without receiving any assistance from anyone else.'"

Flavian paused then continued the story, "The Fates had weaved their will into their wheel and prepared to cut his string—"

Zosime tensed and her mind unbiddenly returned to her newest nightmare and her ears were buzzing too loud for her to hear the rest of the story. All she could hear were the crones' taunts and the sound of shears cutting non-stop.

Snip! Snip! Snip!

Her fingernails dug into her biceps as the sound echoed louder and louder in her mind.

Snip!

Snip!

SNIP!

Zosime then flinched when she heard a loud crackle from the fire, and she looked up to find Flavian laughing.

"My aunt hates that story." he said with a wave of his hand.

Zosime blinked and looked around, seeing the others seated in different positions than she remembered.

She must have missed the rest of the story. She realized than wondered. How long had she been reliving that nightmare?

"Your aunt, the general, hates a story about rebellion?" Balthasar noted dryly.

"Did it live up to my audience's expectations?" Flavian asked with an air of superiority.

"You might be rehired." Alec said.

"And you?" Flavian demanded to Nicholas.

Nicholas only continued fiddling with the knife in his hand and shrugged, "It was satisfactory."

Flavian opened his mouth to protest when Zosime suddenly said, "I'll take first watch."

"Me too." Anastasia volunteered a moment later while everyone else froze in surprise.

She could still feel Dryas's concerned eyes on her and sensed the others' bewilderment at the abrupt change of subject. Everyone exchanged inquisitive glances with each other before Balthasar quipped, "I think our queen is hinting that we need our beauty sleep, boys."

Flavian, Alec, and Nicholas chuckled at that, and no one said anything else as they started lying down to go to sleep.

She already knew that it was going to be impossible for her to sleep and that she needed to brace herself for a long night. Her mind was still reeling from the fact that the Fates had just visited her dreams and the last thing she had seen before awaking was one of the women giving her a smile while playfully waving shears in front of her.

As if ready to snip the chord and end Zosime's life prematurely.

CHAPTER

23

Zosime thought the dawn would never come until she finally saw the first rays of dawn streak across the horizon. Anastasia hadn't protested when Zosime insisted on taking watch all night, but she refused to sleep when Zosime ordered her too, insisting she would keep watch with her queen. Zosime didn't have the energy to fight her and just shook her head in irritation as they waited out the night in silence together. Once she saw these rays streak across the horizon, Zosime and Anastasia began waking up the others and packing up camp. Zosime wanted to reach Palapao as soon as they could today and didn't want to waste precious seconds by letting the others sleep in. It wasn't long before they started walking and, to her relief, she only had to wait a couple of hours before they started seeing other people around. Zosime tried engaging these strangers in conversation, but they would only duck their heads and avoid her path, to her great surprise and increasing unease.

She couldn't figure out why people were so angry when they saw the red cloaks and why they were so afraid of them. It didn't make any sense to her since they were Leondrians, defenders of Midrios. They had protected Midrios from foreign threats and they had even defeated Typhon a few years ago. And yet, everyone went out of their way to shoot them dark looks or walk as far away from them as they could.

She tried to distract herself by studying the countryside around her and was stunned by its dreadful state. Unlike the vibrant green trees and proud mountains of Leondria, the ground here was marred. It was lined with cracks and such sharp dents that it looked like it would never heal. The land, like its people, also felt broken and angry.

Anastasia grew quieter after passing by the first crater which distressed Zosime since she felt that she had finally started to get to know her, and she suddenly shut back down. She suspected that the mood change could be attributed to returning to Palapao and hoped it would only be temporary. But she didn't know yet how long they would be here and couldn't shake the well of darkness she felt from her.

Zosime saw the rudimentary beginnings of a stone wall being built when they approached Palapao and was surprised that this city-state didn't have large, imposing walls with a front gate like the ones encasing the Hearth back home. What stunned her was not seeing any guards in sight and how they were able to walk straight inside without being stopped.

She sensed Dryas's concern as he stepped closer to her while Anastasia and Balthasar walked in front of them as they meandered further inside. Instead of a housing and barracks section close by the gates, Palapao had several rows of stalls where many people were clustered around and the whole area buzzed with noise.

But these weren't food stalls where vendors supplied nourishment to hungry warriors. Zosime's eyes widened when she saw that people were actually quarreling with the distributors behind the wooden stalls, instead of just being handed piping hot food on a plate. She tore her gaze away from these arguments and looked around her. There were a few buildings straight ahead of them and structures all over the place with no organization, as if the city-state grew faster than expected and they compensated for this change as quickly as they could.

She felt a hush creep over the crowd as they passed by people who took in their golden shields and bright red cloaks. Not much time passed until people automatically ducked out of their path and she caught Anastasia and Balthasar grimacing at each other.

"Ho! Leondrians!" a voice cried out and they turned to see a trader who must have been in his late teens waving them over.

"What are you doing, Christos!" a trader in the stall next to him hissed.

"Don't worry about it, old man." Christos retorted and his face brightened when they approached him while the older barterer mysteriously vanished. "How do you do?"

"Well." Balthasar replied. "You?"

Christos looked a little thrown by the brief response but quickly recovered, "It is a fine day. I have no complaints, none at all. What about the rest of your fine group?"

"We're all well." Zosime said and Christos frowned, studying her closer. Eyes widening, he breathed, "Are you—"

"We're seeking information." Anastasia interjected, more curtly than what was polite. "Would you be able to help us?"

Christos frowned and Zosime sensed his flash of recognition. He suddenly stiffened but his hard smile indicated that he wanted to keep up the pretense of civility.

"That'll cost you." he said coolly with the stiff smile still in place. "What do you have to trade?"

Zosime quickly looked at the others and Balthasar handed over the bag he had tied next to his sword. Christos took it eagerly and, after scouring through it, his smile dropped.

"Cooked meat. Old apples." he said curtly then pushed it back to Balthasar. "I know you have something better. Let's work out a deal."

"It's good meat." Balthasar insisted. "Food is always a prudent choice."

"If you were previously vetted and I knew how you handled it." Christos crossed his arms in irritation then his eyes gleamed a moment later. "But what about your shield? It looks well-crafted."

"Not for sale." Zosime said defensively, more than a little offended.

She was a Leondrian. Selling her shield would be paramount to treason and she would rather die than be parted from it, let alone selling it for a quick piece of information she could acquire in other ways.

"Are you sure?" Christos pushed. "One could buy quite a lot from trading it."

"She has spoken." Balthasar said firmly.

Christos hesitated for a moment then switched gears, "What about your red cloak? Winter may be over soon but one could always use extra layers for next year or to be put to other uses in the spring."

This wasn't quite as disrespectful as asking to sell her shield but was still an objectionable request. The red cloak was earned after a decade of shedding blood and countless sacrifices, not something that was casually given away to a stranger who didn't deserve to wear it. Zosime's first instinct was to tell him no, but she found herself hesitating.

Sensing a deal on the table, Christos said, "I'll make it worth your while. The cloaks for information and fresh food."

Zosime twisted her lips for a moment and Christos added with a wave of a hand, "Winter will be over in a matter of weeks. You won't need it to keep you warm. You'll forget you even had it in a few days."

Dryas then reached up to unpin his red cloak from his shoulders and Zosime raised a hand to stop him, "Do not sully your honor, Dryas."

Christos leaned forward and asked, "What honor is there in a piece of cloth? You won't need it and it'll be a fair trade."

"It is no trouble, Z—my queen." Dryas said, his eyes not wavering from hers.

"It is." Zosime protested.

"I have no objections parting with my cloak, my queen." Balthasar piped up and started reaching towards his shoulders.

"Stop." Zosime ordered and he froze.

She returned her attention to Christos and insisted, "We'd be grateful if—"

"I have babes to feed." Christos replied impatiently then demanded. "Do you have anything worth selling?"

Zosime retorted, "We have food, we have ribbons, and we can offer our protection services—"

"Waste of my time." Christos muttered before turning on his heel and vanishing from sight.

Zosime looked around to find most of the market had been deserted then turned to suggest to Balthasar, "We can try another one."

"No harm in trying, my queen." he agreed but Zosime didn't fail to notice the look of grim resignation on Anastasia's face.

It was as if she had been expecting this, Zosime thought in bewilderment to herself. But she sensed how everyone else in the group felt as surprised as she was by these reactions.

They walked over to the nearest stall that still had a trader in it. But when this trader saw them approaching, she brusquely told the customer she was with that she was closing for the day then fled the area. The customer glanced at them and quickly hurried away when Zosime opened her mouth to talk to her. The whole group looked at a loss for words for several moments before Balthasar finally cleared his throat.

"My queen." Balthasar said quietly. "Perhaps we should—"

He was interrupted by the sound of approaching sandals, and they turned to find a male who must not have been older than sixteen stroll towards them then make the sign of the gods.

They returned the gesture and Balthasar greeted, "Good afternoon, friend. I'm Balthasar and these are my traveling companions." Balthasar gestured to her and said, "This is—"

"I am aware of who travels with you." the boy interrupted shortly after glancing into Zosime's eyes.

Anyone who couldn't sense Balthasar's emotions wouldn't have known how irritated he was with the look of fury that this boy gave Zosime, but he still managed to ask cheerfully, "How may we help you, friend?"

The boy returned his attention to Balthasar and stiffly replied, "I am Governor Theodoros, one of the governors of Palapao who bid you welcome to our city-state. I was sent to ask you if you would like to join us for lunch as our personal guests."

Zosime couldn't have planned this better than if she tried, even if she did feel a flicker of wariness from Balthasar whose face never outwardly wavered from geniality.

"We would be honored to break bread at your table, Governor Theodoros." Zosime replied politely.

Theodoros didn't deign to respond, only holding his hands behind his back and leading them to the tallest building straight ahead.

"How long have you been a governor?" Balthasar asked cheerfully.

"Since Typhon's attack." Theodoros replied tersely and Zosime sensed his unbridled anger. "After my family perished from his flames."

Balthasar hesitated before replying, "Your loss is felt by all—"

Theodoros's eyes slanted as he looked sideways at him and hissed, "Is it?"

"Yes." Anastasia said and Theodoros glanced over at her.

"By you, maybe." Theodoros allowed, a shade less rudely.

"Do you remember me?" Anastasia asked quietly and he nodded.

"I don't forget a face, especially one that saved my life." he said but the hardness in his voice didn't dissipate.

Balthasar tried again, "How has rebuilding been going?"

"Well. Do you not see what progress we've made?" Theodoros asked acidly.

"Yes—" Balthasar faltered.

"Or does it leave much to be desired?" Theodoros interrupted.

"Palapao's governors have done a fine job." Balthasar insisted.

"Rebuilding takes time, and you didn't see what it was like before." Theodoros disagreed.

At this point, they arrived before a plain marble building with several white columns. It was much taller than the Heart but still looked designed for functionality, which Zosime approved of, and they followed Theodoros inside. Balthasar gave up on initiating any more attempts at conversation and they wordlessly trailed several steps behind the angry boy. He led them all the way down the hall then opened the door for them, gesturing for them to enter.

"Welcome, guests." a dozen people that must have been the other governors greeted when they walked inside. "Please, join us."

Zosime sensed the boy's simmering disdain as he walked past her and joined the others at the table. Each one of the governors introduced themselves and her party did the same, although she could sense that they already recognized her and Anastasia.

"Are you Perleros's boy?" Governor Agapetos asked Dryas once all the introductions were over, and they were served their meals.

"Yes." Dryas answered a little stiffly then gestured to Balthasar. "And so is my brother."

Governor Agapetos nodded and replied, "You're his spitting image." When Dryas didn't reply after a few moments, he continued, "I remember meeting him twenty years ago. What a force to be reckoned with."

Balthasar smoothly cut in for Dryas and said, "You honor us, Governor. Were they under good circumstances then?"

Governor Agapetos leaned back in his chair and took a sip of his wine before replying, "Very pleasant circumstances. I could tell right away he was a devoted subject and leader." he raised his glass towards Zosime then returned his attention to Balthasar. "Which looks like a trait he passed on to his sons."

Zosime sensed tension clinging to the air when the others noticed that Theodoros was glaring at her and hadn't touched his meal. Governor Dionysia, who was sitting next to him, whispered in his ear but he ignored her as he continued scowling at Zosime. He was clearly the youngest person here since the other governors looked like they were anywhere from their late twenties to early fifties.

"How is your journey going?" Agapetos asked but was cut off when Dionysia whispered something again in Theodoros's ear and he resolutely shook his head.

Theodoros seethed back at her, "I don't care about the consequences."

Thinking it was best to get this over with, Zosime asked, "What's on your mind, Governor Theodoros?"

"My queen—" Anastasia murmured.

"He was just leaving." Governor Dionysia said quickly.

"No, I wasn't." Theodoros shook.

Agapetos pleaded, "Please—boy—"

"Are we just going to pretend all is well and forgiven?" Theodoros blazed.

"This is not the time, place, or manner to act this way, boy." Governor Gaios reprimanded.

"It's governor, not boy, Gaios. And do you not want an explanation?" Theodoros demanded turned to face Zosime. "Where were you?" He slammed his hand against the table. "The legendary warriors? The two descendants of a goddess who stood by and did nothing while we were being slaughtered by Typhon! You come here ignoring everything we suffered, breaking bread with us and claiming to be our guests. For thousands of years, your people have claimed to be Midrios's protectors but you stood by while so many were ripped apart and Typhon razed our fields to the ground. No wonder the gods have forsaken us."

"Careful!" Governor Chares snapped in warning. "Else our guests get offended by something *construed as an insult.*"

Theodoros abruptly rose from his seat and Zosime honestly believed that he was going to leap across the table to attack her for a long moment. Then he unexpectedly made the sign of the gods before declaring not a little sarcastically, "Please excuse me, friends. I must beg your forgiveness. I am not feeling well, and I must go rest."

Every word was flawlessly polite, but its delivery was dripping with hostility, including the way he stalked out of the room.

The room was at a loss for words for a moment and she sensed severe distress from all the governors.

"He had to take his family's place too young, Queen Zosime." Governor Dionysia said quickly.

Zosime replied as smoothly as she could to show that she had not been insulted, "You have been most welcome, governors."

She could feel their relief and Governor Agapetos asked warmly, clearly overcompensating for Theodoros's rudeness, "Is there anything we can assist you with, Queen Zosime?"

"There is." Zosime inclined her head then inquired. "Have you received any concerning reports from the northeast?"

Zosime waited with bated breath as the governors frowned and they turned to confer quietly with each other.

Governor Chares said slowly, "The tribes around Karkaros have been more active lately."

"Bloodthirsty murderers." Governor Agapetos bit out. "I would avoid taking that route."

Not what she was looking for, Zosime thought impatiently to herself.

"Have you heard anything about any other threats that may be coming from the northeast?" Zosime asked.

"Not at all." Governor Dionysia replied. "Unless there's something you've heard that we haven't."

Zosime turned to Governor Agapetos, "Not even about Afshin?"

He frowned and responded in a puzzled tone, "He died. Twenty years ago, by your late father's hand."

"Are there any concerns you would like to share with us?" Zosime pressed when she felt flickers of unease from all the governors.

"Of course not, Queen Zosime." Governor Agapetos said smoothly but Zosime felt his discomfort despite the calm exterior and the smooth lie that followed. "Nothing at all."

CHAPTER

24

"How are you, father?" Daphne asked and Perleros glanced at her.

She may not have been his actual child, but he thought of her as a second daughter after she married his oldest son. It was custom for in-laws to be called by the same endearing terms one used with their blood family because marriages bonded two families together into one. There were no "steps" or "in-laws."

There was simply family.

Daphne had made a great addition to theirs and he was proud to have her as his second daughter. She was strong, thoughtful, and a perfect fit for his oldest son. Their offspring should prove equally strong, he thought, as he contemplated what his first grandchild would be like. He had waited for this moment for decades ever since he and his closest friend had learned their wives were with child at the same time. They had talked about becoming brothers by the laws of gods and mortals if their children grew up to marry each other.

To Perleros's great worry and alarm, it was not long afterwards that King Atreo had started to change, and he had ultimately lost the battle to madness.

Zosime eerily reminded him of her father with their thirsts for adventure, constant jokes, and willingness to put everything on the line without a second thought. Vasiliki was much more like her mother with her superior discipline, quieter demeanor, and the deep, introspective looks on her face.

Only the Fates knew if either or both daughters would start exhibiting signs of madness, but Zosime so often reminded Perleros of her father that he had kept a particularly close eye on her all her life to see if there were any signs of madness lingering under the surface. He had seen his friend slowly descend then plummet into insanity and he dreaded the thought of seeing these two girls he had watched grow up suffer from the same illness.

He then remembered that Daphne was waiting for him to tell her how he was doing but he wasn't about to burden her with his problems.

"The gods bless us with a beautiful day, daughter." he finally responded. "How are you?"

"Always well." she said cheerfully.

Perleros noted the dark circles under her eyes, but he didn't comment on them. He knew all too well the toll of having a loved one gone for long periods of time, but she was a Leondrian and could manage it.

"I would love to get a snack from the vendors if you can spare the time." she suggested after a few moments of silence.

He reflexively opened his mouth to say he didn't have the time then caught himself. While he had a tremendously busy schedule most days, he was no longer trying to lessen the vacuum of a missing monarch which gave him some free time today. He had long ago learned that his time in this life was finite, and he then thought that he would regret not taking her up on her offer.

So, he responded to her request by offering his arm to her and her knees wobbled slightly as she stood up from the chair before resting a hand on her stomach. Perleros knew that they would still have to wait a while before she would be due to deliver but, based on how large her stomach already was, his grandchild would grow up to become a strong Leondrian. The thought made him smile proudly for a moment before he regained control of himself as they walked outside into the cold air.

"I heard news about Balthasar from some vendors this morning." Daphne smiled as he closed the door behind them. "It's old—weeks old— but the group has been seen in Palapao."

Perleros kept the surprise off his face but was grateful for the update, patting her arm he still held as he helped her walk down her house steps. This past year had exemplified Leondria's poor intelligence gathering skills, which was a weakness they needed to overcome. Collecting information had never been their strong suit and staying within their borders for twenty years as they had found out this year had only worsened the problem.

He was reminded daily of his failures, but he had done his best for twenty years to serve his people and obey Lady Meraki's final orders to him. She had been a steady presence in Leondria before King Atreo died, but he had been shocked to see her when they spoke right before she disappeared for two decades.

He had remembered the rage that had propelled him forward in their hunt for Spyridon for stealing the twins right before he last saw his goddess. Thankfully, they had found them at the holiest place in Midrios, and he had felt no remorse in cutting down the traitor Leondrians who had assisted this so-called holy man in kidnapping the King's children.

After slaying these traitors, he had then turned to Spyridon, ready to haul him back to Leondria to make an example out of him. To strike the worst kind of fear in the hearts of lions as a stark warning of what happened to traitors.

Before Perleros could approach him, a bright light had suddenly scorched his eyes and Perleros had been forced to turn away until his vision returned. He had blinked rapidly—wondering how Spyridon had done that and preparing to chase after him—before realizing that Lady Hermione stood protectively in front of the so-called holy man.

"My Lady!" Perleros had exclaimed in awe then hastily made the sign of the gods.

"I forbid you to kill this man." she had declared, her body glittering brightly with power.

It was unthinkable to question a goddess, but Perleros—unsure if he heard correctly—had only blinked and repeated, "My Lady?"

"Was this holy week not made in my honor?" she had demanded, her melodious voice sharpening in displeasure.

"Yes, my Lady." he had replied.

"I forbid any further bloodshed." she had ordered, and he was relieved that her voice wasn't filled with wrath. He had heard too much rage from gods in his time and he didn't know if his nerves could handle hearing such powerful fury again.

"Yes, my Lady." he had said and resigned himself to the fact that he would have to let this filthy excuse of a person go.

She had dropped her hand then unexpectedly closed the distance between the two of them, whispering in his ear, "Listen to the wind and answer when she calls."

Before he could speak, Lady Hermione had taken a step back and vanished from sight. The world around them had then seemed a much darker place in her absence, despite the rising sun. Perleros had sheathed his sword as Spyridon smiled in triumph and strolled towards the lake. He had begun to bend over two wooden objects when Perleros, eyes widening in realization, shoved him aside and knelt before the two tiny, wooden boats. He had nearly wept in relief when he saw that his friend's daughters were alive and unharmed.

"Look at the marks." Spyridon had instructed in a haughty tone and Perleros had flashed him a look of deepest loathing before looking back down at the infants.

His mouth had then dropped open when he saw that they had both received the mark of the Queen then whispered, "It's not possible."

"Oh, it is." Spyridon had laughed and said in a superior tone like he alone had all the answers in the world. "The gods have spoken."

Perleros had then risen to his feet and walked over to the holy man, looming over him with his hand resting on his sword's hilt.

"You are no longer welcome here." Perleros had warned menacingly. "The gods spared your life once, but they won't do it again if you ever trespass on our lands again."

"Do you think I care for my life?" Spyridon had scoffed. "Everything I do is for the gods, and if they demand my life in their service, then so be it."

"Do you think your cause will outlive you?" Perleros had taunted then threatened. "Your followers are dead. So, you can fail and never be reunited with the gods if you ever return or you can flee and continue in their service."

Perleros hadn't been able to stop his lip from curling in disgust when Spyridon froze. What a weak, pathetic hypocrite, Perleros thought to himself. He had then frowned when Spyridon's eyes rolled into the back of his head, and he had been immobile for several long seconds before his body sagged and he opened his eyes again.

"The wind has spoken." the holy man had whispered then straightened.

Perleros would never dare to defy Lady Hermione, but he had clenched the hilt until his knuckles went white before demanding, "Get out and never come back."

"Long may they serve." Spyridon had proclaimed while glancing at the twins before calmly walking away, not even sparing a glance back at the followers he had condemned to death.

The words had haunted Perleros, but he had only unclenched his grip and picked up his friend's daughters. They had then quickly but carefully began riding back to the Hearth with the loyal Leondrians who had accompanied him, only stopping when they made camp for the night.

In their concern for the twins' health, they had built a tent around them and Perleros insisted on being the one to keep watch all night beside them. He had already failed them by not protecting their parents and from preventing them from being kidnapped but he could not trust anyone else to watch over them.

The night had come early—an early sign of impending winter—so he hadn't known how long he had kept watch until he saw a flash of white light. He had reached for the hilt of his sword then froze when he saw that Lady Meraki now stood right in front of him in her full glory. Her tan, olive-colored skin radiated brightly, and her brown hair was braided down her back and tied together with a white ribbon. An old, red cloak had hung from her shoulders, and she had been wearing full battle armor which only furthered Perleros's concern about an imminent war with the gods.

"My Lady!" Perleros had whispered in shock then quickly stood up, his eyes widening when he noticed that her hands were still stained red from Atreo's blood.

"My time here grows short." she had said brusquely.

"Yes, my Lady." he had replied even though he did not know what she meant by that.

Her red-brown-yellow gaze fell on the children for a long moment before redirecting her attention towards him. It was hard to meet those eyes that reminded him so much of the friend he had just lost but he didn't look away from his goddess. Without warning, she had taken a step forward and clutched his arm so hard that he was sure that she had broken something.

"My line must remain Leondrian at all costs. Stay in Leondria's borders and remain vigilant for threats." she had commanded, her fingers leaving a dent in his forearm.

He had ignored the pain and only said, "Yes, my Lady."

Her eyes had then flared bright red, and she had warned, *"Beware Apistia. Do not trust her with them."*

Her eyes had flickered back to the girls, and he nodded to show her that he understood. In another flash of light, she had vanished and that was the last time that he had seen his beloved patron goddess.

His Lady had given him orders and he obeyed the best he could, but he sometimes wondered if he failed to properly follow them. He wondered if he effectively prepared the twins for their roles as queens. It was desperately clear they were lacking the experience needed for the position with Vasiliki wanting more time than she had to make decisions and Zosime not thinking about consequences when she acted. He wished that a long mission with Anastasia and Balthasar would positively influence the rash queen and that Vasiliki being the sole voice in a room would give her the confidence she needed to lead. She had been doing better with acting faster and giving commands which gave him hope.

What did concern him was that they hadn't heard further reports about Zosime's progress. They should have been further than Palapao, but they were probably being diligent with stopping at multiple villages and were likely slowed down by the winter weather.

"He is strong." was all Perleros said in response to Daphne when she looked up at him expectantly. "Balthasar will perform his duty remarkably, and he'll be home soon."

He had full confidence in his son. This was a perfect opportunity for Balthasar to come back with honors to hasten a promotion to the officer corps. He then idly wondered how Dryas was doing but he hoped the trip would be a good experience that taught him how the world worked.

"General." two aides approached him and Perleros already prepared himself to be dragged away.

The aides remained silent, and it only took him a moment to realize why they had sought him out.

Daphne's eyes softened in understanding, and she reassured him, "We'll grab food another time, General."

Perleros didn't waste time with niceties and followed the two aides out of the busy section of the Hearth and hurried towards the Tower.

One of the two guards standing by its one entrance said, "The Council demands your presence, General."

The guards opened the door for him and stepped to the side to give him enough room to enter. He said nothing as he stepped over the threshold and the guards closed the doors behind him, leaving him in pitch-black darkness.

He carefully took a step forward until he felt the first stair then slowly climbed to the top floor. He did not fear the dark but not having any visibility made his skin crawl as he recalled past instances of being ambushed.

He ignored his howling knees and thought that growing older was its own test of strength. He paused for only a moment when he finally reached the top step where he knew the Council would be waiting for him then walked onto a wide landing. Torches lined the walls which provided enough light to enable him to see his surroundings again. He blinked as his eyes adjusted and then he saw all the Council members waiting for him in a single line.

"Your report on the queens, General." they intoned together.

There were no names here, only titles. Perleros would only be "General", and the Council members were only "The Honored Nameless Ones." Through some strange secret training, those who joined the Council somehow acquired the ability to lose all sense of self, so they somehow moved and spoke at the same time. All with the same cadence, rhythm, and pitch. It was an uncanny thing to see, and it was supposed to be a testament to how well they lived up to their duty by being the ultimate role models for Leondrians.

They were supposed to, at least. Perleros hadn't failed to notice worrisome signs in recent years, such as the Council encroaching on the queens' power and not respecting their authority. The most recent transgression in his opinion occurred when they didn't return their kneels at their coronation to illustrate mutual respect and cooperation during their reign.

He had noticed small changes over the last couple decades. Since they didn't have a monarch for twenty years, the Council had steadily expanded their power. Perleros had done what he could and obeyed where he couldn't argue, but he was deeply troubled at how far they would be willing to go.

Perleros made the sign of the gods and said, "Queen Vasiliki rules Leondria while Queen Zosime is gathering intelligence to confirm if there is a threat from the northeast to determine if we should prepare for war, Honored Nameless Ones."

"We rule Leondria, General." they hissed and Perleros bowed his head.

Another troubling sign.

"You did not stop her." they accused, a hint of anger in their collective voices, even though this was not the first time they had reprimanded him about it. "Tell her that she required *our* approval to do such a thing."

"I offered my counsel, but she gave me an order." Perleros responded respectfully.

"A General who cannot control a new Leondrian is no General." they said and Perleros kept his face blank even if his eyes flickered around him.

"I will follow the Council's command, Honored Nameless Ones." was all he said in reply.

He heard a strange buzzing for a few moments before it suddenly ceased and they said, "A queen who does not listen is no queen. A general who does not inform us of such updates and forces us to acquire this information through other means is no general."

Perleros kept silent and did not voice his objections. They would not get a rise out of him, and he would take their insults without complaint.

"Any signs of madness from the queens?" they asked and Perleros felt his blood run cold.

"No, Honored Nameless Ones." he denied.

It was true that he hadn't seen any symptoms from either of them, but it was a lie to say he hadn't seen any troubling signs.

"Leave, General." they ordered and Perleros was careful as he turned around and headed down the stairs.

As he left, he could have sworn he heard them murmur, "Any more signs of disrespect and we will need to step in."

He hastened his pace in case they said anything else that he was not meant to hear. He pushed the door open when he reached the bottom step, and the bright light of day seared his eyes when he stepped outside.

Perleros feared no man; he was not afraid of death, war, or pain. What did concern him was Leondria's future if they were attacked and they were still divided like this. Everything he had held together for twenty years was slipping through his fingers and the idea of everything he valued in this world falling apart made his heart start beating erratically in his chest.

He didn't know how to live in a world where he wasn't serving Leondria and the prospect of losing it terrified him.

CHAPTER

25

Dryas would have done anything to avoid disappointing Zosime. He only wanted to serve and honor her, but he had to admit that he wasn't entirely sure where he stood in her life or with the group on this mission across Midrios.

He hadn't expected her to invite him to come. While he knew Zosime very well from a decade of staying in close quarters together, there were still times that she surprised him. No other first year Leondrian would ever have been given permission to go on such an important mission, and he knew that any misstep could cost him with the others.

He made sure to stay focused and disciplined throughout the mission. To show Zosime and Balthasar that he could handle the responsibility. That he wouldn't joke around too much and he would embody Leondria's virtues. He wouldn't let them down by acting too familiar with Zosime or even giving the appearance that he wasn't taking the mission seriously. Not that he didn't enjoy listening to Flavian when he told stories every night or smile at Alec's and Nicholas's banter.

It had been a gift to have all this time with Zosime and Balthasar, but he was concerned about people's reactions when he returned home. He would either be treated with honor for accomplishing this task or be spurned for being so favorably singled out. Dryas got along well with other Leondrians, but he had heard the occasional rumor about him being close with the queens. Nothing too malicious, but he was worried that these rumors would only grow worse.

He then thought about Vasiliki and hoped she was bearing her duty well all alone back home. He knew she had been struggling with all the new changes in her life, but his thoughts soon returned to Zosime, who he was the most concerned about now.

She was never well-rested, but Dryas couldn't help but notice that she had been getting less sleep than usual lately. He couldn't shake the feeling that something was bothering her that she wasn't telling anyone about. He knew the exchanges with the man with the cart and Theodoros had bothered her, but he believed that it was something else that was keeping her awake lately.

But those two interactions had been eye-opening for Dryas. They had been instructed time and again about their duty to protect everyone as Leondrians and how important their service was to Midrios. Yet, if they were truly perceived as protectors, they wouldn't have received all those fearful and angry expressions. He had quickly realized that they weren't the beloved protectors their superiors had always led them to believe and the rest of the country's opinion of them would pose a significant obstacle if war was truly coming their way.

It also worried him that Midrians seemed divided with each other in every interaction he had observed in the villages they had briefly visited and even Palapao.

He was sure that Typhon's rampage didn't help their image but that alone wasn't enough to explain the reactions from people outside of Palapao. He had then concluded that something must have happened that Perleros hadn't told them about. Again.

He knew Balthasar didn't understand his frustration towards their father. He was the eldest child and obeyed Perleros's commands without a second thought, even after their father stood by and did nothing while his mother wasted away. He had never expected his father to be perfect, but his failure to do everything in his power to try to save her made his blood run cold every time he thought about him.

Dryas understood how important duty was, but his father never cared about how his family was affected by each action he took. It wasn't his father's commitment to duty that infuriated him so much. It was Perleros's breach of loyalty that he would never forgive, not to mention his obsession with the family legacy. Balthasar was happy with Daphne and was a great leader but that didn't seem to be enough for Perleros.

At least he was on the other side of the country, Dryas thought savagely, far away from him.

They had left Palapao after their failure to find someone with information about Afshin. Not even the governors could assist them so, after a few weeks of hoping a trader would be able to help them, they had decided to not waste any more time there and go further north. The bitter cold winds hadn't ceased but the snow was melting faster with each passing day, so Dryas knew winter was winding to an end.

The end of winter meant they would be able to move faster but Dryas still mentally prepared himself for trouble as they crested the end of the mountain chain and began heading east.

They were about to enter tribal territory, and Dryas remembered the governor's warning about them being violent. He knew he needed to be extra vigilant here, to sharpen his eyes for the most miniscule of details. It could be the difference between life and death, and he would never forgive himself if his failed to notice something that got Zosime killed.

She had still not recovered from whatever was bothering her, so he decided to talk to her about it since she needed to be focused before they entered hostile territory. There was a time when he wouldn't have hesitated to say anything to her but that was before she became his queen. The only thing he hadn't been able to tell her was how deeply he felt about her. He lost count of how many times the words were on the tip of his tongue when he stopped himself. He worried that she wasn't ready to hear it since she had so much on her plate, especially now that their relationship had permanently altered.

Balthasar went to great pains to remind him of that. No, he couldn't go visit her in the Heart whenever he wanted. No, he couldn't go up and talk to her in the morning before her meeting with her generals. No, he couldn't joke around with her or smile at her anymore.

She was his queen now. She was a great one too, filled with fire, passion, and a desire to serve Leondrians. He knew she needed to temper her spirit a little, but that would come in time. He knew his father didn't appreciate this aspect about her and he was now reaping the seeds he had sewn from his litany of failures. If Perleros had been willing to bend the rules just a little, then this transition wouldn't have been so hard on his friends.

Dryas wasn't arrogant enough to think that a general's job was easy, but he was certain that he would have done things differently. He would have slowly exposed Vasiliki and Zosime to the demands of their position so they could have learned how to manage their duties long before their coronation. He would have allowed them to fight Typhon when it looked like the end was near, instead of ordering them to remain behind just because they were Trainees.

He wasn't rigid like the older generations. Times had changed and Dryas was convinced that Leondria needed to adapt if they were going to survive. He didn't know why the people in charge didn't understand that. He supposed that was the biggest divide between his generation and the older ones: the recognition for the need for change. But they weren't old enough yet to enact that change and they would likely have to wait years before they could. Had to wait until the older generations were dying off and waning in power.

Dryas thought about all this as he looked for his opportunity to speak to Zosime, but it was not the easiest feat to get her alone when they were part of a small group that stayed close together.

Today was different though since Anastasia and Balthasar had gone hunting while Nicholas and Alec went searching for a nearby stream to replenish their depleted water. Dryas knew it was now or never when he, Zosime, and Flavian were building a small pyre with the sticks they had collected half an hour ago.

He put another stick on the growing pyre and looked up at her before stating, "Queen Zosime."

"Dryas." she replied then straightened. In a serious tone that suggested that she sensed his concern, she asked, "What's on your mind?"

He didn't want to talk with Flavian next to them to overhear the conversation, so he casually suggested, "Want to gather more sticks with me so we don't have to gather more after dinner?"

"Of course." she agreed without hesitation and gestured for him to lead the way.

"We'll be back in a minute." she told Flavian who had raised his eyebrows for a moment then shrugged with indifference.

They walked just far enough to be out of sight when Zosime asked, "What is it, Dryas?"

He took a breath to compose himself then confessed, "I'm concerned, my queen."

She gave him a humorless smile and said, "I know."

"You haven't been sleeping well." he pointed out.

"I never sleep well." she retorted, but the dark circles under her eyes had never been so pronounced before.

He gave her a disbelieving look and pushed, "I know something is on your mind, my queen."

He could just barely see a muscle twitch in her jaw when she replied stubbornly, "Many things are."

He took a step closer—one step too close to be construed as a concerned friend—and whispered as he stared intently into her eyes, "My queen."

He could see the flame of defiance in her eyes, mixed with some emotion she was wrestling with. A part of him was hurt that she didn't think she could trust him but, knowing her, she didn't want to burden him.

"You can tell me anything." he continued. "At any time and I'll be here. But if you don't want to talk about that, we can talk about Palapao."

Her chin lowered and she opened her mouth before closing it a moment later.

"What happened to Theodoros's family is not your fault." Dryas said.

Zosime stiffened and shook her head slowly, "I have a responsibility, and I didn't live up to it. A boy's entire family was slaughtered. Too many people were murdered because I didn't do anything."

"It's not your fault." Dryas insisted. "You obeyed your orders, and you couldn't do anything then."

Zosime shook her head again with an exasperated sniff and Dryas knew that she was still blaming herself based on how many lives she could have theoretically saved.

"You were being a good Trainee who listened to her superiors. You *couldn't* have done anything then." Dryas asserted. "But now you can. Just make a promise to yourself to act now that you have the power to do something."

That got her attention and Dryas prided himself on being able to speak Zosime's language when she slowly nodded.

"I can do that." she whispered before vowing fervently. "I will do that."

His heart squeezed in admiration, and he murmured, "I lo—"

"My queen! Dryas!" a voice called out and Dryas instinctively took a few steps back as Balthasar strolled up to them without a care in the world.

"We're cooking rabbit. Again." Balthasar laughed then put a hand over his chest. "My favorite, my queen."

In that moment, Dryas inwardly cursed Balthasar's name for his poor timing.

"Not as good as lamb." Zosime replied dryly as she crossed her arms.

Balthasar rested a hand on Dryas's shoulder and steered him away from her, "I can help Dryas with gathering more sticks for the fire, my queen."

Zosime nodded coolly and said, "Whatever you need to do, Sergeant."

Dryas recognized that all too familiar expression on her face when she had read someone's emotion and was pretending not to let on that she did. He clenched his fists in anger as Balthasar practically shoved him forward as Zosime walked back to camp. He wasn't a little kid that could be pushed around by his older brother anymore, even if his older brother outranked him.

Scowling, Dryas said, "Bal—"

"You need to get serious, brother." Balthasar interrupted.

"I'm serious where it counts." Dryas disagreed, hurt that his brother hadn't noticed how hard he had worked to make him proud during this mission.

"Not with this." Balthasar clarified before declaring. "You need to accept she doesn't love you back."

"She does." Dryas disagreed as his heart started pounding in indignation.

He knew beyond a shadow of a doubt that she loved him and considered him her closest friend.

"Not like you do." Balthasar corrected in a heavy tone. "Do your duty: find a wife and start a family after we return."

"Speaking for father again?" Dryas accused angrily.

"No," Balthasar said, and Dryas blinked in surprise. "He would rejoice if you two were betrothed."

"What do you know about it?" Dryas demanded. "Do you know what you interrupted? I was finally about to declare myself and you ruined it!"

Balthasar looked down and sighed, as if interrupting Dryas's proclamation of love had pained him instead of Dryas.

"You need to do your duty, but it would kill you if you married her, assuming she even agreed to it." Balthasar finally said. "There's a reason you never told her how you felt before, Dryas."

"She just became queen and was told war was likely coming to our doorstep." Dryas replied angrily. "I wasn't about to push her on another life changing issue, but I was finally going to tell her how I felt before *someone* interrupted me."

"I spared you." Balthasar responded evenly, sounding even more pained. "Even ignoring that issue, brother, there's something you don't know about their family."

"She is my family!" Dryas seethed. "No matter what she chooses to do."

He expected Balthasar to push back but, to his surprise, Balthasar only sighed heavily again and remarked, "You are so much like father."

Rage soared in Dryas's veins and his voice was a shade too soft to be taken casually when he proclaimed, "I am *not* like him."

"Self-deception is for the weak." Balthasar chastised. "You need to move on and pick a suitable wife when we get back. One who will actually love you back."

"Loyalty isn't weak." Dryas countered.

"Don't misunderstand me, brother." Balthasar snapped. "It's beneath you. All you're doing is hurting her, yourself, and Leondria."

His brother's words cut Dryas deeply and had more truth in them than he wanted to admit to himself. As deeply as he loved her, an instinctive part of himself recognized the expression on her face before Balthasar interrupted them. An expression that was part fear, part concern, part wariness, and all pain.

"Being distracted is undisciplined." Dryas finally said tersely. "I need to gather more sticks for the fire."

Dryas turned his back on his brother who didn't follow him as he walked away. He didn't know what tomorrow would bring but he feared that it wouldn't be anything good.

CHAPTER

26

"Watch everything and make as little sound as possible. We don't know what we'll be walking into, so we'll be going at a fast pace with no stops." Zosime ordered and everyone made the sign of the gods in acknowledgment.

Anastasia watched her queen closely and listened intently as she crept forward beside her. All they needed to do was to cross through this final portion of Midrios and traverse the Karkaros mountains then they would be in foreign territory. But they first had to pass unnoticed by the tribes and they didn't want to take any chances now. Not when they were this close to leaving and being within reach of accomplishing their objective.

Anastasia wouldn't permit anything to happen to her queen, so she kept a hand on her sword, ready to pull it out at a moment's notice. The terrain here was even more mountainous than back home, and it was hard to see anything clearly past the next hill. That would work both in their favor and against them. They weren't familiar with the area but both sides would have poor visibility. She hoped that, if her group couldn't see any wandering tribes, then they wouldn't be able to see them either.

She kept her ears sharpened for any threat and listened like all their lives depended on it. Zosime was true to her word and walked much faster than their previous pace but not so swiftly that the others couldn't keep up. Hours passed in silence and Anastasia kept an eye out for anything unusual. While Queen Zosime's ability to sense impending attacks was a useful power, it didn't seem to be the most consistent on how soon it warned her of imminent danger.

So, she kept a close eye on Queen Zosime, like she had throughout their journey as Perleros requested, and had been impressed by her selfless drive to help others without a thought for herself. But she had grown concerned about the queen ever since the day that they ran into the man with the cart.

Unlike the others who had never left Leondria, Anastasia wasn't surprised by the Midrians' hostile reactions. She had seen the looks on the survivors' faces after she slew Typhon and knew there would be resentment towards them for failing to act sooner. She knew their disgruntlement would only worsen when they didn't stay to help rebuild. To help get them back on their feet before withdrawing instead of letting them wallow that much longer in misery.

It was never her intent to soar through the ranks as high as she did in the aftermath of such tragedy. She had wanted to become a Leondrian her whole life, but she had to confess to herself that the revelations she had during the Trials still haunted her to this day.

How she missed mama and her comforting warmth. Mama did what she could to protect her and had given her important survival lessons before she left for Training. Anastasia dearly missed her and wished that mama had lived long enough to see her don the red cloak after passing the Trials.

Anastasia suddenly raised her head, frowning. She snapped her head to the left and peered into the distance and wondered if the noise she had just heard had been real. Her eyes narrowed then widened when she saw a shadow high up on one of the tall hills.

Not just one, she realized, as she stared at it closely. She could just make out the outlines of several figures who weren't moving, as if they were carefully tracking their progress. As if ready to ambush them at any moment.

"My queen." Anastasia murmured and Zosime tilted her head towards her slightly. To show that she was listening without being obvious about it. "We have lurkers."

Everyone moved their hands to the hilt of their swords and started to move faster when Anastasia muttered, "Keep the same pace."

They slowed down slightly but Anastasia feared that, between her stare and their reactions, they had showed their hand. She glanced out of her peripheral to look at the figures on the side of the mountain, but they were gone. Anastasia clenched the hilt of her sword even tighter and stared resolutely at the looming Karkaros mountains.

They were so close.

Each step brought them nearer and she feared they were on the brink of disaster. That those lurkers would strike when they were on the precipice of succeeding.

She took a step and looked around. Then she took another step and glanced around again. Step, look. Step, look. Step, look. This was eerily reminding her of the fight with Typhon when they had arrived at the remains of Palapao right before he unleashed a deadly attack.

Was that smoke and burning flesh she was smelling now?

She told herself to snap out of it and focus on the present. She couldn't afford another flashback like the one she had at the bonfire a while back. She sniffed again and looked to the right where she saw a village in the distance.

She and Balthasar shared a look, and they simultaneously shook their heads. They could stop to ask if they had heard anything—which was unlikely based on their previous encounters—but they didn't want to stop now with someone watching them. Especially considering that any random villager could head straight south and report their movements to the Apistians. They directed their attention back to the mountains and took a wide birth away from the village.

She could hardly believe their luck when they found themselves at the base of the Karkaros mountains and they practically let out a sigh of relief when they did.

She and Balthasar now looked at each other and he grinned at her. She smirked back and gave him a nod which only broadened his grin. They had known each other for years since they had been in the same Training class together, and while she had always respected him, she thought even higher of him since they left on this operation. Anastasia had many acquaintances but now it seemed like she had made a new friend which meant more to her than she could ever possibly express.

Balthasar appraised the group then said wryly, "Let's climb."

Zosime stiffened and Anastasia recognized the look on her face immediately. She immediately unsheathed her sword and spun around, seeing a woman in the distance who had spotted her queen. Anastasia channeled every threat of violence into her posture and the woman quickly turned away, pretending she hadn't seen them.

"Take the queen, Balthasar." Anastasia ordered, not bothering with niceties.

"Anasta—" Zosime began but was cut off when Balthasar shepherded her forward with Nicholas and Flavian.

"Go." Anastasia commanded when Alec and Dryas lingered behind the others. "I'll cover you."

Dryas still hesitated before she insisted that he leave to protect Zosime. He then begrudgingly left her behind and began climbing the mountain with the others. She stood in place for several minutes, waiting for a group to ambush them but nothing happened. She didn't move for a long time—probably for around an hour—before she decided it was safe enough to turn her back to anyone who may be lurking out of sight behind her and rejoin the group.

She sheathed the sword and began the trek up, surprised to find the pass narrowing the higher she climbed. Anastasia felt someone watching her again and her brow furrowed, looking around before glancing up to find a pair of godly grey eyes following her every move.

She glared back until those godly eyes disappeared and she shook her head vehemently in a mixture of anger and disgust.

She moved quickly to catch up and found them waiting, relief emanating from their faces when they saw that she had returned to them safely. The reunion was short-lived because she immediately suggested that they keep pushing forward. She wanted to put as much distance as she could between them and whoever had been watching them earlier.

It wasn't until the sun was teetering on the horizon with its pale golden rays desperately clinging to the sky that they decided to stop for the night. They didn't sleep much that night and maintained a quick pace throughout the next day, only stopping to camp at nightfall. Only one more day passed in this manner before they neared the base at the other side of the mountain.

When they arrived, all knew to expect treacherous and dangerous threats ahead of them. Anastasia saw Zosime square her shoulders, and take a deep, silent breath in. No one uttered a sound, and they only hesitated briefly before their sandals crossed into foreign lands.

PART
FOUR

CHAPTER

27

Alastair knew better than anyone the different levels of fear and how each one distinctly impacted people. The less fear someone felt, the more effort he had to exert to inflict pressure on them. The greater their anxiety, the less time he needed to put in to sway them, especially the witless who were susceptible to succumbing to the smallest pressure points. He did have to be careful in how far he intimidated them in case someone's distress was so great that they snapped and lost all their usefulness.

The key was to apply the right amount of pressure and to act when the time was right to optimize effective responses.

This principle was especially true with the situation at hand, and he had to wait before being able to make his move. The Senate had agreed to extend an offer of alliance, and this necessitated sending a messenger over to that barbaric city-state across the mountains. But no one wanted to be the lamb that was offered for the slaughter so their last several meetings had been unproductive as Senators viciously debated who to send to be Apistia's voice.

They would never admit it but most of them were too terrified to go to Leondria themselves. They gave their rationales that Senators were too valuable to send, and they couldn't possibly leave their constituents un-represented in the middle of the legislative session. But Alastair saw these proffered justifications for the flimsy excuses they were.

There was a consensus that they couldn't trust this task to just anyone and that they needed someone canny enough to negotiate a relationship with Leondria while maintaining favorable terms for Apistia. Alastair would have gone himself, but he knew it would be a grievous political blow to himself that Sophie would only exploit to her advantage.

He knew exactly who he wanted to send as soon as the Senate agreed on the alliance, but the time was now ripe to send him. If he had offered him up sooner, he knew his suggestion would have been shot down immediately and questions would have arisen even further regarding his judgment towards Leondria.

The looks had only grown worse since the rumors spread of Queen Zosime leading a group of Leondrians around the mountains that separated Leondria from Apistia. He noticed how the atmosphere in Apistia electrified, and he saw panic in many Senators' eyes as they agonized on whether there would be a repeat of what happened twenty years ago.

Most of them had only been able to breathe easily again when she had inexplicably turned east towards Karkaros instead of marching south towards them. The stranger part was that she hadn't been seen in Midrios since. He had initially found it puzzling that she would bring a small group with her to leave Leondria before a few key pieces of information sprung to Alastair's mind:

1. Queen Zosime only led a small group, not any substantial portion of her forces.
2. If she was last seen by the eastern border of Midrios, then they were remarkably good at hiding (which evidence indicated was not the case) or they had left Midrios.
3. There must have been something outside the country she badly needed if Queen Zosime went herself. Only the desperate and the unwise would have done such a thing so there must have been something she really needed.
4. She left Midrios with the group after the strange encounter Alastair had with Angelos.

Once he had connected these dots, it became painfully obvious what she was doing. Angelos must have talked to the queens about Afshin, and she was now trying to determine if the threat was legitimate. He thought it was foolish for someone of her position to go on such a mission when there were high odds that she would be killed or kidnapped for leverage.

Once that became clear, Alastair recommended to his fellow Senators that they needed to finally implement their plan to reach out to Leondria.

Especially since the early tides of spring had arrived which would make a messenger's journey over there much easier. He reminded them that Queen Vasiliki remained in Leondria and one queen would be easier to reason with than two. He urged them that now was the time to strike.

There were still concerns but his reasoning held up. Alastair could see the fear that drove their decision—which disgusted him—but he was pleased that he played his cards right and had been able to pick the messenger without losing political capital. Now Alastair just had to ask the man if he would be willing to go.

So, after this latest Senate meeting, Alastair found himself heading straight to the ships instead of going home to change first. His sandals clicked against the docks as he passed by several ships until he reached the one he wanted.

"Cap'n!" a familiar male voice cried out as he approached.

Alastair smirked and drawled, "Adonis. You and the boys drink all my liquor yet?"

Adonis winked while leaning over the edge of his ship with the others watched with reactions that varied between amused exasperation and indifference, "Once we find the rest of the stash."

"I only hide it because you ingrates drink it all without leaving me any." he muttered as he walked aboard.

"Is it time for another mission?" Adonis asked excitedly.

"No." he replied. "Where's the Lieutenant?"

Adonis raised an eyebrow and teased, "Where do you think, cap'n?"

Alastair laughed and shook his head as he followed his hunch where he thought his second in command would be.

"I recognize that look in your eye." Adonis noted as he followed close behind him. "You have something."

Alastair waved a very dignified hand as he walked down the steps into the cabin section of the ship and said, "Go be productive or drink where I'm not looking and set a bad example for the others."

"We'll be waiting for you, cap'n." Adonis grinned, lingering a few steps behind him on the stairs before heading back up. "I doubt we'll have to wait long."

"Don't drink all my liquor!" Alastair called back which resulted in a rumble of laughs up above and he resumed strolling down the wooden halls. It was a short walk to Sofoklis's cabin, and he knocked expectantly on the door.

"I thought you said they wouldn't bother us." a female voice complained from within.

He then heard a shushing sound and rustling from inside before his lieutenant opened the door.

"Sir." Sofoklis greeted solemnly in a clearly disheveled state.

Alastair appraised the tangled hair and what appeared to be a blossoming bruise on his neck for a moment before stating, "Let's grab a drink in my cabin."

Sofoklis was silent as he closed the door, and they walked the short distance to Alastair's cabin. Alastair gestured for him to sit in the chair by his desk and began ruffling through it. Those miscreants had found some of his stash and he had to stand on a chair and push a slightly discolored wooden beam in the ceiling up and away before reaching into a secret compartment to grab some of the good stuff.

After spending most of his days around Senators who had nothing better to do with their time than listen to themselves talk without saying anything of substance, Alastair enjoyed the stoicism of his second in command. It was nice to sit in silence now and again with someone who thought things through before speaking. Sofoklis was quiet as Alastair poured them drinks and he raised a glass to his lieutenant before taking a long moment to savor the rich burn of alcohol going down his throat.

After letting the silence sit long enough, Alastair raised an eyebrow at Sofoklis and gave him a cheshire grin before taking another sip.

"I'll tell her to leave, sir." Sofoklis finally said.

Alastair laughed and reassured him, "No need to get rid of her just yet, Sofoklis."

It wasn't an uncommon occurrence for the men to come back with girls to impress them with the ships and spend a night or two with them in their cabins. So long as it didn't interfere with their duties, he honestly didn't care what they did, and it did help alleviate tensions that often arose between people who spent too long together in close quarters.

Sofoklis peered at him with a look that only an old friend could give then asked in a matter-of-fact tone, "How can I assist, sir?"

"We're sending a messenger to Leondria in the hopes of establishing an alliance with them." Alastair said.

This was hardly news, but Sofoklis's eyes widened slightly in understanding, and he replied slowly, "I see."

They had both joined Apistia's fledgling Navy in their adolescence and, after everything they had been through together, Alastair would never make demands to his second in command. Sofoklis usually didn't hesitate when Alastair requested something from him, but there were times when he needed a moment to consider the situation before committing himself to a particular course of action.

"Precautions need to be made." Sofoklis finally replied after looking down at his drink for a long time. "But I'll have the boys ready by dawn."

Alastair shook his head and corrected, "This isn't a task for the rest of them."

Sofoklis frowned and looked at him warily.

"I will acquire anything you need." Alastair said then explained. "I need *you*—someone who can do the job and give honest assessments of the queen and the other Leondrians to me—while also limiting my tracks here."

Sofoklis leaned back in his chair as he thought the matter over then raised his drink in a mock toast, "To walking into the lion's den."

Alastair did have reservations about sending one of the few good men that he trusted to a dangerous place. Alastair didn't know what to expect from the queen who stayed behind while her sister went across the country, and he would never forget the last king of Leondria. Nor could he forget how his inhumanly red eyes raged with madness right before he murdered his father right in front of him.

How red would this queen's eyes be when she perceived an insult? How willing would she be to work with people so different from her own?

Alastair finished the rest of his drink and rose to his feet, "You should enjoy the rest of your afternoon."

Alastair waggled his brows at him and Sofoklis finished his drink in one long gulp before standing, his face still drawn in deep contemplation.

"I saw Adonis eyeing that wooden board the last time he was here." Sofoklis warned before heading towards the door. "I would find new places for your stash, sir."

"Thank you, friend." Alastair said after a moment, but his appreciation wasn't for the advice on where to hide his liquor.

Sofoklis hesitated at the door then turned to face him, his brown eyes glittering in determination, "I'll leave for Leondria in the morning. I'll see that your long-awaited wish is finally done."

28

It may have been mid-morning, but Abdul was already weary from the toll of the day. He blamed this fatigue on his old bones, which had endured too much hardship after sixty years of life. His joints now complained every time he stood or exerted himself too much, but he didn't bemoan the pain of old age too much since it was miraculous that he had survived this long. Let alone with all his limbs intact.

His body could protest all it wanted, Abdul thought to himself, but he was determined to make the trip to the local village, especially now that spring had arrived.

He had two very important errands to run, and he smiled when he made it to the outskirts of the village. He smiled when he saw the brilliant shades of violet peeking out among the emerald blades of grass and slowly knelt on the ground. He then carefully cultivated the most beautiful of them, thinking about how delighted his granddaughter will be when he returned home with a basket full of her favorite flowers. He could also picture the outrage on his sons' faces when they discovered that he went into town on his own again, but they worried too much about him.

He raised those stubborn mules too well. Abdul may have been too old to hunt or farm anymore but he could still do his part.

His knees wobbled as he stood, and he groaned when he bent over to pick up the wooden basket. This excursion had once been so easy and painless, but he was all but hobbling by the time he walked into the middle of town to buy some goods to take home.

He walked straight to the busy market and found his gaze wandering to the westward mountains in the far distance, the ones that separated his country from some foreign land he had never visited before. He had heard in his youth that wrathful gods lived just across those mountains, but he was concerned with the threat coming for them from the east, not the strange people in the west.

Abdul haggled with a merchant for a few minutes before they agreed on a price. He didn't want to prolong his stay here longer than necessary since it was becoming more dangerous by the day as more people fled here. Many of them were good people who were desperate to live their lives in peace. But some had evil hiding behind their soulless eyes who wouldn't hesitate to take advantage of others for self-gain.

He had seen this once before twenty years ago and it seemed that history was repeating itself. Only he feared that this would be so much worse than before.

He quickly took the food and spices, carefully placing them in his basket next to the flowers. He was ready to return home when he heard a buzzing in the crowd around him. He looked around then his eyes widened when he saw seven people entering the market. They wore red cloaks, had golden shields wrapped around their arms, and had swords and daggers strapped to their sides.

Abdul was just about to turn away to mind his own business when he saw a young man named Karim on the other side of the street. Based on how intently the young man stared at this group before whispering to his friends beside him, Abdul could sense trouble brewing.

Karim was a menace who lorded his strength over others, but he also wasn't the smartest man he had ever met. Attacking a group with weapons hardly seemed like a good idea to Abdul but perhaps he thought he could surprise and overwhelm them.

Abdul was tempted to cry out to these red cloaks to warn them of Karim's band of mercenaries but then he saw a woman in the group stiffen. Moments later, Karim's hands reached out towards her. She turned towards him, her hand already reaching towards her dagger, when one of the men beside her punched Karim in the face so hard that it sent him sprawling into the dirt.

His group of mercenaries then attacked and the man who had punched Karim sprang into action. The other red cloaks quickly pulled out their weapons and defended themselves against the dozen in Karim's group who had launched themselves at them. Abdul clapped a hand to his mouth when he saw Karim stir slightly on the ground and looked up to watch the man who had hit him.

When the man turned his back to him to block an attack from behind, Karim retrieved a hidden dagger from his pocket and leapt to his feet. He stepped forward and a knife arced through the air, straight for the back of the man's neck. Abdul thought for sure that he was about to watch this man die when he successfully kicked the adversary in front of him so hard that he fell to the ground. Then, the man quickly spun back around, used one arm to push the knife away, and used the other to bury a dagger into Karim's eye. Karim screamed before collapsing and Abdul finally looked at the other red cloaks who had quickly dispatched the rest of the mercenary group.

"Gods' blood, no one will talk to us now." a different male wearing a red cloak swore.

Abdul glanced around and realized that he had been so enthralled in the fight that he didn't notice how most of the market had been abandoned.

He realized he needed to depart immediately and took a step to leave when the man who had punched Karim called out, "Sir?"

Damn him and his curiosity. He thought he had learned better after all these years, but apparently, he hadn't. He toyed with the idea of leaving anyway then thought better of it after watching these armed red cloaks take down a larger group with ease. Abdul cautiously walked towards the man who he could now see had river-colored eyes.

He expected the river-eyed man to say something else when the woman who had been the target of Karim's attack spoke, "I am Queen Zosime of Leondria, and this is Sergeant Balthasar."

"Abdul." he replied. "How—er, may I help?"

"We wanted to ask you something." she said, and Abdul frowned in bewilderment.

Seven strangers strutted into town, killed a dozen men, and now they wanted to ask him a question?

He watched them warily before she continued, "Have you heard of any threats to the east?"

Abdul stiffened immediately and he exhaled without meaning to, "Afshin."

That seemed to grab their attention.

"Tell us more." she encouraged.

Abdul shrugged, "I don't know what to tell you that you wouldn't already know."

"We come from a country to the west." the river-eyed man—Sergeant Balthasar—said as he gestured towards the far away mountains behind them. "We know nothing, save his name and that he may be a threat to us."

"He is a great threat." Abdul asserted.

"Do you have any proof?" Balthasar inquired.

Abdul straightened and asked indignantly, "Besides my word?"

The group looked at each other for a moment. Perhaps they didn't know that a person's word meant everything in this country. It certainly meant the world to him.

"Yes." Balthasar said then added tactfully. "Any information you have that we could tell our people would be greatly appreciated, even with a man of unquestionable honor like you."

Abdul raised his eyebrows and asked skeptically, "Didn't you see the refugees here?"

"We just got to town, friend." Balthasar said respectfully. "We left our country's borders weeks ago and this is the first real town we have encountered since."

Abdul blew out a breath and relaxed when he realized these foreigners weren't insulting his integrity. He considered their odd accents and dirty clothes which indicated that they must have been living outdoors for a long time. These strange people with their strange gods hadn't been seen in his country for a very long time and likely did not know everything that had been happening in recent years.

Abdul finally advised, "If you want to see his army for yourself, continue heading east. But he only takes obedient slaves and soldiers. He slaughters anyone else who defies him. But you will be in for a long journey if you wish to see him with your own eyes, especially if you continue on foot."

"So, he *does* have an Army?" Zosime pressed.

"Yes. I've even heard rumors that he's building the largest army the world has ever seen and has a formidable navy." Abdul confirmed. "I've never seen so many refugees flee this far west before, not even when his father razed our lands twenty years ago."

"Do you have any more information about him?" Balthasar asked.

Abdul shuddered, "Just that he has won every battle against those who rejected his demand for fealty and has done horrible things to the survivors who defied him."

"Is there anyone who can corroborate your claim?" a blonde woman in their group asked.

Abdul used his free hand to gesture all around him, "You can ask anyone in town." He cleared his throat when the group looked at each other and added, "I don't know who your gods are or what they stand for, but I would pray to them for mercy. If I was a younger man, I would run as far as I could."

"We don't run." Zosime declared. "We fight."

"Then you'll die." Abdul stated matter-of-factly. "But if you are determined to do so, then return to wherever it is you call home and prepare."

He waited expectantly for more questions for a few moments then turned away when they remained silent, resolving to himself that this would be the last time he came into town. Town brought nothing but trouble and his family was all that mattered to him with whatever time he had left.

He hoped to pass away in his sleep long before war returned to their doorstep and that his sons could leave without worrying about leaving him behind. He didn't think he would be lucky enough to survive two wars, but Abdul would not leave his home at this age. If that meant being cut down, then so be it. He had lived long enough as it was.

Abdul couldn't stop thinking about the conversation on the way home and his heart grew heavy in his chest. He didn't wish that strange group of red cloaks any ill will, but he didn't like their odds of prevailing. At least he had warned them and now they knew who was coming for them. He hoped that they would change their mind and run as far away as they could, because when Afshin inevitably reached them, no one would be safe from his wrath.

CHAPTER

29

"Have you ever thought about what it means to rule? Vasiliki inquired.

"My queen?" Jedrick asked in surprise.

Vasiliki paused for a moment from the stroll she had been taking up and down the landing of the Heart on that chilly spring morning and repeated, "Have you?"

"I wouldn't know anything about it, my queen." he replied quizzically.

She resumed her casual pacing and stated, "You are my protector, correct?"

"Yes, my queen." he said.

"You have been my instructor?" she asked.

"Only with horses, my queen." he corrected with a very small smile.

"Advisor, then." she amended.

"Yes, my queen." he agreed.

"Aren't rulers the protectors and advisors of their people?" she pointed out.

He cocked his head to the side for a moment as he considered the question then said, "Protectors and leaders, yes."

"We are meant to lead by example, certainly." Vasiliki conceded then asked. "And we make final decisions, but don't we only advise them?"

"I don't understand the question, my queen." Jedrick admitted and she stopped mid-step.

"What do you think the difference is between them and us?" she wondered aloud. "Why they're down there and we're up here."

"We're all Leondrians." he answered a moment later, still clearly confused by her line of questioning. "And you are our queen."

She looked down and didn't reply.

"Are you alright, my queen?" he asked.

"It has been a productive morning." she said then returned to her pacing. "Makes one wonder about the state of affairs in the world."

"No news about Queen Zosime is good news." Jedrick said sympathetically a moment later.

Vasiliki shrugged, "She'll be back when she's back."

Truthfully, she hadn't thought about Zosime in a long time. She no longer glanced at the gates every other hour in the hopes that her sister would stroll back into her life, and she had learned to stand on her own after months of ruling by herself. But she had grown more preoccupied by questions that had consumed her thoughts since childhood and was disappointed that she hadn't received satisfactory answers.

She took a few steps forward then stopped as she surveyed the Hearth. Her morning had been busy with resolving conflicts from residents which would have once been daunting for her, but these strolls had proved invaluable to clearing her mind throughout the day. Viewing the city and the mountains in the distance somehow grounded her to reality that helped her manage the demands of her day-to-day tasks.

"Everything looks so much smaller from up here, don't you think?" she asked.

"Yes, my queen." he agreed but she didn't think his heart was in the conversation.

He was a great warrior, but she decided to stop bothering him with philosophical questions and merely looked out into the horizon. She tilted her head when she saw Orrin run towards them, and she gestured for him to approach.

"My queen." Orrin greeted breathlessly.

"Report." she said, curious why he had rushed over here.

"There's a messenger at the gates, my queen." he informed her with a grim expression.

"Who?" Vasiliki asked with raised eyebrows. "Another servant of Spyridon?"

Orrin tensed slightly and slowly shook his head, "A messenger from Apistia."

Vasiliki blinked and it took a long moment for her to compose her thoughts before she replied, "Where is he now?"

"At the gates. He's being watched by the guards." Orrin answered.

"Good." Vasiliki remarked then followed up. "Has he been searched?"

"Yes, my queen." he confirmed.

"Check him again for weapons." she instructed, and he nodded.

Vasiliki turned to Jedrick and ordered, "Gather the generals."

Her mind raced as she strolled back inside. It had taken all her control to maintain her composure and she would have been less surprised if she had been told that Lady Meraki had walked through the gates. She hadn't heard of an Apistian ever visiting Leondria before and didn't know much about them, except that they had a culture that emphasized scholarly pursuits and that their home was founded by Lady Apistia.

She remembered the generals' reactions the last time they had a messenger that they didn't get a chance to screen first, so she was resolved not to repeat that mistake. She didn't know yet if Angelos's claim had merit, so she wasn't inclined to take any similar message at face value until Zosime returned. But she wasn't about to turn away someone with potentially important information either, not without at least hearing them out.

Jedrick quickly muttered instructions to some servants inside the Heart then followed Vasiliki into the meeting room as they waited for the generals to arrive. Only several minutes passed before they all hurried inside the room and made the sign of the gods.

Vasiliki didn't waste any time with preamble and announced, "I called you in to inform you that we have received another messenger."

Perleros leaned forward and Oscar stiffened while the rest blinked rapidly in surprise.

"Is he in the other room?" Thea asked slowly.

"No." Vasiliki answered. "He is still being held by the gates and I wanted him to be cleared first before inviting him in to deliver his message."

Everyone relaxed with that statement until Vasiliki added, "Once you do clear him, I wish to hear what he has to say."

"Do we know who he is yet?" Perleros asked.

"Just that he is from Apistia." she replied, and the room froze with shock.

"Apistia!" Oscar exclaimed in indignation.

"We can't trust those snakes." Perleros declared softly but vehemently.

"Vet him then." Vasiliki said calmly. "And we can hear what he has to say with my generals beside me, of course."

A muscle twitched in Perleros's neck, but he gave Vasiliki a nod of acknowledgement as he leaned back slightly. She suspected that this course of action wasn't exactly what he wanted to pursue but it had enough safeguards to placate him. It was at least better than springing a stranger on them like last time.

She inclined her head towards them and walked out of the room, giving them time to adjust to the idea. She was having a hard time believing that having emissaries come here from two places they never received messages from were coincidences. She knew that Leondria and Apistia didn't interact with each other due to their different cultures, but she was also having a hard time understanding her generals' reactions. Jedrick was her silent shadow as she proceeded with her duties of the day, but she found herself distracted by often wondering when Perleros would tell her that the messenger was cleared.

Vasiliki was dying with curiosity by the time dinner time rolled around and she found herself sitting at one of the bonfires beside Daphne with no update on the situation. She was now only weeks away from her due date and her enormous belly looked uncomfortable. Her cheerful demeanor never wavered but Vasiliki could see some physical changes—how the rest of her body had lost weight and the persistent dark circles under her eyes—that indicated that she wasn't bearing the stress of having her beloved away well at all.

She did possess a certain strength and wisdom that Vasiliki deeply admired about her, and she fostered a secret hope that Balthasar would return just in time to see his child come into this world. She knew that stress could exacerbate pregnancies, and she wanted her friend to have an easy delivery.

She still enjoyed sitting at the bonfires most nights, but Flavian had left a vacuum when he departed with the others. People would still share personal stories or humorous anecdotes, but no one could match his ability to tell stories. Especially considering how the tension from Angelos's visit still lingered in the air around them.

Nor could her people fail to notice Zosime's absence, and Vasiliki often heard her sister's name mentioned in conversations from nearby Leondrians. She finally sighed when she heard Zosime's name mentioned for the dozenth

time, and she realized that her mind was too preoccupied about the messenger to be good company, so she asked Daphne if she required any more
assistance for the night. Daphne good-naturedly waved a hand and insisted
she would be fine, so Vasiliki ended up leaving early.

Her mind was too laden with thoughts to permit her to sleep well over
the next couple of days, but she dutifully got out of bed each morning and
mechanically went through the motions. On the third day with no update
from her generals, she found herself prowling around the Hearth right after a morning workout. She couldn't bring herself to go to one of the bath
houses at the peak of bathing hour, so she wandered instead. Jedrick hovered
a few steps behind her, and she wondered how he always knew when to give
her space and when to stand beside her.

Vasiliki frowned and halted in her tracks when she noticed Perleros
exiting the Tower. He blinked furiously, as if his eyes needed to adjust
to the sunlight and Vasiliki found her gaze meandering up the Tower's
high walls. She had never been inside before, but it must have been very
dark if it was taking this long for Perleros to adjust to being out in the
sunlight again. She watched him take a few steps forward before their
gazes met.

His eyes widened for a moment before he recovered himself and walked
over to her with the polite greeting of, "My queen."

"General." she replied with an expectant tone.

Perleros glanced at Jedrick who said, "General."

"Would you like to head to the Heart, my queen?" Perleros asked.

Vasiliki nodded, and they set out in that direction with Jedrick following at a far enough distance behind them to not overhear their conversation.

"Do you have an update, General?" Vasiliki asked.

Perleros was quiet for a moment before stating, "He claims to be from
Apistia."

"Yes." Vasiliki said patiently then followed up a few moments later
when Perleros remained silent. "Did this claim pan out?"

"He had a seal from a Congressman Alastair of the Apistian Senate."
Perleros replied.

"Did he say what the message was?" Vasiliki inquired, her curiosity
growing.

Perleros didn't answer right away, and annoyance bubbled in her chest.

It wasn't enough that Zosime's thoughtlessness ruled her life and now her advisor wasn't telling her everything.

"General." she chastised coolly, and his eyes flickered back to her.

"He wishes to speak with you, Queen Vasiliki." he replied darkly. "About establishing an alliance with Apistia."

"That would be helpful for a war, if an enemy is truly coming to our shores." Vasiliki said thoughtfully.

"They can't be trusted." Perleros insisted.

Vasiliki frowned, "What has he done that is untrustworthy?"

Perleros only shook his head vehemently before reiterating, "He is an Apistian."

Vasiliki wasn't content with such an answer, so she pressed, "Do you have any evidence he is untrustworthy?"

"Apistians can't be trusted, my queen." Perleros claimed. "They're dangerous, seal or no seal."

"Is there any evidence of wrongdoing?" Vasiliki pushed and Perleros shook his head. "No poison? No hidden dagger? No accomplices waiting to ambush us?"

"No, my queen." he responded quietly.

She shook her head in disapproval then asked, "Where is he?"

"Under custody." Perleros replied promptly.

She was ordinarily so careful not to ask too many questions and to maintain her composure, but she couldn't stop herself from snapping, "Still? Don't they have resources we could share?"

She didn't understand what the problem was but there was this growing suspicion in the back of her mind that he was keeping something important from her.

"Is there something you wish to tell me, General?" she asked in a calmer voice despite her rising frustration. "Something from the past that gives you cause to believe that we shouldn't trust them?"

Vasiliki crossed her arms and stared at the general she had deeply respected her whole life.

He hesitated a beat too long for honesty before replying, "No, my queen."

Vasiliki stared at him for several seconds before finally shaking her head furiously. She had done everything that was asked of her with no word of complaint. She had been pulled in so many different directions without proper guidance or experience and she had done her duty because she had operated on the assumption that he was doing his best to help her.

But now she had had enough.

"Bring him to me unharmed." she ordered.

"My queen—" he began, alarmed.

"He'll have breakfast with me in an hour." she interrupted. "I need to clean up first."

She stalked away, leaving Perleros behind as she went to the nearest bath house and Jedrick stood guard outside the doors. She was grateful when she walked inside and found that it was empty, pleased that she wouldn't have to answer any questions. She shed her sweaty clothes and stepped into the warm blue waters. She could already feel her muscles begin to loosen as she sat down on the marble steps and deeply inhaled the rosy oils that now coated her skin. She dunked her head under the water and quickly resurfaced, not liking having her face underwater for too long.

She usually didn't need longer than a quarter of an hour to bathe and re-dress, but she took her time now, wanting to be as relaxed as possible before meeting with this messenger. She didn't know what Apistia would want from them, but she doubted it would be as surprising as a man committing suicide after warning them of impending war.

Would they confirm the report or universally contradict it? Did they want Leondrians stationed in Apistia to protect them?

She let her mind churn with possibilities and eventually dragged herself out of the warm pool to dry herself off and put on clean clothes that servants had placed in cubicles positioned against the walls. She stared at the white ribbons that remained in the cubicle then raised her chin. She usually didn't bother spending too much time on her hair, typically tying it back in a ponytail and moving on with her day. But her hands flew as she weaved her hair into multiple braids that converged into one plait in the back.

She put on her sandals then strolled out of the bathhouse. Jedrick followed her as she walked down the street to the Heart and proceeded straight into the breakfast room. She noticed how two plates and plenty of food had already been placed on the table when she entered the room. Jedrick posted himself in the corner closest to Vasiliki, but she didn't sit down yet as she waited.

She steeled herself when she heard footsteps a couple minutes later and straightened her back, so she stood as tall as possible. She didn't quite recognize the voice that came out of her mouth—the one that was cool and self-assured—that said, "Bring him in."

Perleros walked in and was accompanied by a man who was a little taller than average height with dark brown hair, bronze-colored skin, and light brown eyes. He was lean and wiry, but Vasiliki noted the way his muscles shifted with each movement. Not in an obviously strong way like Leondrians who spent all their time training for war, but he was clearly someone who spent time out in the sun and worked with his hands.

"Welcome." she said.

"I am honored to be here, Queen Vasiliki." the man replied, making the sign of the gods backwards.

She didn't comment on the gesture and instead returned the sign in the correct form before asking, "What is your name, friend?"

"Sofoklis." he replied.

Vasiliki sat down and gestured for him to join her, "I'm sure you are weary from your long journey. Help yourself."

Sofoklis replied in a tone that was not rude but with a hardness that made Vasiliki blink in surprise, "I wouldn't dream of eating before my esteemed host."

Vasiliki would ordinarily have insisted on eating last, but she appraised him for a long moment then glanced at Perleros. Her general only folded his arms and stared intently at Sofoklis which only cemented her belief that she was missing something important. He had been frosty to Angelos and now to Sofoklis which was peculiar behavior from him. He had never been the type to have drawn out conversations, but she had never seen him be disrespectful before.

She looked back to the Apistian and grabbed various pieces of food then poured herself a full cup of wine. She raised her cup towards Lieutenant Sofoklis, who mimicked the gesture, but he didn't take a sip until Vasiliki had taken a few gulps and began eating her food. She felt his eyes tracking her every move like a hawk, but he did seem to relax ever so slightly as she ate more breakfast.

"How was your journey?" she finally asked after she watched him pick up a piece of bread and take a bite from it.

"Uneventful, Queen Vasiliki." he replied and then plopped a grape into his mouth. "The seas were kind to us."

Interesting. He must have sailed around the edge of the mainland then walked the remaining distance to Leondria instead of going through or around the mountains.

"What kind of work do you do in Apistia?" Vasiliki followed up, genuinely curious. "Are you a fisherman?"

Leondria didn't have any ships and, while she had no interest in spending her days at sea, she did wonder if he enjoyed such a profession.

"Not quite, Queen Vasiliki." Sofoklis responded. "I am the Lieutenant on Captain Alastair's ship. He has entrusted me with this mission as his second in command."

Vasiliki blinked and Sofoklis added after seeing her expression, "In the Apistian Navy."

She didn't know the Apistians had a Navy or any sort of military at all.

"Your Captain sent you here to send a message on behalf of Apistia?" Vasiliki tilted her head to the side. "I thought it was a congressman who sent you."

"The Captain is also an Apistian Senator, Queen Vasiliki." he explained.

"Do you enjoy your post?" she asked, finding herself growing more intrigued, and he smirked before taking another bite.

"The men could use some work. They do enjoy making their Lieutenant's life more difficult when they can." he said wryly.

She frowned and repeated, "The men? Not the men and women?"

"Our ship has an all-male crew." Sofoklis replied, and after Vasiliki's eyebrows rose, he elaborated. "We do have female sailors but less women in our area volunteer to enlist than the men."

Vasiliki wasn't sure if she heard correctly and she clarified, "Volunteer? Do you not conscript?"

"No." Sofoklis replied warily but he tilted his head slightly which made her think he was bewildered by her line of questioning. "People decide whether they want to join, but if they do, they are bound by contract to stay for a predetermined period of time."

Vasiliki leaned back in her seat in shock and murmured, "I see." She had never heard of such a thing before, and she quickly tried to hide her disconcertment. She took a sip of wine then asked, "What prompted you to volunteer, Lieutenant?"

"Misspent youth." he replied promptly with a serious expression. "So, my choices were to join or die."

Vasiliki's lips tugged themselves upwards in amused bitterness, but she refrained from smirking at the last second. Now that was a sentiment she could understand.

"How is Leondria doing?" he asked, and she hoped that he hadn't noticed the expression.

Perleros immediately cleared his throat in warning and Sofoklis turned slightly in his seat to look at the general. When he did, his tunic shifted, and Vasiliki was able to see some angry welts that were now blooming on his chest.

"Did you run into trouble on your journey?" she asked, concerned, and gestured to the marks.

Sofoklis glanced down briefly at them then shifted back to his original position. He stared at her intensely, as if trying to discern her inner-most thoughts, before slowly stating, "Some trouble, yes. But nothing I couldn't handle."

His eyes flickered to the side where Perleros stood, and Vasiliki frowned deeply.

"I trust your troubles will now be over, now that you are a guest of Leondria." she stated firmly. "Under the Queen's protection. And, to answer your question, Leondria is enjoying the spring's fine weather."

"I would think it too tame of a season to interest such renowned warriors." Sofoklis said.

"Our spirits thrive in the hardships of winter, but we do enjoy the beauty of spring." Vasiliki replied in an amused tone.

"We prefer the summer." Sofoklis said a moment later, as if he wasn't sure whether her last statement was a joke. "There's nothing quite like Apistia and its brilliant blue seas under the sun's unfettered golden rays."

Vasiliki tried imagining such a sight and confessed, "That sounds beautiful. It seems your misspent youth was a blessing for your current fortunes, Lieutenant."

The side of his lips twitched upwards for just a moment before he stated, "The Captain has uttered the same sentiments to me before."

Vasiliki took another sip of wine then asked, "Was your Captain acting in his military or senatorial capacity when sending you to us?"

"The two positions are interrelated for him, but I was sent on behalf of our Senate with my Captain's recommendation. Our Senate heard of your coronation and has been deliberating how to reach out to you about our city-states becoming allies."

Interesting, she thought. So, they hadn't wanted to just provide information or to ask for resources from Leondria.

"My coronation was several months ago." she said slowly as a suspicious thought rose in her mind. "And your Senate has just now sent you?"

Sofoklis somehow smiled while still looking grim and remarked, "Our Senate takes deliberations … seriously."

He took a sip of wine and Vasiliki's eyes flickered to Perleros. He was as still as a statue, but he twitched ever so slightly, as if he was trying to shake his head with as little movement as possible. She looked back to Sofoklis and pursed her lips as she thought through the implications of his statements.

"So Apistia fears war too." she noted, and she saw something dark flicker in his eyes that she didn't recognize. He was silent for a long moment before she added, "To the east?"

"We do desire an alliance," he said and the darkness in his eyes faded. "We believe that we stand better odds of surviving a threat together then divided."

That made sense to her, but this was a major decision to make without her co-queen's knowledge. Then again, Vasiliki had no idea when her sister was coming back from the mission that she had joined at the last minute. It seemed nonsensical to wait until her sister returned when she may not return for several more months. If she even came back at all. But this alliance could shape their lives for years to come so it was not a decision to be made on a whim.

"I'll think it over." Vasiliki finally said, rising to her feet. "Give me a few weeks to give you my answer."

"That's all we can ever ask of you, Queen Vasiliki." Sofoklis bowed his head.

She inclined her head back in a show of respect and said, "I hope you enjoy your stay here in the meantime." she looked at Perleros and added briskly, "Show our guest to his room and make sure he has everything he needs."

Perleros's face darkened but he obediently said, "Yes, my queen."

"Welcome to Leondria, Lieutenant." Vasiliki said to their guest then strolled out of the room with more questions than answers.

CHAPTER

3∅

Zosime had never truly experienced fear until she was seventeen years old. She had felt it second-hand from others, but she had never personally experienced it herself since she had always been much stronger and faster than everyone else and had an inner alarm system to warn her of attacks. So, she never had anything to be scared of for most of her life until she sensed Typhon's impending escape, and it looked like all would soon be lost.

That was the first time she had been struck with terror. She had tucked that panic away when the Leondrians triumphed over the monster and moved on with her life. At least she had until she had been forced to confront her fears during the Trials.

She hadn't known how to process these feelings, and she had been on the cusp of failing when she had miraculously pulled through and survived. The nightmares had followed her since that fateful night, which had only worsened when the Fates had visited her dreams. She hadn't really slept since, her eyes springing open the second she thought she heard eerie cackles or the sound of a machine whirling. She could naturally triumph over most mortal beings, but she had instinctively known how small and powerless she was against the Creature and the Fates.

This was the third time that she had been struck with terror but now she thought it would settle irrevocably in her heart. That she would forever be haunted by this feeling and never live free of it. She had been both re-signed and comforted when they ran into Abdul because it meant that the threat was real but at least the mission was almost over.

They had also talked to every villager who was willing to speak with them, and they all confirmed Abdul's report that Afshin was coming, and he was building the largest Army the world had ever seen. Zosime had then spoken to Balthasar and Anastasia, and they all agreed that they had heard enough.

It was time to return home and prepare.

They had set off for Midrios the next day and she felt Dryas's and Anastasia's continued concern for her. Dryas tried to be there for her by being supportive, but he hadn't sought her out again since that one night when he had almost told her he loved her. Zosime had sensed that he was about to spill his feelings, and she had been so relieved when Balthasar interrupted him. Such a confession wasn't something she could deal with right now and she treasured him too much to break his heart.

She wasn't worthy of Dryas, and she never would be.

That and she hoped Vasiliki would find a suitable man to marry so she would never have to. All she had cared about was being a Leondrian, not being someone's wife or mother. That was a problem for the future though. She just needed to focus on getting back and readying her people for war.

She was relieved that they could finally quicken their pace since they didn't have to worry about meticulously combing through surrounding areas to find villages in search for information. They made good progress as a result, and it didn't take long before they found themselves before the Karkaros mountains again. She had sensed Anastasia's weariness when they started hiking through the passes but this feeling faded when they stopped for the night. No one was particularly happy given the grim news, but everyone was elated about the prospect of soon returning to Leondria.

"I can practically smell home." Flavian smiled.

"Is that your stomach talking?" Balthasar grinned and the others laughed.

"I've heard it speak in tongues before. I think it might be trying to talk to us, Sergeant." Alec smirked.

They were all sitting by the fire for an added layer of warmth for the mildly chilly night, but they didn't huddle over it as they had during the winter.

Flavian rested a hand on his stomach and bowed, *"We* can practically smell home and are grateful for your attention, Sergeant."

Nicholas noted where Flavian's hand rested then looked at Balthasar, "You might make it back in time, especially with our faster pace."

"Knowing Daphne, she'll either have given birth a week ago and has everything sorted out or she won't deliver for another month and will insist on picking the name." Balthasar said with an adoring smile.

"Do you have any names in mind?" Anastasia asked.

"I'll leave that to her." Balthasar stated and waved a hand. "I'll be happy with anything." His eyes grew distant, and he continued thoughtfully, "We'll need to move with particular swiftness tomorrow."

"Yes," Zosime agreed quietly then added. "But they did see us last time and didn't attack."

"They may not be as hostile as the Palapao governors made them out to be." Balthasar allowed then asked. "Did you read their intentions?"

"They were too far away for me to sense their emotions." Zosime answered.

"I waited for an hour before climbing the mountain and no one approached." Anastasia remarked. "And they were studying us long before that."

"So, they watched us then ignored us?" Flavian said slowly.

"You're not sensing any sort of attack, my queen?" Balthasar asked and Zosime shook her head.

"We should still move quickly through, just in case." Anastasia advised.

"Yes." Balthasar agreed. "The sooner we're back home to deliver our message, the better."

A piece of burning firewood cracked which sent shooting sparks into the air.

"We'll leave by dawn." Zosime decided. "And move quickly and quietly."

"I'll take watch." Balthasar announced and Zosime shook her head.

"Rest." she said pointedly, sensing the radiating pain in his back. "I'll take watch."

She wanted him in the best shape possible for their journey. She had occasionally sensed his physical discomfort throughout their mission and, while he never once complained, she could tell it really bothered him some days.

She felt his chagrin, but he only bowed his head and said, "Yes, my queen."

"I can take watch instead." Dryas offered and his eyes dropped to the heavy bags under her eyes.

"Rest." Zosime snapped then bit her lip. In a much kinder tone, she added. "You all need the rest more than I do if we'll be increasing our pace even more tomorrow. I'll be fine."

She sensed his worry, but he didn't contradict her.

"I know I don't need the beauty sleep, but I'll take it." Flavian smirked. "I certainly know that Sergeant Balthasar needs it more than I do."

Balthasar flashed him an exasperated look which was tempered by the amusement that sparkled in his eyes.

"You don't want your kid to think they have a rotten turnip for a father, right?" Flavian joked and Balthasar shook his head. "It's bad for their self-esteem."

"He's not wrong." Dryas shrugged which prompted Balthasar to casually push him off the log they were both sitting on.

This sent everyone into raucous laughter and Dryas shot back up to his feet. She had sensed some tension between the brothers since the night that Balthasar dragged Dryas away from her, and she hoped this was a sign that their relationship was mending.

"I take it back!" Dryas held up his hands then added slyly. "I meant to say a rotten tomato, considering all the wrinkles."

"Need better reflexes than that, little brother." Balthasar said then patted the empty spot on the log.

Dryas took his seat again and elbowed him in the side which made Balthasar swipe at his arm. The group didn't stay up much longer after that and everyone, but Zosime and Anastasia fell asleep.

After an hour, Zosime whispered to her, "You can rest."

Anastasia shook her head and whispered back, "Not a chance. You protect us and I protect you, remember?"

Zosime looked down but couldn't stop the small smile from forming on her lips. They stayed up all night together in silence and they both began shaking everyone else awake when the sky began to lighten to a watery grey. They ate quickly then finished the final trek down the mountain, but Zosime could no longer disregard the massive headache pounding at her temples. Nor could she ignore her vision blurring at the sides as they walked past the mountains.

She suddenly wondered when she had last slept, and she honestly couldn't remember when that was. Her stomach was now recoiling from the food she had eaten, and she wanted to do nothing more than to fall to her knees and throw up.

The exhaustion was taking over so much that she scarcely realized that she was back on Midrian soil. All she knew was that she had to keep moving. She could survive today if she just put one foot in front of the other. They didn't stop for lunch and continued their hard march as they hurried quickly through tribal territory.

Perhaps she should get some sleep tonight, she thought idly, as she stumbled over her own feet.

Her head was pounding so hard she couldn't even think straight, and she thought the day would never end. She was having a hard time differentiating between errant thoughts and noises she heard around her. She even thought she was hearing a faraway bell ringing and she shook her head as she tried to clear her mind. But the bell only grew more persistent until it suddenly went silent, which prompted Zosime to stop in her tracks.

Anastasia immediately froze then her head whipped to their left, clearly hearing something Zosime hadn't, and cried out, "Guard!"

But the order hadn't come soon enough since they were suddenly ambushed by a couple dozen people lying in wait behind the tall hill right beside them.

The attackers were fast and Zosime furrowed her brow as she attempted to keep her shield high and draw out her sword. Each attacker fell when they approached, and she felt the never-ending onslaught of death. It encompassed her completely, clouding her senses, and she knew that her maneuvers were only growing clumsier and more deficient.

She kept enough presence of mind to slay the attackers in front of her, but she missed the dagger of the man diagonal to her until it was almost in her right eye. She couldn't move fast enough to dodge it altogether, but she was able to pivot just enough for it to only slice a part of her jaw and cheek. Blood spurted from her face and her arms collapsed from both pain and exhaustion. She barely registered the second attack but knew she wouldn't be able to move fast enough to evade death again as the dagger hurtled towards her throat.

She sent a mental prayer to the gods to watch over Leondria and her sister right before she saw a flash of red. Her eyes widened when she saw that the blood was spurting from Balthasar who had just dived in front of her. The knife that was meant to take her life was instead plunged into the right side of his chest.

"NO!" Dryas screamed.

Anastasia sent an elbow into her attacker's face and used one hand to slash down her opponent while using the other to throw a dagger into Zosime's attacker's face.

"My wife." Balthasar gasped as they both fell against the ground.

Zosime's mouth dropped open, and her skull felt moments away from cracking when she saw his fingers spasming. His lips mouthed the words he didn't have the strength to say: *tell Daphne I love her.*

"I'll tell her!" she promised with tears leaking from her eyes. *"I'll tell her! I'll tell her!"*

"How is he?" Dryas demanded frantically. "Is he still alive?"

Zosime could only take in shallow breaths, and she looked up to see Dryas kneeling in front of her. She quickly glanced around to find that all the attackers had been killed then blinked when Anastasia effortlessly pushed Dryas away. Anastasia first studied Zosime's face then nodded to herself when it was clear that her wound wasn't life-threatening. Anastasia then efficiently began checking him for any other signs of injury and, when she didn't find anything, returned her attention to the knife protruding from his chest.

Zosime could feel death hovering over him, ready to clutch him in its inviolable embrace. She counted Balthasar's breaths as his chest slowly rose and fell then asked Anastasia, "Should we keep it in?"

Anastasia shook her head, "If we keep it in, it'll fuse to him and do more harm later."

"Should we take it out then?" Dryas asked, stunned.

"Not yet. We need to get out of here first." Anastasia lifted Balthasar's limp body in her arms. Her blue eyes were blazing when she hissed, *"Run."*

Zosime was jolted into motion, but she could barely feel her legs when she struggled to stand. She knew she was stumbling more than she should and she just watched Anastasia who was sprinting well ahead the others. Zosime soon lost all track of time, and she was scarcely aware that dusk had arrived when they finally stopped.

Anastasia gently placed Balthasar on the ground then ordered, "Flavian, Nicholas, build a stretcher. Dryas, Alec, start a fire."

Zosime could only watch as Balthasar's eyes fluttered and didn't realize that Dryas had returned to his brother's side until he whispered, "I'm here, brother."

Anastasia removed the dagger that was strapped to her side and put the blade in the small fire Dryas had just built. When the silver morphed into a brilliant orange, her hand wrapped around the hilt of the blade protruding from Balthasar's chest.

"Keep him still." Anastasia instructed and Flavian, Alec, Nicholas, and Dryas held down his arms and legs. Her eyes then met Zosime's and she asked with a pointed look at the red fabric, "When I give the signal, can you apply pressure to the wound, my queen?"

Zosime nodded and Anastasia took a single breath before ripping the blade out of Balthasar's chest. His eyes flew open, and he began to thrash before they tightened their grips over his limbs.

"Now!" Anastasia cried and Zosime used the cloth to apply pressure to his chest.

She could feel the blood begin to soak through the cloth, staining her hands red, so she only applied more pressure until she didn't feel any more liquid seep through.

Zosime gently removed the rags to confirm that he had stopped bleeding a minute or so later and gave Anastasia a small nod. Anastasia then grabbed the blade from the fire and pressed it against Balthasar's chest. Zosime wouldn't have been surprised if everyone in Midrios heard his screams of agony.

"I'm here, brother!" Dryas repeated over and over, each time louder than the last so he could be heard.

Balthasar's screams finally abated when Anastasia removed the blade, and they waited for what felt like days before his chest slowly rose again. Zosime let loose a staggering breath and couldn't stop her hands from shaking. He was still alive.

"We need to go." Anastasia urged. "If we don't get him to surgeons, he'll die."

"Should we go straight to Palapao?" Dryas suggested wildly, his eyes wide in desperation.

Anastasia gently placed Balthasar on the stretcher and said quietly, "They've barely reestablished trade. Even if they did want to help us, I doubt they'll have surgeons skilled enough to save him."

"Leondria is his only chance." Zosime said numbly then said more forcefully. "Let's go."

Anastasia picked up one side of the stretcher and Zosime picked up the other, and they started running as fast as they could.

CHAPTER

31

A couple weeks had passed since Lieutenant Sofoklis's arrival and Vasiliki was still puzzled by him. She wasn't sure what she had expected from an Apistian, but she found herself growing more curious about him and his home.

She wondered what Apistia's values were. She knew they appreciated intelligence, but she didn't know what made them tick as a people. She wanted to be able to promote cooperation between Leondria and Apistia, but she was utterly in the dark on what they valued and what they considered to be grievous insults.

She didn't want to say or do the wrong thing to jeopardize any potential alliance. She also dearly wished that Perleros and the others would be more forthcoming with her about their dislike of Apistia. Without any evidence to demonstrate that Sofoklis was untrustworthy or that any alliance between them would be unsuccessful anyway, Vasiliki was leaning towards accepting his offer.

She did notice how closely Sofoklis watched them which only further increased her own curiosity about him. She often found him watching the Leondrians work out in the morning, stroll down the streets throughout the day, and listen closely to them at the nightly bonfires. He had caused quite the stir after his arrival and she could see how coldly the older Leondrians treated him, even if they were never outwardly rude to their guest.

The younger Leondrians and the children were fascinated by him. Some would go out of their way to strike a conversation with him, but Vasiliki could tell they were thinly veiled attempts to pry information out of him about Apistia. When she thought they had bombarded their guest enough, she politely told them to leave him be until it was just Sofoklis, Vasiliki, and Jedrick at one table.

"I hope they haven't infringed on your dinner too much, Lieutenant." Vasiliki said and he shook his head.

"Not at all." he disagreed thoughtfully. "They don't want for enthusiasm, to be sure."

"You're our first Apistian guest." Vasiliki said then paused. "Well, technically, the second."

Sofoklis raised an eyebrow, "Technically?"

"We had a guest earlier this year who was from Apistia, but he wasn't sent by your Senate." Vasiliki explained.

"Is that so?" Sofoklis asked blandly but something about the way he tilted his head made Vasiliki uneasy.

"It was—" she hesitated. "Quite the affair."

"Was he a thoughtless guest?" he asked, and she looked down for a moment.

"Not at all. In fact, I think about him most days." she said heavily. "It's dreadful what happened."

"I hope he was not too poor of a representative for Apistia." Sofoklis apologized. "And I hope his behavior does not prevent us from establishing better relations in the future."

Vasiliki frowned, "His behavior?"

"Did he not—" he hesitated for a moment before finishing. "Offend his host?"

"He bewildered us, for sure. But he offered no offense." Vasiliki remarked.

He frowned in turn, and it looked like he was looking for the right words before he responded, "When did he leave? I don't recognize anyone who might be from Apistia."

Vasiliki blinked a few times in confusion before stating, "He's dead. I thought you would have heard about that during your stay here."

"No one has said anything to me, Queen Vasiliki." he corrected respectfully. "If I may ask, what happened?"

Vasiliki cleared her throat, not wanting to offend him, so she said carefully, "He came to our gates one day with no warning, looking disheveled and like he had been on the road for a while. My sister let him in as our guest, so we gave him food and wine. Then we had a meeting with him and the generals since he said he had a message to deliver to us and he—" she faltered for a moment. "He warned us of Afshin, second of his name, but we didn't really believe him since he had no evidence or allies to support his claim then he pulled out a dagger—" Sofoklis's eyes widened as she finished. "And he stabbed himself in the chest. He seemed adamant that it was the only way for us to believe him, but he acted too quickly for us to stop him."

Jedrick looked down uncomfortably and Sofoklis was quiet for a while before declaring, "That sounds like quite the ordeal."

"It's why you haven't met Queen Zosime yet. She is leading a group on a reconnaissance mission to confirm or deny the threat." Vasiliki said.

He gave her a look she couldn't decipher then turned his gaze away. Vasiliki glanced over at the Leondrian who just finished telling a funny story and asked, "Would you like to share any anecdotes? We would be delighted to hear from you."

"I do not have the liveliness required to tell a story properly, Queen Vasiliki." he said then added. "I am more than content listening to the others."

Jedrick's eyebrows temporarily rose in surprise, but Vasiliki only nodded, "However we can make your stay here comfortable, Lieutenant."

Sofoklis stared at her for a moment with an expression of studied puzzlement and wonder. His gaze then cooled when he saw something behind her, and Vasiliki didn't need to turn around to know who he had just been staring at. Sofoklis never failed to address her or her guards with flawless etiquette, except for Perleros.

"Excuse me a moment, Lieutenant." she said and Sofoklis nodded graciously.

She gestured for Jedrick to stay by their guest as she stood, tuning out someone's retelling of the First Passage as she walked over to Perleros.

"Do you have any updates for me?" she asked.

"Just that the Council wants to be included in any decision, my queen." Perleros said.

Vasiliki cocked her head to the side and stated, "I sent a runner to inform them of his presence after he arrived, but they didn't respond. They are welcome to discuss it at length with me."

Perleros kept quiet before eventually responding, "Phrasing matters, my queen."

While the queens held immense power in Leondria, only the Council could approve official alliances and make declarations of war. Vasiliki had taken their silence as either acquiescence to any proposed alliance or as a sign that they were waiting for more information before responding. She had also seen Perleros exit the Tower recently which only reinforced her belief that they would not be against any future partnership with Apistia.

"I would try again, my queen." he suggested then emphasized. "And ask for their opinion."

She didn't understand why she would need to explicitly ask them for their guidance, but she didn't see the harm in it either.

Her voice was hard when she assured him, "It will be done in the morning."

She hadn't forgiven him for hiding something from her, and she wasn't about to let him forget that fact any time soon. He opened his mouth to say something when they heard a loud gasp of pain that made Vasiliki whip her head towards the source of the sound. Her eyes widened when she discovered Daphne bending over at one of the tables and she and Perleros hurried over to her.

Cheeks flushed with sweat and her fingers clutching her stomach, Daphne gasped, "The child is coming."

CHAPTER

32

Zosime was no stranger to blood, being a woman and a warrior. It was something she was accustomed to seeing regularly and had never really bothered her, but she couldn't stop glancing down at her red hands and the droplets of blood that dripped down her face onto her clothes. She couldn't shake the painful fact that her hands were still stained with Balthasar's blood.

She had lost all track of time, and she didn't know any more if she was awake or if this was one long nightmare that would ever end. There were times she could have sworn she saw one of the three crones standing just ahead of them with the cruelest smile on her face. Then Zosime would blink, and she would vanish.

She and Anastasia never stopped running and they soon left the group behind. Dryas didn't quite catch up to them, but she could hear his pounding footsteps somewhere behind her. Never once slowing or stopping. She could barely feel her own feet anymore—she felt utterly disconnected from her body—and she could scarcely drag her gaze away from her hands.

She was responsible for this. If she hadn't been so slow, Balthasar wouldn't have taken the dagger for her. She was the one who was supposed to be protecting them, and she had failed.

You're a failure. She thought to herself. YOU'RE A FAILURE.

The words only grew louder in her mind with each step she took, and each struggling breath Balthasar wheezed. She didn't know what kind of queen she was if her people were the ones who had to save her, instead of the other way around.

Zosime stumbled again and Anastasia's head turned around to glance at her. Something flickered in her eyes, and she quickly returned her attention forward until all Zosime saw was her billowing red cloak and flowing blonde hair. Zosime caught herself on the next step and she gritted her teeth in a mixture of rage and frustration.

"Halt!" Zosime exclaimed and Anastasia immediately stopped.

"My queen?" she gasped.

"Put him down." Zosime ordered and they gently put down the stretcher.

Anastasia turned around to face her, clearly confused and repeated, "My queen?"

"I sense something." Zosime murmured.

Anastasia blinked and rested a hand on the hilt of her sword.

"No, no, no." Zosime continued muttering with rapid shakes of her head. "Not a threat. I sense something."

Anastasia frowned but Zosime could see the rising alarm on her face.

"I sense something!" Zosime insisted, her voice indistinguishable from a hiss.

She scrambled around Balthasar and hurried several paces forward, searching the area around them for a few minutes.

"We should keep going, my queen." Anastasia finally said when she didn't find anything.

Zosime only shook her head adamantly and barely noticed Dryas when he caught up with them, his chest heaving from the effort. He frowned as he stared at them then he turned to ask Anastasia in an exhausted pant, "What's happening?"

"Where are the others?" Anastasia asked.

"Fell behind." he replied, still panting. "Ma'am, why aren't we still running?"

"The queen ordered us to stop." Anastasia replied and Zosime whipped her head around to look at her.

"Someone's coming." Zosime insisted, eyes wide.

She sensed Dryas's panic, and he suggested in a breathless voice, "I can carry him, Zosime."

This felt like Typhon all over again. Why did no one ever believe her? Why did they look at her like she was moments away from destroying everything?

She couldn't stop herself from letting out a screech and returned to looking around. Anastasia and Dryas glanced at each other, looking at a total loss for words when Anastasia's eyes suddenly widened.

"Do you hear something?" Dryas asked.

Zosime followed Anastasia's gaze then sprinted forward.

"My queen!" Anastasia called out and followed her.

Zosime ignored her as she continued charging forward then leapt directly in front of a buckboard being dragged by two large brown horses.

"Woah!" the man sitting at the front of the buckboard cried and pulled on the reigns to avoid running her over.

The horses whinnied in response and dug their hooves into the ground, narrowly stopping in time to avoid hitting her.

"What are you doing?" the man yelled indignantly then froze when he saw her red cape and golden shield.

"What's your name?" Zosime demanded.

The man began shaking when he looked into her eyes and he stuttered, "P-P-Paraskevas."

"Of where?" Zosime barked.

"Palapao." he shuddered when he saw her blood-stained hands. "You just passed it."

She had been so lost in her delirium that she hadn't even noticed where she was.

"Do you know any surgeons?" Anastasia asked, catching up to them.

"Surgeons?" he repeated hoarsely.

"Do you, or don't you?" Anastasia grilled.

"No." he stammered.

"Are there any in Palapao?" Anastasia pressed.

"I don't know of any." he whispered.

Zosime didn't have time for this. She stalked around the horses until she stood beside him and ordered, "Get off the cart and leave."

He didn't move until Zosime's expression hardened into a glare and she rested a hand on the hilt of her dagger. Anastasia looked at her in shock but remained silent when Paraskevas clumsily got off the cart and quickly backed away from her.

They needed those horses now and she didn't care how badly she had to scare Paraskevas to get them. She hastily cleared out all the crates of fruit in the back of the cart and gestured for Anastasia and Dryas to lay Balthasar down in the now-open space.

Dryas clambered into the back with his brother while Anastasia and Zosime climbed into the front. Zosime turned the horses to face the opposite direction then snapped the reigns against them a few times until they were galloping at full speed.

"Hold on, big brother." Dryas pleaded. "We're almost there."

Zosime usually loved the feeling of a horse galloping beneath her but now the hoof beats just felt like heart beats. Each one reminded her of how much Balthasar was struggling to breathe, of the knife cutting into her face, and what little time they had left to get him back home.

They were almost there. With the horses outrunning the wind without taking any breaks, and not caring who saw them, they could make it back in time.

She just felt the *pulse, pulse, pulse* of the hooves and vaguely heard Dryas whispering to his brother. She inwardly cursed the jostling movements of the cart and wondered if Balthasar felt any pain from the constant vibrations. She tried to push these thoughts away and focus on what lay before her. The landscape flew around them and Zosime's head perked up when she finally noticed they were back in Leondrian territory.

They could make it! She thought hopefully to herself. She knew they could. They were now so close to the Hearth where the surgeons would be waiting and could save him. Zosime had faith that Balthasar could make it and then the surgeons could patch up whatever was broken inside of him.

"My queen." Anastasia suddenly said and Zosime was snapped out of her reverie.

"We're almost there." Zosime replied heatedly and she felt a nervous giggle rise in her chest. "He can make it."

Anastasia touched her arm a moment later and repeated in a tone that was much older and heavier than her years, "My queen."

Zosime shook her head and kept her eyes resolutely on the road ahead of her and repeated firmly, "He can make it."

Anastasia's hand moved so quickly that Zosime couldn't react when she wrenched the reigns away from her and brought the horses to a stop.

"He needs you, my queen." Anastasia said quietly.

Zosime hesitated—not wanting to believe what she was saying—before she slowly twisted in her seat to find Dryas bent over Balthasar, his shoulders shaking.

"Dryas?" she whispered.

"Zosime." Dryas murmured and she couldn't miss the tears that were streaking down his face when he raised his head to look at her.

But it wasn't her name that he was really saying. It was a call out to the abyss to try to fathom something that was beyond human comprehension. It was a plea to his queen to return the life of someone precious to him even if such a request was beyond the power of a mere mortal like herself. It was a prayer to watch over a warrior's soul that was now wholly in the hands of the gods.

33

There were two great battlefields that Leondrians ever encountered. One involved facing the enemy with shields and weapons in hand while the other was fought on the infinitely more perilous ground of childbirth. Vasiliki was no expert in bringing new life into this world since she had never been with child or assisted midwifes in the process before.

Despite her inexperience, she could only feel rising concern for Daphne as her face contracted with agony and blood continued flowing from between her legs. Vasiliki felt the stakes of this moment in her bones, but she could only helplessly wipe away the sweat from Daphne's brow and ensured she had as much water as she desired.

It had been days since she and Perleros had rushed her away from the bonfire and the child was still no closer to being born. Daphne's parents hovered close by, and Vasiliki was only growing more worried for her friend's welfare when her mother's face slowly transformed from shining pride to horrified concern. This worry was only reinforced by the midwife, whose lips had been drawn in a tight line for the past day.

She had heard that labor often lasted several hours but that it could take up to a few days in rare cases. Daphne was now on day three and Vasiliki no longer had any reason to believe that this was a conventional birth.

"You're so strong." Daphne's mother whispered in her ear, but Vasiliki didn't think that her daughter had heard her, based on how glassy her eyes were. "My strong girl."

Vasiliki stepped away to give her some space and murmured to the midwife, "Is there anything further you require?"

"Some more water and clean cloth, my queen." the midwife responded quietly, and Vasiliki inclined her head.

She walked out of the house and blinked in surprise when she found Jedrick and Sofoklis waiting for her.

"My queen." Jedrick greeted solemnly.

"Can you get some water and clean cloth?" Vasiliki asked him and he bowed his head in acknowledgement before hurrying away.

"Queen Vasiliki." Sofoklis said respectfully then, after taking in her tangled hair and the dark circles under her eyes, asked. "How is she?"

Vasiliki hesitated before replying, "She's enduring, Lieutenant."

She turned when she heard the door opening behind her and the midwife strolled out and bowed her head.

"Did you need anything more?" Vasiliki asked urgently. "Besides water and clean cloth?"

The midwife was quiet for a moment, swallowing in trepidation before answering, "No, my queen. There's nothing else."

Sofoklis frowned then asked shrewdly, "Is the baby in breach?"

The midwife raised her eyebrows in surprise then confirmed, "Yes."

"In breach?" Vasiliki asked.

Sofoklis's face was neutral, but his tone was sympathetic when he explained, "The baby is supposed to be born headfirst. It is in breach when it is positioned with its feat downwards."

"I have done what I can to reposition the child." the midwife said heavily. "With no success."

"Why does that matter?" Vasiliki frowned. "This way or that way, so long as the child is born."

"If the feat come out first, then the weight of the body will put so much pressure on the neck that the bones will break." she explained.

Vasiliki recoiled in horror then inquired, "Is that why you've been massaging her belly?"

She nodded and added, "I thought it best if Daphne didn't know and focused on delivering."

None of them spoke for several moments, the air heavy with implication, before Jedrick quickly returned with a new water pouch and several pieces of clean white fabric in his hands.

"Can you take them inside?" the midwife requested, and Jedrick nodded as he did so.

When he was out of earshot, Vasiliki shook her head and addressed the midwife with grim resignation, "Water and cloth won't help, will it?"

"The water will help with the thirst and the cloth will be used to clean up more blood, but no. It won't solve the underlying problem." she replied softly.

Vasiliki turned away from them both as she struggled to compose herself. She closed her eyes and took a deep breath as she ignored the stinging in her eyes.

"You can continue trying to reposition the babe." Sofoklis suggested but Vasiliki suspected he was asking out of kindness instead of a genuine belief that such an idea would help.

"It's been three days." the midwife said. "If the babe hasn't repositioned itself by now, it's not going to. And, even if I could, she's lost a lot of blood. Her body won't hold out much longer."

She shook her head sadly and sighed heavily before going back inside. Vasiliki didn't move for several more seconds as she focused on overcoming the lump in her throat so she could trust herself to speak without weeping.

"I hope you don't feel we've been neglecting our duties to you, Lieutenant." Vasiliki finally stated as she turned back around to face him.

"Not at all." Sofoklis said sympathetically.

"I haven't forgotten about you and your objective." she added quickly. "I'm still mulling it over."

"I completely understand, Queen Vasiliki." Sofoklis insisted. "I'm sorry."

She blinked in surprise and her mouth dropped open slightly. She had never once had those words said to her before. Not here, where actions were valued above all else and words of apology meant nothing. She realized a moment later that she was probably being a substandard host who was doing a poor job of representing Leondria.

"Don't hesitate to ask if you need anything, Lieutenant." she finally replied as Jedrick walked back outside to rejoin them. She turned to face Jedrick and asserted, "Make sure he is well provided for."

"Yes, my queen." he said then added softly. "I would go in now before it's too late."

Vasiliki hung her head for a second and she took a deep, shuddering breath before nodding in agreement. She gently patted his shoulder a couple times in appreciation and hauled herself inside, barely having the strength to lift her feet to continue walking forward. Her heart felt like a boulder in her chest that was weighing her down with each step she took. But took them she did as she forced herself to face what she most dreaded.

Losing a dear friend.

Vasiliki opened her mouth to speak when she approached Daphne one last time then closed it when words failed her.

She was shocked when Daphne's eyelids opened weakly and she asked, "Is my husband here yet?"

Dear gods. Vasiliki thought desperately to herself. What was she supposed to say to that?

"Is my Balthasar back?" Daphne croaked.

Vasiliki fought back another round of tears and stated, "No word yet."

Daphne moaned then muttered, "My love, where is my love?"

"Daphne." Vasiliki said gently and rested a hand on her shoulder in her best attempt to comfort her. "Balthasar is on his way back now. Do you doubt your husband, one of our best warriors?"

Daphne didn't seem to hear her, and Vasiliki could no longer ignore her ashen complexion. The hairs on the back of her neck stood up as Daphne's breaths grew shallower until she suddenly stilled. Vasiliki couldn't explain the alien feeling that was rising in her chest and scarcely heard the wails from the parents who could not hold in their grief.

Daphne had lost the war without even holding her child one time.

Vasiliki numbly turned away from the grieving parents and found herself outside before she even realized that she had left the house. She couldn't hear anything over her heart pounding in her chest as she shuffled towards the Heart. An idle part of her brain began planning, thinking of the pyre ceremony she would need to orchestrate soon. She flinched and came to a stop when a bright light hit her eyes. She blinked rapidly and turned her head away from the rising sun, amazed that a new day had come but that everything in her world had now changed.

"My queen?" Jedrick asked softly and she flinched again, forgetting that he followed her from the house.

"Tell the Lieutenant I accept his offer of an alliance." she said numbly.

"Yes, my queen." he replied then suggested. "After you've rested, we can arrange a lunch with him to talk—"

"Now." she added softly, and he reluctantly bowed his head before hurrying to the Heart.

She didn't see the point in delaying the inevitable any longer. She had sent two runners to the Council without receiving any response, she hadn't been given any legitimate reason by her advisors not to pursue an alliance, and there was no telling when her sister would return to discuss it with her.

"Queen Vasiliki." a soft voice called out and she turned to find Perleros standing behind her.

"She's gone." she murmured, and his face seemed to age another couple of decades.

She never got the chance to hear his response when she heard multiple people shout, "*Queen Vasiliki! Get Queen Vasiliki! Queen Zosime has returned!*"

CHAPTER
34

Dryas didn't know why his hands were shaking so badly but he couldn't keep them still as he stared into his brother's unseeing eyes. He had never before felt so exhausted and wired at the same time and he didn't know what his place in the world was anymore. He was and would always be a Leondrian, but he didn't know who he was outside of that anymore.

For as long as he could remember, he had looked up to Balthasar as an example of what kind of man he should be. When they were separated during Training, Dryas had often thought of what his brother would do and envisioned what kind of advice he would give in any given situation. Then, when they were reunited after the Trials, he had turned to him for guidance and companionship.

Now, there would be no more solace or counsel from the man he had respected more than any other, even if their last one-on-one conversation had been words of anger. There would be no more daily lunches or joking around the bonfires. There were no more possibilities, only the void that had just ripped open in his heart that Dryas now thought would never close. The only thing he could do to prevent it from opening any further was to honor his brother's last request: *Look after Daphne and my child. Live up to your duty, brother.*

He had dully wondered if his niece or nephew had been born yet and a part of him wished the child would be a boy so it would almost feel like he had his brother back. Balthasar had been the father figure that Perleros failed to be, and it was now up to Dryas to be the male role model for his niece or nephew.

"I will." he had whispered back, and Balthasar's body slackened, as if the promise had brought him much needed peace.

Balthasar had done everything for him, and he had only fallen woefully short of his expectations. He had missed the chance to make him proud when he was alive, but he would make it up to him now.

It wasn't long after that Balthasar lost all capacity for speech, and he only mouthed the name *Daphne* over and over again before his body finally stilled.

Dryas would never have predicted that his entire world would change in the back of a cart under an open sky. In the stories he had always heard, such things always seemed to take place under much more dramatic circumstances. Like in the immediate aftermath of a great battle, while being cradled by a devastated lover, or in front of the gods after rewinning their favor. The mundaneness of the situation just further deepened his shock and made it feel so unreal.

But the sweat dripping down his back was real. The jostling of the cart was real. The grief that was tearing him apart from the inside couldn't have been imagined.

"May we live to die free." he had murmured before the tears began to spill over. "Goodbye, big brother."

That's when he heard the sweetest voice call out into the void and he looked up to find Zosime staring at him, looking stricken. His brain was moving too sluggishly to compose a response and all he could do was murmur her name. Her face dropped even more, and she buried her head in her hands.

"We're close to the Hearth." Anastasia said heavily. "We can give him a proper pyre and funeral rites there."

"Daphne should be with him, too." he added quietly.

At least Balthasar had died protecting the most important person in the world to him and his brother would not have to wait long before his soul was sent to the heavens to dance among the stars. Dryas could find some comfort in that.

"No, no, no." Zosime began muttering and he felt his heart crack even more.

She didn't look too far away from death's door either with her bloodied face and he could tell that she was about to lose it when she started tearing uncontrollably at her hair. He glanced wildly at Anastasia who reached out a hand towards Zosime, who only slapped it away.

"No, no, no." Zosime hissed.

"Zosime." he murmured, having no idea what to do next.

She started to rise from her seat when Anastasia suddenly flashed out a hand and hit her on the back of the head. Zosime's eyes went blank, and Anastasia caught her before she fell over.

Dryas almost cried out in outrage before Anastasia whispered, "She hasn't been sleeping. She needs rest to face what happened."

She carefully picked Zosime up, stepped out of the cart, and walked to the back before gently placing her on Dryas's lap.

"Watch over her." she ordered firmly but not sternly.

"Always." he said in an undertone as he wrapped his arms protectively around her.

Anastasia hesitated for a moment as she looked at him then at Balthasar's body. She looked like she was going to say something for a moment but was ultimately silent when she walked back to the front. Instead of climbing in, she gave water to the horses from the animal bladder she had tied to her side and patted them on the side of their necks.

"I know you've had a hard journey." she stated, and Dryas marveled at how she talked to them like they could understand her. "I know you're tired, but it was necessary. I only ask for you to hold on for another day before you get proper food and rest. Are you willing to help us?"

The horses whinnied then snorted, raising their heads then bringing them down like a nod of agreement.

Anastasia inclined her head in appreciation and said, "Your service won't be forgotten."

She then climbed back in and gently urged them forward. He felt the jolt of the cart as they moved forward, but instead of galloping at full speed, they only trotted. He didn't complain, knowing that there was no more need for speed now that the emergency had passed.

"They're very intelligent creatures." Anastasia said a few minutes later.

"Horses?" he asked numbly but he didn't take his eyes off Zosime's weary face.

She was starting to regain some color in cheeks which relieved him, but she still looked like she needed to sleep for a full week. Her eyelids weren't fluttering like they usually did when she slept and, if she hadn't been taking the occasional deep breath, she could have been mistaken for a corpse.

"Yes." Anastasia confirmed. "Have you interacted with one before?"

"No, ma'am." he replied softly.

"They're like our queen." Anastasia claimed and Dryas frowned before she explained. "They can sense people's emotions when they're nearby."

He swallowed before asking, "How?"

"I don't know." Anastasia shrugged. "But those who spend enough time around them know it to be true. Just watch how they react when they're around people feeling different emotions."

"Ma'am." he murmured.

"Horses around desperate riders act like the world is about to fall apart around them." she continued. "Horses around angry riders can never keep still. Horses around anxious riders look like they're about to be attacked. Horses around happy riders prance." She didn't speak for a long moment before finishing. "Horses around sad riders are often quiet and stare into the distance."

"I see." was all he had the strength to say.

"It's the same with people, I suppose." she added. "When mama died, father would either pace around the house or sit still for hours without moving."

"What did you do, ma'am?" he asked so quietly he thought she hadn't heard him for a minute.

"I was in Training at the time." Anastasia replied. "I didn't have the luxury of time to feel my grief. But all I wanted to do was lie in her arms or to have my father show me that there were still hills worth chasing."

He swallowed before inquiring, "Does it change?"

She didn't respond for a long time until she finally answered, "It will always be with you, but it won't always feel as heavy as it does now."

She didn't volunteer any more information and Dryas knew better than to ask more questions, even if he had the energy to. He was surprised he got as much from her as he did but, even if her voice was still one of hard steel instead of the gentle caress of a light wind, he was grateful she talked to him. They didn't speak as the hours passed and she asked the horses to quicken their pace just enough so they wouldn't be stopped by any farmers on their way to the gates.

"Zosime." he murmured in her ear as the gates grew closer, thinking that she should be awake when they returned. "We're here."

He gently shook her, not wanting to aggravate the slowly scabbing cut on her face, until her eyes finally peeled open, and she croaked, "Dryas?"

"We're here." he repeated gently, and he almost shuddered at how close he had come to losing her. "We're home."

She blinked several times and winced as she began to sit up. He was sure she was feeling every ounce of pain that she had ignored from all the recent strenuous physical activities, and she gingerly rubbed the back of her head. To his immense relief, the unhinged look in her eyes had faded and she only looked dejected and befuddled, instead of being moments away from losing all semblance of control.

"Who goes there?" a stern voice demanded, and it took a moment for Dryas to recognize it belonged to Orrin.

"The queen is back." Anastasia called out.

He heard several shouts that Queen Zosime had finally returned and the cheers that followed quickly faded into silence when they saw Balthasar's body in the cart. A minute later, Anastasia pulled on the reigns, and they slowed to a complete stop. Dryas looked up to find a disheveled Vasiliki standing in front of them, her hands stained with what was clearly blood. He clenched his jaw when he saw Perleros standing beside her, and he savagely wondered if his father would feel any remorse for valuing the family legacy more than Balthasar's life.

"General." Anastasia said as she got off the buckboard.

"Where is everyone?" Perleros asked softly a moment later.

Dryas stepped off the cart, his sandals hitting the ground with a heavy thud and Zosime took his outstretched hand as she jumped down to join him. He knew she was still recovering from the physical toll she had experienced and was now swaying on her feet.

"There was trouble and speed was of the essence." Anastasia stated. "The others couldn't keep up but are on their way back."

There was a long pause before Perleros asked, "Who?"

"We should go inside, General." she suggested, but he brusquely walked past her.

Dryas glared at Perleros, and his father's eyes widened when their gazes met. There was a heartbeat of silence before he saw the realization in his father's eyes, and he knew that his father was thinking that the wrong son had been taken. A muscle twitched in Dryas's jaw as Perleros ran the rest of the distance to the back of the cart. He watched his father freeze as he saw who was waiting for him there before leaning on the cart for support a moment later.

He heard his brother's voice echo in his mind: *What would you know about legacy or family when you've only worn the cloak for a few months?*

He may not have cared about their legacy, but he knew all about family. Much more than the man who stood inches away from him who had traded his brother's life for the chance to pin an officer's rank to his cloak. Disgusted, he turned away and began preparing himself for what he had to do next. He took a step forward and found the muscles in his legs spasm from the toll of running non-stop for days then spending excruciating long hours sitting still.

He gritted his teeth and limped over to Vasiliki, appraising her appearance for a moment, before asking hopefully, "Has she given birth yet?"

Vasiliki swallowed and said, "She didn't survive."

Dryas bowed his head and resisted the urge to rage against the world for taking his brother and sister so cruelly away from him at the same time.

"Boy or girl?" he inquired, wondering if Daphne had named her child before dying or if he would be able to help pick out the name.

Vasiliki only shook her head, and he felt the void inside him expanding.

"What happened?" she asked as Zosime finished dragging herself over to stand beside him.

"Ambush." Zosime answered dully.

"You need rest, my queen." Anastasia said quietly and a dazed Zosime didn't protest when Anastasia led her away.

Dryas appraised his friend and said kindly, "You look like you need to rest, too."

"Arrangements need to be made for the funerals." Vasiliki replied.

"Funeral." Dryas corrected. "They would have wanted a joint one."

"Done." Vasiliki agreed. "I'll make the announcement. One joint funeral at dusk today." She studied him for another moment then ordered. "Go clean up. You have my permission to use the bath house. I'll handle your father."

A part of him was surprised by how smoothly she was taking this all in stride, but he only gave her a nod as he shuffled forward. He soon found himself inside one of the bath houses and stripped off his sweaty and bloodied clothes. He gingerly stepped into the pool and was surprised to realize a moment later that, for the first time in a very long time, he was alone. Feeling something snap inside of him, he buried his head into his hands and sobbed.

He didn't know how long he remained there or when he finally scrubbed off every trace of dirt and blood off him. He just knew that at some point he had dragged himself out of the warm water and put on clean clothes that were left out in one of the cubicles. It wasn't quite big enough to fit him properly, but they were close enough for him not to care. What was a little discomfort after such agony?

He shuffled outside and frowned when he saw a stranger clad in white and blue clothes standing off to the side of the market street. He wondered briefly what else had happened since he left but he didn't stop to ask questions.

He had a job to do.

He continued forward towards the area where the nightly bonfires were held and stopped when he found a wide enough open space to build a large pyre. He then began to collect pieces of wood and meticulously placed them in the form of a large triangle. It was a slow, arduous process and he worked silently until he turned to find Vasiliki holding an armful of wood behind him. She still looked fatigued, but she must have cleaned up at some point since she was no longer bloody and sweaty. Jedrick stood beside her, also carrying wood, and he felt his throat tighten at his friend's thoughtfulness.

"It's time." Vasiliki said once they had finished building the pyre and she glanced at the horizon.

He followed her gaze and blinked when he realized it was dusk. He didn't know the entire day had come and gone already. She and Jedrick shared a look, and he inclined his head towards her before leaving them alone.

"At least he had you." she uttered softly, and Dryas bit the side of his cheek.

The next thing he knew, a crowd had gathered around them, and he felt a surge of irritation when he felt a tap on his shoulder. He spun around then almost lost his composure when he saw that it was Adelphie who had interrupted him in his grief. Her brown eyes blearing with tears, she wordlessly handed him the torch she had been carrying, its orange flames radiating like a beacon in the twilight sky.

He looked down as the bodies of his brother and his wife were placed on the pyre and he took a few steps forward to set the bottom of it aflame. It took a moment for it to catch but then the flames grew steadily taller and brighter, and he watched the smoke rise towards the sky. He almost flinched when he heard his sister begin to sing, her typically sweet voice utterly consumed by mourning for a loss that would be felt by them for every moment of every day.

He prayed that he would be able to protect her where he had failed to do so with their brother and that he would see Balthasar and Daphne's souls dancing together among the stars in peace at last.

CHAPTER

35

Perleros had battled with the worst kinds of pain in his life and thought that, after everything he had been through, he could survive anything. That wistful delusion was dispelled when he saw his oldest son's lifeless face and devastation shredded his soul apart in a single second. He was unsure how he remained standing throughout the pyre ceremony, but he found the strength to stay on his feet. Even after Adelphie began singing. He wanted to reprimand her for that, but he refrained from doing so at the last moment.

There were only so many times he could see the accusation in Dryas's eyes, and he didn't have it in him to see it again. Not today. He waited for Adelphie to finish her song of mourning before he approached his son and placed a hand on his shoulder, but Dryas only shook him away angrily.

"Look at what your ambition has wrought, father." Dryas scorned.

Adelphie didn't say anything, but her eyes flickered between the two of them before Perleros shook his head and walked away. He scanned the crowd for the next person he wanted to see then strode forward when he saw an exhausted Anastasia lingering on the outskirts of the crowd.

"General." she had stated quietly.

It wasn't her sympathy he wanted, but a thorough explanation of what happened and how the mission went catastrophically wrong.

"Let's talk." he ordered, unable to stop a little of the anger he was feeling from bubbling to the surface.

She nodded solemnly and suggested, "My house?"

He didn't object and followed her as she led him to her home and let him inside. He sat at the table while she poured wine into two cups and handed one of them to him. He stared at his without touching it and

Anastasia fiddled with hers for a minute before suddenly raising it to her lips and swallowing every drop in it.

"Balthasar saved her life." she said quietly, and he looked back up at her.

She then began recounting the events of the mission and walked him through every decision they made. Perleros scarcely registered the news that Afshin would soon be coming for them as he waited for the part he was most desperate to hear. She only hesitated for a moment after mentioning how they crossed the Karkaros mountains back into Midrios before talking about the ambush.

"We moved fast." she whispered. "I did what I could to get us out of there and to bandage him, but we were just too far away."

Perleros heard the regret in her voice, but he found it miraculous that Balthasar survived for as long as he did. He should have died days ago but he held on much longer than any other person would have expected him to.

That was his son, he thought proudly to himself. A fighter just like his mother.

There was a hole in Perleros's chest that he knew would never heal and would haunt every step he took for the rest of his mortal life. But he also couldn't permit his grief to outwardly consume him since too many were counting on him.

"You did everything you could." he finally said, and Anastasia slumped in her seat. A muscle twitched in his jaw when he forced himself to ask, "Did you notice changes in Queen Zosime's behavior?"

She immediately stiffened at the introduction of this new topic but replied carefully, "She hasn't been sleeping."

"How is her mental capacity?" Perleros continued to question.

"Fine." Anastasia replied curtly.

"Did you see anything of concern?" he followed up, not convinced based on how terrible the girl looked when she returned home.

Anastasia paused for a moment and eyed Perleros carefully. Finally, she responded protectively, "She just needs rest."

"Anastasia." he said softly. "I'm not asking you to insult our queen."

Her posture relaxed infinitesimally but her eyes remained guarded.

Perleros sighed. He knew that he would have to disclose more in order to put the warrior at ease and he swallowed before remarking, "You've been in leadership long enough. There's something you should know."

Her face smoothed out until she gave nothing away and only stared at him silently, waiting for him to continue speaking.

"King Atreo went mad before he died." Perleros stated. "Have you seen any such signs from Queen Zosime?"

She stared at him for a moment then unexpectedly stood up and poured herself another cup of wine. She looked down into the goblet for a moment then murmured, "The day grows even wearier." She looked back up at him then asserted sternly, "She only needs rest, General."

He couldn't fault her for downing the second cup of wine as rapidly as she did and pouring herself a third when he began telling her about the recent development with Apistia.

"Queen Vasiliki accepted his offer today." he finished, and he fiddled with his cup, toying with the idea of drowning his sorrows. "For better or for worse, we're going to have to deal with *them*. I'm calling a meeting tomorrow to discuss next steps."

"Yes, sir." she replied softly.

"I'll see you tomorrow." he declared, placing his untouched wine back on the table before he silently and quickly left the house.

Perleros's body felt heavy as he started walking towards his house. He reminisced about the time he met his wife, when all three of his children were born, and other all too fleeting moments of happy memories. But he couldn't stop himself from recalling much darker points of his life, especially when he thought about the Apistian who lurked in their walls.

He could never trust those silver-tongued snakes across the mountains who had probably just bided their time to make their move since that terrible day almost twenty one years ago. He could distinctly remember how the ground around him had been wrecked by a small earthquake that had knocked him off his feet. Perleros would still see those wrathful golden eyes that had burned brighter than the sun before mysteriously vanishing.

He recalled rising to his feet after those eyes disappeared and shuffling over to his king's body. How young he looked now, in his memory. His old friend's eyes had been wide but unseeing, his usual red-brown-yellow irises now just a dull red.

"*What did you do?*" Oscar had roared and only then had Perleros glanced up and looked at him and the other two Leondrians who had witnessed it all.

"Time for us to go." was all Perleros had said and had quickly shut the king's eyelids to hide the red irises.

Oscar's face had contorted with rage, but he and the others moved quickly to pick up the king's body.

"*Cowards!*" a female voice had shouted. Perleros hadn't bothered to reply to the taunt and focused on the task at hand. What was that Senator's name? Sophie?

Perleros had known leaving would cause a litany of problems but staying would cause even more. So, he hadn't looked back at the boy, his father's body, or the three shaken Senators as they hurried away. He had only tightened his grip on his king's body as they ran back to the others who were waiting at camp a couple of miles outside the city.

After they had walked past the two guards with the king's body in their arms, he announced to the stunned people in camp, "Our king is dead. Ready to leave in ten minutes."

Perleros helped put the king's body in the back of a cart while the others sprang into action to pack up camp.

He had leveled the full weight of his gaze on the non-Leondrian responsible for carrying supplies in the cart and warned dangerously, "Drive carefully, as if your life depends on it."

The man had paled and nodded vigorously. Perleros had then turned away but didn't have time to react when Oscar stepped up to him and whispered venomously, "You killed him, Perleros." Oscar's eyes had gleamed darkly before hissing, "You lured our king there and—"

Perleros had meant to maintain his stoic demeanor but, in that moment, he couldn't stop himself from snapping, "Don't speak of things you'll never understand, Oscar."

Oscar's face had hardened before spitting, "We'll see."

They had moved out a couple of minutes after that and Perleros had hardly noted the time or the passing miles until they arrived at the gates of the Hearth. He and a few others had taken a boat to return the King home as quickly as possible while the rest of the Leondrians would be crossing the mountain pass to return home. Perleros hadn't looked back as he forced himself forward, dreading his inevitable confrontation with Cora but knowing she couldn't hear the news from anyone else.

"Perleros—" Thea had called out when he had stalked down the halls of the Heart, but he ignored her as he approached the door to Cora's chambers.

He had then knocked respectfully and waited a few seconds before gently opening the door, "Cora—"

He had stopped dead when he saw her on the bed, her body too unnaturally still to be confused for someone alive. Thea had sighed from behind him, and he turned to see her grave expression.

"You're a day late." she had said softy. "She died last night."

Perleros had drawn in a breath and then asked, "The child?"

"Children." Thea had corrected. "She had twin daughters."

"*Had*?" Perleros had demanded.

"Has." she had corrected then asked a few moments later after looking around. "Where's King Atreo?"

"The king is dead." Perleros had said numbly, feeling little else besides how heavy his body was and wanting nothing more than to lie in bed with his wife in his arms.

Perleros had ignored Thea's intake of breath then walked into the chambers and knelt beside Cora's body. He hadn't known if her soul was still hovering nearby or if it was wandering the Hearth in search of her husband. All he had known was that her soul was still tied to this mortal plane since her body hadn't been burnt or buried. He had then hoped that she was still in the room, just out of his mortal sight so she could hear him make her one last promise.

"I failed to protect him." he had whispered then vowed, "But I promise to look after your children."

Perleros had made the sign of the gods as he rose to his feet again. He had frowned as he walked around the bed then surveilled the rest of the room.

"Where are the children?" he had asked as dread rose in his chest.

"Vasiliki and Zosime were taken to be cleaned then Spyridon wanted to pray for them to receive the gods' blessings." Thea had explained. "I was just about to check on them."

His temper flaring, he had asked, "When was the last time you saw them?"

Thea had then answered, "Last night. They needed my help with—"

His fists had clenched, and he had known instantly that something was wrong. It was simply too much of a coincidence for the children to not be here after everything that had just happened.

"We need to find them." he had ordered, and Thea had wasted no time in acting.

"Let's go." she had responded.

They had searched the Hearth frantically but there had been no sign of the children or Spyridon. They had eventually found them and taken them back to safety, and until Angelos had walked to their gates, Perleros hadn't heard from Spyridon since he had banished him.

These memories and recalling how that little Apistian boy cried plagued Perleros throughout the night and for most of the next morning. He could still hear it faintly when he walked into the generals' meeting room and watched when everyone else entered. They gave him sympathetic looks and nods of acknowledgement but said nothing as they waited for their queens.

Vasiliki joined them a couple minutes later, her eyes lingering on Perleros for a moment before she ordered, "Report."

Perleros grunted and replied, "The Council—"

He stopped when he saw Zosime come in with Anastasia beside her. She looked remarkably better than when she had first returned, looking nowhere near as dazed and disheveled. Vasiliki only glanced at Zosime for a few seconds before looking back at Perleros and waved for him to continue.

"The Council wishes for a group to go with the Apistian as a gesture of good faith." Perleros finished. "Before approving the alliance."

There was a long ring of silence in the room before Vasiliki announced, "I'll go."

"I'll go with you." Zosime added a moment later.

"It is too dangerous for both of you to go, my queen." Oscar insisted. "Especially with the close call you had with no heir."

Vasiliki gave Zosime a side eyed look before pointing out, "You just returned, and you haven't established the same diplomatic relationship with him as I have."

"I am not convinced that either of you should go." Thea interjected. "But if you *both* go, there will be no queen here to look after Leondria."

"I am looking after Leondria." Zosime disagreed. "By ensuring a war alliance succeeds."

"It will succeed." Vasiliki said with a certain sharpness in her tone that made Zosime blink.

"My queen—" Thea began, and Vasiliki held up a hand.

"This isn't like the last time." Vasiliki said. "I won't be doing dangerous intelligence gathering to foreign lands. This is a diplomatic mission across the mountains. How else can we satisfy the Council and ensure that an alliance will succeed unless I go as Leondria's representative?"

Thea closed her mouth and reluctantly nodded.

"If she goes, I go." Zosime persisted.

Perleros knew there would be no changing their minds, but he couldn't stand the idea of both of them going after everything that happened. So, he squared his shoulders and announced, "I will accompany the queens with their personal guard."

Perleros hadn't dared to leave Leondria in the past couple decades but now he didn't dare to stay behind with both his queens leaving, especially since they would be accompanied by that Apistian naval officer.

He had a vow to uphold to protect his friends' daughters and he could keep a better eye on them if he went with them.

"Inform the Lieutenant we'll be coming with him to Apistia." Vasiliki ordered then added a moment later. "We leave tomorrow."

CHAPTER

36

"My queen!" the room cried out.

"We need to move." Vasiliki said. "Why delay?"

"We need to make preparations." General Thea insisted. "And decide on a group to send with you, my queen."

"Our personal guards and General Perleros will suffice." Vasiliki replied. "And we can hunt off the land. It's not a long distance."

"It's not short, Vasiliki." Zosime shook her head.

"You went the long way to avoid going through Apistia." Vasiliki said, without really looking at her. "We should cut straight across the mountains."

"You should have more protection around you." General Thea pressed.

"I'll have my sister and some of Leondria's best warriors." Vasiliki disagreed. "And we won't want to scare them with a larger group."

"Scare them?" General Penelope frowned.

"Yes, unless I'm missing something." Vasiliki raised an eyebrow and noticed how Perleros's and Oscar's faces both darkened.

"We could wait until my nephew returns so you have a few more people with you without bringing too large of a group." Penelope suggested and Vasiliki was surprised by her energy. She had grown quieter and seemingly more confused during recent meetings and Vasiliki had been growing concerned about her continued effectiveness.

"We can't afford to wait for Flavian and the others." Vasiliki said. "We need to cement the alliance, so we have a chance to survive against the tyrant's army."

"The country is divided." Zosime added and there was a mournful look in her eyes. "They don't trust us, and I don't know if we can unite them for war without Apistia's support."

No one responded to that statement and Vasiliki looked at each general in turn for several seconds.

"If there's nothing else," Vasiliki finally said, and after waiting a moment, declared. "Dismissed."

The generals reluctantly filed out and Zosime said after they left, "You've changed."

Vasiliki slowly turned to look at her and replied coolly, "You were gone a long time."

Zosime wouldn't know what these past months had been like for her. Wouldn't have seen her find the inner resolve to give orders when she was forced to stand alone. She may not have been as quick on her feet like her sister and there may have been times she delayed before making final decisions, but she had learned to act much quicker than before.

"You should rest." Vasiliki advised before sweeping out of the room with Jedrick following close behind her.

The rage she had felt so strongly in the initial weeks after her sister's departure had abated but the bitter disappointment she felt towards her still hadn't faded. She was grateful that Dryas had returned safely. But Balthasar was still dead, and the others were lost somewhere north of them in Midrios. Zosime had created such a mess and now she needed to pick up the pieces.

"Queen Vasiliki." Sofoklis greeted when Vasiliki walked onto the landing.

"Lieutenant." she stated as she inclined her head towards him. "How has your morning been?"

"I have no complaints." he gestured around him. "Your lands are beautiful."

"You'll be grateful to return home though." she said, and he shrugged.

"I am honored to be here for as long as your hospitality allows, Queen Vasiliki." Sofoklis disagreed. "It has been quite the eye-opening experience."

"Do Apistians have preconceived notions about Leondria?" Vasiliki asked.

"Just the same as the Leondrians have for us." he replied mildly.

"Then it's untrue that Apistians value intelligence and scholastic thought?" Vasiliki raised an eyebrow.

This made him smirk ever so slightly then he answered dryly, "I was referring to the darker rumors about the depth of our cowardice and weakness."

"Then those who uttered such tales shall be punished." Vasiliki declared, indignation rising in her chest. "Who insulted a guest of Leondria?"

"I can hear without being seen." he shook his head. "No one has disparaged your honor as a host."

She eyed his bright blue chiton skeptically and asserted, "If anyone has insulted you directly, they will be dealt with."

Jedrick cleared his throat and added, "I haven't seen any such undisciplined behavior, my queen."

She inclined her head to him then turned back to Sofoklis, "Then there is much we must learn about each other."

"I already have a much better understanding of your people." Sofoklis said. "And their leader."

"I have given my approval for the alliance." she remarked a moment later.

"I was informed, Queen Vasiliki." he replied.

"But final approval rests with the Council." she added, and his gaze wandered to the Tower. "They have ordered for us to accompany you to Apistia before agreeing to provide it." His eyes snapped back to her as she finished. "We'll be leaving tomorrow."

He looked down for a moment to compose himself before asking, "How many?"

"Five." she answered. "Myself, my sister, our two personal guards, and General Perleros."

His lips twisted for a second at the mention of Perleros then his expression smoothed into guarded neutrality.

"What is it?" she inquired.

He hesitated then walked further down the landing. Vasiliki gestured for Jedrick to wait by the guards and followed Sofoklis as he walked just far enough to be out of earshot before he asked, "Can I ask you something personal, Queen Vasiliki?"

Intrigued, she agreed, "You may ask."

"Do you know what happened about twenty one years ago?" he inquired.

She frowned, surprised that was what he was asking about. She said in an unsentimental tone, "My father died defending Midrios from Afshin the First, my sister and I had just been born, and the gods disappeared."

"That's what I feared." he murmured in a troubled tone.

"Does this have to do with how you act around General Perleros?" Vasiliki guessed as she narrowed her eyes in suspicion.

"I would speak to your general, Queen Vasiliki." Sofoklis suggested.

She had already tried that route with unsuccessful results, and she wasn't about to let this opportunity to find out the truth slip through her fingers.

"Lieutenant." Vasiliki reproached. "You would agree we've established a good working relationship since you've arrived?"

Sofoklis begrudgingly nodded and eyed her warily.

"Do you want this alliance?" she asked.

"The people I respect do." he responded evasively.

"Do you expect an alliance to work if we hide things from each other?" she asked.

He hesitated then sighed before stating, "King Atreo did defend Midrios against Afshin the First, but the story doesn't end there."

Vasiliki frowned, "There were more invaders?"

"No, Queen Vasiliki." Sofoklis corrected. "Just the one. Your people successfully repelled his invasion by Karkaros."

She stared at him intently, waiting with bated breath for him to elaborate.

Sofoklis finally, maddeningly continued, "After the battle, King Atreo marched south with his forces. I don't know his reasons for doing so but he set his sights on Apistia."

"Set his sights?" Vasiliki repeated slowly.

"He marched his forces down and camped them a couple miles away from Apistia." Sofoklis explained, his expression even more wary. "He and a few of his guards, including your general, went to Apistia where they were greeted by some Senators."

"What else?" Vasiliki asked as apprehension rose in her chest.

"He commanded subservience from us then killed a Senator when we rejected his demand." In response to the shock on her face, he added. "From every account I have heard, he had gone mad."

QUEENS & GODS: DARK HORIZONS

"And Apistia still wants an alliance?" she asked, astounded.

He nodded as his eyes flickered to something behind her and she quickly turned to find Perleros standing behind her.

"It's true then." she whispered after seeing the look on his face. "*Why,* Perleros?"

Why did their father do that? Why did he keep such important information from her?

"I live to serve, my queen." Perleros replied quietly.

"That's no answer." she muttered then said to Sofoklis. "You should make your preparations tonight."

Sofoklis bowed his head.

"We leave at first light." she said then stalked away from the Apistian Lieutenant who had just shaken her entire world and the General who hidden the truth from her.

—

Vasiliki usually enjoyed warm spring mornings like these, but her mood was still dampened by the devastating news she had received yesterday. She would occasionally catch Sofoklis glancing at her, but he kept quiet as they strode out of the Hearth. No one spoke after Anastasia suggested that they avoid the most populated farmlands to prevent any overeager farmers from delaying their progress.

She wasn't sure how the naval officer would fare on a land journey with a lot of physical exertion, but he surprised her with his agility and stamina. He wasn't as strong as a Leondrian, but he was able to keep up with them. By maintaining a steady pace and avoiding certain farms, they were able to make decent progress. Only a few days passed before they found themselves at the base of the gods' mountain where they stopped for the night.

Vasiliki soon found herself awoken by Jedrick and she rubbed her eyes before standing, ready for her turn on night watch. She cracked her neck as she walked around and saw Anastasia wake Zosime. Vasiliki watched Jedrick and Anastasia lie down as Zosime joined her on watch but neither of them spoke. Only a few minutes passed before she heard light snoring from everyone, and she found herself glancing up at the glittering night sky in longing.

She honestly didn't know when the song began playing. She just knew that, at some point, she could hear nothing but the sweetest music emanating from the distance. A lullaby that wrapped her in a cocoon of warmth and beckoned for her to come. Without a mind of her own, she followed the melody. The song reached a climax, and her movements slowed until she stopped at the same time the music ended.

She blinked, feeling like she had just woken from the strangest dream. She glanced around her and found her sister standing beside her looking as bewildered as she felt. Zosime opened her mouth when a bright light suddenly pulsed out of nowhere and a woman clothed in white materialized where no one had been there before.

"How do you do, my children?" a soft feminine voice asked, and Vasiliki was now paralyzed for an entirely different reason.

A goddess stood in front of her. A goddess with a smile that was brighter than a cloudless day that promised a mother's unconditional love. A goddess with the warmest almond-colored eyes, with skin that was the richest shade of burnt umber, and hair that fell down her back in long black waves. Vasiliki had never before seen anyone so beautiful.

"I have missed you," Lady Hermione greeted Vasiliki warmly then turned to Zosime. "And it is a pleasure to finally see you again, young one."

Missed her? Vasiliki thought, bewildered. But they had never met.

"Do you not remember, young one?" Lady Hermione asked kindly, and idly tucked a loose strand of hair behind Vasiliki's ear.

"No, my Lady." Vasiliki uttered dumbly.

"You were still a child," Lady Hermione remarked. "But you had wandered away and found yourself too far out in the pond."

The horrid memory of the time she had nearly drowned surged into her mind. She could vividly recall the near drowning itself but only had vague recollections of the events afterwards.

"You saved me?" Vasiliki gasped. "I always thought—"

Lady Hermione smiled kindly, "That a random woman saved you? Or you saved yourself and only imagined receiving help?"

Vasiliki was at a loss for words, "My Lady—"

"Call me mother. Or, in your case, aunt." Lady Hermione gently corrected.

"We never had a mother," Vasiliki muttered automatically.

"Yes, you did, and she loved you very much." Lady Hermione chastised. "Her body just couldn't survive the birth." When Vasiliki looked down, she continued. "I felt her undying love for you when I blessed her pregnancy, and she would be so proud of the women you have become."

Vasiliki blinked at the word women. All her life, she had only been viewed as a child, a Trainee, a Leondrian, and a queen. She had never been her own before and the thought almost made tears spring to her eyes.

"But she died when we were born. How could she be proud of us?" Vasiliki asked quietly.

"Oh, my child," she sighed. "She loved you long before you were born. It is something you cannot truly understand until you carry a child yourself."

Lady Hermione reached up and brushed Vasiliki's cheek, "She loved you more than anything." She then turned and brushed Zosime's cheek too, "She loved you both more than anything and she would have stayed if she could."

Vasiliki opened her mouth then closed it.

"So much death in two decades. How the people, too, have changed," Lady Hermione remarked sadly, her tone turning to that of warning. "Not following the old ways or disobeying our long-given commands without fearing the consequences."

Vasiliki's eyes widened and she asked breathlessly, "Have you come to help us with the war?"

Lady Hermione sighed heavily and stated sorrowfully, "I can't interfere. My time here draws near."

Desperate for more information, Vasiliki inquired, "Why have the gods—"

"I will not go that far, even now." Lady Hermione interrupted with a note of finality then added. *"Make the peace*, my children. My darling nieces."

Lady Hermione's skin began to shine even brighter, and her form glowed so brightly that Vasiliki was forced to looked away when the goddess disappeared in a flash of white light. Stunned, she and Zosime looked at each other.

"You never told me," Zosime whispered.

"I didn't remember her," Vasiliki said sincerely.

"The drowning," Zosime corrected then scoffed. "I always wondered why you dreaded bathing."

"It was during the one time you were sick—" Vasiliki started.

"We need to get back," Zosime interrupted brusquely, and Vasiliki didn't bother protesting.

A heavy silence hung over them as they walked back and Vasiliki stared up at the stars when she returned to her post, her thoughts churning from everything Lady Hermione had told them.

Her entire extended family hadn't abandoned her as she had always believed, and her heart squeezed at the thought. The thought stuck with her throughout the next day when they began climbing one of the mountains and she and Zosime didn't once speak of what transpired the night before. They just continued marching forward and Vasiliki found her mind buzzing when they crossed over to the other side of the mountains.

She had never been this far away from home before, and she was so curious about what Apistia was like. The closer they came, the more her excitement grew. The lands were still mountainous but not as much as back home and she was surprised by how differently the air here smelled. It had a salty taste to it, and she saw birds flying over the coast's rich blue waters. She became so mesmerized by the beautiful sights that she didn't even notice the gates in the distance until Sofoklis suddenly stopped.

"We're here." Lieutenant Sofoklis announced and turned to the group. "Welcome to Apistia."

CHAPTER

37

Anastasia could feel her skin crawling by the time she saw the Apistian gates in the distance. It had been a sober journey across the mountains, but she thankfully hadn't seen those godly grey eyes following her. She watched over her queens carefully, and noticed how Vasiliki became more animated the closer they came to Apistia while Zosime only retreated more into herself. Anastasia was relieved that, besides Zosime being quieter than usual, she seemed to have fully recovered from the arduous run back home. But there was now a persistent, haunted look in her eyes that hadn't been there before.

She would never forget seeing the intensity in her eyes when they raced to save Balthasar's life. She had been a source of strength that helped Anastasia focus on saving him when his burning flesh reminded her so much of the bodies she had seen in the aftermath of Typhon's attack. Even if it ultimately hadn't been enough to save him.

She glanced at Perleros when the Apistian informed them that they had arrived, and she had stood by his side long enough to know that he was currently on high alert. Neither he nor Anastasia needed the Gift or superior intelligence to know that they wouldn't be accepted here.

"The entire group shouldn't approach the gates all at once." the Apistian added which made Perleros cross his arms.

"I'll go with you." Perleros said and the Apistian vehemently shook his head.

"We remember the last time you approached us." he said darkly.

"You won't be going alone." Perleros replied softly but his hardened face left no room for argument.

Anastasia wasn't certain but she was reasonably confident that Sofoklis did not harbor any ill will towards the rest of the group. She didn't think he was planning an ambush, but she agreed with Perleros that he shouldn't return to Apistia's gates alone either. He was a naval officer whose loyalty belonged to Apistia, who clearly didn't harbor any friendly feelings for Leondrians. They did have the advantage of surprise since they had left unexpectedly but she didn't want to take any chances that would unnecessarily endanger Zosime.

But this also meant the Apistians could perceive them as a threat since they showed up on their lands with no warning. Even though they had been the ones to reach out to them for an alliance, she suspected that this proposal was probably made with dispassionate reason than out of any desire to become friends. Her attention shifted to Zosime, and she could tell she was about to say something when Sofoklis cleared his throat.

"Queen Vasiliki." he said. "Would you and your guard like to accompany me first?"

Vasiliki pondered the offer for a moment before agreeing, "I would be honored, Lieutenant."

"Follow me." Sofoklis replied and Anastasia kept her eyes trained on the three of them as they walked towards the gates.

Perleros also kept his eyes trained on Vasiliki and the veins in his hands were bulging from how tightly he gripped his arms when he uttered, "Now we wait."

"I didn't sense any malice from him." Zosime said quietly.

Perleros turned towards Anastasia and ordered, "Use any force necessary to protect the queen if anyone tries anything."

"Yes, General." she said.

She would protect Queen Zosime at any cost and let the gods have mercy on anyone who had to go through Anastasia to get to her queen.

CHAPTER

38

"There will be two guards at the gate who may have questions for you, Queen Vasiliki." Lieutenant Sofoklis warned in an undertone.

She nodded to show she understood as they quickly closed the distance to the gates. They stretched high into the sky and two guards wearing matching white and blue uniforms stood in front of them. She braced herself for whatever was coming next when they stopped in front of the guards and couldn't help but notice how they tensed when they saw her red cloak and golden shield.

She was reminded yet again that her father had attacked them, and she still couldn't believe that a protector of Midrios killed one of the people he was supposed to defend.

Their stances relaxed ever so slightly when Sofoklis stepped ahead of her and one of them said, "Lieutenant?"

"I bring guests for Apistia." he gestured to her and introduced, "This is Queen Vasiliki of Leondria, and this is her personal guard, Jedrick of Leondria."

"Please wait here, Lieutenant." one of them requested.

Sofoklis nodded and said graciously, "Of course."

The guard who had just spoken bowed his head and slipped through the gates that blocked most of her view of what laid inside. Her skin thrummed with anticipation while they waited, and she noticed how Jedrick angled himself just subtly enough that he would only need to make a single sidestep to block any blow directed at Vasiliki.

"Your crew has been anxious for your return, Lieutenant." the remaining guard informed Sofoklis with a smile. "They were about ready to—"

Sofoklis smoothly interrupted, "Let's not bore our guest with such trivial details, sailor."

"Sir." he replied.

The silence grew awkward, and the sailor began to look a little uncomfortable as they waited. Vasiliki was nearly bursting at the seams with questions, but she was also content with the silence, as she knew Jedrick was. They only had to wait several minutes before she saw the sailor who had left earlier push the gate open just wide enough for him and two other figures she didn't recognize to walk out.

One was a pale, middle-aged woman with brown hair streaked with silver and the other was a man who looked a handful of years older than Vasiliki. His lips were curved upwards in a smirk as he sauntered towards them, and his dark beard was trimmed short like the rest of his hair. She had to stop herself from blinking from surprise, unused to seeing such diverse physical appearances. The sailor took his place back at the entrance while the other two took a few more steps forward before stopping in front of them.

"Lieutenant, who are your new friends?" the man asked.

Sofoklis bowed slightly before answering, "Captain Alastair. Senator Sophie. This is Queen Vasiliki and her personal guard, Jedrick of Leondria. Queen Zosime and her two guards are waiting further behind so we could get better acquainted."

Vasiliki inclined her head and said, "It's a pleasure to meet you, Captain. Senator."

The Senator looked at her red cloak and shield with cold, calculating eyes and her lips curled in disdain.

"Queen Vasiliki." she responded coolly and just barely inclined her head back.

"Welcome to Apistia!" Captain Alastair boomed then turned to Lieutenant Sofoklis. "Did you have a safe journey back?"

"I did, Captain." Lieutenant Sofoklis reassured.

"Excellent." the Captain grinned then asked, "How was your journey, Queen Vasiliki?"

"Uneventful." she replied. "Your Lieutenant was more than competent as our guide."

"I'm glad to hear that." he said, and she was stunned when he waggled an eyebrow at her before continuing. "He's gotten us stranded in the open sea before so I was worried he would get lost."

Senator Sophie's eyes flickered to hers when she remarked, "Lieutenant Sofoklis is one of the finest officers in our extensive Navy. We are glad to have him back home to lead our esteemed sailors."

"Thank you, Senator." Lieutenant Sofoklis bowed his head and Vasiliki blinked in surprise.

Those weren't words she often heard since one should be grateful to do their duty without seeking attention or commendations.

"Would you prefer to rest or take a tour, Queen Vasiliki?" Senator Sophie asked after a moment with the slightest mocking emphasis on the word Queen.

"I would be honored to learn more about Apistia." Vasiliki answered seriously, ignoring the slight.

"That is excellent news." Sophie remarked with a sly smile and tilted her head. "You will find Senator Alastair a great guide. His obsequiousness towards guests like yourselves is unparalleled."

The bow Alastair gave her was nothing short of ridiculing when he agreed, "Finer words have never before been uttered, Senator. One can never match your scholarly wit in civilized society."

Vasiliki glanced at Jedrick from the corner of her eye, wondering if this was really the kind of conversations Apistians liked to have and what game they were playing here. He returned her stare for a moment before they glanced back at Senator Sophie who gave Vasiliki another sly smile before leaving without another word.

Alastair gestured for them to follow him as he walked past the gates into Apistia, and she almost stopped dead in her tracks when the full city-state came into view. Vasiliki immediately thought about how the Hearth had been designed in such a way that everything built inside of it would be connected with the idea that Leondrians made up one heart.

What she saw now looked like something straight out a dream if she had the imagination to envision such creations. It was clear to her in that moment that Apistia had been built by the dreamers. By geniuses or madmen who each had their own visions on how to impress the gods or to intimidate other mortals who dared to enter. Everywhere she looked, there was something new to see, as if conformity was the greatest travesty an Apistian could make.

Vasiliki found herself marveling at one building in particular that was several stories tall, scarcely believing her eyes.

"It's interesting work." Captain Alastair said, noting where her gaze landed. "I know the architect and it's his greatest ambition in life to build something so tall that it touches the sky."

Vasiliki blinked and remarked, "Bold."

"There's a lot to see in Apistia." Captain Alastair declared then asked. "Is there anything you desire to see, Queen Vasiliki?"

What a scandalous idea, she thought to herself. Having individual desires almost skirted traitorous territory since Leondrians only obeyed the gods and protected their people. The only desire they were supposed to have was to serve or, if they avoided their duty, to die.

Vasiliki dodged the question under Jedrick's watchful eye and instead asked, "Where's your favorite place, Captain?"

"Ho!" he exclaimed, and he stopped to think.

Her head turned when she heard a beautiful song that she had never heard before. She found herself captivated by it, drinking in every note until the music suddenly ceased when meandering Apistians finally noticed her. She saw how their eyes clung to her red cloak and couldn't miss how many people ducked inside nearby buildings.

"I know just the place." the Captain clapped his hands together. "I think it will be a unique learning experience."

Vasiliki did her best to keep the excitement off her face, hoping she only conveyed polite interest. She could never admit out loud that she was intrigued to see whatever was so impressive that it was this highly ranked military officer and political leader's favorite spot in this fascinating place of invention.

"Lead the way, Captain." she said as nonchalantly as she could.

"Oh, I will." he laughed, and he led them around many buildings and windy roads.

"Here we are." he announced suddenly and pivoted to face an inconspicuous building on their right.

She didn't initially him believe him since it didn't seem anywhere near as impressive as many of the other places they had passed by on their route.

She hid her surprise, not wanting to offend him, before realizing that there was probably something ingenious waiting for her inside.

"Jedrick." the Captain pursed his lips. "Would you mind guarding the door with Lieutenant Sofoklis?"

Jedrick's eyes narrowed before he turned towards Vasiliki who only nodded in agreement. She tried silently conveying that she could break his bones with little effort if he gave her trouble and that she would call out if she needed him. He grunted in reluctant agreement and stood at the entrance, as fierce and immovable as a statue.

"Queen Vasiliki." Alastair said as he opened the wooden door and gestured for Vasiliki to enter.

"After you, Captain." she gestured back.

Even if she was taking some risks to show good faith, she wasn't about to walk first into some strange building she had never seen before.

"Of course." he grinned, unfazed, and sauntered inside.

She closed the door behind her after stepping inside, and immediately found herself enveloped in darkness. She followed him by listening to his footsteps and blinked a few times when they entered a large foray where small candles lining the walls provided enough light to maintain an air of mystery while making it more comfortable to see.

She glanced around her, and her hand almost twitched for her sword when she saw movement against the walls. She stared at something that moved again then froze when she realized what it was she was watching. Now that her eyes had adjusted, she could clearly see lounge chairs placed closely against the walls with patrons in golden masks lying down on them. But what made her jaw drop open was when she noticed people in various stages of undress performing very intimate acts on these patrons hiding their identities.

"Captain?" she asked, recovering from her shock.

"Feel free to wait here or pick your favorite and join us." Alastair chirped then bounded to a room to their left.

Vasiliki slowly turned back to look at the people in the room, most of whom were now staring at her before immediately averting their eyes. Some quickly untangled themselves and hurried away or dragged their partners into nearby rooms. Vasiliki ignored their reactions and walked to the farthest corner of the room while she waited for Alastair to finish his business.

Such places didn't exist in Leondria, but Vasiliki had a good idea of what kind of establishment this was. She saw a young girl, barely a teenager if Vasiliki had to guess, whispering with an older woman while periodically glancing at Vasiliki. The woman fervently shook her head, but the girl ignored her as she strode over to Vasiliki.

"You'd be more comfortable if you sat down." the girl said huskily with lowered eyes. "Or I can take you to a private room."

"I am waiting on—" Vasiliki hesitated. "—the male I came in with."

The girl brushed her hand against Vasiliki's arm, and she automatically took a step back, breaking off the contact.

"He's in a room?" the girl asked, quickly dropping her hand.

Vasiliki nodded and the girl smiled seductively, "He'll probably be a while then. Are you sure I can't make you more comfortable?"

Vasiliki gently but firmly said, "No."

A flash of relief and disappointment flickered across the girl's face, and she bit her lip, her eyes clinging to the shield.

Vasiliki gave her the best reassuring smile she could muster and asked kindly, "What's your name?"

The girl's eyes met Vasiliki's then she froze, horror dawning on her face. She trembled as she took a step back and Vasiliki marveled at the reaction until she realized that her red-brown-yellow eyes were a dead giveaway to her heritage.

She wasn't simply a disliked Leondrian in Apistian territory anymore. She was a queen of the people that the Apistians distrusted. Moving slowly to avoid scaring her further, Vasiliki sat down in the closest unoccupied chair. She gave the girl another encouraging smile and gestured for her to join her. The girl reluctantly followed and sat rigidly in a chair beside her with clenched hands.

"What's your name?" Vasiliki asked again with an even gentler tone.

"Call me Citrine." she squeaked back, and Vasiliki's eyebrows rose in surprise.

"Citrine?" she confirmed, wanting to make sure that she heard correctly.

The girl swallowed and nodded, "It best resembles Lady Apistia's eyes." Following Vasiliki's polite puzzlement, she elaborated. "It's a gemstone. A man from far away gave me one as payment last year."

"It's a fine name." Vasiliki reassured while thinking that the muscles in her face would soon strain from all the smiling she was doing.

But Citrine had to know that she wouldn't hurt her. She wasn't her father.

"This is my first time in Apistia," Vasiliki continued. "It's very different from my home. We don't have nearly as many buildings or visitors as you seem to have."

Citrine slightly relaxed and it was clear that her curiosity was starting to overcome her fear. She bit her lip then asked breathlessly, "Is it true all Leondrians are taught to fight as soon as they're weaned?

"We are taught the fighting spirit from our first breath, but we don't start Training until we're ten." Vasiliki answered, surprised by the girl's burst of curiosity.

"Really?" Citrine breathed. "How does that work?"

"We stay with our families or in communities designed to watch over children if our families are dead or out fighting. Then we go through Training where we live outside for ten years. Then we live in barracks, or in houses if you get married." Vasiliki explained.

"Is every Leondrian born left-handed like Lady Meraki?" she grilled, leaning forward.

Vasiliki pretended not to notice a few of the older workers inching closer to her in her peripheral and corrected, "That's not true, actually. Few Leondrians are born left-handed. Neither was Lady Meraki."

"She taught herself to be left-handed?" Citrine gasped.

Vasiliki nodded seriously, "Yes. It can all be traced back to her union with the mortal Alexandros."

Eyes widening, she demanded, "Really? What happened?"

Vasiliki leaned back in her chair and said, "During her marriage ceremony, she made a God's promise that every act she would make thereafter would be those of love, duty, and devotion. She pledged that every act the hand closest to her heart would make would be in deference to that vow and her right hand would only be used in its defense. He promised her the same and every Leondrian has been trained to uphold this vow."

"And the cloaks?" Citrine pressed. "Why do you wear them? Why are they always red?"

"That's a much sadder story." Vasiliki warned and pretended not to notice a larger group of workers eagerly listening in nearby.

"I like sad stories," she said quietly. "They mirror real life."

Vasiliki paused, ignoring the implication of what a girl as young as herself had to do to survive by working here before continuing, "Lady Meraki and Alexandros were happily married for several years, and they had one child who she named after her husband. A group of mortals who revered her lived nearby. They begged her to train them, but she never had any interest in teaching a bunch of farmers how to be warriors when she knew how precious her time was with her mortal husband."

Vasiliki made the sign of the gods before continuing. "One day, she was called away to a meeting of the gods and, during her absence, mercenaries attacked her home. Lady Meraki heard his cry for help from the gods' mountain, but it was too late for her to save him by the time she returned. She did arrive just in time to save her son. After dealing with the killers, she looked down at her husband's body and noticed the white cloak he normally wore was red from his blood. She took it off him, gave him a warrior's funeral, and has worn it ever since. Afterwards, she turned to her followers and made another God's promise that she would train seven generations of their families if their descendants upheld their vow to protect her lineage. The red cloak became a symbol of this duty."

Citrine's eyes were wide by the time Vasiliki finished then she asked eagerly, "Is that why your sign of the gods is the opposite of what it should be?"

Vasiliki blinked and raised her eyebrows at the girl in question.

"You know—" the girl said, bringing her thumb, index, and middle fingers of her right hand to her forehead, tracing a line down to her heart, making a line across her breast until it reached a point on the right side of her chest, before bringing it back to the same spot on her forehead. "You always think first, you detach yourself from your emotions, you wander through alternative thoughts to analyze ideas, and then make a logical decision."

"Yes," Vasiliki inclined her head, making the Leondrian version of the sign of the gods. "We immerse ourselves in emotion, detach ourselves, wander, and then master ourselves to stay true to our Lady's values."

She cocked her head and stated, "That is so strange."

With a small smile, Vasiliki conceded, "Perhaps."

She glanced up to see Alastair waiting several feet away, his turquoise eyes assessing her. She rose to her feet and inclined her head to the girl and everyone else who had been pretending not to listen before joining him.

"Quite the instructor," he drawled with waggling eyebrows. "And a *modest* one at that."

So, he had intended to make her uncomfortable by bringing her to such an establishment. She almost scoffed, thinking that he didn't know anything about Leondrians at all.

She slid her eyes towards him and said with a pointed look, "You were fast."

She heard him choke on a laugh as she strode away, irritation rising in her chest. She didn't bother to look back at him as she walked to the front door and the sunlight seared her eyes for a few moments before she could clearly see Jedrick and Lieutenant Sofoklis again.

His eyes narrowed, Jedrick asked, "Are you alright, my queen?"

"All is well." she said. "The Captain is merely amused by a joke."

"Oh, yes I am." Alastair chuckled from right behind her. "But I fear you will only be disappointed henceforth after frequenting the most popular site we have to offer."

"Disappointment is the result of mismanaged expectations." Vasiliki said as he walked a few steps forward until he stood in front of her. "I have never been here before, so I have none."

He raised an eyebrow at her and asked innocently, "Can this experience be topped for you then?"

"One can always expect misdirection from those who lurk in the dark." Vasiliki replied, raising her chin. "I will manage my expectations accordingly."

There was a gleam of surprise in his eyes that vanished as quickly as it had appeared.

"Is that right?" he drawled.

She gave him a steady look and said seriously, "I'll keep my eyes open for more eavesdroppers."

"I'll keep my ears ready then." he winked.

Unimpressed, she asked, "Where to next, Captain?"

She was getting the distinct impression that he was studying her, and she saw Sofoklis's eyes flicker very quickly towards him in astonishment before composing himself.

"You have a great variety of options, Queen Vasiliki." Alastair finally said. "There's the Senate building, the amphitheater, Apistia University, town halls, art districts, the telescope, whatever you wish to see."

She had tried her best to keep her face neutral despite her rising curiosity with each place he casually rattled off, but it was difficult to maintain this façade of polite interest towards the telescope. She very nearly asked him if they could visit it before she stopped herself. How her heart yearned to stare at the stars and to study the heavens, but she could not permit herself to succumb to such undisciplined behavior. She reminded herself that she was here to serve her people, not to fulfill her own selfish desires.

"Would you like to see the telescope?" he asked, and she inwardly cursed herself for giving herself away.

"If that is where you wish to go." Vasiliki replied coolly. "But our time would be better spent discussing how this proposed alliance would work."

"You're right. It is too early to go to the telescope. It is best use in the deepest, darkest part of the night when the stars truly shine." he said with a knowing smile.

Feeling Jedrick's eyes on her, she replied a little sharply, "If that is *my host's* wish, I will be honored to oblige. But we should discuss coordinating military forces."

"Do you wish to see our navy?" he inquired, clasping his hands behind his back.

She didn't want to insult his vocation, but she also didn't see the use in visiting a few boats either. What she needed to know was what sort of personnel and support he could provide.

"Do you have any soldiers?" she asked, avoiding his question.

"Why would we?" he cocked his head and there was a shade of darkness in his voice when he stated. "Leondria has the monopoly on that."

"Afshin is amassing the largest army ever seen." Vasiliki pointed out. "We need as many soldiers as we can get."

"Afshin has hundreds of thousands of soldiers and a formidable navy, both of which is only growing as he conquers west." Alastair answered, in a tone one would use to explain how to properly sharpen a sword.

Vasiliki blinked at his blasé attitude then her heart fell when she thought about how meager her forces were in comparison.

"I wouldn't be surprised if he hits a million before he storms our shores.

His forces grow so quickly since many people in the territories he conquers choose servitude over death." he continued in the same tone. "How many Leondrians do you have that are strong enough to fight?"

"All are strong enough to fight." Vasiliki said, not liking what he was implying. "That is what it means to be a Leondrian."

"You didn't answer my question." Alastair chided.

"About six thousand." she replied tersely.

"That won't be enough." he tsked.

"Hence, the alliance." Vasiliki added, her irritation rising.

"I agree." he said blandly which only made Vasiliki's heart pound in indignation. "That is why we proposed the alliance to begin with. But you must admit that the situation does look dreadful. Even with our combined forces, we won't be able to match them."

As much as his attitude grated her, this last comment made Vasiliki's mind start spinning. This couldn't be it, she thought furiously to herself. After millennia of self-governing and successfully repelling the few foreign invaders who dared to invade their lands, it couldn't all just be ripped apart under her watch.

She couldn't ignore how badly outnumbered they were but there had to be a way out of this. She knew her people were formidable and worked best together but there had to be a way to acquire more numbers. But if her soldiers and their sailors weren't enough, she wondered where they could acquire more fighters.

There were hundreds of thousands to a million combatants on their way to invade Midrios and she didn't have enough Leondrians to protect the people she was sworn to defend. She then stilled when an idea popped into her mind, but it vexed her to even consider it.

"You see the solution, don't you?" Alastair asked shrewdly, his eyes boring into hers. When she didn't say anything, he pushed, "Where do we get more soldiers if our Army is too small?"

"From the people." she forced herself to spit out.

They should have been enough. It was their sacred duty to defend Midrios and now they couldn't protect them when it counted the most.

"Exactly." he agreed. "You've spent your entire life inside your borders, right?"

She knew his statement was correct but she didn't appreciate his superior tone so she countered, "Haven't you?"

"No, Queen Vasiliki." he shook his head. "I haven't."

This made her pause, and she tilted her head slightly as she studied him. "Have you seen other parts of Midrios then?" she asked.

"I have frequented some of the islands and northern territories." he responded and the mocking tone in his voice faded. "Has Queen Zosime told you about the division within Midrios?"

"Yes." Vasiliki reluctantly confirmed.

"So, you see the problem that needs redressing?" he raised an eyebrow and, when she only stared resolutely back at him, finished. "How do we prepare a country for war and recruit enough people to fight if we stand divided? Many will flee or bow before a dictator if we don't present a confident, unified force."

"An official alliance between two city-states who detest each other will increase their confidence." Vasiliki said quietly.

Something glimmered in his eyes when he said, "Exactly, and—"

"Senator!" a voice cried out and they turned to find a young woman running towards them. Jedrick took a step in front of Vasiliki as the young woman quickly approached.

The young woman stopped a few feet away from Alastair and stated breathlessly, "Senator Prokopios is calling a meeting with the public in an hour, Senator Alastair. He wants to welcome our guests to our benevolent city-state."

"Is that right?" Alastair said. "We best oblige him then."

The woman kept her distance from Vasiliki and, after giving him a quick nod, ran off.

Captain Alastair returned his attention to her and asked, "How would Queen Zosime like to come inside our esteemed city-state?"

"She would be honored." Vasiliki inclined her head.

"Excellent." Alastair looked at Sofoklis and declared with a smirk. "Bring them in."

CHAPTER

39

Zosime couldn't stop herself from furiously pacing back and forth as she waited for news from Vasiliki. She had been too slow to volunteer earlier when the Apistian asked her sister to go with him and she couldn't stand the thought of not being able to help if Vasiliki was in danger. Despite the frosty reception she received and the months they had spent apart, she wouldn't be able to take it if her sister got seriously hurt. Jedrick was a great protector, but she would feel so much better if she had accompanied them. But she was stuck here and could only occasionally glance up at the sun that Anatole was dragging across the sky way too slowly for her liking.

Perleros hadn't once moved away from his spot where he had watched Vasiliki walk away with the Apistian. His arms were still crossed tightly across his chest and, besides the occasional tightening of his biceps, the only movements he made were the breaths he took as they waited. She felt his devotion and a twitch of regret as he maintained his post. He looked like he would stand there for as long as it took before Vasiliki returned or tear down the city-state with his bare hands if anything happened to her.

Anastasia had found a nearby rock to sit on and had been sharpening her sword since the trio left. Zosime would hear the scrape of stone against the blade every few seconds in a slow and deliberate movement, as if to warn away all those who dared to approach. She sensed something akin to focus from her, but she gave every outward appearance of dangerous nonchalance.

Zosime stopped her swift pacing mid-step when she heard incoming footsteps. She shifted and turned, ready to spring into action when she saw that it was Sofoklis who was advancing towards them. Anastasia casually sheathed her sword as she stood and strolled forward until she was standing in front of her.

"Tell me where she is." Perleros ordered when Sofoklis approached.

She sensed Perleros's flare of anger when he walked past him, ignoring him entirely before stopping in front of her and Anastasia. The Apistian's voice was mild but there was no mistaking the satisfaction she sensed from him when he asked, "Are you ready?"

Zosime's eyebrows rose for a brief moment then she relaxed when she understood that the message was from her sister.

"Vasiliki's given the all clear." she declared.

They may have had their differences lately, but she had never doubted Vasiliki's judgment. A part of her yearned to talk to her about the Fates but they had left so quickly that she hadn't really gotten a chance to tell her about them. But as terrifying as that experience was, what truly haunted her was the prospect of facing her oldest friend again. She dreaded the day when she felt Dryas's inevitable realization that she was responsible for his brother's death. She knew that she would never forget seeing his blood on her hands for as long as she lived.

"This way, Queen Zosime." Sofoklis said and they followed him as he led them towards the gates.

She sensed Perleros's growing concern, but he maintained his cool exterior as they approached the tall gates. She inclined her head at the two young men who stood there, their wariness palpable even if they made no move to stop them as Sofoklis led them inside. Zosime was at first surprised by the tall buildings around her but what shocked her was the immediate bombardment of so many different emotions that it almost made her head start spinning.

Happiness. Curiosity. Jealousy. Rage. Grief. Arrogance. Fear.

She had never sensed so many different things all at once and never so strongly before, but it was fear that she felt the most from them right now.

Fear of her.

Zosime tried to hide her troubled thoughts as she continued following Sofoklis down winding streets filled with equally underwhelming sights. It was easy enough to build something out of nothing but what was impressive was making something that stood the test of time. None of what she saw here was strong or durable like what they had back home.

They slowed as they approached a large white marble building and she saw a tall man standing beside Jedrick and Vasiliki.

"Queen Zosime." the man greeted with a bowed head. "Welcome to Apistia University."

"This is Captain Alastair." Sofoklis introduced. "Who is also a renowned politician in our esteemed Senate."

"You'll make me blush, Lieutenant." Alastair said with fake modesty.

She sensed his pulse of curiosity but what made her eyes narrow was his overwhelming feeling of loathing towards them. She had sensed Sofoklis's dislike and distrust, which had faded somewhat since their first meeting, but it paled in comparison to what this Captain felt. He outwardly feigned indifference perfectly, but she could sense what he really felt immediately.

"Pleasure." she said coldly and ignored Vasiliki's look of exasperated disbelief.

She sensed this curiosity shift to cool assessment even if the smile on his face didn't fade.

"Ah." he said a moment later, as if something dawned on him. "You're one of those."

Sofoklis shot Alastair a disbelieving look and cleared his throat.

"You can read emotions." Alastair clarified.

"She inherited the Gift." Anastasia confirmed in a hard voice.

"Straight from Lady Meraki herself." he added before closing his eyes.

Zosime didn't know how to explain what happened next. The closest she could describe what she sensed was that he somehow grabbed his emotions and dragged them into one place in his chest. She could have sworn that he folded these emotions into smaller and smaller pieces until they were no bigger than one of her fingernails. Then it felt like he crushed them under a sandal until they dissipated into nothing.

He opened his eyes, and she couldn't sense anything from him anymore. There was nothing where, moments before, there had been something. She had felt people tighten the leash on their emotions, but she had never felt someone will theirs away before.

"Did you enjoy your journey here?" he asked pleasantly but she still sensed nothing from him.

It almost made her cringe, and the hairs on the back of her neck rose in unease. She was used to the muted emotions of Leondrians, who valued physical and mental discipline above all else, but she always felt something from other live beings. Except for the Creature.

Blinking rapidly, she responded, "It was fine."

"Excellent." he smiled but she felt no happiness or satisfaction from him. "School is on break, and I wanted a moment to speak with you with less ears around before we head to the town hall for the meeting."

"The meeting?" Zosime asked curtly.

"Did you not tell her?" Alastair turned to Sofoklis with a raised eyebrow.

"I wanted you to have the honors, Captain." Sofoklis replied and Alastair nodded.

"Pardon my Lieutenant. He is extremely thoughtful but not the lo-quacious type." Alastair's smile broadened. "One of my colleagues, Senator Prokopios, wanted to give the Queens of Leondria a cordial welcome to Apistia."

Zosime felt Perleros's chagrin, but he stayed silent as he stared at the Apistians with narrowed eyes.

Alastair's eyes wandered to Perleros, and he asked lightly, "How have you been since the last time we met, General?"

Perleros frowned and she sensed his confusion.

"Don't remember me?" Alastair asked then waved a hand. "No worries. We will just have to get reacquainted and under much better circumstances this time."

The two men stared intensely at each other and Zosime sensed the rising tension in the air until Sofoklis said unexpectedly, "We should be heading to the town hall, sir."

"Right you are." Alastair agreed. "I don't want to miss a single word of his speech, but I should warn you that he is very long-winded."

Anastasia walked closely beside Zosime as they followed him down a couple streets and found a long line of people waiting to enter another large white marble building. This one was comprised of three columns where sculptures of Lady Apistia rested on the top of all three with her hands raised above her head, as if she alone was the one holding up the roof.

Vasiliki cleared her throat and commented, "Remarkable."

"It's not as grandiose as the Senate building." Alastair disagreed.

"Doesn't mean it's not still impressive." Vasiliki pointed out.

Alastair didn't respond and Zosime kept an eye on her surroundings as people in the crowd gave them a wide berth as they advanced steadily closer to the entrance. Some of them, immediately after seeing her, indiscreetly hurried as far away as they could. She couldn't shut out their fear and distrust which only prompted her heart to beat faster and make her wonder why they were so scared of them.

She sensed Vasiliki's resignation in response to these reactions but not surprise, which only confused her more. The man in the cart's terror had shocked her and each subsequent interaction with other Midrians had never dampened her surprise. But Vasiliki was acting like their emotions were to be expected, which was so unlike her. She always sensed her sister's never-ending curiosity when something unexpected happened and she very nearly demanded for her to tell her what was going on.

Then she glanced at the two strange Apistians and held her tongue. She could begrudgingly force herself to wait until they were alone again, but she was determined to know what was happening.

She felt a twinge of unease as they walked inside the town hall and then looked around. She had never seen a room like this before. There were long marble benches cascading down to a small open space at the bottom of the room where a lone speaker was waiting. As her eyes scanned the room, she noticed a group of people sitting on one of the benches by the speaker gesture for them to approach. People moved out of their way with murmurs of "Senator" as they walked down the steps towards them.

"Senator Alastair!" the older man who waved them over greeted amiably.

"Ajax." Alastair welcomed with a nod, and she sensed the older man's delight at being remembered before he asked. "Has anyone given you trouble over the fishing permit?"

"Not since your intervention in issuing me one, sir." Ajax said.

"How about your business?" Alastair followed up, interest sparkling in his eyes even though she still didn't sense anything from him.

"Flourishing, thanks to you." Ajax smiled. "Are you looking for a seat, sir?"

Alastair looked around at the nearly full room and said, "I think we're out of luck, but we can stand in the back."

Ajax's eyes flickered to her, and she felt a spike of fear from him before he offered, "Why don't you take our seats?"

"I wouldn't dream of it, Ajax." Alastair chastised. "Your knees have been bothering you."

Ajax swallowed and continued with a slightly trembling voice, "I can't sit while knowing that my Senator and his guests aren't comfortable."

"We can't take your seats." Zosime added diplomatically. "I assure you we will be comfortable standing for long periods of time."

This only reinforced Ajax's fear but he replied politely, "Please, madam, I must insist."

He stood slowly and the rest of his group, who must have been his family based on their physical resemblances, carefully filed past her. She glanced at the Senator—who was clapping each of them on the back and wishing them a good day as they passed—and was stunned by how well he had feigned concern for them when he still felt like a blank slate.

Anastasia was the first to walk to the farthest empty seat and Zosime sat down next to her. Perleros claimed the seat to her immediate right then Vasiliki then Jedrick then Alastair, and Sofoklis took the last space next to the aisle. She sensed Jedrick's distaste with being seated next to Alastair, but he only gave the Apistian one quick look of dislike before composing himself. Jedrick was the broader of the two men, but she had the distinct impression that Alastair wouldn't be easy to take down in a fight.

Zosime then caught Alastair glancing around the room and saw him chuckle when his gaze landed on a woman with brown hair with silver streaks in it sitting in the very front, two rows ahead of them. For the first time since he crushed his emotions like a bug under his sandal, she sensed a flicker of amusement from him.

"Is she a friend of yours?" Vasiliki asked, following his gaze.

"Are you friends with spiders?" he countered, and Vasiliki blinked.

"Depends on the spider." she said coolly then added before dropping the subject. "Some are useful."

Zosime sensed his momentary surprise then, when their gazes met, all emotions in him disappeared again. The maneuver still made her uncomfortable, but she was relieved he experienced feelings like other humans.

"Esteemed Apistians!" the speaker who must have been Prokopios cried out. "Welcome."

There were murmurs from the crowd and Zosime stared at the man with wispy white hairs on his balding head and overgrown belly that strained the blue fabric of his clothes around his midsection. She felt his apprehension when he glanced at them, but it was his boundless arrogance that caught her attention.

"Apistia is a very old and very proud city-state." Prokopios began and she was surprised by his low baritone voice and steady cadence. "Our ingenuity is so renowned that people throughout Midrios flock to us and it has even captured attention from the curious abroad who come to our shores. No one in the educated world can match our wits. Who else has invented our elegant system of democracy? Who else had the intelligence to institute multiple levels of government as we have? Or to create effective solutions for everyday problems, such as the permit system I created a few decades ago?"

He continued in the same vein for a long time and Zosime honestly didn't know how he could find the words to drone on and on without actually saying anything of substance. It just felt like a huge waste of time that could be better spent elsewhere. They could be patrolling, discussing tactics, or coordinating supplies right now. But he just continued to lecture about their intellectual superiority to the point that she feared the speech would never end.

"But I would be remiss not to mention an equally old city-state, Leondria." Prokopios stated and she could feel hundreds of eyes on her. "We have never been friends and the last twenty years have been especially tempestuous when we have been most likely to declare each other foes." Zosime frowned at the comment and listened closely as he continued. "However, desperate times call for extreme measures and we must ally ourselves with people we never thought we would work with. Together, with Apistia's great strategic mind and the Leondrians fighting our enemy's large forces on the front lines, the gods will smile down upon us, and we will prevail over the conqueror who has set his eyes on our fair country."

Just when she was feeling relieved that the speech was winding towards its end, this relief quickly dissipated when she felt a spark of danger. She straightened in her seat when she heard a faint ringing in her head. Eyes widening, she twisted in her seat and saw that the front door was the only exit out of the building.

"My queen?" Anastasia whispered but Zosime only continued to look around, trying to discover who was about to leap out and attack them.

She saw people start to fidget in their seats and she slowly turned back around to face the speaker as her heart started racing.

"Zosime." Vasiliki murmured.

Prokopios raised his arms and declared, "May Lady Apistia look down upon what she has created with pride and bless our alliance with Leondria."

She opened her mouth to respond to her sister when the ringing suddenly became so loud she could hear nothing else.

"Run." she gasped.

Vasiliki's eyes widened and the two of them rose to their feet, but it was too late. There were confused murmurs from the audience when the floor suddenly started vibrating then began shaking violently. She saw people in the very back have just enough time to push open the doors to exit when the floor throughout the building started cracking. These murmurs morphed into cries of fear, and even her superior reflexes weren't enough to move out of the way when the marble in front of her caved in, swallowing Senator Prokopios whole and sucking Zosime in with him.

CHAPTER

40

Vasiliki lost her footing as the ground in front of her collapsed in on itself, but something grabbed her arm and yanked her upwards before she was dragged into the widening hole. She flinched from the pain of her arm being wrenched in its socket then she glanced up to look at the face of the person who had helped her. Expecting it to be Jedrick, her eyes widened when she saw that it was Alastair who now had one arm wrapped around her waist while using the other to hold on to the marble bench behind them. He must have leapt towards her after she stood up and she marveled at his fast reflexes.

She recovered from her surprise and thought furiously about their options. She knew the bench he was clinging to couldn't remain stable for long and that they would need to find something—anything—before they fell in. She looked wildly around her and saw that the place was in complete chaos. The people in the back half of the town hall were screaming and trampling over others in their attempts to flee to safety.

"ZOSIME!" Anastasia screamed and Vasiliki whipped her head towards the sound of her voice.

There was blood trickling down Anastasia's face and Vasiliki realized with alarm that she must have struck her head against the bench before grabbing it, but her worry for Anastasia abated when her blue-grey eyes sharpened with focus a moment later. Jedrick and Perleros dangled next to her, and Vasiliki followed her horrified gaze down to the ruptured floor.

"Zosime!" Vasiliki bellowed.

Anastasia's face hardened into what Vasiliki could only describe as a fierce expression of protectiveness right before she let go and allowed herself to be swallowed into the abyss. Vasiliki only stared after her and thought there had to be something she could do to help them.

"Do you have a rope?" she yelled over the rumbling.

"Not on me!" Alastair retorted, his face furrowed in concentration.

If she didn't have a rope, Vasiliki told herself, then she would have to make do without it.

"Get to safety, Captain!" she urged then loosened her grip on him. She would just have to drop in and use whatever strength she could to help them down there.

Instead of letting her go, he tightened his hold on her and suddenly shouted, "Give me your cloak!"

"What!" she cried out, astounded that he would ask that of her.

"Gods' blood!" he swore. "YOUR CLOAK!"

She reached up and fumbled with untying it since the ground was still rumbling dangerously but she was able to tear it free from her shoulders a few moments later.

"My queen!" Jedrick called out and Vasiliki shifted just enough in Alastair's arm to grab the cloak Jedrick just ripped off his shoulders and held out for her.

She immediately tied both ends together then let them hang, but when she glanced down, she noticed that the two cloaks weren't long enough to reach the hole.

"My queen!" Perleros called out and tossed his cloak towards her. She caught it then quickly added it to the other two. The third cloak, which was much larger than the other two due to Perleros's height, was enough for the newly made lifeline to dangle over the edge of the hole where Anastasia had fallen in.

"Lieutenant!" she called out and he reached out to take the lifeline from her.

She waited for him to give her a nod then she looked at Alastair.

"Ready?" he asked.

She turned her head to Jedrick and Perleros and ordered, "Go help the civilians in the back get out."

"No, Vasiliki!" Perleros protested.

"Let me go instead!" Jedrick exclaimed at the same time.

Ignoring their objections, she cried out, "Now!"

Alastair then let her go and she allowed herself to fall for several seconds before reaching out a hand and grabbing a piece of red cloth. Now relying on Sofoklis to support her weight, she quickly but carefully used the lifeline to descend towards the hole.

She could feel her hands getting sweaty and the bones in her body vibrating from the trembling all around her. But she only gritted her teeth and methodically placed one hand below the other until she found herself at the edge of the hole. She looked down to find Senator Prokopios, Senator Sophie, Anastasia, Zosime, and three other Apistians she didn't know.

Prokopios's right leg looked like it had been shattered from the impact and the old man was moaning continuously in pain. Sophie's arm was twisted at an unnatural angle, and she could see the blood staining the woman's blue clothes. Anastasia was crouched beside Zosime, who looked bruised and a little dazed but didn't seem to have sustained any other injuries. The three Apistians looked battered and shaken but remarkably didn't seem too hurt.

"Zosime!" Vasiliki shouted and her sister looked up at her with wide eyes. "Send up the civilians!"

"Send up the children first!" Senator Sophie gasped, clutching her arm.

Zosime dragged herself to her feet and grabbed the first Apistian child who didn't look older than eleven. She picked him up and thrust him towards Vasiliki, who then coaxed him into climbing up the rope to safety. She tracked his progress long enough to see him reach the top and noticed that Sofoklis was now sharing the burden of holding their weight with Alastair. She didn't see Perleros and Jedrick holding on to the bench anymore so they must have obeyed her instructions to help the civilians.

"Hurry!" Alastair shouted from above and she gave him a curt nod.

"Send me the next one!" she bellowed and the second Apistian, a teenage girl, didn't need to be told twice.

She hastily moved towards Zosime who hoisted her towards Vasiliki. She took her arm and helped her get a grip on the cloak then urged her to move. She climbed like a wildcat and Vasiliki immediately redirected her attention back down. Zosime was already ready, holding up another girl who looked similar in age to the girl she just sent up. This girl was more tentative, her hands shaking so badly it looked like she would nearly lose her grip on the cloak.

"The Senators!" Vasiliki cried out.

She couldn't miss the dirty look Sophie flashed the old man before she scoffed derisively, "He needs all the help he can get."

Vasiliki doubted he would have the strength to pull himself up or to walk out on his own so she yelled, "Zosime, grab him."

"I won't leave them!" Zosime disagreed.

She snapped, "You're the only one down there strong enough to carry him out the building. Do it!"

She saw something flicker in Anastasia's eyes, but she only urged, "Go, my queen."

Zosime hissed something under her breath and roughly grabbed the old man. He yelped when she threw him onto her back, barking at him to hold on to her neck. She then sprung, leaping high into the air then grabbed Vasiliki's hand. She grunted from the unexpected weight but only pulled them upwards until Zosime was able to grab the red fabric.

"Gods' blood!" she heard Alastair swear as Zosime began climbing with Prokopios clinging to her neck.

There was another crack and Vasiliki saw a fissure opening beneath Anastasia. Sophie neatly jumped out of the way, but Anastasia lost her footing. Vasiliki thought for sure that she would be swallowed whole when Anastasia flung out her hands just in time to clasp the edge of the cracking marble.

"Anastasia!" Vasiliki cried out.

"What happened!" Zosime demanded and Vasiliki glanced up to see her sister halt halfway through the climb.

"Go!" Vasiliki bellowed. "She's fine!"

She could see the reluctance on Zosime's face before she continued climbing a few seconds later. She looked back down in time to see Anastasia haul herself out of the second hole that was now cracking open. Anastasia didn't hesitate to throw Sophie unceremoniously over her shoulder and leap up to grab Vasiliki's hand. She pulled the two women up until Anastasia could grab the cloth and started expertly climbing with Senator Sophie dangling over her shoulder.

Vasiliki was able to catch the indignant expression on the Senator's face before she began climbing back up the makeshift rope. She accelerated her pace after she saw Anastasia carry the Senator over the bench and it only took a handful of seconds for her to reach Sofoklis and Alastair.

"RUN!" she commanded as she climbed over the bench and watched Anastasia put Sophie down. "Help the civilians!"

Sophie began sprinting for the entrance while Anastasia ran to help the fallen civilians on the higher aisles. Meanwhile, Sofoklis and Alastair immediately sprung to their feet but there was a loud crack as the bench split in half and she saw Sofoklis's sandal slip as the ground beneath him began to crumble. She saw Alastair's eyes widen and he reached out to grab his arm but only touched air as Sofoklis began falling.

But Vasiliki was faster as she flashed out a hand in time to grab the fabric around his shoulder and launched him across the room. She saw Alastair's mouth drop open in shock and knew he wouldn't have enough time to get out of the way. So she took a single step forward, picked him up by the midsection, and threw him in the same manner she had thrown his friend.

She then felt the marble under her crumble, and she felt her stomach rise to her throat as she started falling. She then bent her legs, planting her feet the best she could on the big piece of marble that fell with her and pushed off it with all her strength. She soared through the air, but she knew that her trajectory was off when she immediately began losing altitude. She then realized she wouldn't be able to control her landing after flying past a few rows of benches before crashing into one. She heard a loud crunch when her face smacked into the hard marble and blood began spurting from her nose.

"My queen!" she heard Anastasia cry out from the distance.

Vasiliki could barely hear her over the excruciating pain in her face and the rumbling around her.

"QUEEN VASILIKI!" she heard Alastair shout, and she wheezed as she slowly opened her eyes.

She slowly rose to her feet, her body protesting from the sharp pains that were shooting all over her. She knew her time was running out and she looked up to see cracks lacing up the walls and the ceiling.

This place was about to collapse in on itself, she thought to herself.

She kept a cry of pain from escaping her lips and limped sideways until she was back on the steps. She did a quick scan of the room and only found stragglers who were struggling to make it to the front doors.

A young girl whose leg was pinned under some marble screamed as a large piece of the ceiling broke free and started falling directly towards her. Vasiliki sprinted towards her then leapt forward to cover the girl's body with her own. She braced herself for the hard impact when she heard a loud clanging. Still wheezing, she looked up to find Anastasia crouching over her while holding up the large piece of marble that should have just crushed them.

Vasiliki knew Anastasia was strong, but she found herself marveling at how muscular she must be to be holding something so heavy over her head. She saw the muscles in her forearms strain from the effort and her gaze roamed upwards until landing on something that sent chills down her spine.

"My queen." Anastasia said urgently.

Vasiliki couldn't move as she continued staring at Anastasia's wrist. For there was a small scar there, too small for the casual observer to notice, in the shape of a falling star.

No, no, no. Vasiliki thought as memories of the Trials flickered to the forefront of her mind and she recalled the close-up image of an assailant with this unique scar stabbing Zosime in the heart. Why would Anastasia turn on them?

"My queen!" Anastasia pressed.

Suddenly, Alastair ran up to them and immediately lifted the marble pinning the young girl to the ground. The young girl squirmed from under Vasiliki and began limping towards the entrance. Vasiliki's eyes widened when she felt herself being dragged and she looked up to discover that it was Sofoklis who was hauling her away.

Anastasia then dropped the marble where Vasiliki had just been and demanded, "Can you stand, my queen?"

She felt herself jolted into action when she heard another loud crack and Sofoklis immediately let go of her as she scrambled to her feet.

Not looking at Anastasia, Vasiliki shouted, "Go!"

She waited until the others were in front of her to start running. Each step she took was haunted by her confusion and the pain of being betrayed by someone she respected. Her mind raced as she advanced closer to the exit and she thought furiously about what to do next. She was only a few steps away from the front doors when she felt a sudden spurt of agony in her head and the world went black.

CHAPTER

41

Alastair spun on his heel after hearing a gasp of pain to see a piece of marble bounce off Queen Vasiliki's head. He grabbed her arm as her knees buckled and pulled her towards him just in time to avoid being hit by more falling debris. He then threw her over his shoulder as he felt the rumbling around them worsen and sprinted the last few steps to safety. He had scarcely burst outside before the town hall's ceiling caved in and the entire building collapsed in on itself.

"Captain!" he heard his faithful Lieutenant cry out who then hurried forward to help him gently place the Leondrian Queen on the ground.

"Vasiliki!" Zosime bellowed.

"My queen!" Jedrick shouted at the same time.

Alastair glanced around to see Apistians running in various directions, and he scanned his surroundings to find that, besides some cracks in the nearby street, there didn't seem to be any other damage.

"Senator!" Ajax exclaimed while bursting through the panicking crowd. "Was anyone left inside?"

"No." he replied.

He saw Sophie hovering nearby and noticed her lips curl into a sly smile before the Leondrians swarmed him.

"What happened?" Zosime demanded but Alastair didn't dignify such a question with a response.

He only pressed his fingers to Vasiliki's throat and waited several long seconds before he felt a slow thud of her pulse.

"She still lives." he told them then started studying her head wound.

Blood was still leaking from a large gash on her head, and he gently prodded the area to find dents lining her skull. For any regular mortal, he would be certain that they would perish within a couple weeks. But everyone knew that all the male and female descendants of Lady Meraki possessed superior strength, and many possessed other godly abilities. He was still skeptical that she would live but surmised that she at least had a chance of survival.

"We have to get her home!" Zosime cried out frantically.

"Why would you do that?" Alastair raised his eyebrows at her, astonished that was the course of action she was recommending.

"She needs surgeons." Zosime snapped.

Shaking his head incredulously, he pointed out, "We have surgeons here."

"That we would trust with our queen's life?" Perleros growled softly.

"She won't survive a trip back to Leondria without being attended to by professionals." Alastair quipped with annoyance. "And I thought it was Leondrians who killed Apistians, not the other way around."

Honestly, he thought. How dense could these Leondrians be?

This kind of thought process must have been the result of them indoctrinating their young to mindlessly obey orders without developing critical thinking. He couldn't understand why fools would purposefully move to Leondria to spend their lives there as indentured servants. He especially couldn't fathom how people believed their propaganda that they should work for free because the Leondrian government would be close by to protect them.

There were fools everywhere, he thought. But as he looked down at the injured woman beside him, he begrudgingly admitted to himself that she had surprised him. He hadn't known entirely what to expect from her, but he certainly hadn't anticipated seeing the spark of curiosity in her eyes. He had first thought that it was a part of some grand scheme to set him off guard but then he noticed how much she was trying to bury her genuine interest in the telescope after glancing at her guard.

He still despised everything she represented but she didn't seem to be the monster he had anticipated her to be. Not yet at least. He didn't get to the position he did by relying solely on first impressions. What he needed most right now was for this alliance to work and he doubted it would be successful without her, based on Zosime's blatant disinterest in everything Apistian and her open dislike towards him.

"W—" Jedrick began when he was suddenly cut off.

They all looked up when Sophie unexpectedly announced, "MY FELLOW APISTIANS!"

The exclamations of the crowd abated from her announcement, and everyone turned to listen to her. Many eyes widened when they noticed how she cradled her clearly injured arm with bone visibly jutting from her skin and the blood staining her blue peplos.

"The earthquake has stopped." she said coolly, but in a voice loud enough for all to hear. "Now is the time to compose solutions. I have received confirmation that no one was left behind, but we must send the injured to the infirmaries and assemble a crew to clean up this disarray."

Alastair gave Sofoklis a pointed look and he gave him a nod before uttering, "I'll get a stretcher, sir."

Sofoklis quickly stood and ran off, vanishing in the distance. Alastair then redirected his gaze on the fallen queen and started assessing her for more injuries.

"What are you doing?" Zosime hissed.

"It would be important to know if she has any more injuries, Queen Zosime." Alastair said flippantly as he continued his assessment.

He didn't need her "precious" Gift to know she was seething, and he suppressed the urge to smirk. There were times when the façade of the careless Senator was appropriate and there were times when putting on such a persona would be a grave error in judgment. It worked just fine in politics most of the time to demonstrate that his political opponents could never get under his skin. It was truly remarkable how much those blue-robed Senators resembled sharks if they smelled any blood in the water, but this was an entirely different situation.

There were Apistian citizens who would be voting for the next election this summer who were watching him. Permitting himself to smirk at someone's stupidity in the wake of such a serious event would cost him votes. It would also further sour any chance of an alliance between the Leondrians and Apistians succeeding if Vasiliki didn't survive this injury.

"Sir." Sofoklis called out as he ran back with a stretcher.

Alastair and Sofoklis gently moved Vasiliki onto the stretcher and Alastair told the Leondrians, "If it will make you feel better, you can carry her while the Lieutenant leads you to the infirmary." As Jedrick and Perleros quickly moved to take both sides of the stretcher, Alastair added. "I didn't see any other injuries besides some cuts and bruises."

The blonde-haired woman with blue-grey eyes peered at him and he hadn't needed any personal introduction to know that this was the famous Anastasia. Even in the multicultural Apistia, not many in Midrios possessed those bright golden locks and he found himself studying her. He wasn't sure why, but she seemed so familiar to him. She cocked her head at him as she studied him back, and his eyes widened slightly when he suddenly realized why she looked so familiar.

The Leondrians had secrets, he thought to himself while her face darkened. He would tuck away this piece of knowledge to use to his advantage later.

"Show them the way, Lieutenant." Alastair waved a hand. "I'll check in later."

The crowd parted for the Leondrians as they ran to the infirmary while Alastair walked over to Ajax and inquired, "Are you and the rest of your family well?"

"Yes, sir." Ajax confirmed and rubbed his temple. "We were so fortunate to be in the back. We were some of the first to escape."

"That is excellent news." Alastair said, clapping him on the shoulder. He then glanced around and started biting the inside of his cheek.

"What is it?" Ajax asked.

He looked down for a moment, as if sheepish, then stated, "It would be too much to ask of you. Please, go take your children home and recover from this ordeal."

"Senator." Ajax replied sternly with narrowed eyes, in a way that only a father could master. "What do you require of me?"

Alastair gave the appearance of hesitating for another moment before sharpening his focus back on Ajax, as if he was steeling himself forward, and declared, "Your family could help with gathering stretchers and carrying people to the infirmary. The doctors could also use any hooks and thread you can spare. They might also be hungry if you could provide some fish for meals, which I would of course cover the costs for."

"You couldn't possibly cover that much." Ajax replied, aghast.

"The people need help, Ajax." Alastair insisted. "Bill me and I will cover it."

The surprise didn't fade from Ajax's face, but a muscle also twitched in his jaw when he asserted, "No charge."

"That is out of the question." Alastair contended.

"No charge." Ajax raised his chin.

"A business needs to make profits." Alastair said.

Based on how the stress lines on Ajax's face were growing more pronounced, this fact was not lost on him. He then hit one of his children on the head and waved an expectant hand. The rest of his children then began running to grab stretchers or to assist the wounded.

"Kids." Ajax grumbled and added before walking away. "I'll go grab the supplies."

Ajax was a good man, Alastair thought. It would be very helpful to have such a man think the same of him. It would make it easier to ask favors in the future without him asking for much in return.

Such generosity would also undoubtedly help Ajax to expand his business. The man who saved lives in a crises would soon have lines for his fishing stand stretching for blocks. Ajax might finally be able to open the restaurant he always dreamed of and having a wealthy businessman as a friend could only be a good thing for Alastair.

He heard a soft chuckle from behind him and he smoothed his face to an expression of neutrality before he turned to look at Sophie.

"I applaud your steely resolve in the face of what could have been a deadly crises." Alastair said.

She cocked her head at him and replied, "If I were less Apistian, I would be touched by your applause, Senator. I only did my duty by keeping a level head and pointing out the logical course of action forward."

"Logic and ruthlessness can often be confused for one another." he retorted dryly.

"They are but one and the same." she chided but here was a knowing glint in her eyes when she continued. "Only those who permit their emotions to cloud their judgment try to make such a distinction."

There was no mercy in her calculating brown eyes, and as much as he thought that she was a scourge to the Senate, he couldn't help but respect that mind of hers.

"Only those so mindlessly driven by revenge or personal ambition fail to understand nuances." he fired back.

"Oh, young one." she laughed lightly. "If you don't learn this lesson, you won't survive another term."

"I would say the same for you." he inclined his head towards her. "Even the model Apistian would feel sorrow that an institution where they started their career at was leveled by an earthquake."

"You should practice your mental discipline exercises diligently if you hope to one day achieve stoicism or to understand how the world works." she jeered.

Staring into those dark eyes that were scrutinizing him like a child, he said, "I understand exactly how it works. Because even the stoic Apistian populace would be incredibly angered that an institution they held dear was destroyed."

"Not if it was an act of the gods." she countered with a straight face.

"Blasphemous now, are we?" he drawled and those brown eyes of hers glittered. "Last I checked, there were only six gods."

"It's a shame we won't have our last Senate meeting today." she shook her head in mock desolation. "We'll have to see how your alliance fares next term, assuming you win re-election."

She gave him a sly smile and walked away in the direction of the infirmary. He almost clenched his fists but managed to stop himself as he turned back towards the wounded. He spent the rest of the afternoon carrying the injured to the infirmary and coordinating the cleanup process of the rubble. After the sun had set, he told them to stop working and that they would resume first thing in the morning. It was only then that he strolled back to the infirmary to visit the Leondrians.

It was packed when he walked in, but he was pleased to see that no one seemed hungry. He did have to ignore the lingering smell of fish as he walked down the halls until he found the room he was looking for. Which was easy to find when he saw Jedrick and Sofoklis standing outside a door for one of the surgery rooms.

"Sir." Sofoklis greeted and Jedrick stiffened.

Alastair took one took down the hall then surmised, "The rest of them are inside the surgery, aren't they?"

Sofoklis shifted slightly before replying, "Yes, sir."

"Jedrick, would you mind informing Queen Zosime that I am here to speak with her." Alastair requested.

Jedrick stared at him stonily but, after a few moments, slipped inside.

"Do you have a prognosis yet?" he asked Sofoklis.

Shaking his head, Sofoklis replied, "Doesn't look good, Captain."

"But she still lives?" he verified.

"Yes." Sofoklis confirmed.

The door then opened and Zosime, Perleros, and Anastasia walked out. Jedrick must have stayed in the room to keep watch on his queen, he thought.

"How is she?" he asked and Zosime stiffened.

"Fine." she replied tersely, and he thought with chagrin that he would have to go the direct route.

"The alliance is not official, correct?" he asked, cutting all preamble.

"No." Zosime confirmed as her eyes narrowed at him in severe dislike.

"Does your Council expect you to return soon in order to give their approval or will they give it in your absence?" he asked.

Zosime blinked and he saw surprise flicker across her face.

"We would need to return." Perleros answered softly but his eyes were still narrowed with dislike. "They expect us to report back first."

"What is your timeline to return?" Alastair pressed.

He knew he had them when Perleros hesitated before responding, "As soon as Queen Vasiliki is well."

"You can't take her after the surgery." Alastair declared.

His fingers twitching for his sword, Perleros replied, "No one threatens our queen."

"You are." Alastair remarked.

"General Perleros is a faithful servant of Leondria." Anastasia contradicted severely.

"Fine." Alastair shrugged then waved a hand. "Take her once her surgery is done and have her die on the journey back, so you make it back home before your deadline. She's not my queen."

"Once the surgery is done—" Zosime began.

"She'll still be in a delicate condition." Alastair pointed out. "She was only hit on the head with hard marble, after all."

"When will she be ready for travel?" Zosime demanded.

Alastair shrugged again, "If she survives, probably not for weeks. Maybe not even for a few months."

"It would take that long for her to heal?" Anastasia frowned in a mixture of skepticism and concern.

"To see if she wakes up." Alastair clarified. "After that, the doctor will have to see how well her recovery is going. But this would clearly violate your Council's deadline."

"We won't abandon her." Zosime blazed furiously.

"Her guard would obviously stay behind to watch her." Alastair pointed out slowly so they could understand him.

"We can't leave her with one guard." Perleros insisted.

"I'll stay behind, sir." Anastasia offered but Perleros only shook his head.

"You're Queen Zosime's guard. You must remain by her side." he disagreed. "Her safety is paramount."

"Sir." Anastasia inclined her head.

"The two of us will stay while General Perleros and Jedrick return." Zosime suggested.

"That would be a dereliction of Jedrick's duty." Perleros declared.

"Wouldn't your Council be expecting one of their queens to return, not just one of their generals?" Alastair asked.

"I'll stay." Perleros announced a moment later.

Alastair ignored the surge of sharp dislike at the prospect and asked, "Depends if they're also expecting you. Are they?"

Based on the vein throbbing in Perleros's neck, Alastair already had his answer.

"Stay a couple more days but the logical course of action is to cement the alliance." Alastair advised. "Keep her personal guard here to watch over her and return to check on her after they approve the alliance."

She saw Zosime exchange looks with Anastasia before warning darkly, "We will return, with more forces if necessary."

"Undoubtedly." Alastair said mildly.

They gave him distrustful looks before going back inside the room which, Alastair was sure, was a treat for the surgeon.

"Straightforward approach, sir." Sofoklis noted once the door closed behind them.

"They're a straightforward people." Alastair sighed. "I had to speak in a manner that they could understand."

"There's just one problem." Sofoklis stated.

"I know." Alastair muttered. "She has to survive a wound that would be fatal to any regular mortal."

"I'll keep watch here, sir." Sofoklis said and Alastair gave him a grateful nod.

He could depend on the surgeons to do their best with the Leondrians breathing down their necks, but he wouldn't entrust this queen's safety to just anyone. Not when there could be killers who hated Leondrians lurking in any corner.

"Keep her safe, Lieutenant, or the wrath of Leondria will reign upon us." Alastair ordered. "I'll handle the rest. Afshin won't take us without a fight."

CHAPTER

42

I knew the horrors that were waiting for Midrios in the coming years. The sorrows and sacrifices the people would experience without respite. I saw how fatigued Zosime had grown in the past year and how nightmares plagued her every time she fell asleep. The Fates now held their latest victim in their web so making her wait for another visit was a greater source of vicious delight for them than haunting her dreams again right away.

I saw how weary the aging Perleros had become and how he was reliving the horrors of his past. I knew how gravely concerned he was about Vasiliki and how it felt like he was failing to uphold the vow he made to her mother. All of them worried for her safety but only I and the Fates knew exactly how much time she had left. All because of the decisions the Six made over twenty years ago.

I watched Zosime, Perleros, and Anastasia begrudgingly depart Apistia a couple of days after Vasiliki's surgery when they mistakenly thought that they could come back soon after. Her life still hung in that strange in-between state between life and death, but Jedrick diligently observed every breath she took, praying to the gods that she would soon awake. Still, she slumbered while her sister returned home.

The Leondrians were relieved when Queen Zosime returned but their concern quickly grew when they noticed Queen Vasiliki's absence. I saw Zosime shrug off this concern as she focused relentlessly on one goal: to get the Council to approve the alliance so she could immediately return to her sister's side.

She didn't see the slow deliberation of their movements when they left their Tower like I did. She couldn't pierce the veils they wore over their faces to see the decision already marked on their faces like I could. So, she was understandably shocked when they categorically refused to approve the alliance between Leondria and Apistia without providing any justification for their decision.

I turned away from the scene with a heavy heart, unable to watch further. So many would die as a result of their decision. I would come back to watch them again, but my thoughts became so preoccupied with the younger Afshin that, after a few moments of whispering his name, I saw him for myself.

His face was drawn in boredom and his black eyes were dull with disinterest. He sat on a white throne with his legs crossed and one only needed to take a closer look to realize his seat was made from human bone. Bones of all shapes and sizes were fused and stitched together to build a chair large enough to fit this enormously tall man who did his best to tower over other people. He held a dagger in his right hand and the bulging muscles in his arms flexed as he sawed off flecks of bone on the armrest.

"Again," he commanded absentmindedly as one slave cracked a whip against the back of another.

I could hardly stand to watch from that place between worlds where I could see all but none could see me unless I permitted it. I knew he thought that, as the son of an emperor, he was a god reborn. How he treated everyone else as insects and was planning on showing Midrios his full power if they resisted his rule. But he was determined to succeed where his father had failed so he had been patient where his father had been rash. He was taking his time to build his power so he could strike Midrios with the largest Army that the world had ever seen.

"Again," he repeated, barely noticing how red the floor was from the bound slave's spilt blood. "Harder or you switch places."

Tears stained the face of the slave who held the whip, but she complied with the command. The bound slave let out a shriek of agony as the whip sliced an even deeper gash into his back but neither Afshin nor the woman who stalked into the room reacted to this display of pain. The woman didn't deign to look at the slaves and viciously kicked the boy out of her way as she made her way to her emperor.

He looked down at her when she knelt before him and asked, "Commander. What news do you bring?"

"The Divine," she greeted with devotion. "We have conquered another State in the west."

"What about the north?" he questioned.

"Conquered, the Divine." she smiled.

"We can proceed." he said with interest for the first time that day. "Now we can start moving southwest and crush Midrios."

"Yes, the Divine," the commander answered. "There are still several States that remain between our forces and the Midrian border, but we have come farther and grown stronger than anyone else before."

"Yes," he agreed. "We are close, but we will not strike prematurely. Ensure to get regular updates from our spies in Midrios. When the time is right, we will take the false queens of Leondria for the experiment. They will serve, one way or the other, as their father failed to do."

The commander kept her head bowed in unwavering obedience, but the anticipation rolled off her as she waited for her emperor's response. No one reacted when the boy who had been beaten for hours let out a death rattle and his eyes went wide and unseeing. I knew he would be added to Afshin's collection of bones and would receive no rest, even long after his life had ended.

"I can wait a little longer," Afshin finally remarked, not glancing over at the dead boy, and he returned the commander's gleeful expression with a small smile. "Soon, the whole world will bow before me and praise my name."

ABOUT THE AUTHOR

Daring. Curious. Imaginative. Meagan first started writing stories when she was eight years old living on Yokota Air Base in Japan. Inspired by the beautiful cherry blossoms that captured her imagination and the majestic views she saw every day; she hasn't lifted pen from page since.

Printed in the United States
by Baker & Taylor Publisher Services